Keep the faith

Thank you for being on of my prayer warriors!

Persecution

INFLICTED

LaChelle Parker

WestBow Press books may be ordered through booksellers or by contacting:

WestBow Press
A Division of Thomas Nelson & Zondervan
1663 Liberty Drive
Bloomington, IN 47403
www.westbowpress.com
1 (866) 928-1240

ISBN: 978-1-5127-7580-8 (sc)
ISBN: 978-1-5127-7581-5 (hc)
ISBN: 978-1-5127-7579-2 (e)

Library of Congress Control Number: 2017902571

Print information available on the last page.

WestBow Press rev. date: 03/09/2017

DEDICATION

To anyone struggling, wondering why it's so important to keep to the faith, may this book help to remind you that things will not always remain as they are.

Do not be surprised, my brothers,
if the world hates you.
—1 John 3:13 (NIV)

ACKNOWLEDGMENTS

Primarily, I'd like to give honor and thanks to God. Without His guidance and love in my life, the dreams He provides, and the purpose He has placed on my heart, the Persecution series would have stayed an idea and nothing more.

A special thank you also goes to my husband, Matt, for his knowledge in the scriptures and willingness to read my many drafts. Thank you for patiently sticking by my side through this entire process.

I'd also like to acknowledge Lynne R. Waide for her cover idea and initial artwork for the design, my youth group for giving me the drive to publish, and my parents and siblings for their continued support and encouragement.

Last, but most certainly not least, I want to thank my aunt, Maureena Ruff, for putting more time and energy into content editing than I could ever acknowledge and praise. Thank you for your honesty and support, and for not giving up on me. This start to the Persecution series would not be what it is without you. You truly are "The Coolest!"

PROLOGUE

Mirrors are interesting. They reflect the outward appearances without giving away any indication of the inward man. My uniform says a lot about me that I am dedicated, intelligent, a hero to many, a villain to others, but most importantly, it says I am in control. General, they call me, but I am so much more. Those who follow me only fear my power. They will never learn to appreciate the mastermind behind it all. They will never have to know. Not even my son needs to know why I do things the way I do. He need only do what I say and do, without question. He will be the one the world fears for everything he accomplishes. He will be the one whose reign goes on indefinitely.

"Father," my son snuck in beside me diverting my eyes from my reflection to his. He looked very much like me. "Why must we go today?"

"Because today is a special day," I fixed the sleeves on his uniform. Giving him a firm grip on the shoulders I stared him in the eyes, "Today, you find how you are to fulfill the plans set before you."

"It's also the anniversary of Mother's death," I could see the pathetic tears forming in his eyes.

"Your mother was too weak to live. She was not a survivor. She gave up what little strength she had so that you could be stronger. Will you waste her gift by mourning her?" The young soldier swallowed his tears and sorrow. I'll be proud of him…today will change that. I've made sure of it.

"Now then," I said, straightening his collar, "let's get going."

With my guards at my command, assassins would have no opportunity to thwart my plans. Today was too important to leave to chance. We drove to a place far away from the civil life, where men and women made their living off scraps and saps. I knew their games and kept my senses on high alert. If there were any other way, I would have taken it, but my son needed this. My men provided a human wall around us as we parked and walked to a large, covered wagon. Two men searched the inside before we entered. Two more guarded our entrance while the rest secured the perimeter. No one was to come inside until we left.

"Keep your chin up and your shoulders back," I reminded my young soldier as we stepped into the wagon.

"Yes father," he said, fixing his posture. I could hear a slight quiver in his voice. Fear is good. It's easier to mold people who are afraid.

"Welcome," the greeter bowed and stepped aside as we entered the door. "Madam Sybille has been expecting you."

My son knows better than to break formation, but I could feel him inch closer to me with each step. He was already nine. He shouldn't be this dependent. Brushing streamers of feathers and beads out of our faces, we stepped into a darkened room. Candles and incense burned creating a fog of smoke and dim lighting. Beads and jewels outlined the inside of the wagon's cover, and different kinds of cards and statues of mythical creatures decorated the edges of the floor.

At the far end of the wagon, a round table with a purple and gold cloth held a crystal ball in the center. Madam Sybille, an old woman with thinning grey hair, seated herself on one side of the table, eyeing my son. She greeted us by name and held out her hand, "Have a seat boy."

My son didn't move. I cleared my throat. He eased his way to the chair and then looked back at me. With one look, I let him know he was to do everything the woman asked. Then, I stepped back into the shadows.

Madam Sybille grabbed my son's hand and felt over his palm. She reached out and plucked a hair from his head. Sniffing the hair, she struck a match and lit it on fire. She placed her hands on the crystal ball in front of her. "You've come to inquire how you can successfully complete the plans your father has for you."

"Yes," my young soldier muttered.

She paused, leaned in close, and asked, "Are you scared?"

I saw my son's spine stiffen and become straight. With his chin up, he said firmly, "No. Now tell me what I must do." He could be convincing when he wanted to be.

The Madam placed her hands back on the globe and began to hum and chant. Smoke circled the globe. "There is darkness in your past and even darker paths in your future. You have greatness in you that no one has ever possessed. Still, you are weakened by memories that haunt you."

"My mother," my son whispered.

"Yes, your mother," the Madam sighed. "To accomplish your goals you must let go of her." The woman glanced in my direction, "Look to your father for guidance." She reached out and grabbed my son's hand again. Lights flickered. Echoing voices filled the room. The Madam's eyes became vacant while still staring in the direction of my young soldier. "You will take your father's place, but you must find an appropriate heir. He must be born of a Christian woman, a virgin. You will not love her. Only then can you fulfill your destiny."

The room fell silent and dark. The candles suddenly relit and the Madam's eyes were back to normal. The smoke in the globe had disappeared. My son jerked his hand from hers, but stayed seated. The Madam breathed heavily, "Don't be afraid, boy. Learn from your training. When the right prospect comes along, you will know what to do." She looked at me, "I am very tired now. Leave me."

"Let's go," I said and my son fell back into formation. I waited for him to follow the soldiers through the door. "Your work is done," I set the woman's payment on the table.

"He's very impressionable at this age," she slyly grinned. "It would be a shame if he found out the truth."

"Indeed," I turned back around. "What do you want?"

"Business is slow this time of year," she tapped her fingers on the globe. "It's hard to keep food on the table."

"I see," I reached behind me and pulled out my gun. Its silencer was in place. "Perhaps fewer mouths to feed will help." Her fretful eyes begged for mercy. Had she not just tried to use my son's future for blackmail, I may have spared her. The head would be an easy shot, but the heart would send the best message.

"Please," she put her hands out in front of her. "I didn't mean it. I won't tell a soul."

"I wish I could believe you," I put two slugs in her chest, picked up my payment, and left.

The woman's voice wheezed behind me, "A Son to save… a son to rule… a son will make a man a fool."

I had no reason to turn around as she laughed out her final breath. She was too crazy to pay any mind. She had done her job with my son. That's all that mattered.

"Do you understand what Madam Sybille said?" I asked my young soldier on the ride home.

"I think so," he sighed. "I will have to be like one of them. I must convince them I can be trusted so I may receive my heir, but I must never lose sight of my course."

"It won't be easy," I patted him on the shoulder, proud that he came to that conclusion himself. "I'll make certain you don't stray."

CHAPTER 1

The Lord *had said to Abram,*
"Leave your country, your people and your father's household and go to the land I will show you."
—Genesis 12:1 (NIV)

Sirens suddenly blared. A voice boomed from the speakers, "Due to terrorist threats, the U.S. border is now closed. All air travel is canceled." Airport security rounded up the travelers and began prodding us towards the exits. Chaos surrounded us as everyone scrambled to make new travel arrangements. College students, who hoped to experience spring break for all its drunken fun, created havoc as they cursed the situation. One college kid ran into a businessman, not paying attention.

"Watch it punk!" The man yelled.

The kid grabbed the man by his arm, swung him around, and planted his fist into the man's jaw. The man dove at the kid, dropping him to the ground. Two more college boys jumped on the man. No one tried to stop the fight. My friends, Jeffrey and Steven, and I were on our way to break them up when two security guards pulled the kids off the man.

"Get your stuff and go," one of the security guards said, standing between them. The other guard picked up the kid on the ground and shoved him towards his bag. As the kid stumbled on his hands and knees, the guard kicked him from behind. Their hostility must have frightened the boys, as it did me, because the three left some of their luggage behind as they ran away.

Security jostled us right and left while herding us towards the exit. We now stood on the sidewalk at the pickup curb. The scene I just witnessed shook me to the core. That was not how those in authority treated people.

A little girl shoving past me interrupted my thoughts. I was being overwhelmed. I needed to find peace. Squeezing my eyes shut, I attempted a temporary escape. I couldn't block out the noise so I began to sing. It was a trick my dad taught me when I was younger as a way to calm myself down. The lyrics quietly drifted off my lips. My friends, Jeffrey and Steven, sang with me, "When forced through fire, God will cool the flames. His hand will hold to yours all along the way."

Our coming together helped me find tranquility as our voices joined as one. Calmness replaced fear. Relief replaced stress. Unity replaced chaos. We continued to sing and others from our group joined us.

Onlookers passed by on all sides. At first, I only noticed the annoyed glares. Snide remarks came from some who had to redirect their path around us. A handful of militant type youths shoulder checked a couple of us on the outskirts of the group. My voice shook.

I opened my eyes and saw the same child who had bumped into me pulling her mom closer to us while exclaiming she knew this song. She, too, sang along as her mom stood by and listened. I felt peace flowing again through my mind. Other travelers gathered around as we finished our song. Their gentle presence helped me brush away the last of my fear.

Security guards tried to get us to leave. No one moved. I began to pray aloud, "God, we are scared, but we know You hold the world in Your hands. We cling to Your promises, and to Your love. Don't let us lose sight of You."

Phillip, a member of our group, continued the prayer, "Lord, we serve You, and You alone, above all else. Our sole purpose is to glorify Your name and spread the message of Your love."

"If there is anyone here who hasn't experienced Your mercy or Your love, let them feel it right now," Steven added. "You have provided a way for them to receive Your forgiveness through the sacrifice of Your Son, Jesus. Don't let them be afraid to seek knowledge of You through us."

Macy followed, "Don't let any of us waver in these times of trials, but let us grow closer to You. We love You, Father."

When no one continued, Jeffrey ended with, "Be with us all as we depart. Be with our loved ones. Please take this prayer to the Father for us, Lord Jesus, for it's through Your name that we pray."

Together, we all said, "Amen."

Mixed emotions filled the faces surrounding us. Tears flowed down cheeks, arms held loved ones tight, and many thanked us. We received warm smiles, handshakes, and hugs. Hearts worshiping in spirit and in truth caused other hearts to react and it lifted my spirits. Despite the situation, I was encouraged by the responses to the gospel. It didn't matter what denomination or faith background a person had. We all joined as one, in love. Even though fear had brought us together, we knew God's peace would allow us to go our separate ways.

Omar, a Christian in our group raised in a Muslim family, approached me after the prayers ended. "Thank you," he said, "I did not know how to speak up on our situation, but I am glad you could start us off. God will bring good from this, I know. Many passing hearts were blessed today."

"It was more to help my own sanity," I smiled, "but it seems the Spirit always leads me in the right direction."

A hand on my shoulder stole my attention.

"Khris," Jeffrey said to me as I turned around, "this woman has offered us a spring break alternative." He pointed to a woman who had striking silver hair and wore very little makeup. She didn't need it though; she was gorgeous.

"Hi Khris. I'm Joy," she reached for a handshake. The back of her hand had a few sunspots, which made me guess she was in her sixties. It was very smooth and warm. Between her firm handshake and her brilliant smile, she made a likeable, first impression. I was immediately at ease in her company.

I smiled while shaking her hand, "I'm pleased to meet you."

"I know you all had other plans, but if you're willing to work with change in the last minute, we have an alternative option in place of your mission trip."

"What kind of alternative are we looking at?"

"A Christian camp," Joy said kindly. "It's the first of its kind, fit to hold over five thousand people; created for Christians of all ages who have committed their lives to Christ. We hope to strengthen them and send them back into the world refreshed, ready to lead others to discipleship in Christ."

My interest was piqued. "What would be our purpose in attending?" I asked.

"Well, I'm hoping your group can take the place of some of our missionaries who were scheduled to fly in as guest speakers. Apparently, they're not going to make it. I don't doubt, for a second, that God brought us together today. When I met Jeffrey," she signaled to Jeffrey, as if I wouldn't know who he was, "he told me that you are all missionaries. I believe God wanted me to find you."

My heart felt right while she spoke, which persuaded me into thinking God really had planned this change of events. I accepted Joy's offer for myself, but I couldn't speak for anyone else. Steven and Jeffrey accepted right away. Everyone else stood excited and ready as well, except for Macy.

Macy found herself overwhelmed by the circumstances. She chose to leave and be with her family for the week. No one could fault her decision. We prayed safe travels over her and helped to find her transportation home. By the time Macy's rental came through, three hours later, we had all checked in with our families and let them know of our newest plans.

When I called my family, my mom could barely speak. They saw on the news that the border closed and had assumed we were already out of the country. I wish I had called sooner. Suddenly my father's voice came on the phone, "Thank you for calling." Dad put me on speaker. I divulged what information I could. Mom calmed down, and they were both thrilled to hear about our new plans.

"Khristy, be safe," Mom said in a trembling voice. I imagined her warm smile sending blessings my way because I didn't want to think of her being afraid. "Keep God close."

"Always, Mom," I smiled back even though she couldn't see me. Mom never stopped trusting God. The security that Dad's presence brought her probably strengthened her trust. I couldn't talk long, but hearing their voices was enough to push me forward without regret. I missed my family, but God's work called. I promised to check in once we arrived at the camp. For now, I had some paperwork to do with the team.

Joy had a small bus ready for us. Our previous plans consisted of me cozied up next to strangers in an aircraft that could fall from the sky at any moment. Sarcasm dripped in my thoughts, *surely, I can manage sitting next to anyone on a grounded bus for eight hours.* I laughed to myself.

We loaded our gear, having nothing left to stay for, and headed to Salt Creek Mountain Pass Christian Camp.

CHAPTER 2

Accept one another, then, just as Christ accepted you, in order to bring praise to God.
—Romans 15:7 (NIV)

"Do you mind if I sit with you?" I asked Omar on the bus.

"Not at all," he began moving some of his things to the floor.

I threw my bag on the carrier above us, brushed my frizzy, dark curls out of my face, and sat down. "It's been an interesting change of events."

"Yes, it has been. Now we head to unknown territories in our own country," Omar chuckled. "Tell me: do you prefer Khris or Khristy?"

"Khris is fine. I'm used to it by now."

"I heard your friends call you Khris, but on the lists they gave us, it said Khristy."

"They're just too lazy to say my full name," I chuckled.

Omar looked at me as if I was serious.

Laughingly I said, "No, Jeffrey and Steven are close friends. We met at college and have been on several mission trips together."

Omar and I continued to talk. We told stories about our families and mission experiences up until the bus stopped for gas. We had the choice of four fast food restaurants. I knew immediately where Jeffrey, Steven, and I would eat when I saw the Taco Spot sign. Omar politely declined our invite after I introduced him to the "guys." He was fasting, as he said he always does during the first day of a mission trip, praying for the safety of everyone during our travels.

While eating, I shared what I learned about Omar. Jeffrey and Steven talked about those they had met as well. Jeffrey had sat next to Sandra White, an older woman from Oklahoma, and Steven sat beside Riley, a former drug addict. When we finished eating, we said a prayer before loading back onto the bus. I was the last one in line. Joy smiled as I passed her. Eyeing Jeffrey and Steven, I saw that they both returned to their old seats. I, too, decided to return to my seat only to find that an attractive young man now sat in my place. He wasn't from our group. His hair was dark and hung to his shoulders. Brown eyes looked up at me. His lips caught my attention framed by his dark goatee. I always preferred a guy with facial hair.

"Khris, this is David," Omar said, which kept me from ogling, "Joy's son."

"Hello," I shook his hand. I didn't see him come on the bus the first time. I always did a head count on trips; it was my OCD curse. Macy had opted to go home. I probably included David in the count and forgot we should have had one less. Either way, I now found myself in an odd predicament.

"Was this your seat?" David asked, acting as if he was going to stand.

"Yes…well, no…you can sit there," I insisted as I thought of a way out without making him feel bad.

"Are you sure?"

"Yes, I umm…" I fumbled for an answer. I reached up into my bag, "I only came to get my headphones. I really do need a nap." As I searched through my bag above him, the bus started to roll. My headphones fell into David's lap while I caught the seat behind him to keep from stumbling to the floor.

"You okay?" David asked as he turned to try to help.

"Yes," I stood embarrassed.

He handed me my headphones with a laugh, "Good reflexes. I'm impressed."

"You too," I wanted to slap my face. "Well...umm… I'm going to find an open seat."

"Okay," David replied. "Nice meeting you."

"You too," I said again feeling foolish. Then I went back closer to the front where an empty seat called my name. Two seats held single occupants, but I was too self-conscious about playing off the idea that I truly needed sleep. I passed them up to the place where I could sit back and close my eyes. I must have been more tired than I thought, because I slept through the rest of the drive. Jeffrey said he tried to wake me, but thought it was best to leave me in peace.

I looked down at my phone.

"Joy," I asked while flashing my phone, "will we have service out here?"

She looked up and smiled, "Only when you climb the mountains. We do have a landline in the main office you can use."

With five thousand people in one area, I doubted there being much available phone time. I was glad I called at the airport. I had promised to check in when we arrived, but my family would understand. I peered through the window, up at the tallest peak. Perhaps later I could find time to climb it. Not only would it allow me to call my family but, also, it would be the perfect place to spend time in prayer.

Jeffrey came to my seat while everyone in the back exited the bus. He waited on Steven who had said he would get both of their bags. I would get mine once everyone else got off. As usual, Steven was the last one wandering down the aisle. He trailed behind Omar and David. When David came closer, he held up my bag and said, "Delivery for one Khristy Monzel."

"Thank you," I replied as Jeffrey took it from him and handed it to me.

"Figured I would save you the trip," David grinned as he walked off the bus behind Omar.

At that moment, both Jeffrey and Steven sent a sly smile my way while Steven joked, "Oooh, someone has a boyfriend."

Jeffrey added in with a very feminine voice, "Mmhmm, girl you better go catch that man."

CHAPTER 3

God saw all that He had made,
and it was very good...
—Genesis 1:31 (NIV)

Stepping off the bus, I arched my back and stretched my shoulders. As my eyes regained their focus, the beauty of the camp stole my breath. It rested on at least one hundred acres within a vibrant valley of greens and blues with a splash of color here and there. The mountain range that bordered the west side of camp stretched wide and towered high. Its evergreen trees waved hello to us as a breeze combed through their needles. Below the tallest mountain, six large cabins settled around a pond that looked as smooth as glass. Three cabins sat on each side of the pond with a cluster of smaller cabins between them.

A large tent took up a great portion of the middle of the camp, proclaiming its importance. I could hardly wait to see its purpose. Farther down the valley, south of the tent, the ground had a deep, cliff like ledge. Past the ledge, two football fields sat side by side appearing freshly mowed. Bordering the edge of the field, a creek transitioned the rest of the plain into more forest. In the middle of the open fields, a dark circle caught my eye. From where I stood, it just seemed to be a silhouette. I tried squinting through the sun's rays to no avail. The vast layout of the campground left me speechless. No doubt, five thousand people could spend an entire week here together. The parking lot alone could easily fit four or five hundred large busses.

"Let us hope we are not the only adults attending," Omar whispered under his breath, just loud enough for me to hear.

"Of course not," David shocked us, turning to face Omar. "We plan to have Christians of all ages, and we have at least eight hundred adults over the age of thirty who have registered."

"Do you have any counselors assigned to the cabins?" I wondered how this camp would compare to those from my childhood. Looking around I could see the other members of our group equally curious as they turned to listen.

"Not exactly…I mean we have a few, but…" David stumbled for the right explanation.

Joy rushed to help her son explain, "We have experienced

staff assigned to certain areas at all times to assist campers and counselors. They will have staff shirts and communication devices on them. You'll find those men and women already here. There are also certain groups assigned to song leading, meal preparations, clean up, entertainment, and daily messages. Those people will continue to trickle in over the next few hours. Your group will be one of our guest speakers. You'll receive further instruction during the staff meeting about where we need you throughout the week." She then looked at David, "Why don't you show our guests to their cabins and help them get settled." She smiled at us all and then left in a hurry.

"Yes ma'am," David said, pulling our attention back to him. "Grab your luggage and follow me."

On our way to the cabins, we passed the tent that took up so much space in the camp. The curtains on all sides draped so that no one could see what it looked like on the inside.

"What's in the tent?" Gunner, one of our great outdoorsmen asked. I had a chance to talk to him on the first flight. He hoped to open up a Christian deep sea fishing tour later on in his life. He wanted to take people out fishing and preach God's message during their long hours on the water.

"A surprise," David smiled craftily.

The men's cabins, called First, Second, and Third John, were the cabins nearest to us on the north side of the pond. We walked into First John where the guys received first pick of their room and beds. Inside, the cabins looked even larger than they had from the outside. The first door opened into a hallway and, inside the hallway, doors lined up one after another along both walls. Water fountains, bathroom facilities, and showers were located in between every two doors that opened to a bunkroom. The rooms each had one large window in the very back. Bunk beds lined the other walls and the middle of the room, allowing space for fifty people to sleep per room.

Gunner and his friend, Richard, took to the back corner near the window of the first room they entered. After throwing their items on the bed, they left to check out the rest of the camp. The other men entered the same room. Of course, Jeffrey and Steven found bunks next to each other inviting Omar to join them.

"These larger cabins are built to sleep about seven hundred people each," David said with pride. "The smaller family cabins, which we'll pass on the way to the women's cabins, have two rooms and can hold a family of five; though, we can accommodate larger families with extra air mattresses."

The log walls reminded me of the Lincoln Logs my mom gave me from her childhood. As I scanned the rest of the room, David's eyes caught mine. "I can take you and the other ladies to the women's cabins while these gentlemen settle in," he said.

"Thank you," I smiled. As we turned to leave, I threw one of my travel pillows at Steven, who had forgotten his, "We're headed to our cabins. See you in a bit."

We followed David on a trail that passed in front of the family cabins next to the pond. The girls' cabins – labeled Ester, Ruth, and Phoebe – were on the south end of the pond next to a windmill. The location gave us privacy from the other cabins yet, it didn't feel completely secluded. I stood in awe at God's creation around me. My heart yearned for the morning to come quickly; to hear the birds sing their waking songs, and smell the dew on the ground.

David opened the main door to Ester's cabin with his arm stretched out in front of him. "After you," he smiled.

"Ah, chivalry is not dead," said Geneva, one of the older women in our group. She and her sister, Agnes, laughed as we all stepped inside.

"These cabins have the same layout as the men's," David explained. "Except that there are more mirrors on the cabin walls."

"Yes, and we all know how important mirrors can be in the morning," Agnes said with a touch of sarcasm.

I entered the first door to the left and chose the closest bunk to the exit. Agnes apologized for not coming into the room with me, probably because she saw that the men had all stayed in the same room. She insisted that she sleep by the restroom in case of an emergency in the night. Geneva followed behind her, and so did Sandra. Sandra seemed to feel more comfortable with them than she did with the other girls in our group.

Four of the other girls snatched up their own room. That left Jasmine. Jasmine is one of the quietest people I have ever met. She stood in the hallway trying to decide on where to go looking back and forth at the two rooms.

"I like my space. Why don't you go with them?" I smiled. Her eyes lingered more in their direction anyway. Had she hesitated, then I would have asked her to join me. For now, she seemed content as she darted into the other room.

"That was nice of you," David commended. "Don't worry; you'll have a full cabin before tomorrow afternoon."

"Thanks for the warning," I joked.

He gave a nervous laugh.

I took the opportunity to ask, "So what is the tent in the middle of the camp really for?"

"I told you, it's a surprise," he teased. "Don't worry. You'll find out soon enough. I need to check in with a few people. I can give you a tour later, maybe after the staff meeting. Is that alright?"

"I'd like that," I grinned as I let the door spring shut. David was very personable and easy on the eyes. Charm could only get a person so far in the world, but I hoped he had more to offer. It didn't take long to see that he wore his heart on his sleeve… I laughed at myself for thinking such thoughts; to assume I knew him. Maybe I read too much into his gestures. David and I are strangers. Perhaps we could get to know each other over the week. That is, if he even had time to visit.

Shoving these thoughts aside, I rolled out my sleeping bag on the bottom bunk next to me. Having a mattress under my back would be much more comfortable than the hard ground we planned to sleep on in Mexico. "Father, be with the villagers that expected us," I prayed while shoving my luggage bag under the bed. "Don't let them assume that our absence represents Your abandonment of them." I wondered if other countries even knew what had happened.

Again, I had a chance to admire God's creation while heading back to meet up with Jeffrey and Steven. This time I stopped for an extra moment and watched as the sun started its descent in the sky. It still reflected off the glass waters of the pond. It was the setting for a perfect evening. There were no strong winds to disturb the vegetation, though a gentle breeze still rustled the pine needles. The trees reached for the sky, showing their majesty off to the world. Little patches of lilies, blue bonnets, and daisies covered the pond shore, getting as close to the water as possible without drowning. I spotted a trail that seemed to lead behind the family cabins and up to the side of the mountain.

CHAPTER 4

Blessed is the man who does not walk in the counsel of the wicked…but his delight is in the law of the LORD*…*
—Psalm 1:1–2 (NIV)

Jeffrey and Steven met me outside of their cabin with Omar. Busses pulled in as we walked and talked, exploring the camp. Men in dark blue uniforms stepped off each bus, first, and then extended their hands out in front of them. Several people followed, taking the men's hands for balance. We recognized some of them immediately; Christian actors, sports players, authors, musicians, and artists.

A loud booming sound came from the surrounding trees and buildings, "Now that everyone is here, please make your way over to the Tabernacle – the enormous tent – and we will fill you in on the details of the week. You will have time to unload your luggage afterwards, while we prepare for dinner."

At the Tabernacle, we were stunned with awe as the curtains drew open on all sides of the tent. Rows, upon rows of round tables covered the floor. Each table had eight chairs around them, white and purple tablecloths on top of them, and beautiful flower centerpieces in the middle. Scattered around the centerpieces were different colored packets of paper and pens. White lights hung above the tables, giving the room a very elegant look. Rectangular tables, cloaked with white tablecloths and black skirts, held drink dispensers and cups along the sides of the tent.

A stage centered in the front of the Tabernacle was visible to all of the tables before it. Purple and white cloth curtained the stage at its base. Large flower arrangements draped over the corners of the stage, with their vines stretching to the ground camouflaging the stairs behind them. In the middle of the stage was a single glass podium with papers on top of it.

Searching to sit next to someone we all recognized, we were disappointed. Most people came with their own families and friends filling up entire tables. Finally, we settled for a table where an older man and woman sat together. We didn't recognize either of them, but they seemed inviting.

"May we sit with you?" I asked.

"Of course you can," the woman replied. "My husband and I were just discussing the possible need to advertise our open seats."

Chuckling, we introduced ourselves. Their names were Jim and Jan, both very sweet people. Jan had a brace on her left hand and a cane next to her chair. Jim didn't seem to talk much, although, he could hardly form a sentence with his wife's constant chatter.

A man appeared on stage. His voice thundered from the speakers of the tent. "Glad you could all make it. A few are still on their way due to their canceled flights, but we will do all we can to keep this camp flowing smoothly. Are you ready to get this week started?" Whooping sounds, claps, and cheers immediately filled the tent. The speaker let it go on for a few seconds, smiling proudly. Then he raised his hand for silence, "It excites my heart to see how God has blessed this camp with so many strong leaders and jubilant spirits. My name is Glen Roach, my wife Joy and our son David are here as well. I hope you take a moment to meet them before this week ends." The same Joy and David who brought us here stood up from the center table near the stage and waved at the crowd.

Glen continued to speak, but I missed most of what he had to say when someone sat down next to me. I looked to greet them with a smile. The stranger's unique appearance stole a few extra seconds of my gaze. A five o'clock shadow outlined his face, connecting to his brown, crew cut hairline. With black sunglasses hiding his eyes, it was impossible to miss the silver ring dangling from his nose. It reminded me of a bull. Piercings didn't bother me though. Even Jeffrey had them. What disturbed me was the aroma of men's cologne assaulting my senses.

The look on my face must have said *you caught me smelling you,* because the stranger instantly lowered his shades to reveal piercing blue eyes. He winked, "Anthony," he informed. No formal handshake followed, only the dramatic removal of sunglasses and that ridiculous wink. I needed to refocus on the speaker and get that invasive image out of my head.

"What's your name?" He asked quite loudly, when he saw I had ignored his first attempt at an introduction.

"Khris," I whispered without turning my attention from the stage.

He continued to talk as if he couldn't hear Glen Roach addressing us all, "We had a long flight from New York. It was an even longer drive once all air traffic was shut down."

"Hmm," I acknowledged with a nod, keeping my responses short to help him get the hint.

Sarcastically he said, "Hope I haven't missed much."

"It just started." Was he ever going to shut up?

"Oh good, I would have hated to have to ask for your notes," again with the sarcasm.

I didn't reply. I only glanced over to Steven who began snickering. I shot him my best *be quiet or I will hurt you* glare, and looked back up at Glen Roach.

Applause sounded from the audience, filling the room with even more cheers than before. I had no idea what I had missed. I had heard the word, "entertainers," and a bitter taste settled in my mouth…or maybe it was just the smell of Anthony's cologne.

"I don't want this week to be just about entertainment," it was as if Glen read my mind. "My heart is set on letting God in, and letting Him produce in us what He asks of us. Most of our sessions will focus on His will for us throughout the week. If you notice, on each of your tables, there are colored packets. If you haven't already taken one, I'd like to ask you to do that now."

I reached to the center of the table and grabbed an orange packet. Anthony's hand glided against mine. The hairs on my arm rose as I pretended not to notice. Trying to settle my crawling skin, I looked back up at Glen.

"The colors on your folder will determine your group for the week during the majority of our classes and activities."

I hesitated to glance in Anthony's direction. *Please don't let him have an orange folder,* I prayed. He caught me looking and I instantly faced back towards the stage.

"Inside, on the front page, you will see an outline of the camp schedule for your color group. The assigned leaders of your group will have the same colored tee shirt on as the folders. They will help answer all of your questions. If you turn the page, we will go through the camp rules. Though we are all Christians, sometimes we forget that we are held to a higher standard than the rest of the world."

I smiled as I read the first rule; *Guys and girls keep all clothing modest. DO NOT cause your brothers and sisters to stumble. If you have to ask, "Is this okay?" then just go change.*

Many of the rules were simple and followed close to the Ten Commandments: don't swear, don't lie, don't spread rumors, love as God loves, etc. A few recorded the boundaries of the camp and the areas within the camp that were off limits. Others held to the code of morals; don't start fights, don't tear people down, and don't stir up trouble. One other note that caught my eye was that, sadly, the pond was off limits for swimming due to safety reasons - assigned staff would watch the pond at all times to enforce this rule.

Glen ended with a final thank you and a reminder that dinner would start in an hour. David then made his way to the stage and led us in a prayer. When he prayed, it was as if he was alone, talking to God, and not surrounded by thousands of people. It made me almost drop to my knees. I felt peace within my soul, as if God physically stood in the room with us.

I had almost forgotten about the annoyance sitting beside me until I heard, "Wow, glad that's over," followed by a sigh.

I resisted the urge to bite my tongue. "Excuse me?" I blurted out, offended. Had he no respect?

"Don't tell me you were actually interested in all of that," Anthony rolled his eyes as he stood.

"Actually, I was." I challenged his stance. Anthony stood a

few inches above me and doubled my body mass. Part of me felt intimidated, but my other half stood firm, "I don't appreciate your criticism." Anthony didn't pay attention to my comment; he was already off on a different subject.

"Which one is your boyfriend?" He attempted a smooth voice as he pointed at Jeffrey, Steven, and Omar who all visited with Jim and Jan. Jeffrey glanced my way, his eyes asking me if he needed to intervene. He could be protective when necessary, though I figured I could handle this one on my own.

"None of them," I scorned. "Excuse me; I need to join my friends." I walked around the table towards them. Still feeling Anthony's gaze, I shuddered.

Why did I have such a negative feeling about him? This stranger annoyed me in a disturbing and abrasive way. It was more than just his arrogance. Maybe it was that he had no respect for personal boundaries. He came behind me and quietly said, "Okay, I'll see you at dinner then."

I turned to join in the others' conversation, but sadly, Jim and Jan already left to unload their luggage. The guys offered to help them, but Jim declined saying they only had a couple of things to carry. Their absence left me having to catch grief from Steven.

"So, now you have two boyfriends?" He raised his eyebrows at me.

I threw one back at him and corrected, "No, actually, I have five."

They all looked confused.

I gave in with a grin, "He thought I was dating one of you, but I told him I was with the old man." I laughed at the sight of their faces. Omar looked the most horrified at this.

"You didn't," Jeffrey was shocked.

I laughed.

"Thou shall not start rumors," Steven jokingly reminded us of one of the camp rules.

"They'd almost measure up to the rumors in China when we

had the entire second grade class convinced that she was a boy," Jeffrey chuckled.

"Now that was funny," Steven exclaimed. "Who knew teaching English could be so fun?"

"Oh, so funny," I mocked. "It's all fun and games to you two, but I was the one stopped from entering the girls' restroom. It took two hours with the translator to clear up everything."

Jeffrey rolled his eyes, "You're just mad that you didn't think to do it first."

"No, I actually have boundaries," I smacked Jeffrey upside the head. Omar and Steven gave a slight chuckle.

"What was that for?" Jeffrey rubbed the spot where it hurt most.

"I want to prevent you from thinking about spreading such rumors here."

He rolled his eyes again.

"Come on Khris, give us some credit," Steven chimed in. "We would never recycle ideas."

I raised my hands, acting as if I was going to hit them both, but they flinched and ran.

"Come on Omar, before she hits you too," Steven yelled back.

With only an hour between now and dinner, I decided to wait to hike the mountain. Now, I would focus on getting out of the tent without happening upon Anthony.

CHAPTER 5

A friend loves at all times, and a brother is born for adversity.
—Proverbs 17:17 (NIV)

"Khristy," a voice called, raising the hairs on the back of my neck. I dreaded turning around. If that creep thought he could follow me around the rest of this week, then…a smile made its way to my lips as I saw David approach.

All I could mutter through my shock was a friendly, "Hullo."

"Where did your friends run off to?"

"Oh, who knows? They probably went to their cabin to meet someone famous," I laughed.

David gave a sigh, "I wanted you all to meet my dad before he leaves."

"Where is he going?"

"He wants to make an appearance at the other two camps running this week, but he plans to be back on Wednesday."

"How about I go with you to meet him? If my friends show up before he leaves, one of us can introduce them to him," I suggested.

"Alright, follow me," David spun around, and I trailed closely behind him.

"By the way," I tried not to embarrass myself, "I really enjoyed your prayer. There aren't many people, I know, who actually talk so personally with God in public."

He turned with a perplexed look on his face.

I clarified, "People talk *to* God all the time, but they don't actually talk with Him; not like they are really with Him in that exact moment. To me, public prayers usually sound like a formal letter read out loud, but not with you."

"Thank you," David said. "My mom taught me to pray that way. She always said, 'Never believe God is anywhere but right here.'"

"Smart woman," I said.

"Yes, she was."

David's use of the past tense baffled me.

"My real mom died when I was thirteen," he explained. "Her plane was shot down while she was on a mission trip. Joy is my stepmom and a wonderful woman, but having her doesn't stop me from missing my mom."

"I'm sorry to hear that, but I'm glad God has blessed you and your dad with Joy," I smiled awkwardly.

David brushed off my attempt at comfort and exclaimed excitedly, "I can't wait to see her again. Honestly, I hope I can go just as she did; doing something for God. I never want to get so old that I just sit around waiting for people to come see me."

Personally, I never had anticipated my death. If given a choice, I avoid thinking about it.

We waded through a few more crowds of people until David finally stopped, "Ah, Dad," he said. "I wanted you to meet someone. This is Khristy. She and her group are the ones taking the Henderson's place."

"Khristy," Glen turned to give me a big hug. "It's so nice to meet you." He then took a step back, grabbed my hand with both of his, and gave it a squeeze. "I do wish I could be here for your presentation. I look forward to hearing all about it when I return. Where are the others who came with you?"

"Oh they…" I began to say before David interrupted.

"They walked off before I could catch them, but you'll meet them, don't worry."

"I think I can speak for us all when I say that we're excited to see what's in store for this week," I grinned. "It's going to be an amazing experience diving into the scripture and fellowshipping with everyone without the world's distractions. What a wonderful idea God has given you."

"Yes, it is truly amazing what He has done," Mr. Roach smiled, letting go of my hand. "You are such a sweet young lady." He looked at me while speaking, but he winked at David who shook his head in embarrassment.

"Thank you, sir," I smiled. "You're not too bad yourself."

"Thank you, my dear, but don't call me sir. No, just Glen will do." Now he sent a wink my way. "I hate that I can't stay and visit.

We will talk in a few days." He then turned to David, "My ride is already here. With air traffic canceled, I'll be cutting things close, but thank you for introducing us."

They hugged, and then Glen walked away. In those few seconds, I caught Anthony out of the corner of my eye. He stood at the edge of the tent staring at me. I took a quick glance, out of curiosity, hoping he wasn't actually watching me. Better yet, I hoped that he wasn't there at all. Immediately, I regretted looking. Not only was it Anthony, but he was staring so intently at me that I felt the need to shield myself. *Pretend you didn't see him.* I stepped to the other side of David while waving a small goodbye to Glen, "I like your dad."

"He can be embarrassing," David sighed.

"He's a good man though, I can tell."

"I won't argue with that," he laughed. "So what should I know about you?" He walked to a table, and gestured for me to sit down with him. I didn't know if he was initializing an interview, or if this was his way of trying to get to know me.

"Well, for starters, I like to walk and talk instead of sit," I joked, just in case he was determined to stay put. "That is, unless we are short on time."

"We will have just as much time as we would if we sat," he walked away from the table and we headed towards the back exit.

I really did prefer walking. I like to think on my feet. It was more comfortable to get to know him while walking than just sitting face to face.

We came to the cliff that dropped to the large fields below the camp. It wasn't a cliff at all, but rather, a steep slope. A running track circled around the two fields, which is what we walked along while continuing the conversation.

David grabbed my arm as I almost tripped down the slope. Embarrassed, I said a quick "thanks" and got back to the conversation.

"Where are you from?" I inquired.

"About five minutes down the main road from here," David sighed. "I was born and raised in the mountains, and I will probably grow old and die here – just as I've always feared."

"Why do you fear it?" I asked. "This seems like a beautiful place to live."

"I want to get out into the world," he yearned. "I've always envied people like you, who take the chance to travel and do big things for God. I pray, every day, for God to open that door for me. Instead, I'm stuck here, helping my stepmom around the property, because she can't do any heavy work and my dad is always gone."

"Maybe you should rethink what you consider big things. After all, denying your wants for someone else's needs is huge – just as you're doing for Joy. Paul didn't always get to travel when or where he wanted. Think about it. He stayed in prison during most of his ministry."

"True," he said. "You should add that into your speech, if you can. Let the campers know that God's calling doesn't always put us where we desire to go."

"Alright, or maybe I'll ask Omar to cover that. He chose God over his family. His testimony may have a larger impact."

David agreed, "I really enjoyed sitting with him on the bus. His story is inspiring."

Our trek ended and we went up the hill towards the Tabernacle. Looking behind us, I began to laugh at myself. Surely, David thought I was going mad. I hadn't paid it any attention while we were walking, but in the middle of the two fields was a large stack of wood. "When we first arrived," I explained, "all I could see from the parking lot was a mysterious dark circle in the middle of these fields. I couldn't, for the life of me, make out what it was."

David laughed, "Good job detective, you've discovered our bonfire." We continued towards the center of camp. It delighted me to see he could tease me.

The tables in the Tabernacle were now equipped with napkin

dispensers and salt and peppershakers. This, I found, is how the tent would stay set up the rest of the week.

"I really enjoyed walking with you," David said. "I'm going to make rounds and check on everyone to see how the first meal is coming along."

"I enjoyed it as well. Thank you," I replied. The hairs on the back of my neck stood. I wanted desperately to turn and look for the unwanted eyes I could feel watching me as David walked away towards the kitchen.

It was almost time for dinner. The area began to fill up with people. I needed to find my group. I decided to go to the cabin, but first, I would have to look around and see who might be near. Cautiously, I made a 360-degree turn scanning the crowd. Steven and Jeffrey were nowhere in sight. Before passing the men's cabins, I saw Agnes, Geneva, and Sandra. They stood talking with a few other people and signaled for me to join them.

I regretted advancing their way when I saw Anthony. His eyes hid behind his dark sunglasses. He had that same sickening grin on his face as the last time I encountered him. Next to him stood another man, who looked near Anthony's age, and an older woman.

"Khris," Sandra said, "this is Justin, Anthony, and Erica. They're from the Big Apple."

"I know Khris," Anthony said stepping forward to shake my hand. I politely shook it and tried to ignore the way his touch made my skin crawl. "We met at the intro meeting. She sat at my table."

Actually, he sat at my table, I thought to myself.

"That's great," Geneva blindly celebrated. "Shall we go find a seat for dinner before it gets too crowded? We can talk more while we wait."

We turned and headed back in the direction I had just come from – the three older women walked in front, the Big Apple gang strode behind them, and I hung in the back hoping to fade away.

Little by little, Anthony let himself fall from his group until he was eventually walking with me. His hands were in his pockets with his thumbs on the outside of his jeans. He seemed quite normal now, but his first impression still lingered at the forefront of my mind. "When did you arrive at the camp?" He asked.

"Just long enough to find a cabin before the intro meeting," I still searched for a way to escape.

"Well then, without having any time to explore, how about we go together after dinner?"

Cringing, I declined. I saw Omar, Steven, and Jeffrey in the distance. I veered off, ignoring everything else he had to say. It was rude of me, but I didn't care to entertain any current relationship he was trying to build, friendship or other. I ran to the guys, happy to see them. While hugging Jeffrey I whispered, "Did he follow me?"

Jeffrey hugged me back, "No, but he's definitely staring."

"What's going on?" Steven asked seriously, instead of inserting his usual joke.

"He's giving me the creeps," I still refused to look back.

Steven chuckled, "He can't be that bad."

"I can't tell what his intentions are, and I don't like the way I feel around him," my skin crawled just thinking about it. "I don't know what it is, but I get the impression he's leering at me. Please don't let him get me alone," I begged.

"Do you really think he'd do anything?" Jeffrey asked.

"I don't know," I shivered. "Christian camp or not, I don't want to give him the chance. At first, I just thought he was annoying – with how rude he was at the meeting. Now, he is really starting to creep me out."

"No problem. We have your back."

CHAPTER 6

The Light shines in the darkness, and the darkness has not overcome It.
—John 1:5 (TNIV)

We, Jeffrey, Steven, Omar, and I, heard some wonderful testimonies from different staff members while going through the dinner line. Looking for a seat, I saw David on the other side of the tent. He gave a slight wave with his palm and smiled in my direction, but had too much going on around him for us to visit. It looked like he was in over his head, because he soon had to call Joy to help intervene in the conversation. We would have more time to visit, so I didn't mind following my group to the table they chose.

Once again, all tables filled with men and women who traveled here together. We went near the area where we sat before with Jim and Jan. The table lay desolate this time. Not too far from it sat Geneva, Agnes, and Sandra. I assumed the worst, waiting for Anthony to appear, but they were alone.

"Hi Sandra," Jeffrey said, shaking her hand. "What do you think of the camp so far?"

"It's very different," Sandra looked around as she said this. "In a good way," she added.

Geneva agreed. "I'm anxious to see the diversity among the people when everyone comes in tomorrow."

"I never thought I would get to see a place so filled with the Spirit of God in my lifetime," Agnes added.

"Me either," Geneva and Agnes grabbed each other's hands and gave a squeeze. They were sisters, so I assumed they had a deep bond; yet, in that moment, I remembered that neither of them was married. They had both lost their husbands and now only had God and each other. The Spirit struck me to say a small prayer for them, asking that they never have to experience life alone.

"Heads up," Omar said from across the table. Jeffrey and I looked behind us to see Anthony approaching with a tray in his hand.

My back stiffened.

"Peach cobbler anyone?" Anthony said as he approached.

"You are such a sweetheart," Geneva smiled as she reached her hand out for a plate. Anthony handed her a slice, struggling to keep the tray balanced as the weight shifted. He did the same for the other two women.

When he looked at me to see if I would accept his gift, I shook my head and said, "No thanks." Omar also declined. The ladies had already taken a bite out of theirs, before finishing dinner, and complimented it many times.

"Oh, I didn't make it. I just volunteered to serve it," Anthony smiled. "Dessert?" He gestured to Steven and Jeffrey.

"No thank you," Steven replied. "I'm allergic."

"I'll take a slice," Jeffrey said, leaning back so Anthony could place the cobbler on the table in front of him.

Anthony did so saying, "I haven't had the chance to meet you."

I hope they aren't falling for this prince charming act.

"I'm Jeff." Jeffrey rarely introduced himself as Jeff. To teachers and bosses he was Jefferson; to his peers he was Jeffrey. Only to those who he wanted to keep at a distance did he have call him Jeff. It was Jeffrey's way of reaffirming, to me, that he had my back.

"I'm sure Khris has already told you, but I'm Anthony," he smiled at me again and I wanted to vomit.

"No, she hadn't," Jeffrey smirked amusingly. He never actually let his lips rise, only his cheeks with a small, very unnoticeable squint to his eyes.

"Oh," Anthony turned cold and looked away from me while smiling at everyone else. "Well, I hope you all enjoy your evening. I'll need to continue passing these out."

As he left, Jeffrey took a bite of his cobbler. "This really is good," he teased.

"I don't care," I jokingly glared at him.

The ladies across the table looked confused. I didn't plan to fill them in either. The only thing I would accomplish by letting these women in on the details would be spreading rumors and possibly ruining Anthony's reputation among them. Paul warns us against doing such things. For all I knew, Anthony may have actually been a likeable person around others. Still, I found no motive for me to attempt giving him the time of day.

Instead of talking about Anthony to the sisters and Sandra, I smiled across the table and changed the subject. "So," I said, "the food is great here. Do you think they can keep it up all week?" I could always count on weather and food to help me out with small talk.

"Oh yes," Sandra seemed to notice the tension and tried to help me, "I heard there will be salads and burgers during every lunch and dinner, along with a vegetarian option, for those who don't want to experiment with the main meal."

We all began on different subjects after that, and the dinner finished out surprisingly well. I was tempted to find some of the cobbler after I ate my meal, but resisted as much as possible for my own image's sake. That wasn't necessarily the right way to approach the situation, but it's what I did and I can't go back and change it. Not to mention, as much as I didn't like Anthony's presence, I would hate to hurt his feelings if he saw me eating the cobbler.

CHAPTER 7

Blessed are those who have learned to acclaim You,
who walk in the light of Your presence, oh LORD.
—Psalm 89:15 (NIV)

After everyone finished dinner, David directed us to the bonfire, now ablaze, in the center of the fields. We created a semi-circle around the fire and sat on the ground as someone led us in song. David stood up as the song ended. He talked to the entire group while walking back and forth in front of the fire. He had a strong voice. It carried extraordinarily well.

He cleared his throat before speaking again, "Thank you all for being here. Your presence is an encouragement to me. I would like us to spend the night praising our Creator in song after we pray. I feel that this is the perfect time to direct the focus of our hearts and minds on our God. Feel free to return to your cabins if you want some time alone."

David sat back down while different individuals led songs one after another. Every now and then, someone would lead a song that very few of us knew, but I still enjoyed listening to the lyrics and singing them in my heart.

I lay back in the grass behind me, letting the world disappear. I could see the glow from the fire at the horizon of my knees. The stars shined bright above me. I let the silhouettes of people fade away as I imagined being in my heavenly Father's arms. With the world spinning, I felt as if God were dancing with me. He created the stars, the moon, and the sky. God made it all with just His spoken word. He called it good. Then, He made people. On that day of creation, He knew He would one day make me, a woman so unworthy of His love, who chooses to sin daily. Still, He calls me very good. Why, what is good enough about me to be very good? Only God is good and, yet, He continues to dance with me. I try to turn away because I am ashamed of my sin. Nevertheless, He brings peace to my heart saying, "Hush child. I love you anyway."

All of my life I've tried to live for God. I try to love others and do for them all that He asks. I know I must be completely devoted to Him as a wife is to her husband. Then again, as a wife often stumbles, so do I. I forget to seek Him out; not all of the time, but sometimes I fail to look for His direction. For this reason,

I'm glad to have moments like these when I can refocus and hear God accepting me all over again – not that He had ever stopped accepting me. I just get too busy to listen.

About two thirds of the group left after the first couple of hours around the fire. Now, it was almost midnight, but I couldn't bring myself to leave such a wonderful Presence. Steven tapped me on the shoulder, "Jeffrey and I are going to bed. We checked for you, Anthony is nowhere in sight so you should be okay."

"Thank you," I said as we all bumped fists to say goodnight. Jeffrey looked a little pale, but said he just needed to rest.

Omar stayed, sitting crossed legged, staring at the fire. *Was he praying?* I wondered. I moved next to him, sitting in a similar position. I, too, stared at the flames.

"You do not have to wait on me," Omar said softly.

"Oh, I'm not waiting. I'm actually enjoying the peace," hardly any of the group, who stuck around, still sang as a whole. Several individual groups sang their own choice songs, or prayed and talked with each other. Still, the voices melted into a beautiful sound.

"There is definitely something special about tonight," Omar said, "as if God is giving us a calm before the storm."

"Like waiting for the other shoe to drop," I added in agreement while chuckling at our clichés. With a full camp tomorrow, who knew what would be in store?

"Did your friends leave?" He asked.

"Yes, some of them, but you're here."

Omar smiled at me, and then we continued staring into the fire. Fire can do so much damage, but it can also be beneficial. It helps new life to grow, brings light to the darkness, and warms a cold body. Tonight, the crackling from the fire created a calming melody. I couldn't help but think that it was calling out praises to God's name as it stretched its flames higher into the sky than any of us could ever imagine reaching.

"I do not want to die tomorrow," Omar said out of the blue,

"but I will not fight God if that is His will." Omar was the second one to talk about death today.

"I try not to think about death, but I suppose I could say the same," I looked at Omar, hoping he would expound on his comment. He kept focused on the flames.

"Why?" He never moved his head while asking me this.

I swallowed nervously, "When traveling from one country to another, I know what to expect and how people work. I keep my old memories and make new ones, and I know how to adapt to other cultures. I have no idea what Heaven is going to be like, and fear overwhelms me when I think on it too much. I can't wait to meet Jesus, and our Father, and all of the Christians who have walked before us…but…what will we all do, and forever? I can't think about it…" my heart began to race, so I stopped.

"I can see your fear," Omar said, looking at me and placing his hand on my shoulder. "It is okay to wonder, but do not let it engulf you. Hold fast to knowing that, no matter what Heaven is like, it will be better than anything you will know or have ever known on earth."

I grinned, "Why were you thinking of death?"

"In college, after my family cast me away, the house I lived in caught on fire. My two housemates died in it. I should have died with them, but a friend called me to help him when his car broke down on the side of the road. I believe God kept me alive to help my family see the Light."

"They will," I said firmly. It was too strong of an affirmation simply just to speak; I believed God was speaking through me.

"I know that I don't need them in Heaven; I will only need God. Still, I want so desperately to see them there too."

"I understand," I said.

"Father," Omar prayed aloud, "remove all fear and doubts from our minds. Remove the worry and let us cast our burdens on You. Work on our families' hearts; bring mine to You and keep Khristy's with You. Let us bless those we encounter this week. We love You and hope to glorify Your name in all that we do. In Jesus' name I pray, Amen"

I followed with a resounding "Amen," and then watched as Omar stood. We were the last two on the field. He offered me his hand to assist me. I debated on staying, but knew I needed to sleep too. Therefore, I took his hand. "Thank you," I gave him a hug and we headed to our cabins.

Quietly opening my cabin door, I saw only three other beds made. One rested across from mine. I didn't know who slumbered under the pile of blankets, but I was thankful I didn't wake them. I set my alarm for 7:00 AM, with breakfast being at 7:30, and then curled into my sleeping bag. Within minutes, my eyes sealed shut as my body melted into the bed mat.

That night, flames engulfed me. I tried to scream for help. I had nowhere to go. I was stuck, suffocating in smoke. My lungs constricted so tightly that I couldn't even cough. Waking up, I found my sleeping bag wrapped around my head. I violently removed it and took in several deep breaths. The cool air relaxed my lungs allowing me to sleep once again.

CHAPTER 8

Because of the Lord*'s great love we are not consumed, for His compassions never fail. They are new every morning...*
—Lamentations 3:22–23 (NIV)

My alarm never had the chance to go off. New campers joined our room as early as 6:00 AM. Most of them came in and crashed in the bunk of their choice. The door constantly squeaked open and sprung shut, waking me up before I was truly ready. Sitting up, I looked in the direction of the bunk across from mine. The pile of blankets I saw last night now clumped on one end of the bed. Jasmine, the shy girl from our group who first chose to bunk in the room across from mine, now sat with her knees curled to her chest. She looked just as disturbed as I felt. We made eye contact. I stood up and walked her way, sitting near her ball of blankets.

"Let's hope it's not always like this," I tried to joke and get her to smile.

Jasmine looked down as she twiddled her thumbs, "I'm not much of a morning person."

"Why did you switch rooms?" I asked.

"Oh, I'm not big on drama either," she seemed depressed. "Issues with boys and family were all they could talk about while I tried to sleep."

"Well, I'm glad you switched then," I looked past the window in the back of the cabin. "If you can't go back to sleep, you should come with me to see the sun rise."

Jasmine seemed hesitant to leave her cozy bed, still warm from the night, but she arose nonetheless. We both went outside in our pajamas to see the beautiful dawn that God made. The morning chill took us by surprise, chasing us inside for our blankets. Stepping back into the fresh mountain air, I took in a deep breath. Down by the pond, a pier jutted over the water while holding onto the bank nearest to us. It looked rather inviting for us to come join its celebration of the new morning. Jasmine had a hard time waking up with such an early start, but perhaps sitting down would let her adjust at her own pace. One of the camp leaders in a staff shirt watched us carefully from the other side of the pond. Did she think we would want to swim with the weather so cold? We sat down on the end of the pier and she continued walking her rounds.

The sunrise mesmerized me and, judging by the look on Jasmine's face, the radiance of oranges and yellows ascending above the horizon awed her as well. We absorbed every bit of warmth. God painted such a beautiful sky to introduce us to our first official day at camp. Birds began their good morning songs as the trees revealed the magnificence of their greenery. Flowers opened their blooms. Ripples in the water made me smile as water skippers and minnows began to play. *Thank You, Father, for this beautiful day.* The world was now waking to another new start. Everything was clean, new, beautiful, and sinless.

CHAPTER 9

Be self-controlled and alert. Your enemy the devil prowls around like a roaring lion looking for someone to devour.
—1 Peter 5:8 (NIV)

The camp filled up fast with children running all around. Some parents managed to keep their little ones within arm's length, but most seemed comfortable letting their children roam in groups at a farther distance. Adults of all ages, from nineteen to ninety, migrated towards the breakfast line.

I constantly felt eyes on me and kept close to Jasmine hoping the guys would turn up soon. I couldn't find them in the crowd, so Jasmine and I dined at an empty table together. She spoke very little during breakfast. In fact, the few sentences she did mutter were in response to my questions. I wouldn't allow the situation to grow awkward. Our personalities differed, she's quiet and I like to chatter, but we had many things in common most importantly, our faith. I also found out that she aspired to be a nurse and would start her clinical practicum in the fall.

David came to our table anxious and short of breath, "Khristy, I'm so glad I found you. Our afternoon guest speaker won't arrive until tomorrow. I've already rescheduled too many of the other speakers. Do you suppose your group could be ready by two?"

"Yes, I'm sure we can," I gulped.

"Oh, thank you," he looked up to the sky with clasped hands as if to throw a second *thank You* up to God.

I didn't get a chance to say anything else before he ran off. "I should go tell the others," I looked at Jasmine, stressed, realizing that this gave us very little time to plan anything.

"It will be okay," she said calmly. "God will take care of us."

"You're right," I replied, though inside, my stomach still churned. God had control, but we weren't prepared. I couldn't find room to finish my meal. Instead, I began to search for our group to let them know about the change of plans. God managed to humble me by leading me to Gunner and Richard in the breakfast line. They then directed me to where I could find most of the others. *You should have listened to Jasmine,* I criticized myself.

I finally saw where Omar, Jeffrey, and Steven sat at the opposite end of the tent. I sat with them while explaining the change in plans. Jeffrey still seemed pale. We had until two to prepare, but many of the other members of our group decided to stick to the schedule this morning and wait until lunch to work out the details.

At nine thirty, the entire camp gathered at the fields for a meeting. David introduced the scheduled events for the week. Those of us who had shown up the day beforehand helped pass out the camp packets and gift bags with papers, pens, and pocket Bibles. David took charge and spoke in place of his father. He explained how he expected us to be honest, trustworthy, and modest. Since we claimed to be of Christ, they expected us to love like Christ. In our love, we needed to correct others and ourselves in all situations throughout the week.

It comforted me to see such a large sum of people unafraid to claim Jesus as their Savior. This gathering spoke a great deal to me. The outpouring of faith expressed by those choosing to attend overwhelmed my heart.

Released to our morning schedules, we all stood to walk off the field. Butterflies filled my stomach when I noticed David's gentle yet determined stride as he approached me. I knew why I looked for him among the crowd; I believe it's natural for eyes to gravitate to the leader in a group gathering. I didn't understand why his eyes searched for me. Nevertheless, I was glad he joined us. He greeted Omar, Steven, and Jeffrey, and then moved next to me as we all walked back to the camp together. Jeffrey and Steven got a kick out of mocking me from behind. I ignored their childish remarks, and complimented David on his talent for speaking. He, on the other hand, seemed blind to the fact of how good of a spokesperson he was as he continuously named off all of the mistakes he made during his speech.

"Now wait just a minute," I interrupted. "You have a talent. Being humble doesn't mean you can't have confidence in the gifts God has given you." He never replied, which left us at an awkward silence. I only wanted him to see how amazing he was, and how much God was using him.

"Khris!" Steven yelled for me. I turned, half expecting him to have a prank prepared, but instead, I saw Jeffrey sprawled out on the ground. He had fallen to his face. Omar and Steven knelt down next to him, rolling him to his back. They began fanning him. I ran towards them with David close behind me.

Jasmine rushed to help. "What's wrong?" She asked, immediately placing her hand on Jeffrey's forehead, "He's clammy." The nurse in her took charge.

"He just dropped. One minute he was walking and the next he was on the ground," Omar said.

Jeffrey opened his eyes. He smirked, rolling his eyes at me, "I'll be fine ma. Just give me a minute." Though he looked sickly, he still managed to joke.

I huffed back at him. He knew I hated it when he called me that. As his friend, I had the right to worry, but he never saw it that way. Jasmine had us help him sit up. "Have you vomited at all?" She asked.

He responded lightly, while trying to catch his balance, "Just once this morning." Omar and Steven each grabbed an arm and put it around their necks to help keep him steady.

"Get him inside where he can sip water," Jasmine replied.

David also suggested we take him to the First Aid station. "I'll lead the way," he began to walk ahead of us all.

Jasmine and I walked behind them as she whispered to me, "I'm not certain, but I would guess that having vomited and passed out, he's dehydrated. He needs fluids."

"How much water have you been drinking, Jeffrey?" I asked.

He attempted to turn his head back to me, "None of your business." His voice was not strong enough to yell, though he raised it a tad bit.

"No time for jokes, Jeffrey Mills," I snapped. I turned back to Jasmine, "He loves sodas. We always make it a point to force him to drink two bottles of water a day when we go on mission trips. I guess it slipped my mind."

"You're not to blame," Jasmine put her hand on my shoulder. "He's a big kid; he should be taking care of himself. If it's dehydration, he doesn't appear to be in total distress. I think that if he rests today, he'll be back to normal tomorrow."

With a few more seconds going by, Jeffrey started to walk on his own ability again, but the guys stayed nearby. When we arrived at the camp nurses' cabin, they gave Jeffrey a glass of water and place to sit. We could see how weak he was as his hand shook while lifting the glass to his lips. I placed my hand below the glass to steady it for him. Jeffrey tried to fight me. As he lowered the glass from his lips, he immediately jerked forward and threw up. Thankfully, the nurse had already put a trash bin in front of him.

Jasmine looked a little queasy, but held it together as she turned to talk to the camp nurse. Steven stood next to Jeffrey and gave him a swift pat on his back while making jokes about the different things Jeffrey must have eaten. Omar stepped back, looking as if he would lose his breakfast as well.

"Could I get the rest of you to wait outside," one of the nurses ordered. "One or two visitors at a time will be fine."

"He'll be alright," David assured me as we walked out the doors. "Our nursing staff is well trained. They'll take care of him."

"Thank you," I replied.

Then, David looked at the watch on his wrist, "I hate to leave now, but I have a few things to oversee. Will you be okay?"

I smiled, "Of course, thank you."

Sitting on the benches outside of the nurses' cabin, we watched the crowds of people gathering at their different assigned classes and stations.

"Should we get back to our schedules?" Omar asked.

I shook my head, "You can if you want to, but I don't feel up to it right now."

He didn't budge.

Steven went back to check on Jeffrey after a few minutes while Jasmine, Omar, and I stayed silent in thought on the benches.

Before long, I snapped. I couldn't take the stress of worrying about Jeffrey, and of what to talk about in the afternoon, along with constantly looking over my shoulders. "I need a moment alone; away from the crowd," I said, abruptly standing up. "I'm going to go for a hike and call home."

"What about our speech?" Jasmine said, stopping me in my steps.

I attempted to reassure her, "That won't be until two o'clock. I should be back by lunch."

"Wait," Omar said as I started to walk away. "At least give us your phone number in case we need to reach you."

I did so, and then began talking to my Father in Heaven as I waded around and through the sea of people. *Lord, let this walk help to clear my mind. I can feel myself clamming up at the mere thought of addressing five thousand people. Please, provide me with the confidence needed to glorify Your name.*

I walked the trail that began behind the family cabins. The trail became less and less defined as it went up the mountain, but it made for a good path. The further I hiked I still couldn't catch a good signal. I held my phone as high as possible. Finally, two bars appeared. I froze in place, hoping not to lose them, and then pressed the call button. I had already dialed in the house number. Inch by inch I lowered the phone to my ear while trying to keep the signal. The bars disappeared. I took a couple more steps and waited for the signal to return. The call went through this time, but it was all for nothing…

"You've reached the Monzels. Leave us your name and number and we'll get back to you when we can. If you're a telemarketer, don't bother. God bless and have a great day." The recording was my dad's voice, but the last part of it was my sister's idea. She always had witty things to say.

Keeping my arm and hand as still as possible, I readied myself to leave a message. Voices stole my attention beyond the trees and bushes in front of me. I accidentally hung up my phone before leaving a message. The bars disappeared. Signal lost. Holding my breath, I searched the vegetation in front of me for the owners of the voices.

Normally, I would think Steven and Jeffrey were playing tricks on me, but the hairs on the back of my neck stood. I tried to take a deep breath. Suddenly, I felt alone and scared. I closed my eyes. *There's no reason to be afraid.* A shiver ran up my spine. My skin crawled. My senses were on high alert. I no longer heard the voices, but I knew I wasn't alone. My heart slammed against the walls of my chest. Adrenaline coursed through my veins. I thought of calling out to see if anyone would answer, but something held me back. Fear became more profound by the minute. It took every ounce of courage I had not to bolt down the trail I had climbed. I knew I should run back to the camp. Instead, I crept closer to the voices.

"We are set; everyone is here, except Judas. He left without warning. What are our orders?"

As I got closer, I realized I recognized a few of the voices. I watched my steps carefully. I found some shrubbery to hide behind where I could see what they were doing. "Why can't we just go down to the camp and get it over with?" A male voice asked.

"When you turn on the lights, the roaches scatter, and without a leader, another will always rise up," a female replied harshly.

My phone vibrated loudly, causing me to jump a second before it rang. I fumbled to pull it out of my pocket. Even though I had set it to a quiet ring, it still seemed loud in the surrounding shadows of the forest. I willed it to be silent and hesitated for a moment too long. Before I could answer, a hand roughly clamped over my mouth. Trying to take in a breath, my nostrils filled with a chemical smell.

My attacker wrenched the phone from my hand and tossed it away. I tried to throw my elbow into their gut. Legs flailing, I kicked at their knees, groin, or anywhere where I could make contact. I was becoming weaker by the second but kept on fighting to get away. He was holding me so tightly that I couldn't get a breath. I panicked. Instead of struggling, I let my body go limp. My attacker rewarded my cooperation by forcing me to the ground. All the while, his hand remained firmly around my mouth and nose. Blackness swam at the edges of my vision. Then…all went dark.

CHAPTER 10

Dogs have surrounded me; a band of evil men has encircled me...
—Psalm 22:16 (NIV)

I awoke with my face in the ground and my body up next to a tree. It took me a moment to remember where I was and why I was on the ground.

I heard Erica's ugly voice, "We can't go in yet."

"They'll notice she's missing," Justin argued. "We need to do something."

My body hurt. I didn't know how long I had been unconscious. I started to sit up but something told me, *be still. Just listen.* My eyes finally managed to focus on my captors. Their backs were to me, which was a small blessing as immense pain coursed over my body as if I experienced a beating. My hands and feet had a stinging pain as if they had fallen asleep and were trying to wake up again. Places on my face felt like they were being jabbed by needles. The worst was the soreness in my midsection. Someone must have kicked me. As I continued the inventory of injuries, I realized I had yet to discover the worst. The throbbing in my pelvis consumed my thoughts and my eyes hazed over…*stay still and don't move. Just listen.*

My head and heart pounded with anxiety. *Stay still,* I commanded myself.

"We can't make any rash decisions until we know why she's here," Erica said.

Justin responded, "So we're just going to wait and let the entire operation fall apart."

"Who's in charge here?" Erica growled.

I labored to sit up. The gravel shuffled beneath me, causing all heads to turn in my direction. I froze. I wasn't sure if I should let them know just how afraid I really was. I tried to look unconcerned but then, I saw Anthony step from behind the group and revulsion replaced fear.

Erica stepped directly in front of me. Her dark brown eyes peered into my soul. "Oh look, the spy is awake," she grunted. "Why don't you make things easy, and tell us who all knows you're here."

I sunk back into the ground like a worm with three hungry birds towering above me.

Erica knelt down beside me and pulled a knife from her boot. She touched the cold steel to my cheek and threatened, "Or will we have to make you talk?"

"No one," I blurted. "No one knows I'm here."

"Good, then no one will miss you," she reached her hand for my head, pulling it back to expose my throat.

Anthony reached and caught Erica's wrist. Warm blood slid down my cheek as the blade nicked my skin. "She could be useful," Anthony said as Erica glared at him. "We need to wait."

Erica was not happy about Anthony's interruption, but she listened to him anyway. I couldn't tell who was in charge. The tension between them was electric.

"Khris," a voice called out for me.

I desperately wanted to reply to Omar in the distance. No doubt, they would kill him too. Anthony gave Justin a nudge. He stalked off in the direction of Omar's voice. I couldn't let him harm Omar. I pushed aside my pain and threw myself forward at Justin. I caught his leg mid stride and held firm. I gripped as tight as possible to keep Justin from going any further and pushed aside all of the pain within me.

"Please no," I begged. "I'll get rid of him."

"You're in no position to bargain," Justin huffed as he kicked me and then shook me loose as if I was nothing.

"Khris," Omar called again. "Where are you?"

I sobbed, "Please, I'll do anything."

"Ah, she's got a soft spot for the Muslim," Erica scoffed.

I looked back at Anthony. "Please…"

Anthony looked at Erica, who stepped forward and called off Justin. She then looked at me and sneered, "Get him out of here, and back to camp, or we'll kill you both." She held her gun out and signaled for me to go. I wasn't willing to test their honesty, but I had to try something.

"Omar," I said, as I stepped through the thickets. I tried to stand straight and force all the pain and emotion off my face.

"Khris," he smiled in relief. "When we could not reach you by phone, Jeffrey and Steven both insisted I come find you. I thought they might kill me when they found out I let you come up here alone. You left so fast though…" His smile froze and then dropped. "What is wrong? You look like you –"

"I'm fine," I lied. I was anything but fine. I heard movement from the bushes behind me. I knew that Erica probably had her gun pointed at me, or worse, Omar. I thought of grabbing him and running. "I'm still trying to get a signal out here. I need to talk to my family, so I was going to go a little further up the mountain. I promise I'm fine."

"You appear anything but fine. You look death stricken." Omar ignored everything I said. "Maybe you are sick too, and what happened to your face?"

I raised my hand to wipe off the blood. "Nothing is wrong with me," I snapped. I hated to be so short with him. "I just need to be alone, and I'm concerned about Jeffrey. Please, go back and take care of him."

"He is resting. I can wait with you," he insisted. Omar was so kind, which was exactly why I needed to get him out of here.

"I promise, I'll be back soon," at that moment, I could see his eyes fixate on my phone, which lay on the ground. When he looked back at me, about to say something, I shook my head discretely. I knew of the eyes watching me and I was terrified they would know what Omar had just seen. My expression turned cold and my voice dripped with anger and impatience, "Just go. I want to be alone. I don't need you to wait. Go back to camp, Omar," I lied angrily.

Realization flickered across his face. His tone became tense, "Okay, I will go back to camp, but they will hate me for leaving you here."

My voice wavered as I held back tears and smiled, "Steven

can't hate you, and Jeffrey will be too sick to do anything. Besides, they know how I am."

"Should I tell them anything?" Omar asked. I didn't know if he was hinting at me to speak in code, or if he was just helping aid the cover.

"Just that it looks like it might storm, but I'll try to be back before it does," Jeffrey, Steven, and I had planned that code to warn each other in times of danger. A surge of hope entered my heart. If only the guys would remember what it meant. We only talked about it once.

Omar paid no attention to the clear skies above. I was relieved when he turned his back and started towards the camp. I sighed and thought *I've gotten away with it.*

Those watching me darted past me. Erica grunted, "Do you think we're stupid?"

"Run!" I yelled to Omar, right before something struck me in the back of the head.

"I have her. Retrieve him quietly," Erica growled at Justin and Anthony. They ran at speeds I never would have guessed they possessed. All I could do was pray they tripped before they reached him.

Struggling against Erica's hold, I felt like a child against a bear. I pushed away or, so I thought, when Erica swung a leg over and straddled me. When my head hit the ground, flight or fight took over. I began to swing my arms and fists and let them hit her wherever I could. Erica blocked most of my feral jabs until I gave a painful thrust of the hips, which knocked her off me. I turned to crawl away. Like a magnet, she rolled back, this time grinding my face into the ground. A searing pain came to my back as her knee dug into it.

Erica began to laugh, "Is that all you got, maggot?"

"What do you want with me?" I yelled at her. Everything about her radiated evil.

"I want you to disappear," Erica replied with extreme malice.

"What have I done to you?"

"You live," she spat, as Anthony and Justin approached with Omar in their hands. He was still alive, though badly scraped. Erica's hand twisted itself into my hair and then pulled me to my feet. The pressure on my back ceased, but the pain remained where her knee had been. With every yank of my hair, a new pain invaded my head. The gun in my side stopped me from squirming.

"Now what…?" Justin complained. "This isn't how things were supposed to go."

"Shut up," Erica snapped at him. "Let me think."

Meanwhile, Omar and I looked at each other's pain with empathy. "What is happening?" He whispered, as the three fought to yell over one another.

"I'm not sure."

We listened to them argue repeatedly about what to do with us. Death was certainly a recurring theme, but they had a problem with people noticing our absence.

"They will know we are missing within the next fifteen minutes," Omar interjected. "Khris is expected to talk to everyone about her mission trips. If she is absent, they will know something is wrong."

I tried to get Omar's attention. My eyes pleaded with him to stay quiet. He was signing his own death warrant.

"So, we have fifteen minutes to figure out what to do," Erica said, letting Omar feel the sting of his plan backfiring.

"Or you could let us go, and use that time to leave and never return," I sassed.

"Do you think you're funny?" Erica jerked my head back.

Then, as if a light bulb had turned on, she pushed me to the ground and kicked my already hurting abs.

"Go," Erica, said, "make your speech." A grim smile formed on her face with her eyebrows cocked.

"What are you doing?" Anthony shouted.

I wouldn't go anywhere without Omar. Where was the trick?

As soon as she put her gun to Omar's head, I knew. "Make your speech. Don't start any commotion. Mention nothing of us. If you can follow directions like the good little Christian you think you are, then your friend will live. If not, well…"

"Khris, do not worry about me. Just go," Omar said. I couldn't help but remember our conversation last night. He didn't want to die; he said so himself. Yet, he was so willing to sacrifice his life now.

"Omar is expected to make that speech with me," I pathetically attempted to keep him safe. Even if we had targets on our heads, there was still a better chance of escape than if either of us were in these monsters' hands. "If he's absent, he'll be missed too."

Omar's scowl told me to stay quiet, but I had to try something.

"You seem like a smart girl," Erica remarked. "Convince them he has stage fright. Tell them he's sick. Just figure it out, or he dies. It's as simple as that."

"That's it?" I asked, realizing I had no other option. "I go down and help the camp run normally, while you and your goons hold Omar hostage. If I slip up, he dies. If not, the week goes on and you eventually kill us all off?"

"Guess you'll have to find out," Erica kept her gun firm on Omar's head.

I begrudgingly accepted her terms and held to the possibility that we still had a chance to escape. I began to walk back down the mountain. I should have just sacrificed us both right then.

"Not so fast," Erica stopped me in my tracks. "Farrell, go with her."

Justin released Omar into Anthony's full custody, and then accompanied me down the hillside. He didn't lay a hand on me, nor did he say anything. I watched as he concealed his weapons in his clothing. He tucked his gun inside of his back waistband, behind his shirt, and his knife he hid in his boot. I knew I couldn't challenge him physically, so I would cooperate until I didn't have to…

Half way down the mountain, my mind began to take in, fully, all that had happened. This wasn't a game. I got the distinct impression that Omar and my lives were not the only two in danger. Whatever I did from here on out affected every single life in the camp. People like Jim and Jan, and everyone else we had met, depended on me. They didn't even know danger was coming. I didn't even know what was happening, but in my heart, I knew something sinister was imminent.

"Don't even think about running," Justin threatened.

My palms sweat uncontrollably, and my body shook; perhaps he assumed it derived from a nervous tick, ready to bolt. Never had that thought crossed my mind. Now that he said it, I considered it as an option. Might the members of the camp perceive me crying wolf? They would see me as the world saw Noah when he tried to warn them about the flood. They'd laugh at me and whisper among each other, wasting what precious time they had to escape. No, I had to warn them in a way they would understand. God provided me with the perfect opportunity to do that by giving me this chance to stand on stage in front of all five thousand people.

The moment I stepped back into the campground, fear of failure punched me in the gut. The weight of desperation was on my shoulders. That thought made my stomach sour and bile rise in my throat. I swallowed my angst. How could I even be sure they hadn't killed Omar already? I pushed my worry about him aside. I had to warn the campers. I could not live with the thought that I didn't do everything in my power to inform them. I had an obligation. Hope sprang up within me when I saw the empty fields and cabins. My hope faded when I noticed the sound coming from the Tabernacle. Everyone had already gathered inside. A single, timid voice cracked through the speakers.

CHAPTER 11

"...do not worry about how you will defend yourselves or what you will say, for the Holy Spirit will teach you at that time what you should say."
—Luke 12:11–12 (NIV)

My entire mission group sat on stage, except for Omar, Jeffrey, and Jasmine. I hesitantly walked towards them, but David blocked my path before I could go any further. He was flustered, "Where have you been? Your team started ten minutes ago. We tried to stall, but Steven had to begin without you." David glanced at Justin and then back at me, "Where's Omar?"

I swallowed hard, "He's… not feeling well either." I hated lying.

"I'm taking his place," Justin added. My blood boiled with anger; never in a million years would he be able to replace Omar.

"Okay, well…" I could see the stress of the week already weighing down on David. If only he knew.

"Breathe," I placed my hand on his shoulder while taking in a deep breath myself. "Give God the control. The only people who know we're a little mixed up in our plans are you, me, and the ones on stage."

David let out a sigh, "Please, just tie it together. So far, we've had introductions and slight sharing of experiences. Most of them have been too quiet to hear, or buckled their knees when they saw the crowd."

If the situation were different I, too, would have probably cowered in fear of the masses. I had prayed earlier for God to give me the courage to speak. Forced by gunpoint wasn't exactly what I meant, but now the lives of everyone here were more important than my worries. I confirmed with David that I would do my best. Justin followed me as I walked up the steps and took a seat next to Steven.

"Good acting," Justin mocked me. "Keep it up."

"It wasn't an act."

Steven sent a fist bump my way to acknowledge my presence. Justin took the seat next to me, which undoubtedly belonged to Jeffrey. Two other empty seats waited for Jasmine and Omar.

"Isn't that Anthony's friend?" Steven leaned over and whispered.

Feeling Justin's eyes on me, I answered with a nod.

"Where's Omar?" He asked.

"Not feeling well," again, I lied. I pretended to be listening to Richard Jones speak. My answer satisfied Justin for now, and Steven never once questioned its validity. My throat swelled closed and my eyes searched the crowd while my heart pleaded to God for understanding on what to do.

Most of the people sitting in front of us listened respectfully, but their faces registered confusion. My ears received Richard's story about growing up on a farm, but none of his words held meaning. I looked at his body posture, slouched, fidgety, and timorous. In his hands was a piece of paper with smeared ink all over it. It was obvious that he was reading his speech causing him to slur into the microphone.

I searched down the line of chairs on stage, and saw everyone with their heads hung low. Each failed attempt to share their message left the next speaker less assured in their abilities, vanquishing all confidence. We hadn't prepared for this. We prepared for hands on and one on one work. Even Steven, who sat next to me, had the posture of a doubting man. I suspected that he attempted a few jokes and received only pity laughs.

Richard sat down, sweat falling from his brow. Chelsea was next. She refused to stand. Steven looked at me with an expression screaming for help. After looking high, praying for God's gift of speech, I stood up and stared at the crowd. Movement in the very back of the room caught my eye. Anthony and Erica entered the Tabernacle with Omar in front of them. They didn't sit down. Instead, they walked to the very center of the tent, in the back, and focused all eyes on me.

Silence hung over the room like a dark cloud. A few coughs attempted to prompt my speech. Even David, who sat in the very front, cleared his throat a few times. God had given me my opening.

"Do you feel that?" I said into the microphone with as steady a voice as I could muster. Not sure if they heard me, I repeated myself. This time I could hear myself on the speakers. "Silence is something well known to all awkward situations. Why is that? Who makes the silence awkward? It isn't God, I'll tell you that much. God makes some of His strongest statements through silence, both in scripture and in our lives. Perhaps that is often why we don't feel His presence; we are scared of the silence." I knew my statements were blunt, even harsh, but if I was going to die, I wasn't going to share a whimsical message. I would speak of reality, no matter how ugly.

"Sometimes we make the silence awkward, because we don't know what to do in its presence." Omar squirmed in the back. Fumbling for what to say I desperately tried to regain my composure. "I'm sure you've already noticed, but those of us on stage are not great at filling in the silence, especially when we're put on the spot."

Laughs came from behind me, and smiles crept to the faces in the crowd.

I cleared my throat. I stood straighter and, with a deep breath, continued my thoughts, "We were all created with different strengths and weaknesses. What if I told you that the group behind me could work nonstop from sunup to sundown? There would be no complaints no matter the climate, terrain, location, or conditions, not because of their strength or durability, but because that's what they've spiritually prepared themselves to do. Would you agree that our strengths and abilities come from God?" I received a few responses from the crowd, but not enough to satisfy my ears to know if they were listening. I repeated my questions.

"Amen," the crowd said. A few children even managed to yell it out without their parents' permission. Their joy brought a smile to my face.

"Good, then I would like you all to give a hand of thanks to everyone up here, for simply taking the chance to speak in front of you today. Had we more time to prepare perhaps our speeches could be better, but regardless they are well intended. Not to mention, I am to blame for most of the lack of preparation. Therefore, if you must, you can boo me off the stage later. For now, I want to thank you all for stepping up," I spoke this last line to everyone on the stage, except for Justin. I made it very clear to him through my glare that he was not welcome.

The room filled with applause for everyone sitting on stage. As the crowd celebrated, those who felt like failures before now raised their heads. Spirits were renewed. Now, perhaps I could focus on strengthening the soldiers before me.

"Thank you for your support," I said, trying to silence everyone once again. "It really is an honor to be here with so many brothers and sisters in Christ. I can't wait for God to reveal why He has gathered us together." Erica's threats flashed through my mind. Now would be the perfect time to destroy us all, yet, they were waiting for Judas. Who could that be? Was he here as a wolf in sheep's clothing?

"In a crowd like this, it is practically impossible to ignore the fact that God's presence is among us. It's amazing to know how many different worlds we have all come from to meet here. Yes, we all live on earth, but how many different cultures are represented?" It was a rhetorical question, but the people in the room began to view those around the tent as if really seeing them for the first time.

"I know this week is just beginning, and we prefer to have more time to step out of our comfort zones. Still, how much time do we really need? Now is that moment. Now is the time. Make every second count. Encourage your brothers and sisters in Christ as they did in Paul's time. They gathered to lift one another up and remind each other of Jesus' salvation, not for entertainment or as a vacation. I challenge you to keep these thoughts in your mind. Right now, God could be preparing us for the storm of a lifetime." I looked back at Steven. I had hoped he heard between the proverbial lines. If he had, he gave no indication. He only nodded in approval of my speech.

Justin tensed, but when I continued, he settled down. Erica and Anthony still held Omar captive, threatening my every move. I continued, "Think about it. What good is it for us to know what God has said, if we don't put His words into practice. A sword is of no use to a man if he only studies its appearance, yet never wields it. Likewise, our faith works the same way. We can put on the Christian image for as long as we want, but we can't help lead a single soul to salvation if we don't put it into action.

"For example, if a man named Judas came in here, threatening to kill anyone unwilling to denounce Christ," I saw Erica cock her head and flashed a warning with her evil eyes, "would you take up his offer, or lay down your life?" No one seemed shocked to hear my question. "Of course, you have all heard this question many times before." The menacing look remained firmly on Erica's face. "I want you to seriously contemplate that question. Matthew 10, verse thirty-three, tells us that if we deny Christ, God will deny ever knowing us. Are you willing to give up heaven, which we know will be pain free and without suffering, for a lifetime on earth? It's not worth it. This life could end today. Heaven is eternal."

A few amens arose from the crowd. I looked back again at Steven, wondering if he caught on to anything I was saying. Still, he sat oblivious.

"Let me tell you a story," I continued. "My friends and I missioned in China. Our group had to be small. Our presence needed to stay a secret. We were there under the guise of teaching English; however, at night we led Bible studies. The attendees were the same kids we taught during the day." Again, I looked behind me; Steven remembered our trip. "They risked everything to come and see us. Their parents weren't with them. In fact, if their parents knew they were coming to a place where we spoke God's name, the kids would have suffered a beating and we would have experienced our first arrest in a foreign country. These kids came to us because they could see the hope that came with accepting God as their Father and Jesus as their Savior. Life was worth risking if it meant learning, just that much more, about their Father in heaven.

"One night, a boy came to us with bruises on his arms and legs. He showed up late for our study, and we immediately stopped what we were doing to tend to him. He wouldn't let us help him and instead, begged us to continue our teaching. He didn't want to miss a single moment of God's message because of a flesh wound. He was hungry for God's peace.

"How many of us could say we'd do that? How many times have we woken up with a cough and used it for an excuse as to why we need to sleep in, instead of attend worship?" The faces of the crowd became solemn. "I ask you to judge your heart honestly. I didn't tell this story to tear us down, but rather to build us up. See, the hope that this child found in God is the same hope that lives in you and me. It's the hope of Jesus, who has saved you from the worst fate possible. I want you to think of the joy and hope this boy held dear, and place that same newness of life within yourselves. Do it right now. Don't wait until after I finish. Let God be the one to fill you up once again."

Seeing the faces rise back up into smiles helped me finish my story, "My friends and I found that boy's hope that night. We praised God as we have never praised Him before. In fact, we praised so loudly with those children that we decided to come up with a code to help us know when danger was approaching – just in case we ever ran into such a problem in the future – because we just knew that we would get caught that night." I looked back at Steven, "Do you remember that conversation?" I asked him.

Steven laughed away and nodded his head, showing the crowd he remembered it all. Then, like lightning to his brain, he caught on to everything. He sat taller, readying to make a move. I quickly turned to the audience, trying not to let Justin know the conversation that Steven and I just had. Looking to the back, I saw Erica signaling for me to hurry.

"Thankfully, God protected us that night," I said, trying to appease my captors. "He has continued to protect us ever since." I saw, from the corner of my eye, Steven get up, walk off the stage, and leave through a side door in the tent. I looked back nervously at Justin who did the same to me. I shrugged my shoulders. He stayed seated. In the back, I noticed Erica send Anthony away.

"Until today," I continued loudly, sweat starting to form on my brow. Anthony stopped in his tracks, stunned. I had to think of something quick to keep him away from Steven. I saw Erica's gun shove deep into Omar's side – or at least I assumed that's what made him squirm. Even then, he gave me a look of confirmation to continue. My moments of silence no longer brought awkwardness to the room but rather, anticipation. They waited for me, but nothing else left my lips.

Movement came from behind me, as the crowd's eyes grew wide. I turned to see Justin with his gun pointed straight at me.

"Are you ready to die for your faith?" He asked loud enough for all to hear. Gasps came from the crowd. Why was no one running?

"Yes," I said, staring him in the eyes. Though it was only one word, I stood behind it with my entire being.

Justin took a step towards me and placed the cold barrel to the center of my forehead, "Last chance to change your mind."

"I will not deny my Savior," I shouted at him, "no matter the cost." I only hoped that this example would remind everyone else to stand firm in their faith.

Justin pulled the trigger and the click of the gun sounded through the speakers. I opened my eyes to see him lower the gun and put it back behind his belt. Turning to the crowd, he spoke into the microphone, "Her faith does not waver. Will yours?"

The crowd jumped to their feet. A thundering applause filled the tent. I couldn't believe it. Everything they had just seen was merely a performance in their eyes. Did they not hear the threatening tone of Justin's voice? He wasn't challenging them; he was trying to intimidate them… wasn't he? Frustrated with their reactions I searched for Anthony. I barely caught glimpse of him leaving the tent. That wasn't enough time for Steven to get away. I needed to do more.

The men and women with me on stage applauded as well. Had they all lost their minds? Quickly, I turned to leave, but Justin's hand caught my arm. He came close to my ear, "try something like that again, and I'll be sure to leave the clip in the gun." I met his eyes with all seriousness. "Now take a bow."

I refused to do any such thing, but he practically forced me into it. Pulling away from his grip, I left the stage as fast as I could. I had to push through the pain of pins and needles in my legs and abdomen. Whatever had happened on that mountain, while I was unconscious, left a pain I had never known. I was able to focus on my message while on stage and blocked out the pain. Too many lives depended on what I had to say. Now that I needed to move, my body reminded me just how injured it was. When I caught a glimpse of Anthony as I burst from the tent, I rushed to stop him. He must have seen where Steven went. Just as I was about to tackle him from behind he spun and backhanded me across the face. My vision blurred and went black for a second or two. When I regained my focus… evil, itself stared back at me.

CHAPTER 12

"Blessed are you when people insult you, persecute you and falsely say all kinds of evil against you because of Me."
—Matthew 5:11 (NIV)

Erica spat in my face as she flung Omar into Justin's hands. Her fingers gripped my neck, "Do you think this is a game?" To Anthony, she ordered, "Find that boy. We can't have any loose ends."

"Check the nurses' cabin," Justin quietly advised. I moved to stop Anthony, but Erica tightened her grip, digging her nails into the flesh of my neck. I reached up to pull her hand away and glared at Justin for snitching. He wouldn't make eye contact with me, the coward.

Erica's focus came back on me as she raised her gun with her other hand towards Omar's chest. "I should kill him right now."

"No," I gasped. I had messed everything up. Because of me, my friends were all going to die.

"However," she added, as she hid her gun and released me, "you have Farrell to thank for his quick thinking."

Justin stood tall as she praised him.

I could hear David's voice coming from the Tabernacle. For the moment, the masses stayed corralled in one area. If he was wrapping up the session, I needed to keep Erica focused on me until the group dismissed. A song of praise began to sound out from the Tabernacle. Perhaps David wasn't releasing them after all.

"We did what you asked," Omar disputed. "No one in the camp suspects any trouble. Let us go." He had to know that such an option never existed for him or me. By freeing us, Erica would risk us warning the camp before they could carry out their plan.

"Do you call what she did in there, following orders?" Erica's scowl turned to me as she pistol-whipped me in the side of the head. The pain of the gun hitting my skull dropped me to my knees as she let go of my throat. "I don't believe for one second, that that was your planned presentation."

"What do we do now?" Justin asked, stealing her focus from me.

Erica's face flushed, if possible, with even more fury at his question. Her hesitation gave away that she had no idea how to answer him. "We wait for Tereski to get back with the other one. In the meantime," she looked around, grabbed my arm, and pulled me to a bench where she forced Omar and me to sit, "you two stay here. Don't move a muscle, or Farrell will end your lives."

Justin took the knife from his boot and concealed it in one hand, while keeping pressure on the top of Omar's shoulder. Omar grimaced. I hadn't noticed his dislocated shoulder until now. It was no wonder why they were able to subdue him so easily. I couldn't imagine the pain he felt.

"Your speech was very inspiring," Omar said through his gritted teeth. "I am certain everyone was encouraged." He looked as though he could pass out at any moment.

"You're welcome," Justin said from behind us with a sly grin.

I quickly looked away, filled with despair, "I'm afraid it was all entertainment to them."

"No," Omar reached his hand to touch my arm. "They..." He pulled away and cringed as Justin pinched his shoulder.

I stared at Omar sympathetically, wanting to apologize for getting him into this mess. From the distance, Anthony returned empty handed. Erica became livid. "Where is he?" She growled.

"I searched everywhere," Anthony became a submissive puppy in her presence. "The nurses' cabin was abandoned. I ordered the others to widen their search." He stood as a scolded dog would with its tail tucked between its legs.

There were more than these three?

Omar's eyes met mine in a quick glance. Our friends were safe. Help would come soon if they could stay out of sight.

"At your six," Justin warned.

Everyone hid their weapons and looked towards the tent. I turned to see what he was talking about; David strode our way. *Not another one*, I thought to myself. I really didn't want to see any more friends brought into this mess.

"That was brilliant," David said, coming to shake Justin's hand.

I shuttered to see them corresponding.

"We work to the best of our abilities," Justin smiled and then looked at me.

"Khristy," David gushed out, "you stole the stage. There's no doubt that you had the campers on the edge of their seats."

I didn't know how to reply. I couldn't even fake a smile.

"Oh," David finally noticed Omar next to me. "I didn't expect to see you here."

Justin still held to his shoulder, but acted like someone leaning on a friend. Omar didn't make a sound. He just nodded his head to acknowledge David's presence.

"David," Erica pulled his attention to her. It sickened me to see them all so nice. "When is your father returning?"

Lie to her! I screamed inside.

"Two days," David smiled, "that's when the real fun will begin." He looked back towards the Tabernacle, "I'll let you finish out here. I just wanted to be the first to thank you, Khristy, for your cooperation today."

I winced. What did he mean by *my cooperation?*

David shook hands with everyone, thanking them for their help. Then he went back towards the tent. Justin, Anthony, and Erica all looked at me. If it were Jeffrey and Steven here, I'd expect to hear some smart remark, but I just waited for another punishing blow.

"Well done," Erica mocked with a silent clap. Then, she gave an order to Anthony and Justin, "Rally the rest of the men. Keep them out of sight until the signal is given." She looked at Omar and me, "Take these two with you."

"Wait, no," I shouted. "You can't just…"

"What do you want with this camp?" Omar interrupted.

Justin popped Omar in the mouth and stood him up while Anthony jerked me to my feet. I shoved him back, trying hard to pull away. His very touch revolted me. The more I struggled the tighter his hands gripped my arms. "Let go of me." Getting one arm loose, I swung. Anthony caught my hand, spun me around, and shoved my head toward the ground. Then he bent my arm behind my back, causing a searing pain to shoot through my shoulder.

"That's enough," Anthony pulled my other arm behind my back as well. He gripped both of my wrists with his one hand, and used his free hand to grip the back of my neck, forcing me to stand straight.

"Until further notice, your people are a national threat," Erica sternly informed. "We're here, under strict government orders, to monitor your camp. As long as things continue to run smoothly, you have no reason to worry. If we don't recover your friends, we will use any means necessary to keep this camp subdued. You two are now in the custody of the United States Government for attempting to aid a possible terrorist threat. Fight all you want, but remember, you'll be taking everyone else down with you." Erica haughtily turned and walked to the tent, while Justin and Anthony drug Omar and me back up to the mountainside.

"We aren't terrorists," I screamed and fought for my freedom as they forced us forward. They couldn't seriously think we were like the crusading knights of the 12th century.

"Save it," Anthony snipped. "You're not fooling anyone."

"What have we done to deserve this treatment?" I tried to sink my heels into the ground. My shoes only slid across the grass.

"You, Christians," Anthony spat, "control people with fear, only to take from them their very lives. You preach freedom of choice, but then control the minds of your victims. You, and others like you, are juxtaposing yourselves into all areas of our government, trying to break us down. We've already discovered and imprisoned hundreds of your sleeper cells. Don't think for one moment that we're going to drop our guard at your pathetic attempts to make us think you're ignorant."

I looked at Omar completely dumbfounded. Anthony made no sense. Since when did we become the enemy? The "world" was our enemy; I never thought of us as being theirs. I most definitely never viewed us as a threat to our own country much less anyone else. We teach love… I quit dragging my feet. Fighting was useless, especially if they already prepared for us to be hostile. Maybe, we needed to use our time in their hands as an opportunity to prove them wrong.

“Christians are not trying to trick people,” Omar defended. “We put the cost of commitment on the table for all to see, just as your military recruiters do.”

Justin snidely remarked, “Christians trick people in to blindly following someone who can’t be seen or heard. At least our recruiters let us know exactly who we’re working for.”

“Do they?” I questioned. “You may see your boss just as we can see our preachers and elders, but do you have any idea who you really work for? Whose orders are you truly following by doing all of this?”

“It is not Erica’s,” Omar said. “I doubt two men would follow the barking orders of a woman without a higher power behind it.”

Justin pinched Omar’s collarbone causing him to wince as his eyes began to water. He must have struck a nerve with Justin. Perhaps these two didn’t like taking orders from Erica.

“Stop that,” I attempted to rush at Justin. I couldn’t stand him hurting Omar. Anthony gained full control over me as I, too, began to feel pressure into my collarbone. For a moment, I thought it would break. A searing pain coursed throughout my torso and neck. I couldn’t move. I could barely help myself let alone Omar. Anthony’s steel grip clamped down on the perfect nerve, rendering me defenseless. Debilitating pain rushed over me every time I tried to squirm out of his hold.

We reached the tree line and the trail that would lead us back up the mountain. I looked back, searching for a glimpse of at least one witness. At this point, the rocks and trees were now aiding our captors by hiding us. Would anyone know we were gone, anyone except God? It seemed so much easier to stand on stage and stare death in the eye with Justin's gun pointed straight at me, than to dwell on the things to come. I knew I could trust God, but I had no idea how far He would ask me to go.

"Omar," I said, not caring if the others heard. "Thank you."

"For what…?"

"In the short time that I've known you, you've become a great friend and an even greater example of faith. I thank God for allowing us to meet, especially during this time."

"Likewise," Omar smiled. "I hope that you know your courage has not gone unnoticed."

"Or unpunished," Anthony added in as Justin smacked Omar.

I recoiled at the sight of his pain, but tried not to give them the pleasure of seeing tears.

Anthony scolded, "You two need to shut up. Your God isn't going to save you now."

"Even if he did show," Justin huffed, "he wouldn't be able to get past the two of us."

Omar examined our surroundings with a smile, "God is already here; patiently waiting."

"His timing is perfect," I smiled. I know we held the short end of the stick, but I loved listening to Omar. He had no fear in his voice. His heart stayed focused on God. I tried to mimic his confidence; I wanted them to see nothing but peace on my face. Worries continued barging in as I witnessed the abuse heaped upon Omar. Justin ran him into the side of a tree, slamming his head into a low hanging branch. I couldn't stop my tears, but I held back the sobs. If I didn't start cooperating more, they'd kill Omar before the sun set.

At the top of the mountain, we stopped at a familiar area. It was where they first took me captive. Why had they brought us back here? Justin walked over to a bush and pulled out a hidden bag. Inside, he retrieved a few large zip ties. Handing a few to Anthony, they used the zip ties to cuff our hands behind our backs. They placed us against a large tree, reminding us that running would inevitably end in our death. We were to stay put until further instructions. While Justin stood guard over Omar and me, Anthony made two phone calls. He spoke in a code that neither Omar nor I understood.

The night crept in and we both grew tired. After the hours of sitting, our bodies now ached all over as if we had been crammed in a box for days. My neck was stiff as a board. My chest felt restricted with my hands still behind my back. Shifting our bodies did no good. It only created more pain and discomfort. I would purposefully create some of my own discomfort in order to keep myself awake, but even that plan seemed to stop working, so I attempted to talk with Omar. Whispering, I asked, "Do you think the camp will notice the empty nurses' cabin?"

Before he could reply, Anthony interjected, "Not a chance. We already called in for a few replacements. Camp should be running as smooth as it was with you there."

His arrogance irritated me. They assume that we are like trash, disposable. Soon enough, someone will miss us. Questions will start to rise, and rumors will begin to spread.

Eventually, the chirping crickets lulled me into a state of relaxation. My eyelids were so heavy they'd have to be pried open. Likewise, my body was too weary to waste time and energy trying to stay awake. Perhaps with a little rest, I could think straight and then, maybe, Omar and I could devise a plan of escape.

CHAPTER 13

But Ruth replied, "Don't urge me to leave you or to turn back from you. Where you go I will go, and where you stay I will stay…Where you die I will die…"
—Ruth 1:16–17 (NIV)

Omar refused to sleep. Noticing my droopy eyes and bobbing head, he insisted that I rest it on his good shoulder. I realized, at his kind gesture, who Omar reminded me of: he looked at the best in the world, held firm to his faith through all trials, and always elevated others above himself. Though letting me lean on his shoulder would seem insignificant to most people, his kindness reminded me of my father. Tears welled up in my eyes.

On long road trips, Dad always sat in the back seat with my sister and me when we would get tired. He would still talk with Mom, who loved to drive, but let us girls rest on him while we fell asleep. Though they looked nothing alike, Omar and my dad had a very similar way of showing others they cared. These thoughts are what allowed me to sleep, in spite of the danger around us.

The sun began to rise behind the trees. Even though it stayed hidden from my eyes, there was no doubt of its existence. The forest life awoke and began to greet the day by singing their songs while the nocturnal creatures settled in for a nap. Despite the beauty, my restraints reminded me of our situation and left a bitter taste in my mouth.

I sat up and looked at Omar. His eyes reflected the burden of his heart. I felt selfish for sleeping. I should have woken up and let him rest. Yet, like my dad, Omar wouldn't have slept. He would have kept watch. Noticing perspiration drip from his brow, I asked, "Are you feeling okay?"

He gave no reply, though I worried the answer was, *no*. The morning was too cool to sweat. Looking in the same direction as him, I saw three more men standing with Anthony and Justin; one was tall with thin blonde hair, next to him stood a redhead, and the third seemed old and frail. They were discussing schematics of something, but I had come into their conversation too late to identify.

"What's going on?" I asked.

A moment of silence passed before Omar choked out, "They were here all along."

"Who…?"

"The men who plan to attack the camp. From what I can tell, they have been planning this for a while."

"Attack? What about Steven and Jeffrey, and all those people… the children?" My heart pounded.

"Khris," Omar sounded very grieved. "You need to listen. Militant men and women have disguised themselves as part of the camp staff. Others moved in overnight."

"Maybe they're just here to observe us like Erica said."

"Not likely," Omar frowned. "Not with how they were talking. Their lips are full of hate and disgust towards Christians. Someone has been filling their heads with lies. They think we are trying to take down the government from the inside out. We need to get back down there and warn the ones we know we can trust."

The truth hung between us like a heavy fog. Most likely, we would die before we could reach the camp, but we had to do what we could to warn them before the attack occurred. I nodded my agreement as my shoulders dropped in defeat. I didn't want to die, but I knew I would have to accept this as my fate. I wanted to cling to the hope that had lingered in my mind. Straightening back up, I asked, "How will we get free?"

His eyes motioned behind his back. He had scraped up a sharp stone, and was using it against the zip tie on his wrist. There was very little force to go by, but it seemed to be working. It's no wonder why he was sweating.

"Lord," Omar prayed, "give us quick feet, loud voices, and plenty of courage. Protect us so that we may warn the others before it is too late…"

The redhead looked in our direction, "What are you whispering about?"

Now I began to sweat. Neither of us responded. The redhead stepped in our direction, but Anthony stretched out his arm to stop him. "Leave them," he said. "They can't do anything."

Glaring at us, the redhead stayed put. He eventually refocused on Anthony and their previous conversation.

I took in a deep breath. *Okay God,* I prayed, *if this is how it must end. Please give us the courage to see it through, and to glorify You in the midst of everything about to happen.* I looked at Omar with confidence.

"No matter what happens, you will always keep God first, right?" He asked, readying me for our final trial.

In no way could I ever push God aside in my life; not after everything that He had already done for me. "Absolutely," I confirmed.

"Will you also remember my family in your prayers?" Though Omar's question seemed odd, I realized he spoke as a man ready to die.

I nodded.

"You are a wonderful child of the Most High. I am so glad to have met you," Omar's arms slightly jerked. He broke the tie, "I cannot wait to meet you again."

Realizing, too late, what he was doing my eyes began to scold his every move. I couldn't say a thing to stop him, or it would give him away. He planned to go alone, and leave me here unharmed. *Oh Omar, please don't leave me here.*

"Forgive me," Omar slid the stone into my fingers. I tried to grab his hand and hold him still, but he had more strength than I did. Quickly, while the men had their backs to us, Omar bolted away. It didn't take but a few seconds before they noticed his escape. Anthony acted swiftly, ordering Justin and the others to retrieve Omar.

Justin ran past me before I could make a move, but as the others came, I threw my body out in front of them. I had no way to grab to their legs, but I could pose as an obstacle. I immediately felt a boot to my forehead as the redhead tripped over me. I watched him scramble to get up. The others hurdled over my prone body.

The older man tripped over the redhead, falling headfirst into a tree while the blonde continued his pursuit.

I tried to scream out for Omar. The blow to my head rendered me unable to speak as the world spun around me once more. Everything blurred. I tried to keep my eyes open. *Don't pass out again,* I screamed inside. I wanted to see Omar escape. Suddenly and violently jerked up from the ground, I felt the dizziness take over…

CHAPTER 14

Arise, Lord! Deliver me, my God!
—Psalm 3:7 (TNIV)

I had no clue as to how long I blacked out this time. It seemed like only seconds. I realized there was no one around me. I tried to sit up, but my head pounded and felt like I might pass out. I could feel chills as my body readied to vomit. Panicked, I almost forgot where I was. *Wait... Omar.* I frantically searched. The frail old man still lay on the ground where he tripped. Did I kill him? I gagged at the thought and quickly looked away.

My hands were still zip tied behind my back. A rope kept my ties bound to the tree behind me. With all my might, I tried to break free. Then, I saw it – the stone that Omar used – it was nestled in the groundcover, about an arm's length away. My arms were useless, but my legs were not. I attempted to stretch out my foot to pull it back but I came up a little short. I pulled harder against my restraints. It felt like my arms might come out of their sockets. I didn't let that stop me from stretching further. Reaching with all my might, I finally managed to scoot the stone under my body with my foot. I eventually moved it closer to where I could scoop it up with my hands.

Thank you father, I breathed a sigh of relief. As I exhaled, a gleaming object caught my eye. It hid beneath the pine needles, just past where I first uncovered the stone. What could it be? Voices approached, leaving me with no time to investigate. Instead, I kicked more groundcover on top of the item, hoping to keep it hidden. Why? I honestly don't know.

"I had it on me, I swear," the redhead's voice came through the trees. Anthony and Justin followed him. The blonde haired man was missing, but a new man, short and plump, appeared with them. Everyone stopped and stared when seeing me awake – everyone except for the redhead, that is. He was still frantically searching for something.

"So you chose to come back to us again," Anthony's maniacal voice sent chills down my spine.

Trying to ignore his presence, I looked for an escape.

Anthony laughed, kneeling down to my eye level, "No one is

coming to save you." Then, he reached to Justin's boot and pulled out a dagger, still wet with blood. "Your friend may have killed one of my men, but Farrell, here, took quite the initiative to end any future threats." He positioned the blade so close to my face that I could smell the blood.

"You're lying," I spat, pulling my head back. I would not let him take, from me, the hope that Omar was warning the camp no matter how clear the proof was; Omar was gone and so was the blonde-haired person. The fresh blood on the blade had to come from someone. No, I would not let myself fall into their trap... then again...

"You told us that Christians are peaceful. I've had nothing but trouble from you. Now, two of my men are dead because of you," Anthony watched as I looked at the old man on the ground.

I did kill him. I couldn't keep down the vomit.

Anthony didn't move. "His blood is on your hands, and now, so is your friend's blood." He wiped Omar's blood on my shoulder and I immediately broke down. He laughed as I cried. Then he gave the knife back to Justin who returned it to its sheath within his boot.

I kept telling myself, *pull yourself together,* but the hopelessness surrounding me was overwhelming.

I became old news as the search for the missing object took precedence. Anthony, Justin, and the one I decided to call "Shorty," their plump henchman, continued aiding the redhead in his search.

Stop this, I commanded myself. *Crying will do you no good. Don't let Omar's death be in vain. I won't let them get away with this.* Channeling my anger, I suppressed my sobs and used the strength and endurance it gave me to still my fingers and cut myself free. Foolishly, my hand would slip or drop the rock, but as I rubbed my fingers along the plastic of the zip tie, I could feel where it started to give way. It would take a while, but I was determined. I winced, feeling blood trickle down my finger. The stone's edges were sharper than I thought. Again, it slipped, slicing my thumb. I forced myself to slow down, before I cut off my whole hand.

The men came back up the trail, and I smiled at them ever so slightly. By no means was it a friendly smile; rather, it lingered as one that laughed in their faces. I didn't know exactly what they were looking for, but I knew where it was. Their precious object lay right in front of their noses.

The redhead took my smile as a threat, and attacked me. He picked me up by my shoulders as high as my restraints would let him, and then slammed me up against the tree. I dropped the stone in the process, and let out a slight whimper. The redhead's eyes turned the color of his hair, or perhaps even the color of the blood now dripping down my back. My skin was no match for the tough bark of a pine tree. "Where is it?" He cursed at me.

"Lune," Anthony commanded, "release her."

"She knows where it is," the redhead persisted. When turning to plead his case, he saw Anthony's gun directed at his forehead.

Anthony didn't need to say anything. The redhead violently slammed me into the tree trunk, letting me drop. Then he kicked through the pinecones and needles near where the object hid. Closing my eyes, I tried not to give anything away. I could feel the sweat on my brow, or was that more blood?

"We'll issue you a new gun," Anthony said, "but not if you continue to ignore orders."

A gun; I could most definitely use that. I scooted myself forward, away from the tree, and stopped where I had dropped the stone that would help me regain my freedom. I shuffled around the needles for a moment, very slowly, so as not to alert anyone. When I found the stone, I rubbed it against the plastic, picking right back up where I left off.

The men stayed nearby the rest of that day. They left the body of the old man alone, never once attempting to bury it, wrap it, or even hide it. *You didn't kill him;* I tried to comfort myself, *his actions led to his death.* Every now and then, I would glance towards the hidden object to see if it really was a gun. The more I looked at the groundcover the more my vision blurred.

My vision wasn't the only thing dropping as the day went on. My lips started to crack and my stomach began to growl. The men all had their readymade packs of food and canteens of water, but never once offered me any. They only looked my way to monitor me. *No movement – no mischief,* they assumed. Oh, how wrong they were.

"She's awful quiet," Shorty chuckled while looking at me. "I thought she was the hothead of the group."

"Not when she's without backup," the redhead laughed.

Anthony's phone rang at his waist side. The laughter stopped. Everyone turned; ready to follow the orders of the alpha. Anthony answered the phone, giving a confused face as he put a finger in his other ear. He began to walk further up the mountain, seeking a better signal, and pointed back at the redhead and Shorty. "You two, with me," he whispered. Then, he very sternly demanded Justin not to let me out of his sight.

Justin had no problem sitting and finishing his meal while the others hiked away. He seemed to enjoy the distance from them. I, too, "enjoyed" their absence as I continued to dig into the tie around my wrists. I froze in place when Justin looked up. He stood and made his way toward me. Had I given myself away? I tried hard to be still and unnerved, but I readied myself for the worst.

The thought of Justin possibly being Omar's killer flashed through my mind, causing a stubborn look to mask my face. Part of me wished he would just kill me too and end my suffering, but I wasn't going down without a fight.

"'Even though I walk through the valley of the shadow of death, I will fear no evil, for [God] is with me,'[1]" I began to quote

---

[1] Psalm 23:4 (NIV)

Psalm 23, making sure Justin understood my refusal to let him control me through fear.

"Do you want to preach at me, or do you want some water?" He lifted his canteen up near to my mouth.

My cracked, desert lips couldn't refuse his offer. Once he pulled the bottle away, I retorted, "Only God can convince a hard heart to give a prisoner a drink of water."

Surprisingly, he gave me another drink; though, this time with a smug look. Then, he turned and positioned himself in his old spot, finishing his food.

"Thank you," I said, humbled. He had no reason to help me, but he did and I was grateful. I went back to cutting away at my restraints, thanking God for the refreshments. I took the water as a sign that God was readying me for escape, just as He had an angel feed Elijah before his long journey.

Feeling along the plastic, excitement rose within; nearly half of the job was complete. Perhaps I could pull and break it, but not very subtly. No, I would continue with the rock until I could make a swift getaway.

Anthony returned with his bodyguards behind him. They prepared to move. "Pack up," Anthony ordered. "We have ten minutes."

Now was the time to act. They were sure to see my progress if they tried to move me. A gust of wind came from between the trees, slightly brushing the groundcover off the hidden object. No one else noticed. It was, indeed, the missing gun. The events aligned so well, I would have been a fool not to act. Every muscle in my upper body tightened as I jerked hard against the zip tie. Nothing happened. I took the rock and scratched at it a few more times. Again, I pulled tight, and this time, *Snap!* The strap popped loose.

I used all my strength and leaped for the gun before I could register my own actions. Everyone looked in my direction, but the gun was in my grasp. I only took a second to shift it into the right position. Now they would see what it was like to stand on the other end of the barrel.

"Stay where you are," I demanded as they reached for their weapons. The redhead stared me down, wondering how I managed to hide the gun all this time. I shook profusely, but refused to let my arms drop.

"You're not actually going to shoot us," the redhead challenged, stepping closer to me. My heart burned in anger. I shot at the ground to keep him away, but scared myself more than I scared him. He mildly glanced down at the small crater I made.

"Turn around, all of you," I ordered. He was right; I wouldn't shoot them. Selfishly, I wanted to pull the trigger. I wanted to avenge Omar, to repay his suffering. A voice, sounding an awful lot like Omar's, whispered to me, *it's not worth your soul.* I couldn't do it; it went against everything I knew to be right. All I needed was to disappear.

They didn't want to follow my orders until Anthony finally said, "Do as she says." His compliance baffled me. It also instilled a sense of authority in me that I didn't have before.

The men didn't hesitate to turn around after that. "Get on the ground," I added. Anthony, Justin, and the redhead all did as I asked, but Shorty only squatted halfway. He froze in place, eyeing the men on the ground. His right arm moved ever so slightly, further out of sight.

"On the ground," I repeated. My voice started to shake. I had to get out of here. Never, in my life, had I ever done something so audacious.

Anthony looked at the short man, and then positioned himself to get up. I had no idea how to deal with their rebellion. This was their area of expertise, not mine. Before I could get an order out, Anthony's body lunged at Shorty, who was attempting to reach for his gun. Things happened so fast after that, that I panicked. Shots fired, though I am not exactly sure who pulled the trigger. What I did know was that none of the shots hit me. I had no intention on waiting to see the outcome of the brawl. My feet carried my body faster than my mind could catch up. The gun slipped through my fingers in the mix of things. I had to leave it behind. Right now, I could only run.

I ran wildly, trying to dodge every obstacle on the ground and in the air. Branches smacked my arms and face as I jumped over every rock and log in my path. I dare not look back, only forward, as my feet recklessly carried me down the mountain. Colors blurred together. Greens, blues, and browns now combined into an array of camouflage. My adrenaline must have been at an all-time high, because I no longer felt sore or fatigued. I only focused on getting away.

Nearly out of breath, despite the burst of adrenaline, my lungs constantly tried to collapse. I searched for a group of underbrush or shrubberies where I could rest concealed. I couldn't hear the men behind me, but that didn't mean they weren't there. *Keep running*, is all I could tell myself as despair started to creep its way into my heart. Then I caught sight of what reminded me of the undefined path I first hiked. Running towards it, a gleam of hope resurfaced. I had been running for longer than I thought.

I didn't follow the trail exactly; I continued beside it, straight for the camp. Finally, I could vaguely see the family cabins through the trees in front of me. *Just a little further*, I encouraged myself. Jumping a log, an extended limb caught my foot and tossed me to the ground. There was no time to start running again…but I was so close… Noticing the log's hollow inside, I rolled into it. Soon, cobwebs and bugs of all sorts covered my body. Through the small gaps in the shrubbery around me, I could see different sections of the forest, and prayed repeatedly that no one could see me. I had no idea what to do next. I needed them to lose track of me. I refrained from yelling for help, because I was not yet close enough to the camp for people to hear me. Anthony and his goons would capture me before anyone could follow my screams. *Oh, if only Omar were here with me. He'd help me know what to do.*

Justin arrived first and I immediately clasped my hand over my mouth to quiet my breathing. He stood directly on top of the log where I hid. Either he found a sturdy area, or God's hands held him up, because I was certain the log would cave. My chest and side pained as I restricted my breathing. Justin looked all around as I heard Anthony ask, "Which way did she go?"

Then, the redhead's voice came, "To the camp, no doubt. She'll be looking to warn the others."

"Then she's no longer our problem," Justin said.

I could hear the footsteps leaving. Justin stepped away and, for a moment, I could have sworn I saw his eyes staring right at me. They seemed to pierce through the log, questioning whether he should say anything. I waited for him to shoot me.

"Move out," Anthony ordered.

Justin's eyes pulled away, and he and the others left in a hurry. Had the enemy just shown me grace, or did God blind him? Either way I was grateful.

Suddenly, I heard a deep, hollow sound and the ground shook beneath me. A giant gust of wind came from the direction of the camp, crackling the trees. My heart dropped. Screams of pain and distress stunned me. The ground shook twice more. I could hear a few trees as they crashed to the ground. I quickly rolled out of the log, back over the cobwebs and bugs. I focused on the screams of terror coming from the direction of the camp. The cries of pure agony and horror enveloped me like a dark cloud. I ran towards the anguish. I had no idea what I would find. Someone had to help. The smell of burning wood hit my nostrils just as I began to feel a lot of heat. Smoke began to engulf the forest but none of the trees seemed to be on fire. Emerging from the tree line, my heart shattered. The explosions leveled every building to the ground.

CHAPTER 15

"Whoever acknowledges Me before men, I will also acknowledge him before My Father in heaven."
—Matthew 10:32 (NIV)

Flames engulfed everything that would burn. Plumes of smoke rose from the flames and rubble. It filled the air, burning my eyes and lungs. The log cabins were gone. I steadied myself for the sight of mutilated bodies. Even with basic first aid knowledge, I felt useless. Surely, I could help someone if there was anyone left to help. With God on my side...*well... was God even here?* I was ashamed ever to let the doubt cross my mind. Of course, He's here. This reeked of Satan's influence. God would help me know what to do. I wouldn't let myself forget that – not now.

I could practically feel the adrenaline, which had kept me going, flowing out of me. Each breath grew shorter and raspier, and pain came rushing though my body from all directions. My face felt as if it had gone through a sand blaster. I can't even describe the pain in my abdomen and sides. I needed to move faster. I stepped in a dark puddle and suddenly felt the need to vomit, again. It seemed to come from underneath a fallen tree beside me where I saw a small foot trapped, barely visible. I clasped my hand over my mouth as my throat clenched. Shaking in fear, I knew what I had to do. I limped to the other side of the fallen tree, where all color drained from my face. I had seen death before, but it was never this grotesque. A child lay trapped beneath the trunk while a lifeless woman clung to the child's small hand.

I pressed my hands tighter against my mouth, stifling a scream. I quickly scrambled away, despite the pain in my heart and body. I was frantic to find a reason for hope that someone else had survived the blast. The thought of being alone with all of this carnage horrified me more than being in the hands of the enemy. Suddenly, I saw death all around me. Birds and small animals lay scattered in all directions. Still, the only people I saw were the young child and woman. Renewed by desperation, I found the energy to begin my search for the living.

I darted behind a large piece of shrapnel as gunshots sounded in the distance. They rapidly repeated, drowning out more screams. Any objects big enough to hide me became a cover as I made my way to where the men's cabins used to stand and then, to the Tabernacle. I could see black specs in the open fields. People were moving in, shooting at the ground. It took me a minute to realize that they might be shooting the survivors.

The Tabernacle, a place of peace and conversations, was in flames. The devastation before me nearly dropped me to my knees. Stumbling through the scene, my nose resisted but could not avoid the scent of burning wood becoming more rancid, like that of burning flesh and hair. The ground stained dark red. I searched for life but only encountered death. An occasional groan or sob caught my ear. I turned frantically this way and that just trying to find those that needed help. I dare not call out because of the armed men that might hear me. A faint whisper reached my ears. The voice was unrecognizable, but what was said was clear, "Khris." I froze in place, searching for the source. I heard, "K…K…Khris," followed by a lightly sputtered cough. I searched through the ashes until I finally found Omar lying in a pile of rubble.

I stammered, "Oh, Omar."

He tried to smile.

I burst into tears, wanting to scoop him up in my arms, "I'm so sorry I brought you into all of this." Seeing him alive bought tears of joy and confusion. What happened after he got away? I should have been here sooner to help him.

"It's okay," he coughed blood. I rolled him on his side to help keep him from choking. His agony caused me to lay him gently back. I moved so his head could rest in my lap and gripped his hand with both of mine. "I warned them," he smiled with another cough, "but I was too late." He wheezed for air, "They caught me," he wheezed and coughed some more.

Ripping what was left of a shirt from one of the limp bodies beside us, I tried to wrap Omar's arm. "They took the kids… we could not stop them." He began to close his eyes.

I held him tighter, "No, Omar. Look at me. Don't go yet. I can get you help. Just stay with me."

He looked at me, almost empathetically, with tears in his eyes, "I do not want to, but I am ready." He coughed as I cried. "I am sorry Khris."

I pulled his hand closer to my heart, not wanting to let go. I tried sucking in my sobs, knowing I had no choice, "It's alright." If God were calling him home, then at least he wouldn't have to suffer any longer.

He continued to cough, causing him to squeeze my hand harder. I felt Omar's body slightly tremor as he took his final breath. He looked away from me with a smile. Eternal peace had found him. This world could no longer burden him. His smile faded fast, but was enough to remind me to look ahead. The sound of gunshots returned; they were almost here. I had nowhere to run or hide. The only thing I could think to do ashamed me, but I did it anyway. I rolled Omar's body on top of mine, and tried to pull in a few others. It was my only chance.

I froze when I heard the footsteps enter the vicinity, stepping on the dead without hesitation. A few groans would come, and gunshots soon followed. My eyes closed, and I slowed my breathing as best I could while talking to God.

Please, don't let me die if I still have purpose. Don't let me endure all of this destruction for someone just to kill me. I don't know why this is happening, or who's responsible. I know You will be triumphant. You have promised that much. Just please...

Suddenly, a boot kick to my thigh interrupted my prayer. Holding my breath, I tried not to make a sound. The weight and shelter of Omar's body suddenly lifted as someone pulled him from me. Forced to roll over, I found myself staring up the barrel of a rifle.

"Get up," the holder of the gun said. "Get up," he commanded louder. I struggled to stand, trying not to show fear, staring him in the face – well, the black mask that covered his face. Everyone holding a gun had that same mask. It looked like a cloth material with goggles over the eyes, and plastic lips that frowned across the mouth. There was no telling the men apart. The one threatening me moved his head up and down, looking me over once or twice. Then, with the barrel of his gun, he shoved me, turning me around, "Walk," he commanded, pushing me right over Omar.

He continued shoving me, poking and prodding me like a calf, making sure I went the right way. I could see the fields in the distance, completely torn up and unrecognizable. They looked more like a war zone than the clean cut fields I had seen upon arrival. Other masked men gathered survivors, like me, from their hiding places. They pulled one injured man from behind a broken table. He was missing his left hand. The man in a mask holding him looked to another man in a mask who wore an orange patch on his shoulder. They exchanged a few comments. Then, without warning, the man with an orange patch shook his head and shot the injured. Other bodies were also being rolled over, or picked up, and then shot. They were only gathering hostages with full limbs.

The man led me to the field where we had had the bonfire. That night that started this entire week, Omar and I talked about how peaceful things seemed. He said that God was preparing us for a storm. I never imagined that storm was the genocide of Christians. Now, instead of gathering in the field for a "pep" talk, we found ourselves corralled like animals, heavily guarded by masked men with their guns pointed at us. Surely, they didn't plan to kill us…at least not yet… there was a reason they separated us from the injured.

"Sit down and shut up," the man pushed me within the beaten down crowd of sobbing and hurting brothers and sisters. Guards circled all around us, keeping us from going anywhere. As I looked around, I recognized a face or two, but couldn't put names with them. Loved ones held each other close. Some held hands with their heads bowed, probably praying inwardly so as not to be heard speaking. The majority of the crowd, on the other hand, kept yelling out, demanding the masked men give back their children. The masked men constantly smacked them to the ground until they silenced their cries. Any who tried to defend another were also kicked and hit repeatedly and a few, killed.

A little way to my left, I saw David. His arms wrapped around a crying girl. She couldn't have been over sixteen. I walked towards them, seeing no one else I knew, until a guard practically slammed me to the ground. "Sit down," he grunted as he continued walking through us all. I hadn't seen him approaching me.

David looked at me as I sat up and maneuvered my body a few inches closer to him. He still held the crying girl in his arms. I looked at her and back at him, he lowered his eyes and whispered, "Her younger brother was ripped from her arms and her older brother was killed in front of her. They let her live."

I was dumbstruck, unsure how to grasp the evil before me. None of the persecution I've witnessed in other countries could buffer the shock of seeing it in my own country. Christians, living in a land with freedom of religion, now found themselves persecuted. Masses had died here today. Did the government start this, or did these people have their own agenda? These guards and murderers weren't wearing official military uniforms, at least not the U.S. military that I could remember, but they performed like a trained militia…like Nazis.

"Have you seen my friends?" I whispered.

David shook his head in sorrow, "Only Omar, who snuck in to warn us. Once we understood it wasn't a game, we tried to get everyone out to the busses. I tried to play it off as a part of our activities so as not to alert the enemy. I'm not sure what gave us away. Omar was in the tent when…" He stopped.

"I know… I saw him," I said, as the butt of a rifle hit my shoulder.

"Shut up," my abuser grunted, slapping my face with his hand. Then he continued through the mix of terrified people.

David's right eye was black and swollen as could be. I assumed I looked the same. My face was a little numb, but when David looked for hope to hear that Omar survived, I had to shake my head in regret.

"I'm sorry," David whispered. Then, after a moment of silence, he asked the question we all wanted to know, "What do they want?"

I shrugged my shoulders and we both looked out into the crowd. There were no little ones among us, only children about thirteen or older. Women were rare as well. I caught a glimpse of Agnes, but I feared for her; she looked too frail to withstand any more beatings. Her sister, Geneva, was nowhere near, and neither was Sandra. Agnes just kept her head low with her hands on the ground. There were very few older people rounded up with us that I could see. I couldn't help but wonder if they were only gathering the strong ones for slaves. Perhaps these men were part of an international slave trade.

"I'm sorry," David repeated, though this time he wasn't talking about Omar. "We should have taken your warnings more seriously."

"It's easier to recognize a warning in hindsight," I tried to help. "I would have assumed the same."

"I should have seen the signs; you were screaming for help up there."

I tried to let him know that we couldn't change what happened, just as the butt of a rifle slammed into both our faces. After that, we stayed silent. I watched David hold the crying girl close to his side. I took this time to look for an escape. We waited for hours watching as the guards brought in more prisoners, but none of them looked familiar. I wondered if these mercenaries caught my friends as well. If so, Jeffrey was very ill, Jasmine small and frail, and Steven… well, he may be the only survivor if he didn't attempt to defend the other two. It seemed that the enemy had easily decreased our numbers. A camp that started out five thousand strong now shrank to approximately five hundred. Surely, they hadn't killed everyone who was missing. David and Omar both admitted to getting a warning out to the campers. Perhaps some of the escapees reached their freedom. I wonder how many kids the enemy managed to capture.

Once the masked men had cleared the area and corralled all the survivors, they forced us to stand up. I kept an eye on Agnes as she stayed down on the ground. *Get up,* I silently commanded her. *Get up before they kill you.* One of the men pulled her up, but she kept her hand clenched to someone else's arm. It belonged to Geneva. I couldn't tell if Geneva was alive, but Agnes clung to her as if she was. I could see a guard approaching them. I wanted to warn her, but within seconds, he pulled out his pistol and shot Geneva in the head. Agnes' heart had to have torn to pieces. She loved her sister. I screamed for her, running to her side.

"No, my dear sister…my sister," she sobbed. I swung my arms around her neck and held her close while she clung to her sister's hand.

The vile creature that shot sweet Geneva then put the gun to Agnes' head. "Please, stand with me," I whispered to her. She let me pull her to her feet. I knew she needed to keep walking or they'd quickly kill her too. Agnes was despondent and in shock. I still practically had to carry her, but she moved. They lined us up, men in one line and women in another. David handed the girl to me. "Take care of her," he quickly said.

Here I stood, with two crying women and no sign of help, or hope. We had no inkling of what would happen next. One thing I knew was that refusing to obey orders would result in a beating.

"Denounce your faith," a voice roared out, "and all of this will end. Refuse and you will suffer."

My heart pounded. Impulsively I yelled, "Don't listen to them. God is worth it!" The two in my arms looked up at me. "Stay strong!" I shouted even louder.

"Silence," a voice rang in command as a man came marching my way, "or you will be first." He stopped and stared at me through his mask.

"Don't deny Christ," a man's voice yelled further down the men's line. The guard turned and signaled one of the men to go to the voice.

"Stay strong," cried Agnes aloud.

"Shut up," the man attempted to hit her, but I intervened. I let go of the young girl and shoved the attacker back before he could get in his full swing. My actions only caused more anger towards me. He regained his posture and grabbed my throat, a feeling I hoped would never grow familiar. With his gun to my head and my oxygen cut, he demanded, "Deny your, so called, God."

"Never," I gasped.

He pointed the gun at Agnes, "Deny your faith… or she dies."

Agnes looked at me with no fear or regret. She just smiled. She was ready, just as Omar was ready. Her sister was waiting. Our Savior was calling. The moment I refused his command, the guard pulled the trigger and Agnes dropped to the ground, dead. Her eyes stared heavenward. Even though sorrow threatened to overwhelm me, I found the strength to remain defiant.

The guard dropped me and put his weapons to another woman's head in our line, "What about you? Will you deny Christ, or die?"

The woman, crying and shaking her head no, stepped away from the man. Then she pulled her teenage daughter behind her. The man snatched her daughter, and held the gun at her mom's head.

"No," the girl cried. "Let her live, please."

"Say it," he tightened his grip on the gun.

"Don't listen to him Anne," her mom begged her not to succumb. Then she pleaded to the guard with tears streaming down her face, "Have you no heart?"

"Tell me you don't believe in your God," the guard demanded of the girl once more.

"I don't believe," the girl whimpered. I could hear the click of the gun's hammer hitting an empty chamber. The guard lowered the gun and then quickly lifted it with a loud shot to follow. The bullet tore the through the daughter's heart. Her mother, screeching, scooped up her daughter's body and cradled it like a baby. Tears mingled with blood as they soaked into the mom's shirt. Some men from the other line fought hard to get to her side, but the guards swatted them back. I couldn't believe my eyes. We had no escape. No matter what, we were going to die at the hands of these vile people.

"We will let your afflictions end," the man said, "if you deny your supposed Savior," he held his gun back at me, grabbed my hand and squeezed it open, "and if you refuse, then you will suffer until you do." He lowered the gun to my hand and shot through the webbing between my thumb and finger, leaving a bloody hole.

I stood in shock, never experiencing a bullet wound before. I wished for it to be one big nightmare that would soon go away. A man behind me held me while another used more zip ties on my wrists like cuffs. Even if I could cut through these as I did before, I had too many guards watching my every move. David's girl, who clung to my arm until they pulled me away, kept a close eye on me, but never moved.

"Stay strong," I said to her right before they took me to a different spot to stand.

"If anyone chooses to deny, let him or her come forward," I could see everyone stand firm, and my heart rejoiced through all the pain. Then, I heard six shots – perhaps a few did fail to hold to the faith. After that, the masked men put the same bullet hole through the right hand of everyone who remained standing. After each shot, the men would take the wounded, zip tie their wrists, and bring them to the same area where I stood. They still kept the men and women separated, which pained the loved ones who wanted to comfort one another. We all held our good hand over our injured ones as shock wore off and pain increased. I couldn't move my hand without feeling a sting. Thankfully, the heat from the bullet sealed most of the blood flow.

CHAPTER 16

"Do not be afraid of what you are about to suffer. I tell you, the devil will put some of you in prison to test you, and you will suffer persecution…Be faithful, even to the point of death, and I will give you the crown of life."
—Revelation 2:10 (NIV)

The young girl David asked me to watch over found her way back to me after receiving her punishment for refusing to deny Christ. Tears streaked her face. David followed not too far behind, concerned, no doubt, for her safety. When he tried to talk to her, a guard smacked the back of his head, knocking him to the ground. The girl and I both attempted to kneel and help him up, but the guard pointed his barrel at us. Then he kicked David and said gruffly, "Get to the back of your line."

The girl turned in David's direction, but I quickly reached out my hands to stop her. Though restrained, I could still pull her in beside me and keep her under my wing, so to speak. I let her tears fall, not that I could stop mine either. I doubted anything I said or did at this point would make a difference. All my years in and around ministry could never have prepared me to handle such an extremely violent situation as the one I faced now.

My eyes focused on our persecutors. We couldn't explain away their actions as terrorists who invaded America, because when they spoke, they spoke fluent English – not just proper English, but cultured English with a variety American accents. My next thought, was that they mistook us for a different religious group; then again, their demands and insults were specifically against God following Christians. The repeated fear that sat rooted in the forefront of my mind was that there was a chance of this being a government, sanctioned genocide.

Now, the shutdown of the border was more suspicious than I originally thought. The attack was seemingly coming from our own government. Perhaps it was a coincidence, but not likely. What is surprising, besides this whole nightmare, is that these people knew exactly when, who, and how many attendees this specific camp would have. If this is a sanctioned operation, then what should we expect next? What was the purpose of sparing us now? I mean, why not kill all of us? They had killed the rest of our brothers and sisters. No, I wouldn't let Satan trick me into blaming anyone until I had more information or proof.

The voice of the man who murdered Agnes sounded out from the middle of us all, "For conspiring and aiding in terroristic acts, you are all hereby charged and sentenced to life in prison. From here on out, you obey my men and me. What we demand of you, you will do. If you attempt to escape, you will lose a finger for every man it takes to hunt you down. If you are caught plotting, you will lose a finger for every person you interact with. If you believe yourself to be too weak to carry on with your assignments, we will use you like lab rats until you denounce your god. Your reward for denying your, so called, god will be a bullet to the head, a quick death. There is no escape.

"Men and women are not to converse until all daily work is done. Men must work alone and women will work in pairs. This is not your normal prison. You will not get three square meals a day and we will not tolerate whining and groaning. Your children are now ours. Your freedom ended when you became an enemy of this nation. You claim there is a Hell, well, welcome to it."

The one speaking stepped down, and a new man in a mask stepped forward to give us our first orders. He wore an orange patch on his shoulder, just as the one I had seen in the Tabernacle. Glancing at the man who had just welcomed us all to Hell, I noticed he had a red patch on his uniform. Perhaps that's how they distinguished themselves between commanding officers and the enlisted.

"Where you stand, right now," the man in a mask said, "is where you will bring every fleshly thing that no longer has breath." His words were revolting. Those were my brothers and sisters. He called them *things*. It was unacceptable. I wanted to plug my ears and not hear anymore. I wanted to run. I wanted to scream, fight, and hurt every one of these evil demons. I wanted revenge for every single life they took. I wanted…hot tears streamed down my face. "You have twenty-four hours to place them here. To repeat; men, you work alone. Women, you work in pairs. Any disputes or actions other than cooperation are better left in your head or it leads to painful consequences."

That ended his commands. Everyone stood staring at him and the guards around us. How did it come this far? Their level of hatred didn't form overnight. Now, as if losing our brothers and sisters, our Christian family, wasn't shock enough, they demanded we move their battered and bloodied bodies. We are a society that buries our dead. We don't stack them like cords of wood. My anger burned as my thoughts continued. They never said what would happen to us if we didn't stack all of the bodies in time. Nor did they say what they planned to do with the bodies – that was up for us to speculate about in fear.

"Move," a voice demanded, followed by multiple gunshots. "You're wasting daylight."

That caused the crowd to scatter in haste. Immediately, they caught people trying to escape. I never turned to watch, but I heard every blood, curdling scream. I followed the obeying crowd and walked towards the tent of death. The guards around us kept barking orders, "Two women to a group. Men work alone." I kept the girl with me, and David walked closely by us. They had everyone pick up the first body we found. David's first dead body was that of a small child. She couldn't have been more than five years old. David's tears flowed freely down his cheeks. I saw the anguish it caused him as he scooped her in his arms.

Our eyes met. David visibly swallowed hard and shoved all emotion to a place inside him. The next look pleaded with me to do the same. I nodded. He turned and went on his way. Together, the girl and I picked up a body missing its legs; I grabbed the torso, for her sake, and told her to grab the arms, but I could see her breaking down.

"Look at me," I said gently. "What's your name?"

"Angelica," she paled, looking as though she might throw up.

"Angelica, look at me," I repeated.

She did.

"Breathe, and don't look at the body. Just grab the arms and I'll guide you back. Just look at me." After a few seconds, she finally did so. I grabbed the belt, still attached around the man's waist. Then, we lifted the body as best as we could as we stood. "Ok, now keep your eyes on me. You walk backwards and I'll tell you when to step sideways. Just look up at the sky and talk with me." She did as I asked, after glancing at the body, and then quickly jerked her eyes back up to the sky.

"What do I say?" She asked.

"Tell me what you see up there."

"Smoke... lots of smoke."

"Step to your left," I said, to help her avoid tripping in a hole. "Now, step back to your right. You're doing great. Tell me, do you see any clouds?"

"I can't tell...wait, there's a few."

"Perhaps God will send us rain..." I paused, seeing a group ahead of us drop their body as it slipped through their fingers. "Take three steps left again. How old are you?"

"Sixteen."

"What does your father do for a living?" I asked my question before thinking. Her father may have died in that explosion.

"He's a carpenter," she replied, emotionless.

"Does your mom work?"

"She's a teacher."

"Keep looking up," I reminded her, "you're doing great."

We made it back to the area of the bonfire where the others had already laid a few bodies. Guards instructed us where to go and drop the bodies. We placed ours on the ground, beside a woman with holes in her chest. These men were malicious. Such harshness was unnecessary. How dangerous was this woman to deserve an entire magazine unloaded on her? Surely, one bullet was enough...but they weren't interested in ending the torment. The leader said so himself. They wanted to add to our afflictions.

They gave us no time to rest. On our second trip, Angelica and

I worked together to carry a young boy; it seems that they missed a few children in their kidnapping. Then, we picked up a woman old enough to be my mother. Our fourth body was an older man who scared us when we heard him gasp for breath as we attempted to pick him up. We sat him back down, and tried to get him to speak. Upon opening his eyes, I recognized him as Mr. Jim. The man my friends and I met the first night here. He looked so pale now.

"Is there a problem?" A man in a mask came out of nowhere.

"He's still alive," Angelica cried.

Following her desperation, the man took another innocent life. He leaned his face in close to Angelica. I could practically see his sneer through his mask, as he coldly said, "Not anymore. Now move."

Jim no longer felt pain, but Angelica did. I could see her grow more anxious, looking for a way to escape. "No," I said, "Angelica don't."

"They killed him. They're going to kill us," she said on the verge of a panic.

"You can't control that. You can only control your actions. Now grab his feet."

"I can't," she cried.

"Grab them!" I shouted harshly.

She did so, out of fear, and I wished I could take it back. She needed compassion, not anger, but my anger only came from worrying about her. If she ran, they would definitely catch her. No, I didn't plan to stay here forever, but we had to be smart about it. There was no use in running, not while they looked to hunt us down. If we cooperated long enough, until a more opportune time, we may be able to escape with all of our fingers still attached.

"Look," I said, "I get that you're scared. We all are, but there's a reason you and I are still alive. Will you see it through to find out what that reason is?"

We started to pick up Mr. Jim from the ground. A guard loomed in the distance. Had he heard us talking? He paid no attention to us once we headed back down to the pile of dead bodies – a pile of our family in Christ.

For hours, we walked and carried bodies. I eventually grew immune to the smells around us, which helped ease the nausea in my own stomach. As the morning turned to evening, we remained surrounded by a sea of violence. The explosions that had rocked the camp left its footprint. Now, the gun toting, masked men goaded us to erase the evidence that it had ever happened. I stopped counting the dead. There were too many and it only pulled me down into a spiral of despair. The pain from my bullet wound would cause my hand to slip every now and then, but I managed to keep working. Angelica was slowing down as well, but I wouldn't let her give up. To be honest, we both needed water and rest. Then again, so did everyone else.

A whistle through a megaphone sounded out across the camp. They summoned us to gather around the commander with the red patch, who had first spoken to us. I recognized him first by his voice. It was more distinguished from the rest of the voices, with a slight rasp to it – as if the man behind the mask had once been a smoker.

In front of the commander, they forced a dark skinned man to kneel. The commander tightly grasped the man's hair. His head lifted high for all of us to see his bloodied face. His hands matched in color. He held them close to his chest. It took a moment before I realized that he only had a thumb remaining. "Some of you have refused to take my instructions seriously," the commander shoved the man to the ground. "When I said no plotting, I meant it." He stepped on the man's hand that still had one thumb. The man cried out in agony. "When I said not to attempt an escape," he dug his heel further down into the man's hand, "I meant it. Perhaps I forgot to mention one last thing," he signaled for a guard who didn't have an orange patch. The guard brought out a woman who I could only assume was the wounded man's wife. "If you dare attack one of my men," he pulled out a gun and pointed it at the woman, "you'll lose a life that is dear to you."

"Be strong baby," the woman cried as she stared at her husband on the ground. "Hold God's truth in your heart." She too, was ready to face death, but at the final moment, the commander shot her husband instead. I jumped. The woman screamed. Her husband died instantly.

"I have no use for a man with no fingers. Now get back to work," he shot his gun towards the sky. We all hurried back to what we were doing. No one wanted to be his next example. I didn't see what happened to the woman, but I guessed they put her back to hauling bodies; given no time to mourn her husband's death. It wasn't right. None of this was. In my history class, we had barely skimmed through the story of Hitler killing the Jews. In church history, I learned about the persecution that came after Jesus' disciples started spreading His message. Now, I could only fear that history was repeating itself. There was no doubt in my mind that this horror would not end with us.

Would there be a future generation to carry on the Christian faith? The enemy stole or killed all of the children. Unless I was mistaken, all of us still here would find ourselves in the ground before the day ended. We had no assurance there would be a tomorrow. All things we worked so hard for in this world were now gone. All I could do was cling to the hope I had in God, in His love, and His promises. The work I had done for Him wasn't a waste. It's why I can be confident in Him at this moment.

Angelica shut down, almost completely. She would move with me and carry bodies, but I could see a glaze over her eyes. She followed me, and did as I did without sound or a sob. She was calloused, with no emotion. I wondered if her soul had escaped and left her body here to suffer. If only I could do the same, but my mind wouldn't stop thinking.

With every dead body we approached, I prepared myself to see the face of someone from my group. I kept a watchful eye on those we worked alongside, hoping for familiar faces to show. I continually uttered prayers to God. Then, I turned over the body of a woman. I gasped without thought as my breath left me. Joy, David's sweet and gentle stepmom, lay at my feet. Half of her body was untouched witnessing with the other burnt half what sin could do to the beauty in the world. I looked around, worried that David would have to see another mother dead. I was too late to hide her. David dropped the body he held and ran to Joy's side. She was gone. It broke my heart to see David's pain. We couldn't do anything to help her.

"I'm sorry," I reached my hand for David's shoulder. My fingers were inches away from his touch when I quickly restrained myself. Any contact could get the three of us killed.

"It wasn't your fault," David stared up at the masked men with a fire in his eyes. Then he lovingly took Joy into his arms. I heard him whispering as he held her close. No tears on his face, just love and then anger. He took her to the graveyard. Angelica and I took the body he dropped and followed closely behind him. I was scared he would try something rash.

Angelica would make small responses here and there, proving she wasn't fully lost within herself. Whatever was going on inside her I prayed it was protecting her from the horror around her. I feared I would turn around and see her body, at any moment, waiting for me to carry her to the grave as well.

Late into the night, after gathering thousands of bodies, they called us back to the graveyard. Our numbers were even less now; perhaps only four hundred remained. I assumed those who were missing were either killed, or were the older ones of the group whose hearts were too weak to continue. Perhaps a few escaped, but my hope for such an answer slowly faded.

The masked men had us circle around the pile of bodies and began pouring gasoline on them. My stomach churned. I couldn't bear to watch as the bodies went up in flames. Immediately, the heat sucked the moisture from my skin. The overwhelming stench of burning flesh and hair encompassed us once again. Everyone backed away from the fire. We needed to get away. After we pushed a small distance back, the masked men forced us to sit. Those who refused to listen were beaten until they fell. I tried, for only a second, to turn my back to the fire, but found myself kicked and hit until I turned to face it. How could they force us to watch this? My eyes closed tight as my hands shielded my face.

A shrill scream caught my attention. My eyes squinted through the cracks of my fingers. A chain reaction started as one woman ran to the fire like one who was trying to run to freedom. Gasps from the crowd and cries for help sounded. After her, went two others. People tried to stop them and yet, more followed suit. The guards only laughed. All bodies lay in the flames as they would in a bed. They screamed and howled, until finally death embraced them.

Angelica jumped to run towards the fiery freedom. I stretched out my hands and grabbed her, pulling her to the ground. A shot of pain went up my arm from where I gripped hers with my wounded hand. We struggled for a few seconds as she attempted to pull away. “Please don’t,” I begged. “We will find another way.” She refused to look at me, and I refused to let go. “I need you.” Angelica slowly began to go limp.

The longer we sat, the less anyone fought. There was no energy to fight. We were on the side of the broken. The heat wore on us. I hadn’t consumed food for almost two days. Even if they had fed us throughout the day, it wouldn’t have mattered; I would have thrown it all up by now. More than food, I needed water. Everyone did. Though Justin had given me a few drinks earlier in the day, they weren’t enough. Sympathy was not a part of the guards’ vocabulary.

Angelica fell asleep with her head in my lap. I stroked her hair for a bit, looking around for David. I couldn’t find him in the mix of the crowd. I chose to believe he was only out of sight, versus the alternative. His faith was too strong for him to give into this chaotic evil. Surely, he would be someone seeking for a way out alive.

The guards all celebrated their successful day, while we mourned and grew weaker. I feared what else they had in store for us, but repeated the same phrase in my head; *God can see us through.* I knew the statement was true, but I was having a hard time convincing myself of it. I couldn't bear to lose my hope in God…yet, I seemed to hope, more and more, that He would take us home rather than see us through the fire.

Later, while I stared down at the ground trying to avoid looking at the flames before me, two feet stood in front of me. The worn and battered shoes alerted me that it wasn't one of the masked men, but I still jumped. I looked up and saw a young woman, perhaps a few years younger than me, holding a water canteen. She knelt down in front of me, and handed it to me, "Here," she said, "drink."

I woke Angelica, but she could barely find the strength to sit up; the poor girl was fatigued spiritually, mentally, and physically. Before I drank anything, I made sure Angelica received her fill. "Thank you," I said as I, too, took a drink.

After a few seconds, the young woman lowered the water from my mouth, forcing me to stop. "You'll get sick," she warned me.

All around the circle, young women carried around canteens, giving their brothers and sisters a drink of hope. I thought of when Jesus told the woman at the well that He was the Living Water. I knew His statement to be true. He would forever be the Sustainer of my life, both on earth and in the afterlife. At this moment, I was grateful for His physical gift of water as well.

Other women also handed out tortillas. They only gave one to each person, but that was enough to raise our spirits. I wondered if the guards used the women to ration out our food and drink in order to keep distance between them and us. They stood at the perimeter of the circle, just watching us. Perhaps they thought we carried some sort of disease. Maybe they even knew that their actions were wrong, and avoided the guilt that came with getting to know us.

One girl tried to give two tortillas to a very weak woman, but a guard caught her. In an instant, they took her away screaming. The weak woman mourned over the girl's capture. She couldn't get up to help. One of the men nearby rubbed his hand on her arm, lending what little comfort he could.

When they brought bread to Angelica and I, I about fell over in shock to see, in front of me, the same woman whose husband the guards used as a public example. She had two cuts on her face, and terribly beaten up knuckles. As she handed me the bread, I took it with one hand and placed my other hand on top of hers. She looked at me with a small smile. "Stay strong," she whispered.

Me…stay strong…? This woman witnessed her husband's torture and murder, and more than likely had her kids taken from her, yet she sought to give me courage. It worked. True Christianity – the kind that follows God through all situations, rather than using Him as a safety net – always seems to bring out the best in His people during the worst of times. Her encouragement rekindled a fire in my soul and reminded me just what I needed to know:

> *And the God of all grace, Who called you to His eternal glory in Christ, after you have suffered a little while, will Himself restore you and make you strong, firm and steadfast.*[2]

Suffering would most definitely come. Nevertheless, God promised us it would end. Our pain would not be for nothing. One day we would find ourselves with more peace than we would ever know what to do with. For now, we must continue through the fire, trusting God would be with us all the way.

---

[2] 1 peter 5:10 (NIV)

I cautioned Angelica to eat slowly, not for the sake of manners, but to help our bodies to get the fullness of the bread's nutrition. Letting it first melt on my tongue before beginning to chew, I enjoyed the savory flavor of the bread. I wondered if this was how the Israelites felt. God constantly handed them over into captivity for their sins; were they as grateful when God gave them such seemingly little blessings? Were we, too, going through this for our disobedience? This may very well be our moment of awakening.

No one but God knew how long we would have to endure this torture. The masked men may know, but they didn't share that information with us. In fact, as far as I could tell, they liked keeping us waiting. It gave them more control.

After eating, Angelica again fell asleep in my lap. Though sixteen, she appeared like a small child. Sleep was the only way she could to cope. As for me, I didn't know what to do, except thank God for putting Angelica with me. Had I not had her to take care of, I'm not sure how I would have survived this most dreadful of days.

CHAPTER 17

Then Peter came to Jesus and asked, "Lord, how many times shall I forgive someone who sins against me? Up to seven times?"
—Matthew 18:21 (TNIV)

I wanted to keep my eyes closed to avoid watching my brothers and sisters burn in the fire. It was no use. Nightmares haunted all thought. Either I would watch the bodies as they burned, or I would see Omar's burnt body behind my eyelids. The stench of burning flesh and hair would not leave my nose. Each breath was full of anguish and loss. I had to quit fighting the thoughts and images that continued to bombard my mind. I hoped that they would go away on their own. When Omar's body would fade, I would see my father. My chest wrenched with sorrow. Oh, how I prayed for God to protect my family from this insanity.

I jolted awake, alert, and ready to defend myself. My heart raced. My skin crawled. Nothing around me had changed; the flames still burned, men and women still mourned, and the world still seemed to refuse to notice. My spirit wouldn't allow me to drop my guard.

The ground had my focus for the rest of the night. Guiding my fingers across the dirt, I drew lines crossing over each other, designing an odd shaped snowflake. When I ran out of loose dirt to move around, I brushed my hand back over the drawing to start over with a blank page. I thought of Jesus, as my fingers caressed the ground, the day He drew in the sand. He did so while the Pharisees tried to get Him to condemn a woman for adultery. Instead, Jesus turned their accusations against them. He picked up a stone, just as anyone would – ready to stone a sinner – but instead of throwing it at the woman, he told the Pharisees, "If any one of you is without sin, let him be the first to throw a stone at her."[3]

I pondered on what Jesus said, wondering what He really meant. Does this command only apply to those being unjust towards others? Could we be justified in casting a stone at our persecutors? The scriptures again reminded me that God doesn't call us to forgive only once, but rather, seventy times seven times.

[3] John 8:7 (NIV)

When it comes down to understanding Jesus' message, He told us that forgiveness needed to be limitless, just as God's forgiveness towards us is limitless.

It seemed impossible to have a forgiving heart towards the masked men, rather than thinking of them with anger and hatred. Even if these men were just following orders, they were still responsible for their actions. It wouldn't be easy to approach them with love. It would require full faith in God, and absolute selflessness. "Father, forgive them, for they do not know what they are doing."[4] Jesus said as He hung on the cross. If Jesus was able to show love to His persecutors and murderers, I suppose it's possible for us to do the same.

The sun broke free over the mountains. The masked men whistled loudly and shot their guns in the air. My body ached. I rose to my feet nonetheless and stretched. I could feel every muscle and joint scream in protest for more rest. I helped Angelica to her feet. Her glazed eyes looked haunted. Others remained asleep on the ground. A couple of people tried to shake their loved ones awake only to have the guards come by and kick them. After a few strong hits, it was obvious that they were dead. The masked men then forced the others to add the bodies to the fire, which still burned low.

The guards lined us up, but, this time, they forced us to work alone. Large trucks drove in to the area where we stood. "You will place all rubble in these vehicles," the raspy, voiced man with a red patch commanded. "You will show your items to the guards as you come back to the field. They'll tell you in which vehicle to put the item. Any bodies found go to the fire. Are we clear?"

Though no one gave a response, he still acted as if we had, and shot his gun into the air. I couldn't walk with Angelica, but I walked behind her, making sure she did what she needed to in order to survive. I would whisper to her every now and then to

[4] Luke 23:34 (NIV)

remind her to grab something; a few times, a guard looked in my direction, but they never attacked me.

The guards down on the field searched through the materials in our hands, one by one, and then sent us to the four trucks on the left. They sent very few people to the truck on the right. That truck seemed saved for all electronic items. They were mostly personal items brought by the campers, which the explosions had destroyed. The rubble taken to the left was mainly bricks, pipes, and wires. Most of the wood and cloth burned up completely, but we had to place any of it left with the pile of burning bodies.

"Any sign of the Ichthys?" I heard a guard ask another.

"Not yet. A few items may prove to be of interest once we can analyze them," the second guard replied. A gunshot jolted me back to work. The two men threatened me, demanding I keep walking. I did so without arguing.

As the vehicles filled up, they would load five men into a truck, with two guards, and drive off. At one point, I saw David get into one of the trucks with four others. At least I knew he was alive, for now.

The majority of us were too weary to run or fight. We all stayed our course and did what our captors required of us. Nevertheless, at the end of the day, people still ended up beaten for the items they were caught smuggling under their clothes. The guards searched us thoroughly, and took all hidden items to the truck on the right. Anyone caught with contraband suffered one lash for anything that wasn't the clothes on their back. Like last night, they gave us all a drink and a tortilla. The guards were the ones handing out the food, and rewarded those without anything to hide with more food and water. Angelica and I were included in this count. Though grateful to have more nourishment, I felt guilty when I saw eyes upon us from the fifty or sixty men and women who had been beat down. It wasn't fair that they suffered such punishment; the guards never once told us we couldn't keep anything, even though I didn't see a reason to keep the stuff in the first place. Even phones left behind were useless. Maybe the mere thought of having something to hold onto from their old life was all that they wanted.

For three more days, we worked like slaves. Everyday more people died. Some were beat to death, or caught escaping, and a few died of heat stroke or dehydration. After those tragedies, the guards started giving us multiple rations of food and water throughout the day – not enough to keep us full, but enough to keep us working. I found it interesting that they seemed to need us more than they divulged.

On the fourth day of our captivity, the guards forced us to fill in all the craters and holes left by the explosions. I couldn't imagine why we were leveling the ground out again. Nothing made sense. They even ordered us to take pails of ash, from the cremated remains of our brothers and sisters, and pour them in the craters. Then they had us pack the dirt in the holes. All day long, we repeated this process, but couldn't finish. I suddenly understood. They were using us to cover up our own murders.

As we sat down for rest on that fourth night, the field felt cold and empty. A hand came on Angelica's shoulder. She and I both jumped. I pulled Angelica in close, readying myself for a fight. I turned around with my fist clenched and gave a gasp of relief to see David. Angelica showed a spark of life as she quickly reached over to hug him, but she still refused to speak. The guards didn't seem to care as much about our personal contact this night. Perhaps they, too, were getting tired of their daily grind.

"She's been this way since the first day," I whispered. "It takes all I have to keep her moving."

"Thank you," David said as he kissed Angelica on the forehead.

We sat in silence for quite some time. I had no idea what to say to him. He hadn't approached us since that first day. For all I knew, he had ignored us for the sake of his own survival. Though I looked for him among the crowd, I never saw his eyes looking for Angelica or me. Even now, David wouldn't let Angelica lean on him – I suppose it was for her safety – so again, she fell asleep in my lap. I stroked her hair as thoughts of despair swam through my head. It was getting hard to stay positive.

David stayed quiet. It was as if he knew something, but didn't want to tell me. He could've had a lot on his mind as well. If he didn't plan to sit with us to talk, then maybe he just wanted to let us know he was okay. Whatever the reason, I found comfort in having him near.

"Where did they take you in the trucks?" I finally asked.

David responded in a whisper, "They had us empty them at a landfill. Any useful items were transferred to another truck and taken elsewhere."

"I heard someone say they were looking for an Ichthys," I said. David could possibly help me understand what that meant. The "Jesus Fish," was the only Ichthys I knew of; a symbol in the biblical times used to help Christians distinguish one another from the people of the world. One would draw the first line in the sand, and the other believer would finish the fish with a second line. When spelt in Greek, ΙΧΘΥΣ, Ichthys was an acronym standing for, "Jesus Christ, God's Son, Savior." I never did forget that Bible class lesson. Even after knowing the history of the Ichthys, I was still in the dark on why the guards were looking for it. David showed slight interest in my comment, but gave no response. It could be that someone had misinformed them.

A couple of hours into another dark and haunting night, David reached his arms up and pulled me in between them to where I leaned back on his chest. With the zip ties restricting him, his left hand held my shoulder while his right hand rested on my arm. My body slightly rested over Angelica's, but she didn't seem to notice. "Stay right like this 'till I let go. Close your eyes and pretend to rest, but listen closely." His cheek rested on my head.

I did what he said. In this position, the masked men couldn't see us talk. They would only see a man trying to comfort a woman. I wondered what was so secret that we had to stay hidden. Others conversed among themselves without any repercussions, but maybe their conversations weren't secret. Did David know more about this Ichthys than I thought?

"We're leaving tomorrow," he said. It was hard to contain my joy. I wanted to ask so many questions but David remained subdued. "Some of the guards are on our side," he finally said. I tried to lift up my head and look around, but he held me down. His strong fingers dug into my shoulder painfully. When I winced, he loosened his grip and let his thumb brush up and down against my skin; a soothing technique that almost let me forget my current troubles.

It didn't take long before I snapped back into the conversation. Which guards would be fighting for us? I had no clue. They were all the same to me. I kept my eyes closed as I listened.

"The guards spoke to me and the other men in the truck over the past few days," David was silent for a long time. I wondered if someone was watching us. A woman in the back screamed for help as a few of the guards took her aside. A small riot occurred. People tried to help her, but the guards soon silenced them. This would happen repeatedly throughout the night. I jumped every time, but David somehow managed to ignore it and continued, "They'll have us doing the same as we did today, which will conclude our work. Except, this time, most of the men have hidden sharp, and blunt objects around the camp which they will retrieve tomorrow." He paused for a minute. "A signal will be given, and we will do whatever we have to for our freedom. The rest of the guards will be caught by surprise; I only hope that's enough."

"It could be a trap," I whispered.

He revealed a small knife tucked away in his pants' waist, "They've given us these for reassurance."

"No," I flinched. I kept my head still and made sure not to move, but I couldn't agree with his plan. "I know they've killed a lot of us, but God demands forgiveness. We don't spill blood for blood." I wouldn't do it. I couldn't do it. "I'm struggling with hatred towards these men, but I can't go against God for my own freedom. Shouldn't we try to break through our captors' hearts with love and prayer before we attempt to kill them?"

"I understand your hesitations. I wrestled the idea within my heart at first, too," he said after a moment, "but it's the only way." I couldn't tell if David's silence was him waiting for me to respond, or if it was to keep our cover, but I refused to take the risk.

"What's been planned is done," David said bluntly. "It'll happen whether you participate or not. Just keep Angelica close. When it happens..." he grew quiet... "I'll be nearby to cut your restraints. If I'm not, you need to run as fast as you can. We'll meet at the top of the mountain."

He pulled his arms from me, and I sat up again. Half of me wished to stay in his embrace, even if the illusion of safety was false. I looked at Angelica, wondering who she was to David. Did she have anyone else worrying about her, to pray for her, in her absence? I looked at David apologetically, letting him know I wouldn't help with the plan. I would however, do everything possible to keep Angelica safe. He gave a nod and looked into the sky. I couldn't see his face, but I felt his disappointment. Looking up as well, I could see the stars shining bright without a cloud to hide them. The world seemed so calm.

CHAPTER 18

Help us, God our Savior, for the glory of Your name; deliver us and forgive our sins for Your name's sake. Why should the nations say, "Where is their God?"
—Psalm 79:9–10 (TNIV)

Once again, gunshots followed by screams of terror awoke me from one nightmare into the next. It felt as if my eyes had only closed for a minute. Yet, the sun is rising again. Today, the masked men were much harsher, calling us names and cursing our God. When King David was only a boy, Goliath, the giant, stood to curse God while challenging His people. No one would stand up to Goliath except David; and David won – he won because he stood for God and not himself.

I wanted to stand up for God… no, I needed to stand up for God right here and now, but I had no idea how. We were prisoners. It would be difficult to stand and bring glory to God's name at the same time. If we fight and kill, then people who hear about this day will curse God's name, not honor it. Returning hate for hate would not glorify God.

As I walked, carrying a pail of dirt, I saw the solemn faces around me, with stooped shoulders, showing they accepted their newfound slavery. Still, some walked with broad shoulders and straightened backs. They tried to blend in, but their faces stayed strong. Though their heads hung, their eyes wandered over their surroundings. They seemed on edge. These men of action were most likely the ones planning the escape.

The atmosphere began to change. There was a charge of tension as men and women alike seemed restless. The need to fight for freedom was palpable and no one seemed to consider forgiveness as an option to win over our captors. They would only settle for blood. *Please God, remind us to check our hearts.* I realized it was easier for me to be ready to forgive since I had not had my children ripped from my hands or murdered before my eyes.

A sparrow's call caught my ear. Others heard it, too, as their heads rose. Another sparrow returned the call, with a slightly different pitch, from farther away. Then, as I was dumping my bucket into a hole, I could hear a third sparrow right behind me. Understanding dawned on my conscience. I dreaded what would happen next. I turned to find the sparrow and instead, saw men and women standing still, tightly gripping the makeshift weapons in their hands. Another whistle chirped louder than the others did.

The war began as the battle cries roared. My heart raced. I ran to take Angelica's hand. "Come with me," I said desperately.

A guard advanced towards us. A bullet passed through him. His body dropped to the ground. Christian men and women were swarming over the masked men, beating them down with pipes and bricks of all types. The retaliators took the guards' weapons and used them against them while many of us ran to the mountain just as David had told us to do. I worked to keep Angelica by my side, but a man grabbed me from behind. I tried to pull from him. His grip was too strong.

"Where do you think you're going?" He scolded.

David rushed to my rescue with his knife in hand. A nearby soldier tackled him to the ground. The soldier had no weapon on him, and fought David for his. Others came to my aid while David struggled for his life. They pulled the man in a mask away from me and beat him until he was unresponsive. Another reached to cut me free. Unrestricted, I ran to Angelica's side and pulled her to run with me. We turned back to look for David. The soldier he struggled with now sat on top of him. David rolled the soldier off hitting the soldier's head on a rock. David drew his knife up high.

"David. No!"

"Get out of here," he yelled back. The hate that consumed his eyes scared me more than the barrel of any gun. I didn't want David to kill him, but I wasn't close enough to stop him. I turned and forced Angelica to come with me. We ran through the trees and up the mountain.

I witnessed the guards, who claimed to be on the side of Christians, attacking their own kind in order to help set us free. Over half of the Christians involved in the fight began to take their weapons with them and run up the side of the mountain as well. Others stayed back to fight, getting help from several of the soldiers. I had no power to stop this bloodbath. All I could do was pray for the people behind us and continue to move forward.

We passed a man in hiding who wrenched Angelica from my arms. She fell to the ground with a scream; the first noise I had heard from her in days. Turning, I saw a man in a mask holding a gun in her face. Angelica backed up as far as she could, until she sat up against a tree trunk. Before I could get to her, the gun went off. His body hit the ground. Angelica was safe.

The shot came from a woman I recognized as Bethany. An image flashed through my mind of her running around with twins while her husband called out to her on the first day of camp. Bethany stood before us now, with no children or husband – only a gun and a vengeful heart. The guard she shot lay at Angelica's feet. Angelica was petrified. We didn't need to say anything.

I took Angelica's hand, letting her run in front of me this time. Behind us, war, ahead of us we saw sanctuary. The guards who were on our side stayed below the mountain to help. The masked men started retreating when discovering the betrayal from within their ranks. We gained higher ground, stealing the upper hand.

I felt like a coward for running while others were fighting for my freedom. "Come on," I told Angelica, pushing my guilt aside. "We need to keep moving. Who knows if more are coming?" She did her best to continue throwing one foot in front of the other.

Images of David stabbing that man kept running across my mind. I have no idea how I would react if I see him at the top of the mountain. Being a part of the escape plan didn't mean he needed to kill. He could have left the man, dazed on the ground, and run with us to safety. Then again, was I really standing for my faith by running, or was I just too afraid to face death? I almost ran into a hanging branch because of my thoughts, but thankfully, Angelica was alert enough to direct me out of the way.

Finally, she softly asked through her heavy breaths, "Where are we going?"

"We were instructed to meet the others at the top of the mountain."

"Then what...?"

"I wish I knew. We need to trust that God has given wisdom to those with the plan." Perhaps God had planned for us to fight back. He often called the Israelites to war in the Old Testament. Still, I had no way to be sure. All I can do is stick to what I feel is right in my heart.

We met up with a man and woman who stopped to bandage the man's feet. Her sandals had broken, so he gave her his shoes, but the rocks cut his heel open. The woman cried, blaming herself for the man's wounds. He reassured her that he was fine. We helped them wrap his foot and stayed with them the rest of the way up. I knew helping them was the best thing to do, but I constantly looked back in fear of the danger behind us. Selfishly, I didn't want to slow down.

"We've only been married two weeks," wept the woman. "This week was supposed to start our marriage off right. I never thought it would turn out like this."

"None of us did," her husband caressed her hand. We couldn't run with his injured feet, but we kept a fast pace walk. The husband stumbled in pain every now and again, but pushed through it with little complaint.

There was no sign of organization when we came to the top of the mountain. People held each other while crying. Some found large stones and branches, clenching them in their fists as if preparing for another fight. Others huddled together in prayer, while a handful sat, emotionless, waiting for a leader. A young boy approached Angelica and I with a small pocketknife, blackened from the fire. He couldn't have been over thirteen years old.

"Can I cut those off of you?" He looked at Angelica, pointing to her hands. "Hold still," he told Angelica as he held her hand and maneuvered the knife between her skin and the zip ties. "It's not the sharpest knife, but it has worked fine so far." He revealed his nervousness through his small talk. At least he found himself a job to keep his mind preoccupied.

Raw skin breathed fresh air for the first time in days as he removed the ties from Angelica's wrists. Rubbing her hands gently around her wrists, while slightly smiling at the boy, she showed her gratitude. I reacted similarly when he cut the ties from my wrists. It was odd; I could feel the absence of the zip ties more than I had felt their presence.

Not knowing what to do next, we anticipated the worst. The few people we talked with knew nothing about the area. We could take a chance and start walking, but not knowing the landscape, we could walk right back into the enemy's hands. Finally, David and nine others came into view. Five were men and women like us, all with weapons in hand; including Bethany, who saved Angelica earlier. The other four were masked men. I hoped they were on our side.

A few daring men within the crowd, about fifteen, stood to block the four possible enemies from coming any closer to the frightened group.

"It's okay, they're with us," David motioned his hands in the air, signaling for everyone to hold back their judgments. There had to be more guards than just these four fighting on our side. My eyes shifted back and forth around the crowd. Just because I didn't see anyone hiding in the trees, didn't mean we were safe.

"How can we trust you? Your family is the reason we're in this mess," a pepper haired man indicted to David as he stepped forward. "Your hired staff made up half of our attackers." He gripped the pistol down at his side.

"I had no idea they planned to attack the camp," David said. "I'm a victim, just like you."

"Then why are you sticking up for them?" The pepper haired man asked.

"Trust their actions, not my words," David urged. "They just defended us against their own men; killing people, whom they considered family, to save our lives."

"Exactly, and have you stopped to ask yourself why?" The pepper haired man stepped closer.

David's voice grew bold, "To save you and everyone else here."

"Or, to find the survivors and make sure we don't make it any further?" The man now had his finger on the trigger.

"If that were the case, they would have let us die back there," David clenched a gun within his own hand. "They are on our side."

"Take off your masks. Show us who you are," the pepper haired man raised his gun at the man in a mask who was nearest to him.

"Drop your weapon," David stepped sideways between them with a gun of his own. It baffled me that he could be so eager to save one life and so willing to destroy another.

The masked man closest to David stepped forward and lightly pushed David aside. "It's okay," he said. Then he reached his hand to his face and removed the mask. My heart dropped, "My name is Anthony Tereski. With me are Justin Farrell, Lorenzo Martinez, and Phoebe Bertram." The others took their masks off and my knees nearly caved in beneath me. The bile rose in my throat and threatened to come gushing out. David looked in my direction as if to try to keep me silent. I didn't know Lorenzo or Phoebe, but I knew Anthony and Justin far too well.

CHAPTER 19

Anyone who hates his brother is a murderer...
—1 John 3:15 (NIV)

"It's a trap!" I exclaimed, quickly standing next to the pepper haired man. He gripped the gun even more firmly. Whispers emerged from the crowd. Some darted away together, not risking their lives. I should've been with them, but David needed to know the truth. "These two, and another, called the attack," I said loud and clear. "They started this bloodbath."

David frowned at me. He shouldn't think I was lying; he saw what Justin did on stage.

"We saved your life," Justin defended.

"Oh. Really?" I had no time to repeat the events. We needed to disappear – without them.

"If we would have released you, you would've been killed."

"Seemed like the opposite to me," I scowled.

Anthony interjected, "Major Simmons would have gotten to you before we did. If you remember, she wanted to shoot you."

"Oh, I remember it all too well. I saw what you did to Omar. You murdered him," I accused. It sickened me to see them winning David over to their side.

"We never touched him," Justin changed his story from when they threatened me on the mountain. I know what I saw. They had shown me Omar's blood dripping from Justin's knife. I could never erase that image.

"Enough," David silenced us. "We need to focus on the present, not the past. Tell them what you told me," he said to the soldiers, ignoring all of my warnings.

Anthony stepped back and looked at everyone still with us, "None of you are safe here. A second team is on their way to clear out all survivors. We need to get far away from the camp."

"How would you know this?" Someone in the crowd asked.

Anthony sighed, "We were with the others, yes, but it wasn't supposed to end like this. Our commanders assigned us to watch, report, and detain until all terrorist threats ceased. At the last minute, they changed our orders to extinguish; not detain. Major

Simmons called for backup the moment the revolt began. We need to go, now."

"How do y'all plan to get these people out without being seen?" The pepper haired man criticized.

David tried to answer calmly, "We can follow the mountain range north until we reach a field. Crossing that field and going through a thick section of pine trees will put you at my house. We have means of transportation there, and can get everyone to safety."

"How do you expect us all to get there?" A man asked.

Another shouted, "Where are we going to go after that?"

Others repeated similar questions.

"We can figure out those details later. It's not safe here," the urgency in David's voice increased. "We need to go as swiftly and quietly as possible, but we need to move now. We'll lead the way." He tried to walk forward and start the procession, but more people wanted to argue with him.

"I'm not going anywhere with those murderers," the pepper haired man said, waving his gun towards the soldiers. Heads nodded in agreement behind him.

Gunshots sounded. Loud voices cried for help. The reinforcements were here, tying up the loose ends at the base of the mountain. I was foolish to assume everyone was here with us. As panic broke out, men and women scattered in all directions. We had no plan of escape, and no one cared to wait for David to lead the way. I hastily grabbed Angelica's hand to avoid losing her in the crowd. Someone else's hand grabbed my arm.

"Follow me," David said, as he turned me in the opposite direction. I hesitated, but went with him anyway. Bethany and the soldiers went with David as well. All the others who had come with them scattered with the rest of the frightened people.

Had I been on my own, I would have gone a different way. As it was, I had no assurance that I could protect Angelica alone. I wouldn't trust the soldiers but, for now, they were safer than those pursuing us…I hoped.

Beside me approached the old pepper haired man, who introduced himself as Darius. A few others followed behind him. "I can't leave the two of you with those men," Darius whispered. "It ain't safe."

"I know it's not," I hesitated, "but David's my friend. I can't leave him with them either. I need him to know the truth about what happened at the camp."

"Then just stay near me," Darius winked, patting the gun tucked in his waste side. "Any sign of trouble, you let me handle it."

"Thank you." The use of guns still didn't sit well with me but, if it kept the soldiers at bay, I had no issue with Darius holding onto it. Still, I prayed he'd never have to use it.

We ran down the backside of the mountain with gunshots and yells dogging us from a distance. A pathetic thought entered my mind, *has the worst finally passed?* No, more than likely we'd be on the run until we jumped the border of Mexico, dug a hole to China, or lay in our grave. When we couldn't hear anything nearby, we stopped to catch our breath. The soldiers were annoyed, but David stayed patient. Darius, and the few who followed him, shared canteens of water they had stolen off the soldiers at the camp. "Here," Darius said while handing me his canteen, "you two take this. Drink it sparingly."

Angelica eyed the water like a hawk. I let her drink first. She put down more than she probably should have, but never spit it up. I took a few sips, trying to remoisten my cottonmouth. Every drop turned into vapor as I let little by little slide down my throat. One of the girls traveling with us began to cough.

"Melanie, are you alright?" A man, with a lion tattoo on his arm whom they called Thad, asked.

Melanie coughed a few more times before answering, "Yes, I just breathed the water in instead of drinking it."

Everyone chuckled at her comment, covering burdened smiles.

Pain and sorrow lay behind us, and fear hampered the path before us. Moments of laughter brought much needed relief to the terror of our situation.

"Let's move on," Anthony interrupted. Fear returned as he made eye contact with me. I pulled Angelica close to my side and took a step nearer to Darius. Everyone stood back up ready to continue the journey.

As we ran, I noticed David constantly glancing back at me. I refused to make eye contact. Confusion clouded my mind. The image of him stabbing that soldier to death scared me. Frustration filled my thoughts as I watched him be so willing to trust these other four – even after I warned him against them. I didn't care if they helped him with the escape plan. He should be more willing to trust me over them.

After what seemed like hours of running, we found a small creek where we could rejuvenate. No one said anything. We were all quiet. I can only assume that the others, like me, were just trying to make sense of things. The soldiers surrounded us as best as they could. They watched and listened to the forest. I noticed Melanie with her head bowed, so I took this time to pray as well. I grabbed Angelica's hand in mine and closed my eyes. I don't know if she did or not, but I drew comfort from her physical touch. Water over the rocks had a calming effect on me. I found my muscles loosening up and my mind focusing on the prayer in my heart.

Phoebe squeaked suddenly. Shock kept us from reacting to the appearance of a silver blade sticking into her shoulder. Our eyes were on her. We weren't ready for the ambush. Men and women leaped into view covered from head to toe in mud, dirt, and leaves. Together, they began attacking the soldiers. Anthony swung into action. He shoved the man nearest to him far back into a tree, then he turned to defend Phoebe. He hesitated to shoot as Phoebe and her woman attacker tossed each other around on the ground. Anthony's uncertainty allowed time for two men to restrain him.

He continued to fight with all his might, but stopped quickly when he looked down the barrel of his own gun. Justin, too, found himself at gunpoint by a female twice his size. The other soldier, Lorenzo, held a chokehold on a poor young boy who had tried hard to subdue him.

"Let them go or I'll break his neck," Lorenzo demanded firmly. Immediately the young boy within Lorenzo's grasp began crying.

"They go free first," Justin's captor said, as she pointed to all of us. She not only had the muscles of a man, but spoke with a tone of one as well.

Anthony shouted at her, "They were never captured. We're helping them." Anthony then looked in our direction. "Tell them we're helping you."

This was the moment we needed. The camouflaged men and women could decide the soldiers' fate once we left…No, I can't believe I would consider sacrificing four lives for my own. I couldn't think straight. I tried to focus on the problem at hand. Maybe…if the camouflaged group would just hold the soldiers until we got away…

"They're with us," David defended them. "They helped us escape the massacre, and now they're helping us get to refuge."

All weapons stayed pointed at the soldiers. The boy in Lorenzo's arm slowly changed color in his face, from pink to purple.

"Honest," David said louder, taking a few steps towards the battle scene, "Those two men," he pointed to Justin and Anthony, "are the ones who told me the escape plan. They explained to me, and other men in the trucks, that they had a plan to help end our persecution. They promised to make sure of it themselves. Today, they stood on the front line while fighting against men who they once called brothers. They are with us."

That explained a lot. Anthony and Justin had plenty of time on the trucks to conjure up a convincing story for David. Guilt slammed me in the chest. Maybe the soldiers knew that the orders they carried out weren't right, and by freeing all the prisoners, they hoped to right their wrongs. If that was the case, then my constant judgments were doing nothing but harm. I just wish I could discern whether they were honestly on our side or stuck around with ulterior motives.

"Neil, please..." the boy in Lorenzo's arms gasped for help.

At that, the man over Anthony stepped back and threw the gun away from him and everyone else. "Release him," Neil said to Lorenzo.

Lorenzo slightly loosened his grip and the boy gasped for air. "All of you drop your weapons," Lorenzo clarified.

"Do what he says, Teresa," Neil said.

The woman over Justin stepped back and threw her gun. Then she looked at the woman standing over Phoebe and said, "Rebecca, it's ok." That woman, too, backed down. The man with his gun on Lorenzo finally lowered his hand and tossed his gun away. Lorenzo let the boy fall to the ground. The boy quickly scrambled to his friends, wheezing, while everyone stood idle unsure of what to do next.

"They have no hole in their hand," Melanie said to Darius, breaking the silence.

I looked down at my hand and brushed my fingers across the bullet wound. It was still tender. We all looked closely at the hands camouflaged with mud and dirt. Teresa confirmed Melanie's observation, "That's because we were part of the very first group who escaped."

So, some did get away. The faces of my friends imprinted on my mind. "Have you run into a group with two guys, Jeffrey and Steven, and a girl named Jasmine?" I choked desperately.

"No, I'm sorry." Teresa said. My heart sank. "Your group is the first we've come in contact with long enough to talk to. We mainly keep in the shadows."

"This isn't a game," Lorenzo reprimanded her. "These soldiers you're going up against are highly trained. You sent a boy to fight... of all things...you could all be killed."

Teresa hissed, "Don't you think we know all of that? Wesley volunteered. We're all volunteers each with our own skills. We obviously had enough strength to subdue all of you."

"Yet, you weren't willing to sacrifice one life in order to end ours. Had we been foe instead of friend, the moment you tossed your weapons would've been the moment you all died."

"My faith in God is more powerful than your threat," Neil said confidently.

"Forgive me if I come across as rude," Phoebe interrupted, "but...." She held her wound as tight as she could. Her pale face screamed for medical attention. The soldiers rushed to help her.

"How did you all escape?" Thad asked our camouflaged brothers and sisters from behind Darius while the soldiers tended to Phoebe. Only David went with them to help. The rest of our group, like me, still seemed hesitant to offer them any support.

Neil answered, "A man came to warn us. There were ten of us when we escaped. I'm Neil, this is my brother Travis," he pointed to the other man who had helped him in attacking Anthony. "Teresa and Rebecca were with us as well. The soldiers killed the others and Wesley joined us later. We were all out by the pond, baptizing a friend. Lee, a staff member, came with us. In the middle of the baptism, a man came running down the mountain frantically telling us to get out and away as fast as we could. He said a war was coming. We didn't know what to do. He was too distraught to be playing a prank, so we ran."

"Omar," I whispered under my breath.

Neil continued, "Out of nowhere, Lee pulled a gun on us and radioed something to the others. Our friend, Brandon, tackled Lee to the ground. The rest of us helped, but in the mix of things, Brandon was shot and we had to kill Lee so we could escape and get Brandon to safety."

"Eight of us stood in the trees watching over Brandon, before realizing he had already died. Banks and the man who tipped us off went to warn the rest of the camp. We saw some of the staff leading the children down to the open fields. The explosions that leveled the cabins knocked us down. After the last one went off in the tabernacle, two brothers attempted to rush in and help the injured. I haven't seen them since. The rest of us went to help the children. We didn't reach them in time. It was as if the kids just vanished. We caught two soldiers off guard, took their gear, and continued to fight. Then, we seized the opportunity to rescue everyone we could when we saw you all fighting back a few days later. When Wesley's mom was killed he chose to fight with us."

"But they're trained soldiers..." Bethany's comment hung in the air between the two groups of refugees.

"Like I said, we each have skills that we bring to the table." Neil put his hand on his brother's shoulder, "Travis and I are hunters. We know the wilderness and our way around guns. Teresa practices all forms of martial arts. She can manipulate her opponent's strength and use it against them with little effort. Rebecca is amazing with throwing knives and other items; she's like our secret weapon when going against Goliath. Even Wesley is quick to his feet. He distracts while we attack, but I'll admit we did slip up today. I thank God that this situation was a big misunderstanding. We know that losing our lives is a probability, but it isn't the goal."

"You could have fooled me," Lorenzo grunted as they brought Phoebe over by us. She was very pale. He didn't dwell on the subject as he said, "We need to get moving."

"Where are you heading?" Teresa asked.

Lorenzo looked at David who scanned our surroundings, "I'm trying hard to find familiar territory. As soon as I can, I'll lead them to my home where we can find supplies to help us."

"Let us scout out the woods before you," Neil suggested. "Any Christian's we find can add to your group."

Anthony interjected before anyone could accept the offer. "We can scout for ourselves," he said harshly. They had obvious reason to hold a grudge against the camouflaged men and women, but refusing their help seemed downright senseless.

"How's your wound?" Rebecca asked Phoebe, trying to cut the tension.

"Deep," Phoebe replied. "You have perfect aim. An inch closer and you would've punctured a lung."

"I was going for the heart," Rebecca replied. "My aim on people isn't near as accurate as on animals."

"What's the difference?" Anthony said. It was more of a statement than a question but Rebecca answered him immediately.

"People have a soul."

Anthony rolled his eyes and tried to move us along. David followed behind them blindly, without question. Angelica hesitated to proceed without me. I took a few steps with her, and Darius followed. The others who stood behind Darius didn't move an inch.

"Could you use more help?" Bethany asked our camouflaged brothers and sisters.

"Only from the willing," Teresa responded.

Bethany stepped up, "I am willing."

"As am I," Thad stepped forward. "It's time we get on the front line."

If Darius had volunteered to leave with them, I wouldn't have blamed him, though he made no motion to go. Melanie stayed with us too. The others, who I knew nothing about, all volunteered to join our brothers and sisters in arms. I'll admit that a part of me wanted to volunteer as well just so I could be away from Anthony and Justin. It was obvious that their hold on David was too strong. I had no chance of convincing him to leave them. Yet, for Angelica's sake, I stayed. I had grown attached to the girl. I knew she was going to need my protection.

It didn't take long before trouble found us. Lorenzo was right. We had stayed too long. Soldiers appeared in the distance. We turned to run the other way, further over the mountain and down its backside. Our camouflaged brothers and sisters, along with their new recruits, did their best to hold off the approaching soldiers while we got away. We heard gunshots, but couldn't tell from which direction they came.

CHAPTER 20

Why, you do not even know what will happen tomorrow. What is your life? You are a mist that appears for a little while and then vanishes.
—James 4:14 (NIV)

David changed directions on us several times throughout the hike. When questioned, he would repeatedly ask us to trust him. He knew of a temporary shelter that we could hide in until the enemy threats subsided. We ran down the backside of the mountain for a short time and then we had to hike up a small mound. This part of our journey was a lot steeper, which slowed us down immensely. Angelica wanted to give up, but I wouldn't let her. Phoebe and Melanie also fell behind later on into our hike. I kept looking behind, listening for more gunshots, but there were none. Finally, we came to a cliff.

I kept silent, all the while wondering if David knew what he was doing. David took eight giant steps away from the edge of the cliff towards a tall aspen tree. Then he knelt and started digging in the dirt, pulling out a rope wrapped in thick plastic.

"I used to hike out here for fun," he said, stretching out the rope and throwing it around the aspen tree. He then folded the rope from end to end, and made sure its midpoint was around the tree, "I took up rock climbing and rappelling when I wanted more adventure." He went back to the hole and pulled out another plastic bag with all sorts of rock climbing equipment. He strategically placed and tied everything to the ropes. "I discovered a hideout one day. It kind of became my vacation home." He stood in front of Angelica and I, and held out a harness, "Who wants to go first?" Angelica took a step back. She shook profusely.

A thud sound turned all of our heads. Phoebe had fallen backwards into a tree. Justin and Lorenzo ran to her side to help her back to her feet. "No," she shook her head. "I need to sit."

"What happened?" Anthony asked as he knelt down beside her with the other two.

"I…I don't know," she passively stared at them. Her tight face expressed the pain she couldn't explain.

"Something's wrong," Lorenzo knelt down to check over her wound. He looked up, almost immediately, and caught Phoebe's questioning eyes.

"I'm not going to make it," she said.

"Sure you are," Justin encouraged. "We can lower you down." The way he said this, and the way the three soldiers looked at each other over Phoebe, made me realize she was worse off than any of us were aware. Was she bleeding internally? I could imagine their regret for letting the camouflaged group go free. Phoebe held both Justin and Lorenzo's hands while her breaths grew shorter. Anthony stayed kneeled nearby.

"It's going to be alright," he said to her. "Just breathe easy."

I know they didn't need us, but part of me felt the urge to talk to her about salvation. I debated in my head long and hard on how to phrase it without upsetting them. When I had finally found what I wanted to say, I was too late. Phoebe's hands relaxed. Lorenzo closed her eyelids. The men laid her head back to rest as they placed her hands beside her. Crossly, they looked up at us.

"Let's go," Anthony demanded. "We're wasting time."

Nothing we said or did could help at this moment. The comfort we found from death came in the hope of an afterlife with God. Any hope I chose to offer would be false. Regret made a home in the pit of my stomach. I shouldn't have taken so long to speak up.

"I'll go first," Darius said to David in the midst of their silence. "I'm not letting one of the girls go first and I can help them get inside the cave safely."

"Okay, slip this on," David handed the harness to Darius. "I've connected a simple eight ring to help with the rappelling. All you'll need to do is choose the speed you want to slide down at until you reach the ledge of the cave. To adjust your speed, place downward pressure on this part of the rope," he showed Darius which part. "Keep your feet out in front of you so you don't rub against the cliff."

As Darius began his descent down the face of the mountainside, I had Angelica lie flat on the ground with me and crawl to the edge. I thought it would help to have her see what she would be doing.

"I can't do this," she whispered as we studied Darius' every move.

"You can," I replied. "Don't worry. It'll be okay."

"I'll slip," she said.

"No, you won't. Even if you did, there are people up here to grab your rope and down there ready to catch you."

She didn't say anything in return. I could see fear getting the best of her.

Darius went down about twenty feet before he found the hideout. It took him a minute to catch his footing. When he did, it was a quick process of getting the harness off and back to us. Melanie went next. She was nervous, but not nearly as paralyzed with fear as Angelica. We watched her descend as well. I went after Melanie. Angelica promised that if she could see me rappel, she'd push through it. As much as I hated leaving her here with the soldiers, I trusted that David wouldn't let anything happen to her.

The harness was tight, but I couldn't complain; it would be saving my life so comfort wasn't a concern. The rope felt old and worn as I gripped it in my hands. It held Darius going down, so I hoped it would hold me. "It will be okay," I reassured Angelica, one last time, and then got in position.

David grabbed my hand before I began my descent. He must have noticed my apprehension. I could encourage Angelica, but not myself. "It *will* be alright," he repeated my assurances. I met his gaze with a smile on the outside, as a flash of his face full of hate went through my mind. I couldn't shake the image of him murdering that soldier.

My legs were fine, but my arms shook the entire time. The rope slid between my fingers easily. It began to burn my hand for a moment as I let myself forget to pull down on the loose end of the rope coming out of the eight-ring. Pain shot through my wounded hand, causing me to let go for a moment. I wobbled in the harness and began sliding faster down the cliff. Ignoring the pain, I again grabbed the rope tightly and slowed my descent. Once steady, I clenched my teeth to the sting and continued down the cliff side. Overall, it might have been a fun experience if we didn't have to worry about dying every few minutes. Every second they spent above the cliff was another second closer to the enemy catching us. I tried to drop as fast as possible, but nearly lost it all when my hand slipped again. This time, I had trouble getting my feet out from under me in time and slammed into the rock. From then on, I went slowly with Darius talking trying to calm me down.

"Steady now," he would say. "That's it, you're doing great." When he finally grabbed hold of me, I let out a breath and clung to his arm until I planted my feet on solid ground away from the edge. Inside the cave, Melanie had already found her way to a seat where she fell asleep against the wall.

Next to climb down was supposed to be Angelica. We waited for what seemed like forever. When I finally called for her, Justin began making his descent instead. My heart sunk.

"Something's not right," I told Darius.

"Just wait," he said, holding his hand to his gun. Neither of us helped Justin get into the cave. When he sent the gear back, we asked where Angelica was.

"They're having problems," is all Justin said, and before I knew it, Anthony made his way down to us with ease.

"What's going on up there," Darius asked, looking as tense as I felt.

"The girl's scared," Anthony replied. "The chicken is going to get us all caught."

My blood boiled, "Don't you dare talk bad about her." I walked to the edge and looked up while holding to the wall. I called for Angelica as Lorenzo rappelled down.

"Be quiet," Anthony hissed at me.

"I'm trying to help," I snapped back. "Angelica," I called, a little quieter. I saw her fingertips creep over the side of the cliff and her head barely popped over to where I could see her eyes.

"Angelica, you can do this." I said, as she shook her head no. "Just put the equipment on and let David guide you."

Again, she shook her head no.

"Listen to me," I demanded, "there's more to fear by staying up there. Trust God… you do trust Him right?" She shook her head yes, but I wanted to hear her say it. "Well, do you?"

"Yes," she finally muttered.

"Then trust He will keep you safe. Put the harness on, get set, and pray until you feel us grab you."

She disappeared. I hadn't a clue if she was running away or gearing up. Two thin, wobbly legs slid over the side, followed by the rest of her. Angelica clung to the cliffs' side like a baby monkey to its mother. She took a beating from the rock with every inch she descended, but she made it down safely. When she finally got within reach, Darius and I helped her to the ledge. Darius was the only one who I trusted to help me pull her into the cave.

David was next and he came down without any issues. Just as he was placing his foot on the ledge of the cave, something gave way. Half of the rope slipped from the attachments. The rope above him came rushing down. He had nothing to hold to as he reached forward to catch his balance and his feet couldn't catch solid ground. I gasped and Angelica squealed. Darius and I were both tending to her, too far away to catch him. He met my eyes as he began falling back, begging for my help. My heart dropped, knowing there was nothing I could do. Like lightening, Anthony, Justin, and Lorenzo were all there to catch him. Anthony took David's hand, Lorenzo grabbed the rope, and Justin gave Anthony extra balance. They pulled David in and threw him into the cave. All of us sat for a good minute with hearts racing in the excitement, except for Angelica, who jumped to David and wrapped her arms around his neck. He hugged her back, eyes closed, breathing heavily.

David's eyes met mine once more, only for a second. I suddenly realized the harshness of my judgment. I was glad he was with us, no matter his previous decisions. The three men could have easily let him fall, but they didn't. They all deserved a second chance. Whether they wronged me, they have all the same privileges to forgiveness as I do.

I walked over to the three men who were sitting on the ground and patting each other on the back. My throat clenched, but I knew I had to say something. Lorenzo saw me first and shushed the two others as I approached. In their silence, I froze when I looked at Justin. What did he do to Omar on that mountainside? They impatiently looked at me and I finally had to close my eyes. "Thank you for grabbing him," I blurted. I couldn't apologize for my earlier accusations, or my actions; not yet at least, but I would work towards it. For now, I walked away to hear Anthony say, "You're welcome."

I didn't turn back. Instead, I went and stood next to Darius who rummaged through boxes that David had stored in the cave. There were jars and cans all over covered in dust and cobwebs.

"When I first found this place there was a scare of people losing their jobs and homes," David explained while helping Darius. "My parents always told me not to worry, but I couldn't help it. I was climbing around, praying for God to help me trust Him, and He showed me this place. It's not big, but it's a shelter. God reminded me that day of how He takes care of the birds and the flowers, and therefore, He won't forsake us. I started bringing canned foods and some necessities to live with, and I stored them out here. That way, if anyone tried to take away our property, we'd have a place to go." He walked to a box on the ground and opened it up. "Most importantly, I stored water," he pulled out a package of water bottles. "They won't be cold, but we all need it." As he passed the bottles around everyone perked up appreciatively.

Darius tried to take a bottle of water to Melanie who was still sleeping against the wall, but he couldn't wake her. I assumed she was exhausted though her coughing persisted. Darius placed the bottle near her hands so she could drink it later. As the bottle touched the ground, his body froze. He picked up her hand.

"Come look at this," Darius said.

I came closer to Melanie and looked as Darius held up her hand. She didn't wake up, or even make a move to show she felt him touching her. As he opened her palm, I could see the bullet wound like mine. It looked nothing like Darius' and mine though. Ours were both scabbing over with a little callous. Melanie's hand was very swollen, and the wound had pus coming out of it. Three bright red lines ran up her arm, looking like a road map with major interstates in red. I can't imagine how we missed these markings before.

"What is it?" I asked.

"Blood poisoning I presume," Darius replied. "She's burning up. I tried getting her to wake and drink, but she won't respond."

"What's wrong?" David bent over to get a closer look.

Trying not to startle anyone, particularly Angelica, I quietly asked, "Do you have any first aid items?"

David dug around in a box and found a small first aid kit. He handed it to me. My heart sank. The kit would be nice for normal cuts and scrapes, but there wasn't anything inside of it to help Melanie. I pulled out antibacterial ointment, gauze, and wrap, all outdated. That would have to do for now.

At Melanie's side, Darius held her hand while I poured a bottle of water over it to try to clean her wound. I tried hard not to transfer her infection to either of us. Using some of the gauze, I wiped the water away and squirted the antibacterial ointment on the bullet hole. We placed more gauze over the ointment and wrapped her hand with a bandage to hold it in place. "Hopefully this will help fight the infection," I said.

"How long has she been like this?" David asked.

Darius replied, "I'm not sure. She's had a cough that comes and goes. Right now she's on fire, and very pale."

"It's spreading way too fast," David shook his head. "I'm not much of a medic. Are any of you?" He asked the soldiers.

We looked behind us to see all three soldiers staring our way. None of them could offer any advice. Lorenzo seemed to know more about blood poisoning than we did, but his line of thought paralleled Darius', "She needs to go to a hospital for proper care."

"Then we need to get her back up the cliff and to a doctor," I proclaimed.

David shook his head, "You know we can't do that."

"Maybe you *won't,* but I certainly will," I said. I felt like I needed to try.

"Your self-righteous behavior is pointless here," Justin exclaimed. "You can't carry her up this mountain alone, nor could you carry her back to a hospital without getting yourself killed."

I stood reluctant, "So we're just supposed to let her die?"

"No," Justin kept too calm of a voice for my liking. He didn't care about her wellbeing, "but we can't endanger everyone here for the sake of one. Try to keep her hydrated and nourished, but it's up to her body to fight the infection."

"He's right," Darius shocked me with his answer, "and … what we need to do now is pray."

My frustration turned to guilt. I should have thought of that first. Instead, I searched for my own answers in a first aid kit. Where was my faith? I needed to remember to keep God first and let Him be in control. Here lately, those things seem easier said than done. I submitted to Darius' response and David did as well. We each placed a hand on Melanie and readied ourselves to pray. A fourth hand reached to touch Melanie's arm as Angelica sat beside me. I smiled at her as we all bowed our heads and prayed.

David started us off, "Father, we trust You. We know You are both Healer and Protector. We see Your faithfulness every day of our lives, though trials and persecution weigh heavy on us…"

All of a sudden, Darius' voice began to whisper in behind David's prayer. At first I thought Darius may be repeating David, but he was praying on his own, "God of Abraham, Isaac, and Jacob, we pray Your blessings on this child. She's in pain without a medic. You made us. You know how to heal us…"

David continued with his prayer, as did Darius. I was relieved to know our prayers would be both separate and unified. I took in a breath, blocking out their pleas to God. Letting the breath out I, too, began to entreat God for His mercy.

"We've gone through so much Lord, and You have brought Melanie this far with us. Why take her now? Lord, heal her from this sickness. Don't let her suffer any longer," I began to hear faint sounds come from Angelica's mouth as she started to pray. I continued to lay out my heavy heart before God, "I'm sorry I forgot to trust You first, but please don't let Melanie suffer for my mistakes. Take this infection from her body. Cast it far away, just as You did to the demons long ago. You sent them into the wild pigs never to return. I know You can do all things, and this situation is no different. You can heal her. I know You can. Please, just place Your healing hand over her."

We continued until one by one our prayers ended. Angelica's voice faded out as she started, again, to fall asleep. David's voice disappeared next. I ended my prayer shortly after David, but Darius stayed with Melanie a long while. I turned my body around to where I sat between Angelica and Melanie. Angelica raised her head onto my lap for a pillow. My right hand stroked through her hair as my left rested on Melanie's arm. I continued to lift up Darius' prayer with him. I felt as if I had said all I could.

Darius seemed to have no problem with repeating himself. He grew quieter as he bent down and touched his lips to Melanie's forehead. Then, he whispered something to her, keeping it secret from the rest of us. As he sat his back up against the wall, he lifted his knees to his chest and folded his hands over them. His head raised up to God as his eyes closed. I couldn't tell if he was praying or resting. Either way, I didn't interrupt him.

The three soldiers stayed huddled in their own little group, talking among themselves. They seemed to have found their way around the supplies as they chowed down on something. Food had no appeal to me at this moment. Every now and then, they would look our way. I couldn't tell if they were trying to offer sympathy or just had nothing else to do. My eyes stayed on David most of the time, but eventually I gave up trying to figure out what was going through his mind. Every time that Melanie would cough, our heads would turn, hoping to see her awake.

That first day in the cave was most challenging. Though I normally enjoyed silence, the silence we experienced seemed filled with darkness. Worry, fear, anger, and hate manipulated the hearts within the cave; or they at least did my heart. As Christians, we aren't supposed to let such things enter our bodies, but my mortal flesh was seemingly too weak to hold my eternal spirit high. Though eight of us crowded within the cave together – five of which were Christians – I still felt alone, without support. We had come together to pray over Melanie, but after that, our bodies stayed while our spirits practically went their separate ways. If this was a foreshadowing of the rest of our journey together, then I wondered the purpose of it all.

It's hard to understand why God would allow everything to happen the way that it has. I always assumed Christian freedoms would end. Still, it seemed like we were blindsided by the signs that should have been evident. In certain ways, our country pulled away from God. They took the Ten Commandments out of courthouses and God's name out of the pledge. Yet, those things seemed minor because they didn't affect the Christian home. Christians still had the freedom to worship and profess God's name at work, home, and school… or so it seemed... Public schools were firing teachers for talking to their students about God, and customers were suing Christian businesses for not complying with requests that went against their beliefs. Perhaps the signs were there. I just never realized that they pointed to this day.

Melanie became worse further into the day. Her coughing

turned to wheezing, the red lines spread further up on her arms, and her hand refused to heal. I stared down at my hand, not understanding the difference between her wound and ours. Maybe Melanie had grabbed something that was already infected. Near the late afternoon of the day, Melanie's body started sweating. She took in short, rapid breaths and still gave no response to any of us trying to talk to her. Her wheezing ceased. Had God answered our prayers?

Darius placed his hand under her nostrils. I held my breath. It became clear as he placed two fingers on her neck below her jaw. She had no pulse…no breath. I tried not to cry as I whispered, "But…we prayed."

"Sometimes God says no," Darius said remorsefully. "At least now she's at peace."

I waited for judgmental comments from the soldiers. They saw us pray for her healing and, now they saw our prayers go to waste. Part of me hoped that God would heal Melanie just to prove His existence to them. Then again, God didn't need to prove anything to anyone.

"I'm sorry," Lorenzo said empathetically. They, of course, just finished saying their goodbyes to a fellow comrade.

I didn't know Melanie very well. I could tell she had a sweet spirit, both gentle and kind, but I knew nothing about her family or past life. I didn't know if someone was looking for her, or if she had been alone this entire time. I didn't even know how old she was. All I knew was that she stood faithful to God. I knew this because of the mark on her hand, and the trusting attitude she had through the journey with us. I didn't feel sorrow because of our loss; she was with God now, just as Darius had said. No, my sorrow came for those of us left here to hurt. God allowed people like Melanie and Omar to wait in rest for Jesus' return. What did He plan to use the rest of us for, or are we just supposed to take test after test as we await our death sentence as well?

Darius and David wrapped Melanie's body in a blanket. I

stayed with Angelica, unsure of how to feel. The bodies we moved in the camp were mutilated. We knew that they were dead, but Melanie looked as if she were merely sleeping.

"The body can't stay here," Anthony said to David. "You know that right?"

David and Darius both looked at each other. "Yes, we know," David, acknowledged. Everyone's eyes drifted to the cliff edge.

I exclaimed without thinking, "Wait, what?"

Anthony ignored me. "We can take care of it if the two of you don't want to," he offered kindly. Justin and Lorenzo nodded in agreement.

Leaving Angelica on the ground, I stood between Anthony and Melanie. "You can't be serious."

"This is a body," Darius explained gently. "It's merely a shell, holding a soul and giving God's Spirit a temple. Those things don't dwell in it anymore. Melanie can't feel or see anything that happens to this body from this point forward."

I stood in shock, feeling betrayed. Now Darius was on the soldiers' side.

"Listen," Darius put his hand on my shoulder, "we don't know how long we'll have to be here. All deceased things decompose and eventually Melanie's body will too. The image to come is one that's much worse than sending her body away. This ain't any different from a burial out to sea. If we could dig a hole for her, we would, but you can see that's not an option, right?"

"Alright," I finally gave in with watery eyes, "but I won't help you." Angelica and I both sat in the far back of the cave.

"We can't waste the blanket," I heard Justin say. I didn't turn around to see what they did. Angelica and I faced the wall with our ears plugged. I hummed within to block out any further noise, and tried to focus on God.

"It's finished," Darius tapped on my shoulder with a solemn face. I turned around. Melanie's body was gone. Just like that, we were down to seven.

CHAPTER 21

Test everything. Hold on to the good.
—1 Thessalonians 5:21 (NIV)

The sun began its descent, bringing a cold chill into the cave. David pulled out thin blankets for us all; the same kind they had taken from Melanie's body.

"They're thin, but it'll help," David said.

Darius smiled kindly, "I could really go for some food."

My stomach instantly reminded me of its vast cavity. Maybe that's why I constantly fought against everyone. I still wondered what ulterior motives led the soldiers to stay with us but exhaustion and hunger, not to mention the fear and horror I had been experiencing, may have clouded my judgment. The events of the past week weighed down on me more than I cared to admit, and they grew heavier by the hour. Nourishment may be exactly what I needed to refresh physically and mentally.

David pulled crackers out of a bag and grabbed a jar of peanut butter. We circled around to share the food. When Darius took a cracker, he lifted it up and said, "May this represent the body of Christ, broken for us."

I froze, unsure of how to respond. My mind focused back on Christ. He had saved us today. What's one day when compared to eternity? I thanked Him for bringing us to safety. Then, I ate the cracker and fixated on His sacrifice that gave me hope even if tomorrow never came.

"Amen," David said. He then grabbed another container and mixed the powder inside of it with a new bottle of water. "Also, let this represent the blood of Christ, which gives us new life and presents us as blameless in God's eyes." He took a drink and passed it to me.

I took a sip. It was a clear substance with a little taste of fruitiness. The aftertaste was somewhat bitter, like an energy drink mix.

I watched as the soldiers questioned what they were doing, but they pretended to take the drink anyway. Nothing left the bottle. They only touched their lips to it before passing it on to the next person. Lorenzo, on the other hand, finished the drink off completely.

I gestured for David to watch the three of them, hoping he would say something, but he didn't seem to notice. I dreaded having to speak up, and could feel my anxiety increase. My face flushed red. The Spirit urged me to talk. I had stayed silent while Phoebe lay dying; I would not stay silent now. Trusting God for help, I opened my mouth and let the question roll off my tongue.

"Don't be offended by me asking this." I grabbed their attention, "Do you know what this is?"

Lorenzo, who I knew nothing about, raised his head and said, "It's to remember the death and resurrection of your Christ."

His comrades looked baffled. I half smiled yet, he had said "*Your Christ.*" He didn't claim the salvation in front of him, though he knew about it.

Darius relieved me as he took charge in adding, "It's more than that. When we choose to become Christians, we make a commitment to walk in the footsteps of Christ each day of our lives, whether we are experiencing blessings or persecution. This," he gestured by pointing to the cracker and drink mix, "what we just ate, is a resemblance of the meal that Jesus shared the night before He let the Romans kill Him. It was a way for His disciples to remember Him and what He's done, and we now continue that tradition." Darius looked at the rest of us, "Christ, before His death, reminded His disciples to stay committed. We also have the responsibility to remind each other of our commitment to Christ during times of persecution. We've lived a worry free life for so long. There's no reason we can't also live a persecuted life for Him."

David, Angelica, and I all nodded. We understood the challenge before us. The soldiers continued eating without speaking. Within minutes, we emptied the peanut butter jar and crackers. In the midst of the silence and licking of lips, the soldiers suggested that we give out the rest of the food in rations. "It would keep us from starving ourselves out in the end. We can take the extra food with us when we leave," Lorenzo said. David and Darius agreed, and so, for the rest of the night, we fasted.

While David and Angelica sat together near the entrance of the cave, I sat with Darius. I found out that he was once married and had a daughter.

"When my wife decided she was tired of being married, she took Camry with her," Darius said to me. "She was only a baby, but she was my world. I turned to women and alcohol after that. I was a sinner of sinners," he sighed. "I never once let my daughter visit and see me as such. When my ex remarried they, too, had a daughter together. Money grew tight for them, so I suggested she let me have Camry back. Then, we could each raise a child. The next day, Camry was on my doorsteps with her suitcase. I realized real fast that I needed to change my sinful ways." He then leaned in close as if to tell me a secret, "There ain't no man who can raise a daughter around sin and expect her to become anything but a streetwalker."

His honesty surprised me. It was hard for me to hold back a grin.

"So, I cleaned up," Darius continued. "I found a two bedroom apartment and a fulltime job. I raised my daughter in Christ and never skipped a worship service. We stayed the best of friends." Another sigh left his breath, "I never did remarry, but I believe there's still someone out there who'd be willing to marry this old man." He gave a chuckle that brought a smile to my face.

"Where is Camry now?" *Please don't let her be one of the murdered sisters in Christ,* I begged God.

He looked out at the cave entrance. "She's in Arkansas with her husband and kids. The first thing I'll do when I get out of here is get them somewhere safe."

"I hope my father has kept my mother and sister safe," I said, wondering where they've managed to hide and if they're suffering the same peril as us.

Talking with Darius definitely helped ease some of my worries.

When the conversation grew quiet in the night, I asked, "What did you whisper to Melanie earlier?"

Darius passively let his expression change to the grin of a wise old man. His cheeks raised as his forehead wrinkled. His voice stayed quiet and calm, "When you feel God calling you home; when you know it's time, don't hold onto this world. Go to God's open arms and never look back." He paused for a moment, regaining his normal composure. "That final blessing will stick with me until the end of my life. My father spoke it to his mother as she lay dying with cancer. Seeing the peace enter her body when he let her go was the happiest I ever saw her. Often, people suffer greater pain in death when loved ones beg for them to stay."

I understood it now. I prayed for Melanie's survival; Darius prayed for her rest. God said no to my prayers and granted his. God, who is Just and Righteous, knew what Melanie needed. He was still in control and He still cared. He showed mercy today by taking Melanie home, rather than forcing her to suffer any longer. Had I remembered Hezekiah at the time of my prayer, I would have known better than to pray more days for her life than God had already set. He sent a prophet to tell Hezekiah when he would die. Hezekiah, like most dying people do, prayed for more time. God gave him fifteen extra years in his life and in those fifteen years, Hezekiah had a son that brought great evil to the throne. He caused terrible pain and suffering upon all of God's people. None of that would have happened had Hezekiah accepted the Lord's fate for himself at the first warning of his death. Remembering this story humbles me before God, "Thank you for listening to Darius' prayers over mine."

Darius smiled.

The stars lit up the night sky. We knew that we would be better off traveling at night, but tonight was too soon. Our worn down bodies needed to rest. We had survived multiple attacks, the loss of loved ones without time to mourn, and the vicious labor of hiding all evidence, all within a week. We needed this night to rejuvenate.

As everyone found their place to rest, I stayed close to Darius and his protection and tried to keep Angelica with me. She eventually went to David's side, and fell asleep next to him. The soldiers slept close to each other, leaving no room for someone to sneak up on them. I tried to sleep once everyone else had dozed off, but my body wouldn't let me. I was still on high alert. The slightest noise jolted me awake. I quickly sat up at the sound of military men marching above us. When looking around, I only saw ants marching across the ground, heading back to their home for the night.

Growing more and more anxious, I quietly walked to the edge of the cliff. The view, even at this time, was magnificent. No matter the amazing things, I've seen in life, I still find myself awed by God's creation. Only He could create this view. The moonlight lit up the trees below. The canyon filled itself with life. The birds all rested for the night, except the owls that were just now beginning to make their nightly rounds. Bats flew past me while scooping up the bugs that swarmed in the moonlight. No animal seemed to notice my presence. If they did, then they certainly weren't threatened. Why would they be? They had an abundance of food and water. Their homes were untouched, hidden in the valley between mountains, far away from my reach.

A set of cold hands touched my shoulders. My breath stopped midair. Anthony's voice sent a chill down my spine as he whispered in my ear, "I could push you right now and no one could do a thing."

I froze in terror, quickly assessing what I could grab.

He let go of my shoulders and sat next to me. I quickly tried to get up. "You leave and I'll shoot," he said nonchalantly.

I stayed seated and desired to be alone among the stars, "What do you want?"

"I'd like to talk."

Yeah right. What do you really want? I kept my face hidden from him, refusing to let him see my fear. "About what?"

"About you," he said as if I should have already known his intentions. "Where are you from?"

I huffed, "Why do you care?" God calls me to love as He loves but, right now, I don't know if I can. Anthony made my skin crawl from day one. Normally, I'd be willing to look for the good in a man. After what they did to Omar, the attack on the camp, and not knowing what has happened to Steven and Jeffrey my heart had hardened.

"It matters because I asked," Anthony said.

I sighed, "I grew up in a cabin in the Colorado Rockies."

"Really," he sounded shocked. "Were you homeschooled?"

It was dark, but I still rolled my eyes at his questions. We aren't friends. We aren't going to be friends. In fact, he'll probably be the one who kills me. For now, I would humor him, but I wouldn't drop my guard. Maybe I could learn more of what had started this whole mess. "I started public school when we moved to Nevada."

"How did you adjust to that?"

I sighed again, and continued to play along, "It was a small school, so I adjusted fine. They let me into their close knit family and a few of them went to our church, which helped us get along well."

"That's good," he was a little too enthusiastic with his response. "Were you involved in any sports?"

My fingers tapped my leg out of impatience, "Volleyball and basketball; coed. Our school was too small to compete with local teams."

"I played varsity football. I was MVP my junior and senior years," he said proudly.

With no other noise to compete with me, I'm sure he heard my mumbled, "Good for you."

He ignored me, "I had it all going for me. I was lined up to go pro and marry my high school sweetheart."

He paused, just waiting for me to ask, "What happened?"

"She was killed by a drunk driver," he said angrily. "I should have been in the car with her, but my father needed my help that day. I had no future without her, so I devoted myself to military life. She was a Christian, too," he said. "How could a God, who supposedly loves His people, be so willing to let them die horrible deaths? I can't and won't believe it. It's pointless. She spent her life trying to please Him and change me – and I *was* considering it. Now, I have no doubt in my mind that she was living for a lie."

"That's not true," I blurted. I couldn't look at him because I might stumble over myself. My tone softened, "She was right, and she will be where she always hoped to be for the rest of eternity; with God."

"I don't believe it," he said firmly.

Would Anthony kill me if I made him angry enough? "If only good things happened to Christians, and not bad things, then people would follow God for the wrong reasons. That's what my dad used to say."

"Then what other reason is there to be one?" He sarcastically remarked.

"It's about knowing who you are; your purpose. You get to know God, and His love, through the good and the bad. You also find a hope in a life after this one."

"Whatever," he begrudged, "that's such a copout answer." He blocked me out.

"Look, I get that it hurts; losing someone you're close to in such an awful way. God isn't to blame though; He's to thank." I didn't turn my face to Anthony, but I could feel his scowl. He wasn't ready for that explanation, but I couldn't take it back. "I'm thankful your girlfriend was a Christian, so she had a happy beginning at her end. I'm also thankful you weren't in the accident with her, and have been given more time to decide–"

Angrily, he interrupted me, "How am I supposed to trust the mouth of a liar? You talk about a god of love, and power, and mercy, and about his followers who have a security at the end of life. Then, you say you're thankful I lived?"

"What's that supposed to mean?"

"You're probably wishing that we would have switched places. Then, I'd be dead and she'd be here, talking with you."

"I've never, in my life, wished death on anyone," I defended, "and I'm not going to start now."

He pulled his feet in from the ledge. Before standing, he again leaned in close, "Then why don't you acknowledge my existence? It sure seems like you're always pretending I'm dead."

"No, I–"

Before I could counter he said, "Oh really? Then look at me. Haven't you been talking with me out of fear, and not out of the kindness of your heart?"

My shame left me unable to respond. As he walked away, I looked over him. He had no weapon on him as his arms rested freely at his side. There was some truth in what he said, but how could he make me out to be the bad guy? He's the one who threatened me before sitting next to me. He was the one who carried out half of the orders that lead to this war. He was the one who killed hundreds of Christians; whether by his own hands or just in association, it didn't matter… Then again, he didn't know God. He was a puppet of Satan without knowing it. I know to whom I belong. I know how God expects me to live. Yet, I treated Anthony with contempt. Jesus would have taken him in, fed him, learned his story, and looked him in the eyes the entire time. *Curse my judgmental attitude.* If Anthony's heart was hardened for good, I'd be to blame.

Ugh… he made me so angry. Anthony had no right to attack me. Why am I the one feeling as if I did something wrong? "*…do to others what you would have them do to you…*"[5] Jesus' sermon in Matthew condemned my own actions. I should have approached Anthony with my issues, rather than avoiding him this entire time, hoping he would leave.

I stayed where I was, apologizing to God. A few moments later, another figure sat beside me. I thought it might be Anthony again so I started to apologize, "Listen I'm sorry about–"

---

[5] Mathew 7:12 (NIV)

CHAPTER 22

Bear with each other and forgive whatever grievances you may have against one another. Forgive as the Lord forgave you.
—Colossians 3:13 (NIV)

"Why aren't you sleeping?" David asked, adjusting his body on the cliff edge more comfortably.

"Probably for the same reason you're not," I sighed.

He smiled, "You had a sixteen year old girl kick you too?"

"Oh, well no," I chuckled, "I just couldn't sleep." There was no point in telling him about Anthony, at least not now.

"I see," he said. "Look, I got to be honest with you." I couldn't help but cringe. I couldn't handle any more confessions. Anthony's had taken its toll on me. Not to mention that David said *got to* instead of *have to.* This was neither the time nor place for a grammar lesson, but my grandma had engrained that rule into me. Nevertheless, I ignored my need for grammatical excellence and listened to the rest of his confession. "I don't know how I offended you, but I'm sorry that I did."

I looked at him, confused, forgetting for a split second that I saw him murder a man. Then, my insecurities about him returned; he's fallen for the enemies' lies. Because of him, I was now constantly watching over my shoulder, even in a place where we were supposedly safe. Looking at the soldiers on the ground and then back at David, I whispered, "How can you trust them?"

David looked at me as if I was the one in the wrong, "You ask that question as if we're on different sides. They just risked everything in order to save us."

"How can you be so sure, especially after knowing that the two of them tied Omar and me to a tree for an entire day? You were even sitting in the front row when Justin held a gun to my head," I stopped talking; worried my raised voice would wake someone.

"Khristy," he tried to calm me down, "they did all of that to protect the two of you."

"They've brainwashed you with their lies," I accused. "I saw the bloodied blade they used to kill Omar. I saw Anthony go with murder on his mind, chasing after Steven. I sat, restrained, listening to them. How can you say they did that to protect me? How can you say that they ever once tried to protect Omar?"

"Your anger is clouding your judgment," David said, making me even angrier. "You've been through more this past week than most people could ever imagine. You've lost people close to you. I know what you're feeling inside, but the mind likes to play tricks on people. Though Anthony and Justin were in your vision this whole time, Erica was the one you needed to be watching. She gave them orders that they had to follow. She was the one calling all the shots. Justin and Anthony did everything they could to keep the two of you alive, but she had people watching them too. She didn't trust them. They also did as much as possible to keep the war at bay. They were finding the two of you a safe passage out when Omar escaped. Justin pulled his gun out on you on stage only because Erica would have pulled the trigger first. Anthony pretended to lose Steven so that he, too, could get away. This entire time, they've been on our side, hoping to take Erica down."

"You weren't even there. They killed Omar after he escaped. He never had a chance."

"Khristy, listen to yourself. You told me you saw Omar after the explosions. They couldn't have killed him. They showed you a knife, not a body." He was right and I knew it. They couldn't have killed Omar. The brothers and sisters we met in the forest said a man had warned them. When I found him on the ground, he didn't have any stab wounds either.

"I don't buy it," I said, ignoring the evidence in front of me, "their eyes were too full of evil."

"They had to be convincing," David tried so hard to defend them. "If Erica or her men would've seen through their lies, then they would've been killed instead of being able to help us escape. Then where would we be?"

I looked down at my hands. He was trying to make this all okay and maybe he was right. They had been helping us since we escaped the camp. I had no way to answer him. My ability to reason was tainted. Nothing made sense.

"You've been upset with me about something else, too, haven't you?" David changed the subject on me, but still managed to keep the focus on me. Oh, how I wished to remove myself from the spotlight. "There's something you're not saying. You haven't made much eye contact with me, and when you do you're afraid not angry."

I paused for a moment, baffled that he even noticed. Then I answered, "I've seen you live two lives and I can't figure out which one is the real you."

"What do you mean?" He inquired.

"I've seen your heart when you give it to God and I see your forgiving nature when you allow yourself to trust three men who…" I looked back and the soldiers and shrugged not needing to repeat their sins. "…Yet, you were so willing to kill a man who couldn't even raise an arm to fight back."

He looked at me as if to say I was wrong, *again*, but I know what I saw – his hand raised, ready to plunge it through the heart of an unconscious man. The blood splatter on his shirt didn't quite scream 'innocent' either…

David grabbed my face, "Khristy, look at me. I never murdered that man."

"I saw you."

"I know what you saw but when I saw your face… you turned away from me… I wondered how I was going to explain myself to God. How could I tell Him I loved my enemy, just as He commanded, while stabbing him to death?" He, too, looked back at everyone sleeping. "I witnessed God's love change a person first hand. When I dropped the knife I took that man's hand to help him up." David pointed to the back of the cave. "Lorenzo has been working to save us since then."

Sucker punched again, I had assumed the worst about David. Guilt weighted my measly apology down as I said, "I'm sorry." I needed desperately to change the subject again. I had too much to process. It was nearly indigestible. "How do you know Angelica?"

"You want the truth?"

Of course, I wanted the truth. Unless he was going to tell me that she is his girlfriend who he got pregnant by mistake because he loved her and her parents wouldn't let them get married because they were too young and didn't know what love was…

David leaned in close. I felt his warm breath in my ear. He whispered so quietly that, at first, I didn't realize what he said, "She's my sister." He chuckled, seeing the shock on my face. He must have guessed the thoughts going through my head. "That's what we tell everyone," he continued. "Her brother and I were best friends growing up...." He veered off into thought. "I can't believe he's gone. She watched it happen, right in front of her…"

"I'm sorry. What they've done isn't right. I've misjudged you these past couple of days. You've handled everything well despite losing those you love. I'm sorry," I repeated. "I'm just relieved to know you haven't turned away from God."

"I'm not the only one who has lost someone close to me," he replied. "Don't sell yourself short. You've proved you are strong in your faith as well. We all have," he slowly reached over and took my hand. I didn't pull back. His touch was more than comforting. It sent a surge of excitement through my veins. It allowed me to feel as if one day everything might actually be as it once was, before the attack. "Do you think your friends made it out?" He asked me.

"I continue to pray that they have, but I'm not sure. They were the first to disappear and no one found them so, possibly…" My mind drifted back to that day. Anthony came back claiming that he couldn't find Steven. Maybe he really did let them go. He wasn't far behind Steven when they left the tent. I only distracted him for a moment. It does seem odd that Steven, Jeffrey, and an entire nurses' cabin could disappear without someone seeing them. Surely, they had help. What a concept.

"Well," David rubbed his thumb across my hand and brought me back from my thoughts, "whatever the outcome, I guess it's better to just leave it in God's hands rather than worrying about it down here."

"Right," I gave a small smile, though not worrying about them at all stood as a challenging suggestion. We both know God's ways are better than our ways. In the Psalms, King David would cry out for God's help and complain about the evil around him, but at the end of his Psalms, he always reminded himself of God's goodness and holiness. He would continue to write about God's unfailing love and incredible mercy, even when he didn't feel it at the time. Perhaps that's what we needed to be doing.

We sat for a bit longer in silence, his hand still holding mine, and enjoyed the moment. I finally started to feel myself doze. My thoughts began to blur together and my eyes grew heavy. Instead of risking falling off the cliff, I looked at David. He smiled. "I'm going to try to get some rest," I said, but I hesitated to move away from him.

He gave my hand a squeeze before letting go, "I pray you find peace in your rest, Khristy."

"Thank you," I stood to leave. My heart fluttered while walking back to my place near Darius. I couldn't help but smile, but I was embarrassed to show it. David stayed on the ledge. I wondered what he was thinking.

CHAPTER 23

But each one is tempted when, by his own evil desire, he is dragged away and enticed. Then, after desire has conceived, it gives birth to sin; and sin, when it is full grown, gives birth to death.
—James 1:14–15 (NIV)

Again, I was jolted awake by stomping feet, and I could have sworn I heard talking. The early morning light took me by surprise. David still sat at the front of the cave with his legs drawn in underneath him. As my eyes came into focus, I saw he had his finger against his lips telling me to stay quiet. Dirt and rocks fell past the entrance of the cave and the voices grew louder. I tiptoed to David's side, slightly hoping he would take my hand again. It didn't happen. Soon, all four of the other men were next to us. They had their guns out as if waiting for an ambush. Angelica still slept; the poor girl.

"Over here," a voice called. "I've found something."

We all held our breath and pulled back into the cave a couple of inches. What did they see?

"She's long gone;" a man said, "definitely been this way for over a day."

"They have to be here somewhere," a woman said. Looking at Justin and Anthony, their expressions confirmed my suspicions. The voice belonged to Erica. "There are footprints all around and none of them leave."

"The only place anyone could have gone was down or around," a man said. "My bet is they were either suicidal or smart enough to cover their tracks."

"I don't believe either," Erica growled. "You three make camp here. The rest of us will split up and look for them. You four take the left bank. Keep sharp and remember; I want them alive."

I couldn't tell if she had a specific group of people in mind, and I didn't really care. The fire in her voice needed to be extinguished. We could hear some of them walking away, and those who stayed continued to talk. "I bet someone else already found them and threw them over the edge."

"Not me," another man said. "If I had to guess; they took their trackers and buried them deep."

"Trackers?" I whispered to Darius. He shook his head not knowing what they meant. We looked at the soldiers who all grew wide-eyed. They walked back to their pile of equipment. Before they could go through it, Darius was at their side holding his gun. "Reveal it but don't touch it," he commanded in a low and quiet tone. Justin gave Darius quite an impatient look for his lack of trust, but then he pointed to their water canteens.

Darius picked a canteen up and checked it. It was a normal canteen; except, not only did the top unscrew but the bottom did too. In the small compartment was a device with a flashing red light. Sadly, it was a brilliant hiding place. After all they had put us through it would make sense for any runaways to sneak off with a water canteen.

"You led them here," Darius accused, almost too loudly. Thankfully, the men above us were still talking. Darius had his gun pointed at Anthony's head.

I rushed in between them and faced Darius. I had looked down the barrel of a gun a few times in the past weeks, but this was the first one I voluntarily placed at my head. "Hold on just a moment," I tried to get him to lower his hand. Justin pulled his gun out and pointed it at Darius; I could see him through my peripherals, but he wasn't my focus. If I could get Darius to stand down, they would too, and no one would have to let those above us know where we are.

"What are you doing?" Darius motioned for me to move.

"They, too, have gone through a lot this week. I'm sure the trackers were the last thing on their minds," I said.

Darius grunted, "Doubtful."

"If they were out to kill us, they would make noise right now, shove us off the cliff, or shoot us. They would've acted ignorant about the trackers instead of finding them for you."

"What's your point?" Darius' hand slightly relaxed, but he still fought for his ground.

"My point is that they may not be with us in our faith, but as far as they've shown, they aren't against us."

"How do we know they didn't help kill all of our brothers and sisters? You said so yourself that these two were in cahoots long before the explosions."

"Maybe they did, but people can change. Don't tell me you haven't offended God before. I know I have. He hasn't struck us dead yet. If you're without sin, then by all means, cast the first stone and shoot." I hoped for his mind to flash back to Jesus, writing in the sand, saying the same thing to the Pharisees. I stepped out of the way and let his gun face Anthony again. Justin tensed, not trusting Darius at all. Darius lowered his hand and put the gun back in his waist. Justin did the same.

"Then, let's at least destroy these," Darius threw the tracker on the ground to stomp on it.

"Wait," Anthony said, scooping up the tracker. "You can't just crush them."

Darius reached and grabbed Anthony's wrist, "And why not?"

"Destroying them sends out a final alert burst signal. What we need to do is throw them over the edge."

We took the trackers out of all of the canteens and tossed them over the side of the cliff. Then, we sat around trying to listen to the conversations above, hoping to hear the men leave. Every now and then we could see a rock fly over the edge as the men above challenged each other to see who could throw the furthest. It was odd to hear them acting like children when the image of monsters came to my mind with each voice. It was a reminder that they, too, were people just like us.

When Angelica awoke, she stayed very quiet. I watched as life slowly return to her with each passing minute. The moment her eyes lit up the most, was when a beautiful red bird landed on the edge of our cave. A bright smile crept on her face as the bird jumped around and pecked at crumbs that David dropped earlier.

Two other birds soon joined the feast. Everyone in the cave watched as the birds fought over the same crumbs. They would constantly chase each other off into the air and return until they cleaned house. When our entertainment flew off, we found ourselves, once again, in waiting. We wouldn't be traveling today, not with the men above.

The soldiers with us gathered, segregating themselves from the rest of us as usual. Could we blame them? David and Angelica pulled out more food for everyone, while Darius approached me to talk.

"Here," he pulled the gun from his waist and handed it to me. "Why don't you hold this for a while?" It seemed as if he had been thinking about this for a long time.

I looked at him in question.

"You're right. God has forgiven me. He takes me in every time I fall, and He turns me around, reminding me to keep moving forward. When I have that," he pointed at the gun now in my hands, "my anger takes over because I have control. I don't want control. I need to let God control me."

"Sounds like you know what you're doing," I replied. I didn't like having the gun in my possession, but if it made him feel better, I would hang on to it for now. Later, when no one was looking, I would make sure to take out the clip as a precaution.

"Looked like you knew what you were doing too," he replied. "You were the last person I expected to jump in front of him."

"All I can say is that God is constantly at work on my heart. Had that scene happened a few hours beforehand, I would've stood behind you."

"What did God change?"

"My outlook," I glanced over at the three soldiers huddled. "We preach love our enemies, yet we secretly hate them," I paused to let it sink in. "I don't want to be a hypocrite who dishonors God's name."

"I feel ya," he chuckled. "The Lord knows I feel ya."

For supper, we each had half a can of cold green beans, a spoonful of peanut butter, and two granola bars. Darius said grace over the nourishment God provided, and the soldiers respectfully ceased their conversation while he did. The men above never seemed to notice our presence.

Angelica and I had a chance to talk for a few moments while she was awake. I steered clear of asking questions about her past, feeling it unnecessary to have her reflect on such things. She had suffered greatly. Now, all I wanted her to think about was God. Still, there was no way I could get the previous week off her mind, especially not with it still so fresh on mine.

"How did you survive?" Angelica asked me.

"I was on the mountain when it happened," I didn't bother to fill her in on the details. What's past was past. The soldiers with us were different people now.

"No, I mean, why didn't you just give up? I couldn't have survived without you."

I smiled, "Without God's strength I wouldn't have been able to survive. I thought about giving up, but He helped me shove those temptations from my mind. I don't know if I would have remained as strong had God not trusted you to my care."

"I wish I had your faith," she whimpered. "I almost denied Jesus, just so they'd kill me and get it over with. I feel so guilty."

"We are all tempted, but as James tells us, it doesn't become sin until we do it."

"I almost did," she argued.

"But, you didn't. That's what counts."

"But–" She tried to dispute again, so I interrupted.

"If a girl *almost* invites a boy into her bed with her, but then doesn't, does that mean she's no longer a virgin?"

"Well…no," I could practically see her wheels turning.

"You didn't deny God," I said firmly. "Because of that, you're faith is growing. It will continue to grow with every decision you make. Don't compare it to mine. Feed it and be conscious of the steps you're taking."

"I wasn't prepared for this when I was baptized."

"Neither was I; I don't think anyone ever is which is why it's important we hold to the Truth we know. Then, when our faith *is* tested, we are willing to let God walk us through to the other side."

"What if there's no way out?" She cried.

I pulled her in for a hug, muffling her sobs on my shoulder. "Listen," I said, "we can't worry about the '*what ifs*'. God holds the future. Let Him handle it. We can only control what we do in the present." I rubbed my fingers across her back and whispered, "Thanks to God, we don't have to worry about more than that." Angelica stayed in my arms a while longer and shielded her face from our onlookers.

David's curious eyes caught mine. I gave a reassuring nod, letting him know Angelica was okay. Darius smiled approval of how I tackled her question. Justin rolled his eyes and turned back to do whatever he was doing before, while Lorenzo and Anthony quickly looked away as if they were embarrassed for listening.

God holds the future in His hands. It sounds so good to say, but it takes a lot out of a person to believe it. I learned long ago, that being empty is the only way we can let God fill us. If I wanted to let Him hold my future, I had to empty myself of all selfishness. Right now, I selfishly held onto my anger, which stood in the way of letting God have full control. The vile things I saw done to God's people left me torn. Even if the soldiers with us were gaining my forgiveness, the ones above me weren't. I couldn't forget the cruel, hateful acts done to us.

I felt this anger once before in Africa. We were building a playground for a new elementary school. Some tribal men, who found out about our work, set the playground on fire. We sent Amina, a little girl caught in the fire, to the hospital with third-degree burns. I despised those men.

When the teacher gathered us all together, we prayed. She prayed to God, thanking Him that the fire didn't kill anyone and, for the week of labor that brought us all closer together. Then, she let each of the kids pray. They repeated thanks to God for different things without a single complaint. One young girl even prayed forgiveness for the men who destroyed their playground. That petition blew me away even more when I learned that she was Amina's sister.

With the leftover supplies and some salvageable items from the fire, we still managed to build a few fun things for the kids to do before we left. Our creations were by no means impressive, but it gave the kids joy all the same. That experience changed all of us who worked that week. I left with tears of joy, not hate, and memories to last a lifetime.

It comforted me that God brought such a memory to my mind. The events of then and now were quite different, but it did remind me that good can come from anything if we will only see it. To let the good spring up in our current situation, I could start by completely forgiving those with whom I would be spending the next few days. What they've done is wrong, but they had no one to guide them in what was right. Maybe God would use our current situation to save these three souls. If that were the case, then it was all worth it; right? I didn't bother letting any more bad alternatives run through my head again. They would do no good.

CHAPTER 24

There is deceit in the hearts of those who plot evil, but joy for those who promote peace.
—Proverbs 12:20 (NIV)

The atmosphere from being stuck in a cave made us more restless. We had no idea how much longer we would be here. The soldiers above gave no indication of leaving any time soon. We had thrown the trackers over the side, so they should have been chasing the signal. If they waited for Erica's return, we may run out of resources first.

David sat with Justin and Anthony. I could only hear bits and pieces of their conversation. I still struggled to trust these guys. I said I would give them a clean slate, but my gut said that I must convince David to leave them. I keep telling myself, *you're being irrational, God is in control,* and that, *I should let go of my distrust.* Still, I can't seem to let go of those hours I was in their custody. I glanced their way and noticed the men drawing in the sand and placing twigs in various places. I didn't know what they were up to, but I doubt they were playing tic-tac-toe. I looked back over at Angelica. She often sleeps and tonight was no different. I'm sure it was her way of coping with the stress of everything that had happened. My worries keep me awake and hers drives her to exhaustion. For now, my body lived in survival mode but eventually it would crash. I was weary to the core and on constant alert. I'm sure I heard every noise right down the flap of bats wings. I definitely heard the men on the cliff above, the whispers of the men inside the cave, and the whimpers of the child in my lap just as clear as the ants marching in search of crumbs.

Lorenzo and Darius talked into the evening. I didn't mean to eavesdrop on their conversation, but it was hard not to hear their discussion in such close confines. As they came to know one another, Lorenzo asked Darius, "How do you subject yourself to Christianity?"

"'Subject' is the wrong term to use, and it's not to Christianity," Darius responded calmly. "I willingly submit to Christ. I'm not a forced slave."

"The whole idea of it is rather feminine isn't it?"

Darius cocked his head, "What do you mean?"

"Well, the constant crying and talking of peace; not war, and love; not hate. Where is the place for a man to be a man in it all?"

Darius' eyes grew wide as he let out a big sigh, "I see... Yes, knowing Christ can stir up emotions, but it doesn't diminish your manhood. It's one thing for a man to be a brute champion, taking as he pleases; it's a completely different thing, for him to "man up" and do what needs to be done. No matter the cost. Any boy can break stuff in anger, but only a man can fix it through love..."

"This is it," David loudly whispered, interrupting everyone. The moonlight shining into the cave was so bright that it made his face glow. He had a victorious smile as he called us to join them. I woke Angelica and we moved next to him. Darius and Lorenzo did the same.

"Leave room for the light," Anthony kept us spread apart so as not to block the moonlight. Revealed, on the ground, was a game plan; one like a football coach would draw out for his team.

"We can't stay here forever," David said. "We know how we're going to get above ground without getting killed."

"I still think we should just wait a day and see if they leave," Justin said a little too loud. We shushed him and then listened above for any movement.

"The longer we stay here, the less chances of survival we have. All we're doing is eating and resting. We'll need this food and water for the rest of our escape," David said.

"Until we get to your house," Justin corrected.

"As far as I'm concerned, we can only depend on what little we have for supplies."

That shut Justin up.

"We have all the equipment needed to get two men topside together. Two sets of hooks are already set from my previous climbs. If we wait until sunrise, that will be our best advantage to climb without being noticed."

"What happens if they hear you, or come to the edge?" I asked. The three looked at each other as Anthony put his hand over the gun at his side. No one said anything. They didn't need to. There was no way their plan would work. The men above may end up leaving as soon as they hear that the trackers had moved. David didn't seem to consider that as an option. He was a man of action. There would be no talking him out of this one, especially with everyone's support. He looked at me apologetically, but I wouldn't accept it. This was murder, again. My hands went up, as I imagined Pilot's did when he washed his hands clean of any wrong done to Jesus. "I'm not a part of this if that's how it's going to end." Angelica followed me.

Darius reached up and touched my arm as I walked away, but he didn't ask me to stay. He knew of my inward battle. He seemed to have made up his mind. Angelica and I sat back, near the edge of the cave with our backs against the wall. She leaned her head on my shoulder and pulled her legs into her chest. I pulled a blanket over us as I listened to the rest of their plan and prayed for God to grant us another way.

"Lorenzo and I will go up first," Anthony said, "one on the left and, the other on the right. David already has hooks set. All we have to do is make sure they're stable. Lorenzo and I will detain soldiers above by any means necessary. We'll send the gear down to the rest of you, the first chance we get. The girls will stay here until we can be sure it's safe, then they will send the food up, and we'll hoist them up last."

For a moment, my heart dropped. They could easily leave us after we send up the food. I doubt I could scale the walls without any gear. Darius wouldn't let it come to that. He'd make sure they helped us to the top. Everyone's heads turned our way. I nodded, letting them know that we'd be willing to comply with that part of the plan.

Once they felt they had worked out the kinks, they began collecting the gear and putting things in place. They condensed all of the food into a few piles, ready for us to sack them into blankets. Looking at the supplies, I found a second option. "How about we give it a day, like Justin suggested?" I said. The men turned and gawked at me as if I had three heads and then, just as quickly, brushed my comment aside and went back to what they were doing. "I'm serious," I said louder. They all tried to shush me, but I continued, "We have a lot of supplies still. It's not going to hurt if we wait a day, eat what we need to sustain us, and then, if they haven't left, we can go with your plan."

It was obvious that David, Anthony, Lorenzo, and Darius were not paying me any attention so I was surprised when Justin spoke up, "I think she's on to something." The room grew awkwardly quiet and he continued, "There are risks in going above ground with the other soldiers waiting. They have the high ground. All it takes is one mistake and we're all dead. If we can manage to stay here one more day, then it's well worth avoiding the dangers."

Begrudgingly, they agreed to put their plot on hold for one day. The tension in the cave tasted sour and somewhat bitter. Justin was now at the bottom of his comrades' list of favorite people and if looks could kill, he and I would be sharing a casket. It was no surprise he came and sat by me after that. God had shown me twice now– once with Anthony, and then again with David – not to jump to conclusions this time. I stayed cautious, unsure of his intentions, and prayed for God to give me the peace within to be amiable.

"I'm glad someone brought them to their senses," I said to break the ice.

He smiled weakly, "We just need time for the situation work itself out." Then he rubbed the back of his neck, hiding his face from the others as he whispered. "You can't trust Tereski."

I scanned the room, "Do you mean Anthony?"

Justin nodded. Anthony had his back towards us, speaking to David and Darius who were both looking in our direction, as if he was telling them the same thing about Justin.

Taken aback by Justin's comment, and distracted by my own thoughts, I found myself completely confused.

"I thought you knew," Justin replied, "and that's why you were always fighting him. He seems to have gotten in your head, but for the sake of this team, you can't trust him."

I listened and compared his warnings to his body language. I couldn't tell what he hoped to accomplish by telling me this. I hadn't noticed his hostility towards Anthony before, but it wasn't a battle I wished to join, "Whatever war you have between each other is your business. Don't involve the others and me. If he's willing to fight with this team, then we're willing to keep him around." I didn't know what else to say.

"That's what I'm trying to tell you. He's not on this team," Justin said, and I looked at him cautiously. "He has a different plan for us all."

"What are you talking about?" I asked. Truthfully, my relationship with them was frail enough that I'd probably believe anything about Justin or Anthony. Yet, I saw a change in Anthony the other night. Justin's warning against Anthony could very well mean that he and Lorenzo weren't to be trusted either. For now, I would listen and keep a closer eye on things.

"I've seen him give out the signals; flashing lights, making bird sounds, and then, of course, with how much of a rush he's in to get out of here. I can almost bet that he's planning to turn us all in for the bounty."

"What bounty?" I sat, lost.

"You, David, and Me," he said. "David's family has secrets that Tereski's team needs, I'm a traitor to my country, and you'll be needed to make David cooperate."

"What about Lorenzo, Darius, and…?" I looked at Angelica, sliding my fingers down her tangled black hair. I'm not sure if I believed him, but I had to ask.

"Everyone else is considered extra baggage. I don't know much about Martinez," he motioned to Lorenzo, "but they probably scratched him off as a dead man long ago. When they see Darius and Angelica and realize how little a purpose they serve, they will kill them."

"Why are you telling me this?" I asked. Anthony seemed to be ignoring us, but I thought he glanced slightly at us.

"I didn't think you trusted me; especially after I put a gun to your face."

"Believe me," I said, making sure he knew where he stood with me, "I don't."

"You don't have to, just be cautious. He can be very convincing. He had two older women in your group fooled by telling them he lost his high school sweetheart in a car wreck."

Geneva and Agnes; I prayed for God to reveal Justin as a liar. If Anthony had tricked them, then that means he willingly led an attack that he knew would kill those sweet ladies.

Justin read my expression. He sighed, "Don't tell me you fell for that story too."

My silence was my answer.

"Did he tell you how he butchered hundreds of your people? Men, women, and children stared down the barrel of his gun if they were incapable of work." I wanted to plug my ears and not hear any more about how my brothers and sisters, children of God, had died. "He's a cold blooded killer, trained to be a killer ever since he was very young. Don't turn your back on him, ever."

My heart pained over the remembrance of the suffering we endured. I wanted the war to end. I needed more proof from Justin, other than him knowing Anthony's *sob story.* He could have heard Anthony talking to me the first night in the cave. Anthony had proven through his recent actions that he was on our side. Justin had done nothing to win my favor. I couldn't fathom Anthony, or anyone, rescuing us from the vileness and devastation at the camp only to lead us towards more destruction. I had an obligation to warn the others...but...something wasn't right. "Why did you stand up for him if you knew all of this?"

"I never..."

"You had your gun to Darius' head," I accused.

He defended himself, "Because Darius could have shot you."

"Since when did my wellbeing become your concern?" I said. Scenes from my time in captivity ran through my head. He showed not even an ounce of pity or help there, so why now?

"What do you mean?" He asked.

"Are you kidding me?" I became frustrated. He acted so ignorant. "You kept me prisoner for an entire day. You had your chance to free me, but instead you forced me to stay put."

His eyes dropped and his shoulders slouched. I took that as signs of a guilty conscience. "Look, you don't understand my situation, and I'm not about to explain it. On the mountain, at first, I failed to protect you or anyone else. My orders were to stand watch, and so, when I saw you I saw my mission. I gave you water though. Shouldn't that count for something?" He paused, as if waiting for me to respond. I refused. "After realizing what torture you and your people would be put through, I tried to protect you."

"Protect me?" I whispered. I was barely able to keep my tongue in check. Fury pulsed through my veins. No one else noticed our argument. It seemed as if they were embroiled in their own heated discussion.

"They would've killed you. I saved your life," he smiled as if he expected a thank you.

My temper blared. "What about Omar? I suppose you're going to tell me you protected him as well?"

"I'm the one who helped to free him," a vein bulged on Justin's forehead. "I killed the other soldier chasing him so he could warn the camp. How else do you think I got the blood on my knife?"

I remembered the events, but saw no reason to believe him. Then, I remembered my escape. I fled down the mountain until hiding inside the log.

His voice interrupted my thoughts. "I even saw you in hiding. I left you there."

I pictured the moment. I was in the log and he stood above

me. I thought my mind was playing tricks on me when I saw him look in my direction, but perhaps he really did see me.

My head spun again. Either Justin told the truth, or he was the one I had to fear instead of Anthony. It didn't matter. At this moment, I wouldn't trust any of them. Anthony was too cocky, Justin was too suspicious, and Lorenzo was too quiet. None of them seemed real.

"Why are you so willing to throw him under the proverbial bus?" I needed more information. I needed to understand. "How do I know you're not with him in all of this?"

"I guess, you really don't," he looked at the ground. "I just hoped you would see me being honest. I've tried to keep you safe this far. It's necessary, now, to reveal everything so that we can stop the real enemy. Major Simmons is the deadliest woman I've ever known. I had to follow orders and play nice. The more I heard Tereski and her talk about the 'filthy cockroach Christians,' the more I looked for a way out. Your group is my way out."

We sat in silence. I stroked Angelica's hair. David told me Erica was the one to be worried about, and now Justin is telling me Anthony and Erica are both the enemies. If he is honest, then going above ground was like signing our death warrant. If he's trying to trick me, then he's possibly instigating trouble for his own good. Either way, warning signs were flashing.

The discussion across the room threatened to become loud and out of hand very quickly. Darius' face flushed red as he spat in Anthony's direction. Anthony lunged at Darius. David stepped in between. Fear for David's safety stole my breath. Anthony continued to push on David. Darius stood his ground, but the situation could turn volatile in the blink of an eye. Anthony took a swing at Darius around David's head clipping him in the ear. David never let go. Anthony was throwing another punch in David's direction. David ducked. When he did, he stumbled into Darius. Darius stepped back and lost his balance. One foot slipped at the edge of the cliff. Pebbles and sand scattered off the edge. Justin intervened by grabbing and driving Anthony against the cave wall, pinning him there. Darius regained his balance. I was terrified that the men above would hear the pebbles falling because of the scuffle on our little ledge.

"Take a breath, Tereski," Justin ordered as quietly as possible. "Let it go."

Anthony's face was red hot. His eyes shifted from Darius, to David, to Justin, and then back at Darius again. "That's enough," Justin repeated.

Anthony glared at Justin even more. Again, if looks could kill, Justin would wither up and die. Finally, he began to calm down. Justin slowly released his grip until Anthony sunk to the ground. When seeing he wasn't going anywhere, Justin moved to check on David and Darius. If Anthony was playing double agent, he did it very well. Throughout this entire display, quiet Lorenzo stayed seated up against the wall, three feet from the fight. He seemed to care less about the situation.

Eventually, Anthony's glare turned to me. He shook his head and rolled his eyes, as if I had some part in their mess. Then, he walked over to the cliff side and stared over the edge. Was he thinking about jumping, or just trying to get someone's attention? He started scuffing his feet on the ground and kicking dirt and rocks over the edge.

"Anthony," I whispered.

He ignored me and continued.

"Tereski quit it," I threw a pebble at him.

He turned to look at me, "What's your problem?"

"You're going to give us away," I said.

He didn't take kindly to my command, but he did stop.

I glanced in Justin's direction. He raised his right eyebrow as if to say, *I told you so.*

Angelica awoke, unaware of all that had happened, and sat up with a gentle smile. I had never seen her full smile, only tears and fear, and every now and then a faint grin. Her lips were dry and cracked, just like the rest of us, but I could see the peace within her for a split second; the peace that I used to feel when waking up from a midday nap in my car – the sun would shine perfect through my window to keep me warm. It was uplifting to see Angelica grasp that sort of respite in the middle of all of this turmoil. As soon as she noticed the reality around her, her smile faded away.

Moving my arm away from her, I leaned in close and whispered, "I need to go talk to Darius and David for a moment. Will you be okay?"

The closer I came to David and Darius, the more unwanted I felt. They sat quietly looking at me, waiting for me to speak, but my lips wouldn't move. I wanted to ask what had happened with Anthony. I wanted to see if Justin was right. Things became uncomfortable as the two looked at each other.

"What do you want Khris?" David's voice was harsh. That was the first time he had called me Khris. Since I met him on the bus, he always called me Khristy. Again, I was speechless. The awkwardness of the moment was unbearable.

"Never mind," I finally blurted and turned to leave.

"You're already here," David sighed. I turned back to face him. "So speak."

"Easy," Darius put a hand against David's shoulder. David's mood instantly changed. Then, Darius gestured to the ground in front of them saying, "Have a seat."

I sat closer to Darius than David, unsure of what else to do, "Sorry to be a bother."

Darius shook his head, "You aren't a bother. We're just all a li'l uptight, aren't we?" He nudged David who nodded his head. "Now what can we do for you?"

I could finally speak after snubbing David's stare, "What were you and Anthony fighting over?"

"Ah," Darius had the tone of a wise old man, "it was nothing.

Quarrels are bound to come when men find themselves trapped together for too long."

"It looked like more than a manly quarrel," I prodded.

Darius paused as David tensed, ready to say something. Finally, Darius said as gently as possible, "It makes sense to wait, as you suggested, but we were all ready to leave tonight. Therefore, in our eagerness to leave the smallest of things are lighting fuses. I said a few things that I shouldn't have all the while knowing they would upset Anthony." He brushed it off as if it was nothing, "I went too far, and I'm not proud of it. Anthony knows this. He'll forgive me, but right now we need our space."

Darius obviously didn't plan to go into further detail, but he gave me the information I needed. Anthony didn't instigate the fight. This gave me less reason to trust Justin's stories.

David stood. Before he left he leaned down in my direction. His face wasn't friendly, nor was his manner, "We could've been out of here by now."

"David," Darius calmly reprimanded.

David walked away and went to sit by Anthony at the entrance of the cave.

Shocked, I swallowed the lump in my throat. The gentleness I saw in David the night before had left him.

"This makes for a long day," Darius sighed. "Don't worry, he won't be upset forever." He then patted my knee and stood to leave. I watched as he sat with Anthony and David. I know Darius meant well, but inside it felt as if he, too, was mad at me. Perhaps the conversation he and David were having, before I interrupted them, was more important than my hurt feelings.

I did my best to sleep for a couple of hours. Everything was peaceful at first. My fatigued body melted into the cave floor. Nature's melody gave a blissful song to fall asleep to, in spite of the worries running through my head. Then, Omar's face appeared. He called my name, but something trapped me, holding me against my will. I watched as Justin stabbed him to death. When

I got free, I ran to Omar's aid. His body looked as it did when I found him among all the other dead bodies. He had only one arm. Looking up, Anthony stood in Justin's place with his gun, smiling. When looking back down, Jeffrey lay in my arms with a bullet wound in the chest. A cold hand touched my shoulder…

I needed to wake up from this nightmare. Suddenly, my body jerked and brought me back to reality in the back of the cave. The sunrise loomed. I dreaded what was going to happen next. When my eyes focused, I saw that Anthony stood at the ledge. He turned and signaled for us to stay quiet. He stepped closer to the edge. I held my breath yet again. I wondered what he was hearing. Throwing my head to the ground, I jammed my fingers in my ears as two gunshots went off.

CHAPTER 25

They come to you in sheep's clothing, but inwardly they are ferocious wolves.
—Matthew 7:15 (NIV)

"Who's there?" A voice called above us.

We had no intention of responding.

"Shut up idiot," a man with a very deep voice bickered.

"It's just us, calm down, Clover," another voice above replied. I let out a sigh of relief.

"State your identity," Clover said sternly.

"P-forty-eight, unit two. Object S-F-A-C."

"You may approach." Clover sounded more relaxed.

"Thought you were going shoot me, Clover," the man approaching said. "We may have found the group you were looking for." I heard the sounds of a struggle as the new arrivals brought their prisoners closer to the ones who had been squatting for the past couple of days. "One girl and two guys, right?"

"Owens, you twit. They aren't the right ones. Get rid of them," Clover ordered.

"No," a new deep voiced man interjected. "We can't be sure. Tie them up over there. I'd hate to see the General's daughter mad at us for killing her prize."

"When is she getting back?" A raspy voiced man asked.

"Let's give her until noon before we help them off the cliff. This is stupid, just sitting out here. I want to kill someone."

"How about this sickly looking one? We could kill him now and roll him off the cliff. She'd never know," Owens said.

"Don't you dare touch him!" A female's angry voice yelled.

"Sticking up for your boyfriend are you?" Clover spoke with a menacing tone. It reminded me of Erica's voice when they first captured Omar and me, *"Got a soft spot for the Muslim?"* My anger flared. All of those hours and days spent in captivity flooded back to my mind. I looked towards both Anthony and Justin. Neither one was innocent, nor did either one really appear to be on our side. I wanted to know whom I could trust.

"Now is our chance," Anthony grabbed the climbing gear. "They're distracted. They won't hear us coming." He tossed one set to Lorenzo and kept the other for himself. I quickly reached out and grabbed Anthony's arm. I wasn't going to stop them, but it didn't make sense to let both of them go up together. I insisted he let David go. Anthony argued it would be better for him and Lorenzo to go first since they had combat training, but I stayed persistent. He hesitantly stepped away from his harness. David questioned me with looks, but never rebutted. When both he and Lorenzo suited up, they began their ascent like professional climbers.

The men above us never missed a beat. The deep voiced man ordered the others to leave the prisoners alone and became their personal guardian. They begrudgingly tied up the prisoners all the while cursing at them and God.

I could hear a female praying to God with all her might. *Good woman*, I smiled. The men that detained them kept telling her to shut up, but she defied them. Her prayers became louder. She prayed for God to open their hearts. Whether she knew it or not, she was helping us. Their distraction became our advantage since everyone topside wouldn't hear our climbers.

"Keep her safe, Father," I prayed.

I watched as long as I could while David and Lorenzo scaled the mountainside. Lorenzo was a lot faster at climbing than David. At the top, Lorenzo raised his head above the ground to see where all the men above us were located. At that same moment, David slipped from his rope. My gasp echoed. He didn't fall far, only a few feet, but my gasp and the rocks falling below him made too much noise. He struggled to reposition himself. His feet kicked at the wall to find placement. He held on for dear life. I looked at Lorenzo, who did nothing to help him. Instead, he pulled himself up over the cliff and never once looked back.

Two faces peered over the edge and pointed towards David. We all ducked back into the cave out of sight. I prayed they didn't see the rest of us. Suddenly a shot rang in my ears. I watched and listened for a sound from David. It was silent. I stifled a sob. If Justin was right, then David was important and they needed him alive. Still, there was no sound. More gunshots accompanied loud shouts. I dared to step forward for a peek. Just as I took my second step, Anthony grabbed my arm. I gave it a violent jerk and moved to the edge. I expected to see David hanging, bleeding in his harness. I choked back my fear and looked up the cliff. I shrieked. A body flew past me. We had a moment of eye contact. He was petrified. I wasn't much better. His eyes pleaded for help. *Lord, forgive him.* I shifted my focus down the cliff but he was gone, lost in the trees and bushes below. A rock nearly took my head from my shoulders and I looked up. David clung to the edge. His feet desperately sought purchase. Gunshots continued above. Lorenzo was alone fighting against those camped on the cliff overhead.

The shots ceased. David froze with half his body lifted up onto ground level. One leg planted firm on a crevice, ready to boost him up. "Drop your weapon," Lorenzo's voice sounded. David's muscles began to shake the longer he held himself still, his gaze fixed on something in front of him. Someone must have had him at gunpoint. A gun flung over the edge. A rugged, unshaven man came into sight as he reached to help David onto solid ground.

After saving David, the man poked back over the ledge with a giant smile, and he then cupped his hand to his mouth and teasingly yelled, "I knew you always looked up to me." Steven was alive. In his best flight attendant voice he added, "We're having some technical difficulties, but we'll be with you shortly." My heart soared with excitement as tears dared to escape my eyes. My friend was alive.

Behind me, Justin paced back and forth as if he was worried about something. The plan was for Angelica and Darius to climb up next, even though Anthony offered to go instead to help the others. I had to make sure Angelica was with someone I could trust and insisted she go first. David would also take care of her. She took a blanket full of supplies with her. Above us, everything seemed to calm down quickly. While Darius scaled the mountain, the others hoisted up Angelica.

I now found myself alone in the cave with Anthony and Justin. *You know what you have to do,* I told myself as I backed up into the cave. I couldn't turn around, not yet. Feeling sick to my stomach, I took in a deep breath. *It's now or never.* I pulled Darius' gun from my waist and let my breath out calmly. I ordered the two men, "Put your backs on the wall." Anthony did. A look of shock crept to his face. Justin acted as if he half expected it.

"I want to know exactly which side you're on, right now," my voice was firm, but my whole body quivered. I prayed they couldn't see my tremor that felt like a 7.0 on the Richter scale. I never thought I would be the one calling the shots. My entire life, my faith taught me to step back and turn the other cheek. At this moment, the thought of putting my friends into any further danger overrode anything I had ever learned in Bible class. I didn't plan to shoot either of the men. I only wanted to know the truth. Someone was playing us for fools. I was ready to leave one, if not both, of them here with the rest of the supplies while I escaped with the others. Knowing that God was with me gave me the strength to run my bluff.

"Khris, what are you doing?" Anthony said as he tried to take a step towards me.

I pointed the gun at him, "Don't come any closer."

Anthony backed up with his hands in the air. Justin, on the other hand, gave a small laugh.

"Is this funny to you?" I asked Justin, motioning the gun back to him.

He burst out into laughter even more, "You've brought doom to us all, you stupid little girl. Do you even have the guts to pull the trigger?" He didn't make a move; he just stood there mocking me. He may have called my bluff, but there was no chance I'd be dropping my guard.

"What's this about?" Anthony questioned. I couldn't tell if he acted dumb, or was truly ignorant of the situation.

"Your time is up, Tereski," Justin now mocked Anthony. "She

wants you to tell her the truth," though he was talking to Anthony, he looked at me. "She wants to hear how you've been playing her the whole time. How all of this is just a ruse to find out where the other Christians are hiding. She wants to hear how you led your team right to this spot, and how there are others coming to take them out any minute now. She wants to hear it from your own mouth, so your death will be justified."

Anthony pleaded to me, "I don't know what he's talking about."

I shifted the gun towards Anthony, and then back at Justin who came closer to me. I took a step back.

"Don't lie Tereski," Justin insisted on being right.

"Khris listen to me," Anthony said with his hands now in front of him. He, too, began to walk towards me.

Again, I took another step back. Sweat dripped down my brow. I backed up too close to the ledge. I needed to do something, and soon.

"He's lying," Anthony continued. "He's the murderer, not me. You saw what he did to your friend."

"Do you really want to point fingers?" Justin's face was flushed with anger. "Tell her what you've done to her. See if she trusts you then."

"Stop trying to manipulate her," Anthony pounced on Justin, pinning him to the floor. They threw punches at each other until Anthony's arm pressed firmly against Justin's throat. Then, Anthony bent down and spoke something into Justin's ear. Whatever he said was enough to cause Justin to pull out of Anthony's grip.

"Quit it!" I still pointed the gun at them. Neither of them paid me any attention as they rolled around fighting, each seeking to gain the upper hand. This was not how I planned this *talk* to go. I stepped away from the ledge and towards them as Justin got on top of Anthony. "Stop it," I tried again. In a panic, I attempted to shoot the ground. Nothing happened. Why did I have to take the clip out? Anthony's fist planted into Justin's face and knocked him away. As Justin struggled to get up off the ground, I had the gun pointed at Anthony. "That's enough," I shouted. "Sit against the wall." The moment was spinning out of control. I just needed to escape. "You too, Justin." He was trying to regain his balance, but before I could say anything else he rushed at me, pulled the gun from my hands and then held it at Anthony.

I froze in place.

"I thought you'd be different," Justin said to me as he spit and wiped the blood from his mouth. Like a mad man, he began to beat his fist against his own skull. "No!" Breathing heavily through his teeth, spit flew everywhere. Again, he beat his head screaming, "No." He took in a breath and then pointed the gun at me. In one swift movement, he lunged at me, pulling me in close, with his arm around my neck. He held the gun right against my temple. The cold steel sent an eerie feeling down my spine.

"Whoa, wait a minute," Anthony approached Justin slowly, but Justin's grip tightened. I pushed away from him, but it was no use. He pointed it back at Anthony, "Come any closer and you both die."

I could have easily ended the situation by telling them the gun was empty, but the longer I stayed in his grip, the harder it became to speak. When Anthony stood still, Justin pulled his lips close to my ear. "Do you want to know the real truth?" He asked.

I didn't have to answer.

"Tereski, here, is too weak to carry out orders. He's a wanted man just like the rest of you. I'd have gladly slit all of your throats. My orders were to follow and track down where the rest of the Christians are hiding. You should have taken me out when you had the chance, because now the two of you are going to die, and then all of your little friends will be next."

"Why?" Anthony desperately asked, inching his way closer. "After all they've done for you, for us?"

"The only thing they've done is infested the earth with lies of a hope that's not there. The only reason they've done anything for you and me is because, they think they're going to turn us into one of them. I'm not falling for their tricks."

I tried to offer a defense, but he only tightened his grip on my throat.

"Ferrell," Anthony took a step forward.

"Don't do it," Justin hesitated to pull the trigger.

The lack of oxygen was slowly weakening my body. I didn't want to lose consciousness, again, and forced every part of me to stay awake.

"Look at her," Anthony said. "Imagine what she's been through. If you must kill someone, by all means, shoot me. The only hate you have against her is the hate drilled into you. I've seen past that, and so can you." Black dots began to spot my vision. I could see Anthony inching closer. "I mean, come on man; look at her. She's no older than your sister."

"Don't!" Justin shouted.

Like an old time film, flashing from picture to picture, I saw Anthony take the gun from Justin's hand, just as Justin had done to me. I dropped to the ground, only I never landed. Unexpected arms caught me. I looked up and saw Steven. He pulled some of the rope from around him and secured me to his side. I tried to help as everyone above us pulled us up, but I had no strength. I watched uncomprehendingly as Anthony flattened Justin in the ground. He now had the gun pointed at Justin, who was begging for his life. Anthony's posture was full of strength and full of hate. The cliff side distorted my line of sight, but the sound of a gunshot rattled my bones. I had taken the clip out of the gun. It was in my pocket… My hands searched but there was no clip. It must have fallen out during my struggle with Justin.

At the top, Jeffrey helped Steven unhook me and I immediately jumped into Jeffrey's arms. My strength was coming back, so much so that I tumbled him to the ground. I couldn't contain my joy. My brother lived, though he still looked weak. Sitting up, I looked around at everyone as Steven and Jasmine crowded me on the ground with a hug. Steven helped me up from the ground and our eyes met. He looked at me as if to say everything was going to be all right now.

Darius stood a distance away, scouting the land. No doubt, he wanted to spot any unexpected company before they snuck up on us. Lorenzo, oddly enough, still stood by the edge of the cliff. He bent over, looking as if he was pulling something up, or rather, someone. Anthony's head appeared at the edge. He must have scaled the wall without any equipment; a trait he had not previously revealed to us that he had.

The moment Lorenzo pulled Anthony to the top; Steven rushed over and grabbed the back of Anthony's shirt to help him to his feet.

"Thank you," Anthony said turning around. "I…"

Steven caught Anthony off guard with a right hook and planted him back onto the ground. David rushed over and grabbed Anthony's arms, holding him as he tried to get back up and fight back. Lorenzo advanced towards David. Darius, who must have seen the fight coming, held him back.

"Stop it!" I yelled. Jeffrey grabbed my hand. He may have been weak, but he held firm.

Steven took another swing and landed it into Anthony's gut while Anthony yelled obscenities at them all, spitting blood on the ground. David struggled to hold Anthony's arms back. I knew, the moment he got loose, Anthony would heave Steven over the cliff.

"It's okay," Jeffrey said to me. "Angelica told us everything." My heart sank. The things she told them were probably what she heard come out of Justin's mouth. I thought she was asleep, but apparently not. I had to stop this. I pulled from Jeffrey's grip and stumbled over to stand in between Steven and Anthony. Steven was just about to throw another punch.

"That's enough," I yelled again.

"What are you doing?" Steven asked.

"It wasn't him. He didn't do it," I said, trying to force David to let him go. Darius loosed his grip on Lorenzo, but kept up his guard. "Justin was feeding me lies to try to get me to leave Anthony for dead. He planned to kill us all off himself. Had I known Angelica heard the conversation I had with Justin, I would have advised her not to believe him."

Angelica's eyes went wide as she realized that Justin had fooled her. She lowered her head feeling guilty. I knew that she felt this fight was her fault.

"You did what you thought was best," I reassured her, "but we've all been manipulated." I turned back to Steven. After a moment of staring him in the eyes, showing him my sincerity, I could see Steven's breath leave his chest and his arms relaxed. He gave David a nod and David let go of Anthony. I expected Anthony to fall to the ground, but he forced himself to stand and ignored his pain. It was obvious he didn't trust that the battle had ended.

"Please forgive me," I said to Anthony, looking him in the eyes for the first time without judgment. He had saved my life in the cave. He had my trust.

He didn't hesitate with his response, "Don't ever take your friends for granted. I have a feeling they'd fight off the Roman Empire just to keep you safe." He gave a slight grin. Without a doubt, I knew they would. They'd do the same for anyone in this group, or so I assumed. One by one, everyone added their apologies, though I could tell they were still a little confused and unsure of what to believe. "I'm glad it's all out in the open and we can be a team now," Anthony replied, "but we can't stay here. Major Simmons will be bringing the rest of her team back. We aren't prepared to deal with the men she has with her."

"I agree," Steven said. "Let's get this gear and get out of here."

I looked around to see what he meant about the gear. Around us were five men in their undergarments zip tied together around a couple of trees. A pile of loose laid dirt made me wonder if the men had taken the time to bury Phoebe since her body was missing. I couldn't tell what state the soldiers were in, whether lifeless or just unconscious. Surely, they were alive or there would be no reason to tie them up.

"It's okay. They're just resting," Jeffrey saw my concern, "It didn't feel right to kill them after Lorenzo knocked them unconscious."

All of the soldiers' armor and weapons sat in a pile, ready for us to wear. We picked up the jackets, bulletproof vests, and masks, and warned everyone to take the trackers out of the water canteens. We unscrewed them all and threw them over the edge of the cliff. They had the three of us, Jasmine, Angelica and me, dress protectively first. Then, the rest of the men split up the remaining gear. Anthony and Lorenzo already had their own, which helped. Jasmine and Angelica both had an extremely hard time with the weight from the bulletproof vests, so they gave them up to Jeffrey and Steven. I was able to wear mine, even as uncomfortable as it was, and then made it a point of staying near the other two girls just in case they needed cover. Together, we stood more confidently than ever before. The worst was surely behind us.

CHAPTER 26

"A new command I give you: Love one another. As I have loved you, so you must love one another. By this all men will know that you are My disciples, if you love one another."
—John 13:34–35 (NIV)

Anthony followed closely by David's side as David trekked us through the endless evergreens. Lorenzo guarded our backs. The rest of us tried to stay quiet, ready to run, jump, hide, duck, or crawl at a moment's notice.

I focused on the ground in front of me, attempting to step lightly. *Thank You Father,* I prayed. *I shouldn't have left that cave alive, but You protected me. I don't understand why You've allowed me to live, while so many others die. I'll probably never understand it, but I thank You. Thank You for helping me to give Anthony a second chance as well. Had I known all of this was going to happen, I may have never accepted this mission at the airport. For whatever reason You've brought me here, please continue to fill me with Your Spirit so that I may fulfill Your will.*

We hiked through the mountain terrain to a valley where a slight stream, too small to drink from, trickled into a puddle dammed by a pile of fallen trees. I dipped my finger in the puddle. The water was cool and clear.

"Let's rest here for a few minutes," Lorenzo suggested, taking a quick look at Jeffrey. Jeffrey plopped on the ground and leaned against a tree. He had a hard time catching his breath, but was the type who would rather fall over dead than to complain about a little pain or discomfort. Still, it said a lot that he didn't argue with Lorenzo by trying to push us to continue walking.

Anthony, Lorenzo, and Darius stood watch, while the rest of us sat on the ground. The last time we rested by a stream our camouflaged brothers and sisters came to our rescue. I doubt that would be the results if another group found us now that we've donned the military gear for protection. I probably didn't need to worry since I'm sure there's no way I looked like a professional soldier. I chuckled quietly at the ridiculousness of my outfit. Still, I prayed we didn't run into anyone.

What I saw as we rested warmed my heart. Jasmine tended to Jeffrey making sure he continued to hydrate. I couldn't help but watch and smile. He never liked getting a lot of attention, but he appeared to like it coming from Jasmine. She took a wet rag and used it to keep him cool, by having him press it up on his forehead. When he glanced at me, he simply rolled his eyes.

"It's about time you let someone take care of you," I chuckled. Jeffrey wasn't amused, but Jasmine blushed. Angelica and I followed her actions, each taking torn pieces of cloth from a shirt that Jasmine carried and soaked them in the water. I handed a rag to Steven and used the other to clean myself, while Angelica took one to David. We did our best to wipe away the dry blood and dirt from our faces, necks, and arms.

"I'm so sorry I didn't see the danger you were in at first," Steven said to me. "You know, back at the tabernacle before any of this got completely out of hand. I should've caught on to the code a lot sooner."

"We made that code up years ago," I shrugged. "I'm thankful you remembered it at all. When you left the tent, where did you go?"

"I went to get Jeffrey," he said. "It wasn't long after that we heard someone rattling the door. I had locked it behind me, but the person on the other side wasn't going to let that stop them. The nurses finally took me serious enough to help Jeffrey off the bed…"

"We all thought he was hallucinating," Jeffrey interrupted.

Steven chuckled, "You should've seen Jeffrey's face when I entered the cabin…"

"You looked like a mad man," Jeffrey laughed, "rushing in, slamming doors, and telling us we needed to hide. For all I knew, you and Khris were in cahoots trying to prank me."

"Well, we weren't," said Steven sarcastically. Then he looked back at me, "The nurses and Jasmine helped me lift Jeffrey off the bed but, the door kicked in before we ever took two steps. Anthony stood with a gun, blocking our exit. He could've easily ended our lives. Instead, he warned us that if we showed our faces back in the camp, he'd have to kill us. Then, he disappeared as swiftly as he had entered."

Jeffrey quickly added, "Jasmine had the idea for us to search the parking lot for an open vehicle." Jasmine smiled lightly, trying to stay humble.

"Right," Steven confirmed, "We assumed we could find help in the nearest town. After searching about thirty vehicles, we finally found one unlocked with the keys under the floor mat. Then, right before leaving, we saw people leading Omar and you across the field."

"Of course, it had to be you who needed saving," Jeffrey sighed, sounding sarcastically disappointed while looking at me.

We all laughed before Steven continued, "Knowing we couldn't leave you in their hands, we sent the nurses to go get help while the three of us found our way around the camp, staying hidden in the trees. The hike took much longer than expected," he turned to Jeffrey, "partially because *someone* couldn't keep up."

"I was dehydrated, sue me." Jeffrey smiled. "Besides, it wasn't completely my fault. You got us lost."

"Yes," Steven sighed. "I turned us around and, for the eightieth time, I'm sorry."

Some things never changed. I smiled at my friends. Despite the trouble, they still razzed each other mercilessly.

"Anyway," Steven said more seriously, "we walked all through the night and into the next morning. That's when the explosions happened, which turned us back in the right direction. By the time we could see the camp, we were too late. There were hundreds of men lining everyone up...the smoke turned the sky black. We knew we weren't powerful enough to go down and help, but we hoped you were still up in the mountains; so we pressed on."

I shook my head, "No. I escaped back into the camp, right after the explosions."

"Not much of an escape, huh?" Jeffrey said. His tone rang with the truth of current reality. We hadn't really escaped at all considering we were on the run.

Steven never missed a beat, "We saw the day you all broke

free and watched as everyone ran up the mountain. On our way to meet with that group, a couple of soldiers ambushed us. A few Christians came to our aid."

"Were they camouflaged in mud and dirt?" David asked.

"Yes," Steven smiled. "You met them too?"

"They tried to help us, not knowing these soldiers were allies," David said. "Most of them anyway," he reminded us of Justin's betrayal.

"Well, we were certainly grateful for their help. They pointed us in a general direction where they had seen other groups headed. We never expected the second ambush."

"Did you see anyone else from our mission group?" Jasmine asked me the very question I dreaded.

"Geneva and Agnes," my eyes lowered. "They didn't make it." My shoulders slumped as I realized that, after that moment, I never looked for anyone else. I stayed more focused on keeping Angelica safe. "As near as I know, they're all gone. The attackers used *survivors, us, to* clean up the bodies of those who were killed, but I never saw anyone."

"What about Omar?" Jeffrey asked. "Did he escape with you?"

My eyes watered as I saw Omar's disfigured body in my arms, "He…" I choked.

"It's okay," Jeffrey said calmingly.

"I'm sorry," Jasmine put her hand on my shoulder. "I know he was a good friend."

"The thing is," I finally let out, "I only knew him for a few days, but he had a huge impact on my life. I held him in my arms during his last moments. I couldn't help him… He reminded me so much of my father. I really miss him."

"How did you *escape* back to the camp?" Jeffrey asked me.

"Omar," I smiled. "He broke free first, after showing me how. He went to warn everyone, trying to give me time to cut free. I ran down the mountain and was hiding in a log when the explosions went off." My mind drifted back to the lies Justin fed me before.

I wasn't regretting leaving his dead body in the cave, but I had to have more answers. The things he said, trying to convince me he was watching out for me, only left me more confused than before. Then, I remembered what he said when he and Anthony were fighting; he was willing to kill any and all of us. Whatever game he had tried to play didn't matter now. "When I reached the camp," I said, "I was too late to save anyone…"

"You saved me," Angelica said. "I would have given up."

"I'd be a murderer, if you hadn't been there," David added.

I saw Steven and Jeffrey go wide-eyed.

"You were defending yourself and all of us," I said. "Even still, I'm glad you chose a different path."

Steven and Jeffrey sent curious glances my way. Both were itching to make a smart remark. I ignored them, meeting David's kind eyes with a smile. Then, seeing Darius walking in the distance, I rinsed the cloth in my hand. "I'll be right back," I said to my friends, leaving them by the puddle. "On second thought, I'll take a couple more," I turned and ripped off two more strips from the old shirt and soaked them in the puddle. Approaching Darius, I placed one of the rags in his hand. "Take this," I said, "it'll help you refresh a little."

"Thank you," he rested the rag on the back of his neck.

Anthony stood off a ways, watching us. I left Darius and went towards Anthony, holding the rag out in front of me as a peace offering.

"Here," I said when I got closer to him.

He reached out and took the rag, "Thanks." Then he brushed it across his forehead.

We stood in silence as I tried to humble myself. I took in a breath, "Thank you for saving my life back there. I'm sorry for everything we've put you through, especially for the way I treated you."

He gave no reply. His blue eyes locked on mine. I felt uncomfortable in his presence and didn't know what to do next. I didn't expect an apology in return, although it would've been nice. I couldn't tell what his silence meant. I know I treated him poorly, but I didn't know how to make up for it. He didn't know how much of an effort this was for me. I still had reservations about him, though I chose to shove them all aside to make amends. I watched as Anthony wiped the rag over the bulge that Steven left on the side of his face. "As a Christian, I should have never allowed my anger to get in the way of showing God's love to someone else. I mean, even though they are the…if I see them as the enemy..." I stumbled over my apology. "Sometimes my worldly mind…well, anyway, I'm sorry."

He stared at me, still refusing to talk.

I continued to let out whatever came to my mind, "I believe you had a heart breaking past, but I also hope you'll be able to see past the human mistakes that Christians make…that I have made."

He nodded, "Even after all of the lies Farrell fed you, you still managed to see the good in me and, you chose to see that instead of the bad. For that, I am grateful."

I grinned, thanking him for his forgiveness. Not wanting to push my limits, I left to find Lorenzo. He was leaning up against a tree, shaking his head as I drew near. "I appreciate the offer," he said keenly, "but I'll keep my filth. It keeps the mosquitoes away." I didn't argue and allowed him to keep his distance. He wasn't willing to trust us yet; I could relate to that.

CHAPTER 27

...But one thing I do: Forgetting what
is behind and straining toward what is
ahead, I press on toward the goal...
—Philippians 3:13–14 (NIV)

"We need to get going," Lorenzo said as he adjusted his gear.

Though sore and tired, we rose to our feet.

"My house isn't too far from here," David tried to encourage us.

About thirty feet into our walk, Jasmine let off a terrible shriek. Rushing to her side, I saw her eyes fixated on a man with a bullet hole in his chest. David, Angelica, and I had seen and carried hundreds of dead, mutilated people. I had forgotten what it was like for death to shock me. Maybe I had grown callous to its sight. Jasmine, on the other hand, seemed greatly distraught. We couldn't dig a hole to give him a proper burial, there was no time, and there was no reason to take him with us. We had to leave his body. I didn't know how to relay that to her.

"Let's keep moving, or we'll end up just like him," Lorenzo had no problem addressing the matter. His comment brought a look of horror on Jasmine's face. Before I could intervene, Jeffrey challenged Lorenzo.

Harshly, he said, "You mock our grief as if this man's life meant nothing. He was a human being, and a brother of ours. You watch your tongue when you're around her, and show some respect."

Jeffrey and Steven could handle death fairly well, as far as I knew, but Jeffrey wasn't one to tolerate disrespect, especially around women. I could see that he and Jasmine had grown closer since the simple checkup she gave him the day he fainted in the field. His fondness of her would explain his sudden outburst. On the other hand, Jeffrey's reaction helped me understand why Lorenzo didn't trust us. He only saw anger and hate exploding from us. Why he stayed with our group, I still didn't know. Now was not the time to ask. I had to do what I could to keep the peace.

"Come on Jeffrey," I said calmly, "let's go. I don't think he meant anything by it."

Jeffrey held a hand on Jasmine's shoulder while guiding her away from the body.

We passed two more corpses on our way. Jasmine couldn't

bear to look at them, but I forced myself to. The longer we spent wandering in the forest the more I felt like I was falling for the lie that we were the only ones hurting. I felt like Elijah, who was hiding on the mountain, telling God he was the only prophet left. The more involved faces I forced myself to look at, the more I remembered we weren't the only ones experiencing persecution.

We came to the open field that David had mentioned without any more problems. No one else was here, yet. If they were, they may have already made it to his house. Mountains surrounded the meadow on both sides. Any other day, I would have been tempted to lie down in the tall grass and soak up the sun while watching the clouds go by. Instead, today, we would be trying to get across the field faster than a deer in hunting season. We squatted in the shrubs. Lorenzo and Anthony scanned the field. Everything was quiet, too quiet.

"It's about half a mile across," David whispered. "If we run our fastest, we shouldn't be in the open for more than three minutes. We can't go around the field. The mountains are too steep and rocky."

"I'll go first," Anthony said. "Martinez, you keep a close eye for any sign of movement."

Lorenzo nodded.

Anthony stayed crouched for a few steps, with his gun ready to fire, and then slowly stood. Taking a few more steps, he looked back at Lorenzo.

"It's clear," Lorenzo whispered to us, "follow Tereski."

One by one, we popped out of the shrubs and began to run across the field. David led the way, while Anthony stayed in the middle of us all, still surveying the field. Lorenzo guarded our backs as he had the entire time, making sure no one followed us. Sprinting, I could feel a twinge in my left foot. No way was I going to let a mild cramp slow me down. I pushed through with a limp. I started to fall behind, but just barely, with Angelica right in front of me. Steven, Jeffrey, and Jasmine, who were behind me, began gaining ground, while Darius stayed close to the front with David.

David and Darius reached the cover of the trees and turned around to encourage the rest of us to hurry. Angelica and I weren't but ten feet from the tree line when my foot completely went out from under me. It wasn't the cramp. It was a mud hole. Panicking, I struggled to get myself free. Angelica quickly turned to help me, but she sank into one too. David and Darius left cover to come help us. They warned Steven and Jeffrey to keep moving and avoid more of nature's traps. Steven was about to argue when Lorenzo commanded, "Get to cover. We don't need to risk anyone else being caught in the open." After that, Lorenzo stood close by with his gun out, guarding us while Anthony secured our surroundings.

"Grab her arms," David told Darius as he reached for Angelica first. "Pull firm with a fixed force. Khristy, stay still until we come to you." While Angelica linked both her arms with Darius', David grabbed hold of her leg and they began to pull. She popped out of the ground like a rocket and the three fell on the ground. After helping her up, Angelica hobbled to where the others were waiting in the tree line. When they came to me, they repeated the same process. My back popped twice as they pulled, and my foot felt as if it would come out of socket. We all flew to the ground just as I saw happen with Angelica.

"Are you okay?" David asked.

I gripped tightly to his shirt, scared to let go. I looked at him lying beside me. "I think so," I tried to move my foot. My ankle felt on fire.

"Good, we need to go," David pulled my hands from his shirt and helped me to my feet. Together, we made it to the tree line. Had someone been following us, our disaster in the mud would have been the perfect time to strike. We proceeded with caution, nonetheless.

The woods were thick. So thick, that we found ourselves

having to crawl under branches or squeeze between tree trunks. When they started to open up again, I could see where a home once stood. If this was David's property, our persecutors leveled it just as they had done to the camp, except no one hauled off the rubble. Ashes covered the ground. Burnt frames and melted rubber was all that was left of the vehicles we planned to use for escape.

David walked through the ashes searching. He kicked over a few scraps here and there. A brick chimney, still partway standing, was all that was left of the living room. Metal bed frames and mattress springs outlined the basics of three bedrooms. Pipes, brick, and a small amount of glass were all that remained of the house.

David kept to himself as he paced across the remains of the floors. I feared he was at his breaking point. Then, he stopped right next to a pile of broken glass and ceramics where an upstairs bathroom must have fallen through and shattered. He brushed his feet on the ground until he cleared a visible spot for the tile floor. I watched, unsure of what to say or do. Darius approached David but, when he placed his hand on David's shoulder, David didn't respond. Instead, he knelt to the ground and began to push back the bigger chunks of debris. Darius soon followed suit and signaled for the rest of us to join.

As far as I could tell, it was just a tile on the floor, left untouched by the flames, until Darius' hands moved some of the ash and revealed a handle. David used his shirt, like a glove, to help get a good grip on the handle as he pulled on it. The floor tried to lift up, but there was still too much debris on top of it. We all pitched in to shove everything aside until David could finally open the hatch in the floor that revealed a dark entrance. A stairway extended below the entrance with a box on the first step. Opening the box, David handed each of us a glow stick to break. Then he led the way down the staircase. Anthony and Lorenzo took one last look around outside before they shut the door and joined our descent. The room at the base of the stairs was full of boxes. David walked to the back corner and knelt down to begin messing with a machine. He pulled on a cord the way you would a lawnmower. It took several attempts before the generator caught and the lights flickered.

"A generator," Anthony exclaimed, "Are you trying to kill us?"

"Relax." David said as he pointed down to a pipe in the wall, "My father hooked it up to where all of its exhaust goes outside. The pipe emerges above ground about three hundred feet away from here. No one will know our location even if they see the exhaust being emitted."

Anthony cocked his head, "You have a hideout in the mountains and another under your house. Are there any other secrets you want to share with us?"

David laughed as he opened one of the boxes, "None that I know of, but this isn't a hideout. My family just never got rid of anything, and my mom liked having the extra storage for her canned goods." He then looked back at the generator. "We can't keep it running all of the time. For now, let's find anything useful in here and put everything else up against the wall. A lot of it will be my dad's papers and things my mom used to keep, but we might find something useful. Also…" David walked back to where the generator was and opened a door. Inside was a dusty bathroom. He smiled at us all as he reached for the sink.

My eyes lit up as he turned the faucet on and water began to gush.

"Let me guess," Anthony chuckled, "there's a separate well for the pipes down here too."

"Looks like it," David brushed off the subject. "Let's take turns while we know it's still working. Angelica, you can go first."

She didn't hesitate. The rest of us began to rummage through the boxes. Most were full of bills, receipts, and tax information, but a lot of it included David's schoolwork and art projects from when he was younger. I didn't realize how much a family could accumulate for just one child. It made me wonder how much of my childhood remained in boxes in the attic at home.

I came across a child's tee shirt that had "Momma's big boy" embroidered on it, I began laughing to myself. The tag said it was a child's XXL. It had David's name written on it. Tucking a part of the shirt into my waist side, I kept it as a reminder for me to comment on it later. I placed the rest of the box towards the "useful wall" in the cellar, thinking we could use the clothes for warmth if it came down to it. We also found boxes of food, antique treasures, expired medicines and plenty more. It seemed like our job would never end, but I could feel the center of the room open up the more we shuffled things around.

After Angelica finished in the restroom, Jasmine took her turn. They both looked rejuvenated. I was next. Hesitantly, I walked into the small, closet sized room. I noticed a mirror above the sink and tried hard not to look at it. As I scrubbed my hands in the water with a small bar of soap, the scab came loose from the web of my right hand. The soap burnt my sores, but it was worth it. I lathered my arms and rinsed them off, then cupped some of the soapy water in my hands and splashed it on my face.

We had just rinsed ourselves at the small puddle, but the soap helped to wash out my pores even more. When I finally opened my eyes, I found myself staring at a stranger. Past the grimy water, where wet hands tried to wipe the dust off the mirror, stood a woman with matted hair and bushy eyebrows. Her baggy eyes with dark circles left her looking older and worn. *Is this truly, what I look like?* I raised one hand up to my bony cheek and poked it. I dare not open my mouth to see my teeth or gums, nor lean in to get a closer look. With others waiting their turn, I decided to finish rinsing off before finding further proof of the trauma I've experienced.

When I exited the bathroom, I saw David messing with a radio. It looked as if he was trying to get it to work or pick up a signal. He let everyone else use the restroom before him. As each person went in to freshen up, the stench of our rotting flesh faded away. In all honestly, I hadn't really noticed it before, but I could actually smell our cleanliness now. Some of the stench would remain in our clothes but we were grateful for what we had. It also seemed that the cleaner we became, the more relaxed we were around each other. Perhaps our time here wouldn't be as tense as in the cave.

David suddenly cursed at the radio in his hands. Everyone stopped what they were doing and gawked at him. David turned to us, without apologizing, and increased the radio's volume.

CHAPTER 28

...Let God be true, and every man a liar...
—Romans 3:4 (NIV)

We sat in silence through David's frustrations. Static filled the room. A loud warning signal caused me to jump. The signal repeated three times, as it would for Amber Alerts or weather warnings, until finally a voice said firmly, "This is a national broadcast. Terrorists have attacked the United States of America. Turn in all reports of questionable activity to your local authorities immediately." The warning signal sounded again and then the voice repeated itself.

"This is good, right?" Jasmine asked. "Now these attacks will stop."

"No," I shook my head. "They're only going to increase."

Jeffrey cocked his head, "What do you mean, Khris?"

"The soldiers aren't the terrorists. We are… Christians are the terrorists."

Jeffrey and Steven chuckled, but their laughter didn't last.

"She's right," Lorenzo confirmed.

My friends shifted in their seats as things began to fall in place.

"We're not the ones committing genocide," Steven said sending an accusatory look towards the soldiers.

"We're not your enemy," Anthony quickly said. "If we thought you were terrorists, believe me, we wouldn't have come this far with you."

"Then the two of you have willingly committed treason against the U.S. to help us," Jeffrey said suspiciously.

"No," Lorenzo replied firmly. "We signed up to protect this country from all terrorists, foreign and domestic, and that's exactly what we're doing."

"We haven't seen you commit any acts of terrorism," Anthony added. "All we've witnessed are men and women defending their rights to live after an attack that should have never happened."

"Then why did it happen?" Darius asked.

Lorenzo shook his head, "I haven't the slightest idea."

"You weren't meant to know the reason," Anthony said to

Lorenzo. "You were just supposed to follow orders. For years now, the government has had moles from within their own sects, selling their secrets, planting viruses in their systems, and worming their way into higher positions with top, secret levels of security. Each time our country captures one of these men or women, they claim to be Christians doing their duty to God. At your camp, we started out surveying your people. We were only supposed to act on orders if we saw proof of criminal activity."

"That's outrageous," Darius exclaimed. "I've never heard of any Christians training to infiltrate the government and it certainly wasn't happening here."

"Which is why we are helping you, rather than turning you in," Anthony said. "I don't know who the real terrorists are, but it obviously isn't who we've been warned against. Why they've chosen to use Christians for scapegoats is yet to be revealed."

"About these moles that you mentioned," David said, "is it possible that one of them called the attack on the camp?"

"Absolutely," Anthony said bluntly. "In fact, I'm convinced Major Simmons is one of them. She's the only one who could've called the attack without anyone questioning her order. I had her under my own surveillance for a while. Then, when everything happened with Khris and Omar my fears became a reality. The only issue was that there were fewer willing to fight with me and more willing to kill for her. Farrell was a part of that number, and I apologize for ever trusting him to come with me."

"You can't beat yourself up," David said. "We were all fooled."

"I should've seen his deception sooner."

"It's done and past," Darius said. "We're here now. So, what are we going to do to stop this injustice?"

"There's nothing you can do," Lorenzo said solemnly. "You're already being targeted. The government, and the non-Christians of this world, will think your attempts at peace are a trick. You'll have no refuge." He kept his attention on the stairs.

"God is our refuge," Darius countered. "As long as we trust in Him, He will bring us through to the end."

Lorenzo sighed as he looked Darius in the eye, "You Christians keep on repeating the same hopeful sayings to yourselves, but do you even know why, or what they mean? You get them from a book written by men, yet you've seen men's capability of evil. How can you trust something so . . . so vulnerable?"

"Men are indeed inclined to do evil," Darius said calmly, "but they're capable of just as much good, especially, if they're with God. Our trust is not in the words of men, but in the God who gave those men the words to write and, most importantly, His Son. Personal experiences have been enough to convict me on the scriptural truths, but even science can attest to the accuracy of the events written in the Bible. Astrologists found a record in the stars when time stopped. Scripture explained this in the book of Joshua. All ancient cultures of the world record a massive flood story, and the Bible can tell you exactly how that flood came and why. Scripture also tells us that God made us from the dust of the earth. Scientists have determined that the base and trace elements that make up our body are from the earth's ground. Of every power that ever existed, God's power has always been the strongest within all spiritual cultures. In America, sicknesses and diseases heal without reason or cause. We know why. You just have to open your eyes. Creation is living proof of God's existence. DNA suggests that all humankind comes from one man and woman. Geologists are beginning to discover things that prove the world younger than they thought. You and I know that science *facts* continue to change, but I assure you that our scriptures have not."

Lorenzo neither nodded his head, nor seemed to tune out Darius.

"For me," Darius said compassionately, "scripture isn't vulnerable. It's proof. Proof that God does exist. The events proven by science give me reason to believe the rest of it is true too. Therefore, when the scriptures say God is my refuge, I follow and trust that with all my heart. When they, the writers of the Bible, tell me to trust and believe and that God will help us through all trials and temptations, I choose to believe just that. My faith will not waiver, no matter what torture befalls us."

Slightly scoffing, Lorenzo said, "I guess, for you that would make sense. It just doesn't cut it for me."

"Then why are you helping us?" Jeffrey asked.

"Like I said, I signed up for the military to help people; to protect our country and its citizens. The actions I saw at that camp were not those of protectors. What I saw was butchery. We have somehow allowed ourselves to become involved in an evil that should never have found place on our soil. Led by a mole or not, I won't be a part of it. I'll forever protect those who can't protect themselves. I assure you, Tereski and I aren't the only ones willing to take this stand. There will be others who rise up to help."

He seemed to know much about God, but refused to embrace Him. Anthony also kept his distance, but I felt as if he at least had some interest in our faith. The radio buzzed again as David found a new station. "Be wary of any suspicious activity in your neighborhoods. Christian sleeper cells are waking. You can identify most of these terrorists by a small hole or scar in the webbing of their right hand. If you see these terrorists, report them immediately."

I rubbed my hand where the bullet wound was scarring. Without a doubt, this was all a set up against Christians and people were too easily convinced that we are terrorists. It was going to be near impossible to prove them of our innocence.

Another voice began to speak. Anthony quickly reached over and turned the station. David puffed up his chest, "What are you doing?"

Anthony put his hands out in front of him, keeping space between him and David, "You've heard enough. There's no need to worry yourselves any more than you already are."

David pushed the radio down flat on its face, “Then what do you expect us to do?”

“We can rest for a night and get moving in the morning,” Lorenzo suggested.

“Where would we go?” Steven asked. “We’re refugees now. Everywhere we go…” Steven didn’t finish his sentence. We all knew what he was saying. There would always be a bounty on our heads.

“Is there anything else here?” Anthony asked. “Perhaps you have a way to contact the outside world. Would your dad have put anything else down here that could help us?”

“Nothing that I know of,” David glanced in Darius’ direction. “That doesn’t mean we have to stop looking.”

“Let’s get to work,” Anthony grabbed a box. The rest of us followed suit.

David seemed very distraught, as all of us were, but I watched him as he ran his hands over the radio. I could only assume he was punishing himself for not having any other answer. Pulling his XXL tee shirt from my pocket, I approached him with a sneaky smile.

“I think this may still fit,” I held the tee shirt up in his face.

David stared at me for a moment and then finally shifted his eyes to the shirt. Immediately he ripped it from my hands and tried to hide it.

“Oh come on,” I grinned, “it’s not that bad.”

“You’re right, it’s terrible,” he said with a straight face.

“I bet you were cute as a chubby baby, like a sumo baby.”

David gave a weak grin but he wadded up the tee shirt and threw it into the junk pile.

“What’s wrong?” I stepped closer to him. “Did you not win any of the sumo matches?”

He laughed quietly, but his mirth quickly faded. “How are we going to get out?”

I leaned against the desk where he worked on the radio.

He sighed, "I don't expect you to know."

Taking a moment to look around the room, I saw Jasmine and Angelica starting a new friendship as they explored through boxes together. Jeffrey and Steven tried laughing their stress away with small talk and jokes. Lorenzo shuffled through the same box repeatedly, watching the stairway like a hawk. Darius never touched a box. He was too busy trying not to let Lorenzo's disbelief derail him. Meanwhile, Anthony stayed determined to find an alternative path to freedom. He examined every paper thoroughly and then would crumple it up when done.

"Maybe we don't have to get out," I said to David. "Maybe we're supposed to be here."

David, too, looked around the room. A slight tingle climbed my arm as he placed his hand over mine on the top of the desk. Color filled my cheeks. His skin was rough, but warm. "You may be right. Perhaps there's still some good to come out of all of this," he smiled, "but we can't stay cooped up forever."

"Where do you hope to go?" I had to ask. "As Christians we are being hunted down. Is it really worth it to continue trying to escape? It may be better to just wait until this all simmers over."

He removed his hand and went back to working with the radio, "You all can, but I won't."

"Why?" I pestered.

He kept his face turned from me and gave no answer.

My heart dropped. He had reacted similarly in the cave. "David," I said quietly, begging him not to shut me out any more. "Is there something I need to know?"

He kept working on the radio. I turned to leave him alone when he whispered, "My father."

"What about him?" I asked, coming back to stand by his side. This time, I reached for his hand and gave it a gentle squeeze.

"I need to find him," he looked at me again. "My mom and Joy have both died. One of them was at the enemy's hands. I don't want that happening to him."

It may have already happened. I refrained from saying this aloud. I, too, have no guarantee that my own family survived. David's desire to find his father was natural, but may be nearly impossible.

"I know he's still alive," it was as if David heard my thoughts. "He won't give up easily. If we got free, he can too," he said adamantly.

I placed my other hand on David's shoulder, "I understand that you miss him, but…"

"It's not about that," he sighed. Then he signaled for me to come in closer as he whispered. "There are more secrets to my family than meets the eye. My father knows something about what's happening to us. I don't know what he knows, but some of the things I've seen and heard tell me he's the one who can show us how to put a stop to all of this."

I was too shocked to reply. Is this what he and Darius were talking about in the cave?

"Please, don't tell anyone about this. I don't want to create suspicions until I find absolute proof."

"My lips are sealed," I smiled. "Tell me how I can help."

"Right now, we just need to get through these boxes and gather anything that can help us to survive."

I went to work without hesitation and searched for all useful items. Our junk stack piled high, but our keep stack was also growing which provided hope. Most of it included clothes and canned foods, but we found a few tools as well. When the generator shut off, we used the time to rest and talk. David broke a glow stick and hung it on the bathroom door so we could find our way. The longer we sat in the dark, the better our eyes adjusted to not needing the generator as often.

CHAPTER 29

"I have told you these things, so that in Me you may have peace. In this world you will have trouble. But take heart! I have overcome the world."
—John 16:33 (NIV)

The supplies we gathered allowed us to stay in the cellar longer than expected. Every now and then, some of the men would go out and search for berries, wild onions, and any other vegetation to improve our diets. David kept searching the radio for information waiting to find that it was safe to put ourselves back out in the open. We all prayed for someone to tell us where to go for sanctuary, but the longer we waited the worse things seemed to get in the outside world.

Inside the cellar, I could see things improving with the soldiers. Darius and Lorenzo sat at the bottom of the staircase most of the time talking. Often, their conversations revolved around Christ as Darius answered Lorenzo's questions and rebuttals. They would also talk about their lives before the attack. Anthony, too, seemed to become more relaxed and open with Jeffrey and Steven, though he still kept his distance when they brought God into the conversation. I did my best to stay out of their way. I had done enough damage already. For now, I kept my focus on Angelica, Jasmine, and David, trying to get to know them better.

When the generator was on, we'd gather and read from a Bible we found in one of the boxes; everyone except Lorenzo and Anthony, that is. When the generator went off, we would talk about the scriptures until the conversation drifted into silence. Lorenzo would often listen in, but Anthony kept quiet and sat in a corner pretending to sleep.

One day, as I shuffled through a box of old newspapers, searching for anything we may have overlooked, my stomach began to churn. I hadn't been feeling sick, nor was there anything around to curl my nose hairs, but something made stomach acid rise to my throat. I stood up and backed away from the box.

"Are you okay?" I heard David ask. Looking up, I saw him staring at me.

Please, turn away. I wanted to say. I knew if I opened my mouth, I'd spew.

Jasmine walked my way but, before she could reach me, I

panicked. I needed an escape. I couldn't bear to think about vomiting in front of everyone. To reach the bathroom I'd have to pass by Jeffrey, Steven, and Anthony. Racing for the stairs, I stumbled up them as fast as I could. My hand pushed the cellar door open. The moment the fresh air hit me, my stomach emptied its contents. I didn't have much to release, just water and berries, but I was still grateful to have made it away from my friends.

"Close the door," I heard Lorenzo shout behind me. "It's still light out." I felt his hand on top of my head as he forced me to duck. The light of the day faded as he pulled the door shut. "Someone could have seen you."

"I'm sorry," I said, wiping the remains of vomit from my mouth. "I just…" Again, my stomach purged and what little I had inside went across Lorenzo's boot.

"The door stays shut in the day," he said, walking back down the steps as if he didn't even see my mess.

Jasmine came up the stairs to me, handing me a wet rag, and put the back of her hand up against my face and cheeks. "You're not feverish," she said.

"I'm not sick," I mumbled. "I think I just need fresh air."

Again, Jasmine felt for my temperature. Then, she checked my pulse, eyes, and throat. "Sick or not, you should lie down to keep well."

Nodding my head, I followed her down the stairs. After letting me rinse my mouth in the bathroom sink, she led me to my bed of clumped up clothes, which I had retrieved from a box. I didn't realize how tired I was until my body lay there for a few minutes. Angelica took it upon herself to sit next to me and stroke my hair. Before I knew it, the world around me passed away.

During my rest, I felt a slight darkness hover over me, a darkness, I couldn't escape. I saw myself from a bird's eye view lying asleep. I knew within that I was dreaming, but a terror still filled me. No one was around me. A light came from above the stairs. Footsteps approached. I couldn't see a face. My body was heavy; I couldn't move. When the first boot stepped off the last stair and onto the floor, a shock of pain came over me. My arms wrapped my stomach as the next boot stepped down. The face was still in the shadows, but I could see a gun pointing at me. The round went off just as I managed to wake myself up.

Sitting in the dark room, I couldn't tell if I was fully awake or still in the nightmare. I didn't feel heavy like before. The darkness around me didn't seem as horrifying either. I searched for a glow stick and broke it. Scanning the room, I could see Angelica near where I would lay my head and Jasmine rested to my left. Jeffrey and Steven slept near our feet. I could only assume David and Darius were the two men nearest them and that Lorenzo and Anthony were the two lumps in the farthest corner away. Allowing myself to breath, I tried to fall back asleep. My stomach continued to feel upset, but I breathed deeply trying to keep it under control. Eventually I dozed again.

I woke up to Jasmine handing me a glass of water. The room wasn't as dark as before, but that's because glow sticks had been broken and spread out across the floor. Everyone was up and talking with one another, while Jasmine tended to me.

"You need to hydrate," she said. "How do you feel?"

"I feel fine now," I replied honestly. "I woke up nauseous in the middle of the night but nothing happened. I think I've been too overwhelmed." I took a drink.

"I am glad to hear that," she smiled. "Now, finish that water and eat something." She placed crackers, fruit, and a granola bar in front of me. "Anything will help at least a little."

"I didn't know we still had these," I looked at her. We had rationed out the granola bars not too long after we first arrived here.

"I kept mine for such occasions," Jasmine smiled.

"Thank you," I replied, popping the fruit in my mouth. After a couple more bites, I felt the color in my face disappear. As Jasmine stood, I grabbed her hand and pulled her towards me, "I really need some fresh air."

"Are you feeling sick again?" She looked surprised.

I nodded and tried to breathe slowly to keep the vomit back. David was the first to see me lean over and he ran with a box in his hand and placed it under my face. "Use this," he said.

I tried to smile at him but then threw my head into the box as all the fruit came back up. Coughing and gagging, I felt a rush of embarrassment for everyone having to hear me. Remembering that David had front row tickets to this whole scene, I kept my head in the box refusing to rise. How could I ever make eye contact with him again? I just wished for him to leave. I felt a gentle hand brush up and down on my back as I gagged a bit more. When I finally felt as if it was safe to resurface, I raised my head and reached for my water. Rinsing my mouth, I tried to drink a little more. This time, it stayed down.

I realized that, eventually, I would have to look up. "Thank you," I said humiliated.

"It's no problem at all," David smiled. As he continued to rub my back, I was sure I heard him whisper, "I'll always have your back." No one else paid me any attention after that, they just kept searching through the boxes. We were bound to go insane if box searching and berry picking were to become our only activities. I didn't do much to help. I just sat near the bathroom in case I had another episode. David sat with me, piddling with boxes like everyone else. I enjoyed his company, though I constantly feared embarrassing myself in front of him again.

"Look what I found," he suddenly exclaimed. We were all excited even though we didn't know the cause of our celebration. David held up a small cassette tape in one hand and a box in the other. "Music," he smiled. "It's old, but it should still work."

Everyone blew him off, going back to his or her own boxes. I watched as David put the tape in the player with a smile. A melodious sound of an old church hymn began to play. In an instant, the room became more alive. Conversations perked up. Small giggles and laughter filled the air. *Thank You, Father, for music,* I prayed.

Feeling light headed, I attempted to go inside the bathroom. Jasmine, who kept a close eye on me all along, came to my aid.

"I need fresh air," I said, as I sat near the toilet.

"Just breathe," she said.

"I can't," anxiety rushed over me.

"Stay here," Jasmine left my side. David turned the music off as I heard Jasmine ask Lorenzo, "Could she please go outside, for just a moment?" The next thing I knew, she was back in the bathroom with me. "Come with me," she smiled.

Everyone's eyes were on me once again, as I walked with Jasmine to the stairs. Their attention didn't help my unease. I wanted them to continue to talk and sing; *please, just ignore me.* Lorenzo stood at the top of the stairs, waiting. Jasmine was my aid while Anthony followed behind us. Lorenzo opened the door slowly and eventually stepped out, signaling for us to stay put. He called Anthony out to help him look around. The air was nice at first, but then I began to smell all the soot and ash.

"This smell is making it worse," I said to Jasmine.

"Lorenzo," she whispered, "can I take her in the tree line, away from the rubble?"

"Call Steven to help Anthony guard the perimeter," he said.

Steven came without hesitation. He and Anthony lead us out of the house remnants, into the trees, and behind a large rock. Finally, I could breathe. For the first time since we entered the cellar, we were outside during the daylight. The men always gathered food at night. Surely, Steven and Anthony were grateful to see the sun.

Jasmine took the time to ask me a series of odd questions as the men walked around to check our surroundings. She asked questions like, "How often have you urinated?" "Do you feel bloated?" "Are you always overly sensitive to smells?" "How long have you felt nauseous?" Jasmine had another question judging by the look on her face, but she didn't want to ask. "Khris, when..."

"Just ask."

"Okay, when was your last period?"

That wasn't what I was expecting. I don't know what I expected to hear, but it wasn't that.

"I...I don't know. It's been a while," I tried hard to think.

"Khris," she took in a deep breath, "I need you to be completely honest with me. Is there any possible chance you could be pregnant?"

"No way," I exclaimed, taken aback by her question. I was pure, and I was going to stay pure until marriage. For her to ask such a question was offensive to me. Anyone else who knew me would know that for me to be pregnant at this moment would mean I was either the second Virgin Mary, or.... My heart stopped. Mortified, my stomach soured again. I felt Jasmine's hand on my shoulder. I refused to acknowledge her attempt to console me.

"No..." I repeated. "This isn't happening."

The first memory of my time in captivity on the mountain flooded back through my exhausted brain. Pain. I had gone to call my parents. I remembered hearing my dad's voice on the answering machine and then...nothing. I closed my eyes and took a deep breath. I remember I had been unconscious and when I came to, I hurt. At the time, I had bigger worries on my mind.

Anthony came around the corner to check on us. A sudden recollection and fury inside of me burst out, "Who raped me?"

He jolted, wide eyed, and stared.

"Who raped me when I was first captured on that mountain?"

He stumbled for an answer, "I...I'm not sure I know what you mean."

"Think!" Hot tears of anger and sorrow flowed down my cheeks, "Who turned me in?"

"A soldier," he said. "I don't know his name. He wasn't a part of my initial team."

My blood boiled, "That's it, just some random soldier?" Again, I felt Jasmine's hand of comfort.

"Yes," he said. "Major Simmons had a few men guarding our perimeter. One of them brought you to her. I had my orders and I left to my duty."

Jasmine was a blur in my vision as she pulled me into her arms. "I was unconscious," I sobbed. "I didn't know."

"We really need to get back," Anthony said softly to Jasmine.

"We'll be there, just give us another minute," she politely sent him away. My tears soaked her shoulder.

"Breathe," Jasmine repeated. "Take some deep breaths." She lifted my chin, so she could look at my face, and wiped away my tears. I held my breath and tried hard to focus. "We don't know for certain. You could have a stomach bug. Let's not jump to any conclusions yet. It will be okay. '[You] can [endure] everything through [Christ] who gives [you] strength.'[6]"

What if I don't want to, endure all things? Was it not enough to have to live the life of a fugitive? Now, in the midst of a war, why this? Why me? How could I be pregnant with some stranger's child and be expected to endure all things? I don't want to deal with this. I don't want to believe it. I don't have the energy. I stood and took in a deep breath. I wiped my hands across my cheeks and said to Jasmine, "Let's go back."

Jasmine called the men and silently walked beside me, while Anthony and Steven followed closely to us. Lorenzo stood at the cellar door, waiting on us. As soon as we stepped inside, he pulled the door shut. It seemed as if all oxygen left the room, but I refused to let it drop me. Everyone stared at me in question. A fake smile emerged on my lips as I said, "I'm okay. I'm good now."

David turned the music back on and almost everyone continued back to his or her old activities and conversations. Jasmine held my hand with both of hers, trying to comfort me.

---

[6] Philippians 4:13 (NIV)

I did my best to keep my mind off myself. I hoped that Jasmine was wrong and it really was just a stomach bug. When she felt content to leave me, Jasmine went to sit with Jeffrey. They were fun to watch and listen to as they talked and joked with each other. I needed their distraction especially since Anthony prowled around like a caged tiger. He didn't try to talk with me much anymore, but he did seem somewhat concerned every time I moved. Then again, so was everyone else. It was as if they all expected my sickness to be contagious.

CHAPTER 30

I can do everything through Him who gives me strength. Yet it was good of you to share in my troubles.
—Philippians 4:13–14 (NIV)

A day later, in the dark room while we all tried to sleep, I felt a hand tap my shoulder. A body sat beside me as I heard Jeffrey's voice. "Are you awake?"

I never had a problem waking up for a friend. "Yeah, are you okay?" I said rubbing the sleep from my eyes. I sat up in the fetal position, wrapping my arms around my legs.

"I've been thinking," he said.

That's all that any of us were able to do. "What about?" I asked.

"How none of this is a dream," I could hear the slight tremor in his voice though he tried to conceal it.

"More like a nightmare," I muttered.

"I never thought this would come to our own country. I mean, I knew it was possible, but I didn't think I would ever see it in my lifetime," he wanted to say more but his voice faded away, as if he hoped for an explanation.

"I don't think any of us thought this would happen in our time," I said. I felt the urge to share my fear for my own possible situation. My stomach began to churn, but I didn't know if that was because I was nervous, or if it was a part of my stomach's new routine. I knew Jeffrey would still be my friend and wouldn't shun me but I had no idea how he would react. Eventually they would all know. For now, I found it a better plan to keep it a secret.

"It is strange though," Jeffrey continued in his thoughts, "to think that we were almost done with college; ready to look for someone to spend the rest of our lives with. Now, we don't even know if we'll see tomorrow."

"Yes, but we're told in scripture never to expect a tomorrow," I slightly joked.

"I just meant…"

"I'm not attacking you," I interrupted. "I meant it more sarcastically than anything. I'm finding myself less afraid to be blunt these days."

He laughed, "No need to apologize, it's reasonable given the circumstances."

"I guess we're all a little more on edge than normal."

"Well, yes," Jeffrey said solemnly. "We've seen thousands of people slaughtered for being Christians. Now, people hunt us like criminals for believing in God. It's turned our lives upside down. Sure, we had warning about things like this in other countries, but, well… anyway, that's not what I meant... I'm talking about your specific circumstance."

I couldn't see Jeffrey's face, he was only a shadowy figure next to me, and I'm sure that's all he could see of me, but I immediately turned my head in the opposite direction. It didn't matter how he found out, though I could assume Jasmine told him. I just needed to know what he was going to do with the information. I didn't want everyone in this group to know. I especially hated the idea of everyone seeing me as a burden. Worst of all, with him and Jasmine assuming they knew the cause of my sickness, how long would it be before it became real? I wasn't ready for any of this. Everything was completely backwards to how it should have been.

My heart beat faster as anxiety enveloped me like a blanket of suffocation. I didn't want to wake anyone up, but I couldn't hold in my fear. I felt Jeffrey's arm come around my shoulder as he leaned in and kissed the side of my head ever so gently, caring for me like the older brother I never had. "God will never give us anything we can't handle so long as we lean on Him," he said. "Everything is going to be okay. Jasmine and I will both be here for you, but so will everyone else, if you just let them." That confirmed his source of information, but it also tore down the wall I was working so hard to build.

Jeffrey gave me a tight hug. Tears rolled down my cheek.

CHAPTER 31

He came to that which was His own, but His own did not receive Him. Yet to all who received Him, to those who believed in His name, He gave the right to become children of God.
—John 1:11–12 (NIV)

I awoke to the generator rumbling to life as David started it up. I immediately closed my eyes when the lights filled the room. Jeffrey still had his arms around me. He soon gave me a gentle hug before letting me go, and smiled when I looked at him. "Your secret is safe with us, sis."

Jasmine squatted next to me with a bottle of water and another granola bar. "You need to keep nutrients in your body," she said. "Try to snack some if you can."

"Thank you," I smiled, "for everything." If I didn't want her to say anything, I should have asked her to keep it a secret. Steven was outside with Jasmine and me when I blew up. He could have also told Jeffrey. He hadn't acted as if he heard what happened outside, but he had to have known. It would be just like Steven not to say anything until I was ready to talk to him.

Jasmine gave me a wink and a smile. "We're always here for you," she said. Then she looked up at Steven, who was coming our way.

"Good morning," he said brightly.

"If it's really morning," Jeffrey laughed. "It's hard to tell without any windows."

Steven laughed, "Oh, my stomach can definitely tell. Breakfast is the only time it ever growls."

As I laughed, I looked at the back of the room and saw Darius sitting alone with a book in his hands. He had it open, but was staring at all of us who were being quite loud. "You should read to us," I said, startling him and interrupting my friends' conversations.

Darius tilted the book so I could see the cover. He was holding the Bible we found our first day here. "I can talk about the scriptures all day long," he laughed, "but ain't no man, or woman, ever going to get me to read out loud."

"Why?" I asked.

"I have a terrible stuttering problem when I read."

"I understand. My sister has that same challenge," I said. "Sorry to put you on the spot."

"What were you reading?" Steven asked.

"John, chapter one," Darius smiled.

Steven started to quote it from memory, "'In the beginning was the Word, and the Word was with God, and the Word was God. He was with God in the beginning. Through Him all things were made; without Him nothing was mad that has been made. In Him was life, and that life was the Light of men. The Light shines in the darkness, but the darkness has not understood It.'[7]"

"I'm impressed," Darius lightly clapped.

Anthony scoffed from his corner, "What kind of hippy are you quoting?"

Darius shook his head, "John certainly has a unique way of putting things, but I can assure you, he was no hippie. He was one of the twelve who walked every step with Jesus during His last three years on earth." Anthony had already blocked Darius out, so Darius turned to all of us. "I always found it interesting that John jumps straight to the point. Jesus is God; he states it plain and clear. He has existed ever since before the creation of the world, and He is our only chance at life. John is constantly letting his audience know that Jesus is the Messiah they have been waiting for. He also reminds us about the many prophecies that declared the coming Messiah and how Jesus fulfilled them all. I can't think of a more uplifting book to read in times of trouble. " He then looked at Steven, "Do you have the rest memorized?"

Steven shook his head, "Not exactly. I could summarize it, but those first five verses always stood out to me the most. So much so I used to quote it at recess in grade school."

"Well then, here," Darius handed Steven the Bible, "I'll let you read it."

Steven read to us all right from where he left off. When he

---

[7] John 1:1–5 (NIV)

started to read chapter three, where Jesus tells Nicodemus he needs to be born again in order to enter God's kingdom, Darius took over, also quoting it from memory, "'For God so loved the world that He gave His one and only Son, that whoever believes in Him shall not perish but have eternal life.'[8]"

He paused, looking at each of us, and never stuttered as he said, "'For God did not send His Son into the world to condemn the world, but to save the world through Him.'[9]" He paused again, looking back at Lorenzo and Anthony. Anthony was playing with the radio while Lorenzo sat near him, but kept his eyes on Darius. "'Whoever believes in Him is not condemned, but whoever does not believe stands condemned already because he has not believed in the name of God's one and only Son. This is the verdict: Light has come into the world, but men loved darkness instead of Light because their deeds were evil. Everyone who does evil hates the Light, and will not come into the Light for fear that his deeds will be exposed. But whoever lives by the truth comes into the Light, so that it may be seen plainly that what he has done has been done through God.'[10]"

I sat amazed at his memory.

"Why do people refuse to come to the Light? Why deny God and keep living a life that condemns them?" Darius spoke to us, but I could only assume he hoped for the ears on the other side of the room to listen. "John tells us why. They don't always enjoy doing evil things. It's because they don't want their sins exposed. What they don't know, is that once those sins are exposed, the sin no longer holds power over them. Satan convinces people that their evils are too great to find forgiveness. It's our job to show them just how powerful God's forgiveness really is."

Anthony dropped, or rather slammed the radio on the desk,

---

[8] John 3:16 (NIV)

[9] John 3:17 (NIV)

[10] John 3:18–21 (NIV)

and picked up his gear. I guess he had had his fill of scripture for the day. Lorenzo stood as Anthony made way for the stairs. "Where are you going?"

"To get some fresh air and secure the perimeter. We can't stay here forever. The longer we sit, the closer we are to starving to death or having someone find us. If I'm going to die, it's not going to be down here, listening to all of this nonsense." Anthony looked at me, as if waiting for a rebuttal.

Darius pushed himself up off the ground, "I'll go with you. I could use a stretch myself."

"I don't need a babysitter," Anthony grumbled.

"No," Darius said, "but a second set of eyes will be helpful."

"Make that three sets," Lorenzo smiled as he strapped on his coat and equipped his weapons. "We'll give you your space," he said to Anthony, "but there's no way we're going to leave you alone in the open."

Darius looked at all of us still sitting on the ground, "We'll be back. Don't eat all of the crackers."

As they readied to leave, we all quieted down. David waited for the three to reach the top of the stairs before he turned off the lights. Lorenzo cracked the cellar door and glanced around. Inch by inch he lifted it up, each time, scanning for movement outside. All of us watched in anticipation as he finally opened the cellar door completely, letting the moonlight shine in on us.

"I thought you said it was breakfast time," Jeffrey mocked Steven in his whispers.

Steven threw a light fist into Jeffrey's arm. When Lorenzo closed the cellar door, we all let out a breath. David turned on the lights. Anthony had a good point. The longer we were here, the more risks we took. I leaned my back up against the wall. Would we ever stop running?

"What's with the soldiers?" Steven asked.

"Not a clue," David shook his head, "They're here to help us, but they don't want anything to do with God, it seems."

"I wouldn't be too sure on that," I smiled. "Darius is breaking through to Lorenzo."

"What about Anthony?" Steven asked. "You couldn't stand that guy even before all of this started."

"It's complicated," I shrugged, glancing towards David. "I keep going back and forth, but I think he just has a hard time seeing how we can be so faithful to each other and to God with everything that's happening. Therefore, he's keeping his distance from us until he figures it out."

"I think he's just studying us," Jeffrey said. "I think he's cynical of our faith. It's as if he's waiting for us to mess up, so he can call us hypocrites and no longer feel guilty about ignoring our conversations."

"Why do you say that?" David asked.

"I'm not sure, it's just a feeling I get. I think that the moment we're all free, he'll be out of our lives without ever looking back. It wouldn't surprise me if he's planning on leaving us now."

I prayed Jeffrey was wrong. We needed all the help we could get.

"I'm so tired of being locked up," Angelica sighed as she gazed at the stairs.

"Me too," I said.

"We all are," David replied.

Angelica then asked David, "When we do get out, will I go back to Mom and Dad?"

I could see David nervously try to come up with a gentle answer. Jasmine responded for him, "I think anything is possible."

"Not anything," Angelica's eyes glossed over as she held back the tears. Her cheeks reddened as she bit her lip. She was thinking of her brother, no doubt.

"Yes, anything," David replied. "Benjamin might be gone from this world, but he will be waiting for you in the next. Right now that may not seem comforting, but God is faithful and we can trust that we will see your brother in heaven."

"I hope I go there soon. I don't want to have to tell Mom and

Dad," she started to cry. I moved closer to her side, pulling her in to comfort her. Though sixteen, she was still a child. Wanting to be with her family made sense, but I don't think she fully understood what she was asking. Then again, maybe she did. Perhaps I was the only one who still struggled with thinking about the afterlife.

"I think we sometimes underestimate the God we follow," Jasmine said quietly. She stared at the ground. "We have lost thousands of loved ones to death, our lives are being threatened, we are hunted like animals, and some of you bare the mark of the captured ones on your hands. Still, we are together and able to talk together about God and with God. We know the fight isn't over, but I think within our hearts, we all have the true peace of God to help get us through anything."

A metaphorical lightness filled the room and our recent horrors were not as dark. We knew we still faced danger, but Jasmine had reminded us of why we came to love God. We all grabbed hands. David started to pray. His prayer was like a Psalm of David from the scriptures, beautiful and elegant, pouring out his entire heart to God. He left it open for us to add in our own supplications.

"Father God, our Refuge and Protector," Jeffrey started to pray, when the cellar door suddenly swung open. Darius stood above us in terror.

CHAPTER 32

...Then Joab took Amasa by the beard with his right hand to kiss him. Amasa was not on his guard against the dagger in Joab's hand...
—2 Samuel 20:9–10 (NIV)

"Come, quickly," Darius loudly whispered. Then he looked back behind him. We sat in shock. His voice grew harsher, "Get out now. It's an ambush."

Angelica, Jasmine, and I all ran for the supplies, quickly grabbing anything we could see. The generator shut off and room went dark.

"Now" Darius was not quiet this time. Jeffrey, Steven, and David grabbed us and we stumbled up the stairs.

Reaching the top, I could see Darius holding his side. Blood covered his hand. He was pallid and short of breath.

"Step back," a woman's voice commanded before I could poke my head out of the doorway.

Darius' eyes widened. I searched the dark behind him and saw a tall, silhouetted figure holding a gun to his head. Darius did as she said, trying to stand straight and ignore the pain.

"Step out of the cellar," she demanded us.

Out I climbed. David followed me. Everyone else somehow managed to slide back into the dark and stay hidden. Knowing Steven and Jeffrey, they were probably making plans. I prayed for their protection. When the woman stepped out from behind Darius, I knew we were the ones who would need protecting. A familiar face revealed itself; it was Major Erica Simmons, 'the General's daughter' as the soldiers above the cave called her. Glass crunched and shuffled across the ground. I became aware of the heightened danger around us. Men with guns surrounded us.

"Where are the rest of your friends?" Erica demanded.

David didn't hesitate. "They're dead," he said.

"What a pity," she was very sarcastic. "I did hope to kill them myself. Is he telling the truth Tereski?"

I clenched my fists. The traitor, where was he? Hiding. No doubt. Immediately, I searched for Anthony's face among the men. He cowered behind two others.

"Yes," Anthony said, not taking a second look at any of us.

"Very well," Erica said, pushing Darius towards us. He was

bleeding badly. David and I both caught him, trying to keep our balance. We sat him on the ground and tried to tend to his wound. Someone had shot him, but there wasn't an exit wound.

Erica walked around us, not caring for anything we did. It was as if she wanted us to save him. David used pieces of Darius' shirt to put over his wound, and had me place as much pressure on it as possible. Erica took pleasure in commanding us to stand up. We wouldn't, at first, until she put the gun back on Darius' head. We each put ourselves under his arms and I tried to keep my hand over his wound.

"Where's the Ichthys?" Erica paced, trying to intimidate us. It was working.

"What Ichthys?" I asked.

"I know one of you knows," she demanded. "Reveal it to me or he dies." The gun was now right between Darius' eyes.

"No, wait." I put my hand up to block her aim. Darius groaned in pain, and I quickly placed my hand back over his wound. "If you'd tell us what it is, we could…"

Erica pointed the gun at me, "Do you think I'm stupid?"

I didn't know what to say.

"Tell me where it is!"

"She doesn't know," David yelled. My head turned to him and, now, so did Erica's gun. "None of us do."

"Well that's a shame," Erica shifted the gun back to Darius, and in an instant my ears began ringing. Darius fell to the ground in agony. Shouting, I dropped down beside him, still holding pressure to his side, as if it could keep him alive. My tears began to wash the splattered blood off my face. *Please, not Darius. Take me instead.* The clothes on his chest soaked in more blood as he grasped for a breath.

I started to pray for healing, "God close his wounds. Don't let him die like this. Please save him…" Hearing Darius' anguish, I could almost feel his suffering. I remembered his whispers to Melanie. Through my sobs, I repeated his father's blessing. "When you feel God calling you home," I choked, "when you know it's time, don't hold onto this world. Go to God's open arms and never look back." I didn't want to let him go but I needed to, for his sake. I saw the peace on his face as he breathed his last. My tears gushed. I wrapped my arms around his entire body. First, I lost Omar and now, Darius. The pain of this loss was too much to bear.

David still stood. I looked at him for answers. He scowled at Erica. She now held him at gunpoint, demanding to know where he hid the Ichthys.

"Let her go," David bargained, "and I'll tell you."

"Do you really think you're in a position to bargain with me?" Erica focused the gun on me but still talked to David, "You tell me where it is and I'll think about letting her live."

"We had a deal," Anthony's voice came from behind.

"Deals change," Erica kept the gun on me. Then she asked David, "Where is it?" She straightened her arm, "Three." Her finger tightened around the trigger, "Two."

David looked at me with regretful eyes.

"One..." Erica pulled the trigger and the ringing in my ears grew louder. David dropped down, reaching his arms out to grab me. As he did, I found the strength to meet him half way. We embraced each other. I expected to be with Darius any moment. Seconds later, I still felt the warmth from David's arms. I heard two more shots and held to him tight. Both of us were bewildered. I felt no pain. Then, when looking to where Erica stood before, all we saw was her body, lying on the ground. Two other men lay on the ground behind her.

No one around us moved, except Anthony who came near with a gun in his hand. All grudges I held against him before swelled back up inside of me. He commanded everyone else to stand down. "Are you okay?" He asked me.

"Of course not," I glared at him. "Darius is dead. Why didn't you kill her before she shot him?"

"I didn't think she would go through with it so soon in the interrogation."

"But she did," I looked at David, "and for what, a fish?"

David bowed his head, "I can't say exactly."

"It's okay," I put my hand on his. It was much easier for me to forgive him than Anthony at this point.

"So you don't know where the Ichthys is?" Anthony asked.

David's anger turned to fury towards Anthony, "It's a Christian symbol that can be found anywhere, but no, there's not any one, specific, tangible item that I've ever held, called the Ichthys."

"That settles it then," Anthony reached down and pulled me up. I struggled for David's grasp, but found myself thrown back. One of the men behind Anthony took hold of me and held me firm. "The past months of following you around, practically starving myself, have been pointless," Anthony begrudged.

"What are you doing?" David readied for a fight. "This isn't you."

Anthony laughed, "It doesn't take much to gain your trust, does it? All I had to do was exploit a few emotions, tell you sappy stuff, pretend, to come to the rescue, and, worst of all, suffer through your pointless religious readings. David, you should have listened to your girlfriend on that mountain."

"Let her go."

"Tell me where the Ichthys is," Anthony demanded one last time with his gun now on me.

"I don't know what you're talking about," David spat.

"Well that's too bad," Anthony smirked as he holstered his gun. "That was possibly the only thing that could have saved your life." The soldiers around us moved in closer.

"Whatever you're doing, Anthony, stop before you go too far," David held his hands up and stepped backwards.

"I crossed that line long ago," Anthony smirked. "I have no desire to go back. I've followed all of you long enough. We play by my rules now." Anthony deceived us all. This entire time, he was playing us like a cat playing with a mouse. "Get down on the ground," he commanded. When David didn't comply, Anthony shouted even louder, "Get down!"

"Only a coward shoots a man when he's down," David backed towards the entrance of the cellar. The soldiers around us continued to move in slowly, with their guns out in front of them.

"I never said anything about shooting you," Anthony motioned once again for David to drop.

"What about Khristy? What will happen to her?" David looked at me with eyes that said he wished to save me but didn't know how.

"She's of no concern to you anymore. My patience is growing thin. Get down!"

David finally began to kneel. As he did, the soldiers jumped to grab him. David was quicker and rolled into the cellar before they could grab him. I saw Jeffrey jump up, seize the door, and pull it shut. Anthony yelled obscenities, trying to get his men to open the door, but my friends had locked it tight. A smile crossed my face.

"Get that door opened," Anthony demanded. He then turned to the man behind me, "Take her to the trees."

"Yes sir," the voice sounded very familiar. Conveniently, for him, he was the only one left standing who bore a mask. Anthony shot the other masked men when he killed Erica. I didn't know what to say, or how to fight back. I didn't want to lose sight of the cellar. I didn't want to be alone with these vile men. I didn't want to know what would happen to me. Jasmine's encouragement swam through my mind, *the fight isn't over yet. My God will get me through this... even if it's by taking me to my grave.*

I struggled hard, kicking and screaming, as the masked man took me to the tree line. To my surprise, we stopped right at the edge. Anthony leaned in close to the soldier and said something in secret. I tried to use that moment to run, but the soldier jerked me back and grabbed a pressure point on my shoulder, forcing me to kneel.

Anthony grabbed the man by the neck and threw him up against the tree. "No harm is to come to her," he demanded.

Again, with no restraints, I tried to run. This time, Anthony was the one who grabbed me with his black gloves, leaving indents on my upper arm. If no harm was to come to me, he must have meant that rule for everyone except himself.

"Sit," Anthony said, pulling me to the ground. I could've continued to fight back and try to grab his weapon, or maybe even run, but I was outnumbered seven to one. My chances of both getting away and helping to free my friends were slim. At least now, knowing he wanted to keep me safe, I had a chance of getting information from him. Meanwhile, I'd do whatever I could to buy more time to escape.

Anthony withdrew a pair of handcuffs from the masked man and stuck one side on my right arm. Zip ties had apparently proven themselves as failures.

"What's this Ichthys you're all so desperate for?" I asked.

He laughed at me as if I was a complete idiot, "If you have to ask, then you don't need to know." He pushed me, forcing me to put my back up against a tree.

"Is it worth a lot?" I asked as he fought to grab my other hand and cuff them both behind the tree.

"Those aren't too tight are they?"

I didn't humor his question and only waited for an answer from mine.

"To some, it's worth more than all the gold in the world," he grinned and turned to walk away. His secrecy annoyed me just as much as the menacing look on his face.

"Why go through all this trouble with us these past months?" I yelled. "Why not just kill us all and search for it on your own?"

"It would've been so much easier, for me, if your *boyfriend* could've just trusted me enough to tell me where it is. Nevertheless, with time cut short and new events unfolding, I'm forced to go with plan B." Anthony smiled slyly, "Unless, of course, he told you. Then you could make everything much easier for all of us, and save your friends from certain death."

"Our death is certain no matter what I say," I spat. His threats meant nothing to me. My friends were safer in the cellar away from Anthony's men.

"No worries," he passed my comment off as if it was nothing. "I've watched David when you're around; always looking for you, walking with you, talking with you. His eyes don't lie. He'll tell me what I want to know."

"So that's it. My lifespan depends on David's feelings for me?" I pretended to sound helpless, praying to gain more information.

"Not a chance," Anthony crouched to my eye level and placed his fingers below my chin. I rolled my head away from him as best I could. "Your lifespan is based on how safe you keep my heir." He looked at my stomach, smiled, and then got up to leave.

My eyes widened. My breath shortened. Surely, he didn't mean… "That's impossible," I muttered. "It's just a stomach virus."

Anthony turned back to me. The face of evil peered through my soul. "You don't really believe that. I can see it written all over your face."

I sat stunned, unable to move, wishing for death.

"You should've trusted your instincts about me but, for my future heir's sake, I'm glad that you didn't."

Heir, that word came again, pricking my ear and snapping me back into reality. "Why?" I asked as my eyes welled.

"Why?" The monster laughed. "You're a self-righteous Christian who thought you were too good for me. How does it feel to be put in your place?"

"No," I said, "this doesn't make sense. You helped us. You let Steven and Jeffrey go free. Why?"

"After your little stunt on stage, Erica didn't trust your friends disappearing so quickly. Their unwanted presence in the camp is exactly what would have caused my stupid sister to command the troops into action. I needed them alive at the time. Now, I don't need them at all."

"Your sister?" I questioned.

"The *chosen* Erica Simmons," Anthony said her name with great distaste.

"You killed your sister..."

"She was only half," he rolled his eyes. "The world is better without her. Father was stupid for deciding to keep her around."

He was evil, pure evil. I watched as men pried at the cellar door and fired multiple rounds into it.

"Any second now, I'll have everything I need. Sit tight and you'll see," he winked and ran his fingers down the side of my face like a lover's caress before walking away.

I shivered with revulsion and anger at his touch. I pulled and tugged against the handcuffs and threw my head back against the tree. *No,* I denied, closing my eyes. *This can't be real. Please, Lord, let me wake up from this nightmare.* Tears streamed down my face.

The masked man came over with water and sustenance. Seeing him stand over me flashed my memory back to the camp; all of those soldiers torturing and killing my brothers and sister. The man opened the water bottle and tried to get me to drink. I refused, figuring I would rather thirst or starve to death before they imprisoned me for nine months. The man, prepared for my disobedience, took charge by grabbing my jaw and forcing the water into my mouth. I had to swallow or drown. I wanted to drown, but my body's instinct won. When he let go, I immediately spit the remaining water in my mouth all over his mask.

"Now listen here you selfish, insignificant worm..." Justin pulled off his mask and...I didn't hear anything else he said, nor did I feel his cold blade up against my skin right away. Justin; His name rushed through my mind but all that came with it was a *terminated* file.

"Surprised to see me?" He placed the knife back into his boot. "Drink," he put the water bottle back up to my mouth. This time, he was smarter, and held his hand over my mouth and jaw and pinched my nose until I swallowed every bit. My mind went all over the place; I could hardly focus on spitting anything back. I stared at his face, hoping to see only a close look alike, a twin perhaps. He had a wound on his right cheek, a deep cut that would likely turn into a scar, but nothing else seemed different.

"How?" I managed to ask after he pulled the water away and let me catch my breath. Then, I remembered; I didn't see the bullet enter his chest. I only heard the gunshot. My mind had played yet another trick on me.

"You Christians are all the same," Justin's voice practically turned to pity, "blind and ignorant. You should've killed him on the cliff."

"Now he's going to kill me, isn't he?"

"Most likely," Justin said casually. His response made me wonder if Anthony said anything to Justin about what was growing inside of me. "It depends on whether or not your friends decide that your life is more important than their precious Ichthys."

"I swear, in all of our time together, no one has ever mentioned a thing like that before."

"I'm not the one you have to convince," Justin turned and looked at Anthony. "Although, I bet that argument won't help your chances."

"At least tell me what it is?" I played the pity card as best I could.

"Farrell," Anthony yelled.

"I can't do that," Justin said as he stood up in attention. "Yes sir," he then walked to meet Anthony and the two went on to talk about things I couldn't hear. Every now and then, they would look at me. While they talked, I pulled at my cuffs and watched the men who were prying at the cellar door. They seemed to give up and began placing something small all around its edges. I laughed at their struggles. It was fulfilling to know my friends were safe.

I stared at Darius' body, which they piled with the other three a little ways away from the door. Part of me grew furious seeing his body disgraced with the others, but the Spirit reminded me that Darius was no longer the man I knew in the flesh. I wished to join Darius. Perhaps my purpose wasn't complete but, if that were the case, then why did God take Darius? He had gained so much progress with Lorenzo. Surely, Darius needed to finish the task… speaking of Lorenzo… He hadn't returned with Darius, nor was he standing with Anthony's men. If they killed him, then perhaps that's why God called Darius home too. *No, you can't think like this.* I reminded myself. *This wasn't God's plan.* God didn't take Darius home; Erica killed him.

Anthony distracted me as he started to yell at Justin. Spittle left his mouth as he got in Justin's face. Justin stood firm, not moving a muscle, until Anthony pointed in my direction. Justin came back towards me with his gun in hand. Then he began to undo my handcuffs. I wasn't too far gone to play my cards. I could be whoever I needed to be right now.

"It seems your ride has arrived early," Justin stood me up and re-cuffed my hands behind me. I heard motors rumbling from the distant road. After a minute or two, we started to walk to the vehicles driving towards us. He gripped my arm tight. I dug my feet into the ground. I didn't want to leave without knowing what would become of my friends.

"You told me, in the cave, that you had done all you could to save me," I said, trying to stall. He didn't turn to face me and kept dragging me forward. "Why not help save me now?" Still he gave no sign to show me he heard me. "Or was all of that a lie just to trick me into trusting *him*?"

"Things are different now," Justin said. He still wouldn't look at me. "You had your chance."

"What changed? I mean, come on. You have the military skills. Let me go free and we can both get out of here."

"Not this time," his answers were too short for me to get a read on him. I almost pulled from his grip but he regained his hold faster than I could run. Finally, I did what I should have done initially and plopped myself on the ground like a two year old throwing a tantrum.

"I'll move when you give me an answer."

He didn't respond, nor did he try to get me to move. He just stood there, breathing…thinking.

"Come on. I'm as good as dead. What's it going to hurt for me to know something?" Inside, I was irate but outwardly, I kept my helpless composure.

"I don't know anything about the stupid Ichthys," he grumbled. His eyes, angry yet confused, reminded me of our struggles in the cave. Something didn't add up.

I shook my head, "I don't care about the Ichthys."

"Then what do you want to know?" He slightly cocked his head.

Everything, I thought. If he had the time to answer me, I'd ask him to start explaining, from day one, how we got this far. I'd want an explanation for every murdered body, but for now, I'd settle for the truth to only one question, "You told Anthony, in the cave, to tell me what he did to me. What were you referring to?"

All color left Justin's face. I couldn't tell if it was from embarrassment or regret. He knew, but I needed him to say it. "Let's go," he demanded.

"Answer me!" I yelled while pulling from him.

Justin glanced towards Anthony and then back at me. "He took advantage of you in a way that no man should," he said. That was enough. His lack of eye contact said the rest.

"Please tell me this is all just a sick prank," I stared at him.

"They wanted to kill you. I convinced them to spare you," Justin acted as if I should be grateful. "It didn't feel right. You were defenseless."

I scoffed, "Right…you didn't feel right about killing me, but you let him rape me and now you're perfectly fine with throwing me to the wolves." My head spun with questions, "You could have left with us in the cave. You could have prevented all of this from happening."

Straightening his stance, Justin said, "Questions are over. You'll find no more mercy from me, not this round. Now, get up." He pulled me hard, practically jerking my arm out of socket.

I attempted to sit back down, but a loud explosion jolted me to my feet. The blast came from the cellar. They completely blew the door away. Justin wouldn't let me run to my friends' aid, but he didn't force me to keep walking either. The two of us stood, staring at the cellar as three uniformed men went through the smoke and down the stairs.

"Protect them," I begged to God. "Don't let them die like this."

CHAPTER 33

Do nothing out of selfish ambition or vain conceit, but in humility consider others better than yourselves.
—Philippians 2:3 (NIV)

"Now comes the moment of truth," Anthony snuck up on me. "We'll see what your friends truly value."

The answer was God; they value God the most. No matter what tricks Anthony thought he had up his sleeve, he wouldn't deter them.

Gunfire echoed from underground. Anthony's men waited for his orders. I, too, prepared myself, begging God to spare my friends. The gunfire ceased. The smoke faded. Through the cellar entrance, a guard emerged. He had no weapon or prisoner in hand. He was the prisoner. My heart leapt. Steven held the guard's arm behind his back, directing him with a gun centered on the back of the guard's head. Another guard walked out with David behind him. Jeffrey held the third captive in the same way.

"Lower your weapons," Steven said firmly.

The four guards surrounding them didn't move.

"They only listen to me," Anthony toyed with Steven.

"Then tell them to drop their weapons or these men die," Steven spoke with authority, leaving no question in my mind that he would pull the trigger.

Anthony rolled his hand in the air in front of him. "Shoot them," he said as if he didn't care.

No one moved.

"That's alright, we'll do it for you," Anthony waved his hand. All three guards fell dead onto Steven, Jeffrey, and David, causing them to lose their balance. In an instant, a battle broke out. The men who surrounded them lowered their weapons and attempted to take my friends down by force. David ducked from his attacker and knocked him to the ground. Steven dodged a few swings and landed a couple back into his attacker's gut. Jeffrey plummeted to the ground with his attacker on top of him. Steven saw Jeffrey in danger. He spun on his heel and tackled the man on top of Jeffrey. I struggled against my restraints to go help them. The longer Justin forced me to watch, refusing to let me go, the more enraged I became.

Anthony whistled and more men from the tree line marched in to help. My friends held their own against Anthony's trained goons. Jasmine and Angelica burst out of the cellar entrance with tools in their hands. Swinging left and right at the guards, screaming and hollering, they managed to knock one out cold. Another caught Jasmine's wrist midair and slung her to the ground. Jeffrey, now on his feet, ran to her aid. Throwing his shoulder full force into the guard's stomach, he picked him up off the ground, and slammed him into what was left of the chimney. Angelica, caught in a grasp from behind, threw her head up into her attacker's nose. He stumbled as David planted his fist in the side of the guard's face. More men continued to surround my friends until they were overpowered. It took two guards each to hold them down. It took three to subdue Steven. Overrun by these malicious men, all five found themselves captive once more. When the guards stood my friends up, Anthony strode towards them.

"Traitor!" Steven and Jeffrey both yelled at him.

"I never left sides," Anthony laughed. "Now, tell me what I want to know about the Ichthys."

No one replied. In fact, all of them reacted the same way I had; with confused faces and unsure answers; everyone except David. As David tried to speak up, the two men holding him pulled him forward.

"Let them go," David demanded.

"What will you give me in return?" Anthony's snake like tone revealed he didn't plan to make any deals.

"You won't get any information out of us. We don't know anything about the Ichthys," David struggled against his restrainers, "but I can tell you who does."

"I already know that," Anthony sounded annoyed and gave another wave of his hand. One of the guards threw a sack over David's head and knocked him unconscious. "That's why I need you alive," a maniacal laugh erupted from Anthony's lips. The guards drug David towards the vehicle where Justin previously had been escorting me. "Dispose of the others," Anthony commanded. The guards immediately threw everyone else back down into the cellar. A few of the other guards already had the cellar door, as messed up as it was, ready to close up the entrance. One by one, they threw scraps and materials on top of the door to weigh it down. They included Darius' body and their dead comrades. A few guards stood next to the cellar, shooting at it every time my friends tried to push the door open.

The vehicle they placed David in drove off the same way it came. I twisted, bit, pulled, scratched, and punched to get out of Justin's grip. He eventually managed to pick me up in a fireman's hold, but that didn't stop me from fighting him. Kneeing him in the jaw, I knocked him off balance, dropping him to the ground. I fell with him. Once on the ground, I gave him a few more good kicks as I rolled away from him. I struggled to stand. Justin didn't stay down long and palmed his hand over my head shoving it into the hard gravel.

"Okay, okay," I tried to get him to lighten up. My head felt as if it would implode.

"Farrell," Anthony growled and immediately he knocked the weight of Justin off me. "I told you not to harm her."

My eyes blacked out for a second as I tried to stand. Everything spun. The guards were now pouring gasoline over the pile of rubble and bodies that held down the cellar door. I could hear my friends' yells from below. Held firmly in place by Justin once again, I felt helpless. I wanted to pray, but my heart grieved too much to know what to say. As if I had no other choice, I began to recite Psalm 91:

"He who dwells in the shelter of the Most High
will rest in the shadow of the Almighty.
I will say of the Lord, 'He is my Refuge and
my Fortress, my God, in whom I trust.'

Surely, He will save you from the fowler's
snare and from the deadly pestilence.
He will cover you with His feathers, and
under His wings will you find refuge;
His faithfulness will be your shield and rampart.
You will not fear the terror of night, nor
the arrow that flies by day,
nor the pestilence that stalks in the darkness,
nor the plague that destroys at midday.
A thousand may fall at your side, ten
thousand at your right hand,
but it will not come near you.
You will only observe with your eyes and
see the punishment of the wicked.
If you make the Most High your Dwelling–
even the LORD, who is my Refuge–
then no harm will befall you, no disaster
will come near your tent.
For He will command His angels concerning
you to guard you in all your ways;
they will lift you up in their hands, so that you
will not strike your foot against a stone.
You will tread upon the lion and the cobra;
you will trample the great lion and the serpent.[11]"

I thought on the meaning of the psalm. It became clearer in my heart. *I will trust in God. No evil shall overcome me.* That doesn't mean that bad things won't happen, but it does mean that no evil will take root in my heart. I pushed my anger, fears, and concern for my friends aside reminding myself that God is in control. Closing my eyes, I took in a breath. The wind started to pick up. Anthony and Justin shifted uncomfortably. They yelled at me to

[11] Psalm 91:1–13 (NIV)

be quiet. I finished the Psalm but God's Spirit flowed through me and again I said it even louder. The wind blew even faster. Opening my eyes, I half expected to see a gun in my face. Instead, I saw Anthony and Justin both in a defensive stance. Anthony had his gun out while Justin had his knife. They looked scared. I glanced around and saw man after man fall to the ground. I didn't hear any gunshots, but I could see the bullet like wounds.

I finished the psalm again, smiling as I saw the fear in their eyes,

"'Because he loves Me,' says the Lord, 'I will rescue him;
I will protect him, for he acknowledges My name.
He will call upon Me, and I will answer him;
I will be with him in trouble; I will deliver him and honor him.
With long life will I satisfy him and show him My salvation.'[12]"

Repeatedly, Anthony yelled at me to be silent. I yelled louder, clear to the top of my lungs,

"He who dwells in the shelter of the Most High
will rest in the shadow of the Almighty.
I will say of the Lord, 'He is my Refuge and my
Fortress, my God, in whom I trust.'[13]"

The butt of Anthony's gun swung towards my face. I had enough time to move, but it still managed to graze my ear. I smiled inside at the fear in his eyes but, outwardly, I wore the face of peace. "God is here. He always has been and always will be. He won't leave me, or forsake me, no matter where you take me."

Another man dropped dead on the ground. Anthony tried to get us to his vehicle, but when the men near it fell one after another, he commanded Justin to fall back behind the tree line.

---

[12] Psalm 91:14–16 (NIV)

[13] Psalm 91:1–2 (NIV)

When we reached it, Anthony grabbed my neck and made me stare into his eyes.

"Call your God off, or your friends die," Anthony held his arm high. "One wave of my hand and your friends go up in flames."

I looked out at the soldiers. Though ten or fifteen had fallen, there were still twenty more with their eyes waiting for Anthony's orders. Did he honestly think God was doing this? Even if God was, I couldn't do anything to stop Him. "Am I more than God; that I can tell Him what to do?" I had no reason to doubt that Anthony would give the signal, but I had no way to stop what was happening to his men. Another man dropped not too far from us.

Anthony commanded me once more, "Last chance. Call Him off, now!"

I screamed back at him, "I can't!" My heart shattered at the look of fire I saw in his eyes. The wind turned into a heavy gust. Anthony waved his hand across the sky. Everyone began to run away from the cellar as one man tossed a match over the stack of junk on top of the cellar door. My heart cried out for justice while the force of the explosion slammed us back to the ground.

Anthony obviously didn't plan on the explosion or he wouldn't have started cursing at his men while trying to stand. Through the echoes in my head, I could feel the world spin around me. My ears rang again, but this time they wouldn't stop. The dirt in the air slammed against my face. *What are you doing? Get up!* I pushed back all of the shock that came over my body. Justin's hand no longer imprisoned me. I rolled to my stomach with my hands still cuffed behind my back, pulled my feet underneath, and jumped up to run. I couldn't help my friends. Running towards the explosion would do no good. At least in the trees, I had a chance. The cuffs pinning my hands behind me slowed me down, but I had a head start.

Dodging trees this way and that, I attempted to leap over fallen logs and tried to keep my balance. The wind died down the further I ran. The ground beneath me moved when my steps disturbed families of rodents and bugs of all sorts. The ground became moist. My shoes soaked in the dew. I stepped on a mossy rock before realizing it and fell flat on my face. Without my arms and hands able to catch my fall, my mouth and cheek planted into a tiny stream that flowed beneath the pinecones and needles. I love seeing how diverse God is in His creation, but now was not the time to sit and marvel. I needed to get back on my feet. I rolled to my side to force myself back up. Two black boots stood in my path. My heart dropped.

"Be grateful I've been ordered not to harm you," Justin said harshly as his giant, bloodied hands picked me up from the ground. He then turned me around and started to march me back across the terrain I had just passed. Dragging my feet didn't work this time. He kept pressure below my arm that prevented me from pulling my weight down towards the ground. Justin seemed to find joy in pulling me through all of the low hanging tree branches and scraping me along the sides of the thorn bushes. I guess, technically, it was the bushes harming me and not him, but I'm not so sure Anthony would see it that way.

"What kind of soldier does this to people," I insulted, "especially in their own country?"

"The kind that doesn't work for the country," Justin sneered.

"You don't have to do this," I tried to negotiate, pulling against him. "There's still hope for you."

"This isn't about me, or you," he said grimly.

"Then who's it about?"

Justin stopped and whipped me around. I met his stone cold eyes. "You're not the only person held captive," spittle from his lips splashed in my face. "Stop acting so selfishly and start thinking about others for once."

Cautiously, I searched for an explanation.

"My sister is depending on me. If I let you go, she dies."

Still confused, I shook my head. I didn't know how to respond. I had fallen for his lies and tricks in the past but there was urgency in his voice, almost desperation, that hadn't been there before. He pulled out a picture from his pocket and showed it to me. A young brown haired woman, close to my age, stood next to Justin in a very elegant blue dress. In the picture, Justin was dressed in a military uniform holding a medal. "I don't understand," I said.

"I was in the Army, long ago, but I'm in over my head with the wrong people. Now, I'm Tereski's puppet. He has my sister. He made that very clear when he pinned me in the cave. I had no other choice but to take the fall. If I don't carry out his orders, Brittany will be at his mercy, and I'll be executed," he put the picture back in his pocket and pulled up his right sleeve. Strapped tightly to his forearm was a small box with wires all around. "This is a tracker," he said. "All it takes is one push of a button from Anthony and my veins fill will poison. He's the only one with a key to remove it."

I dropped to the ground in desperation. He let me go and stood over me, ready for any move I might make. I didn't feel like running any more. My friends were dead. Life as I knew it was over. The only thing left for me, was suffering. "He's forcing me to carry his child," I cried. Justin needed to know the whole truth if he planned to place me back into the lions' den. As the word 'child' left my mouth, the reality of my situation hit me like a punch in the gut. I could no longer deny it. I had the enemy's child growing inside of me.

Justin's upper left lip rose as he snarled. He turned and threw his fist into the tree nearest to him. "No," he repeated this several times waving his hand at me as if he was going to hit me next. "No, you won't fool me like that."

"It's not a trick," I cried. "That's why he's keeping me alive."

"Do you swear this is the truth?"

"Yes," I sobbed.

"On your God's name?"

"God knows it's the truth. I didn't want it to be... I've tried denying it... but I can't."

"Could it be anyone else's?"

Offended, I shouted, "You told me yourself what he did to me on the mountain side. Why deny it now?"

Justin's silence confirmed all speculation. "Kill it. Get rid of it. He cannot have an heir," Justin huffed and puffed.

"It's a child."

"Tereski will raise it to destroy your people and, thus, this country."

I shook my head.

Justin knelt down in front of me, "Anthony needs two things to become supreme monarch of this nation, but he will be a tyrant: The Ichthys, which is some type of item that can supposedly protect Christians from him, and an heir of his bloodline born from a Christian mother. He'll find the Ichthys now that he has David. You need to end this now."

"I can't," I exclaimed. "Let America defend itself."

"It can't," Justin said. "The U.S. is already starting to fall apart. Tereski's people have infiltrated the nation from the inside out. His followers have the upper hand. They're in every leadership position possible. Soon, it'll crumble as every soldier and politician who refused to succumb to a new rule are either killed or taken captive."

I gaped at Justin. Everything he said sounded like what Anthony told us in the cellar. That meant that Anthony was the one planting terrorists into power positions and having them claim to be Christians when their plots unfold. He was behind all of our suffering. If one man could really hold that much power, there's no telling what else he was capable of doing. "What does this have to do with the child?" I asked.

"The only people standing between Tereski and his new reign are Christians. An oracle, witch, palm reader, gypsy type woman told him that your God could stop him, but not if he had an heir from a Christian woman. That *thing* inside of you assures Tereski's success. He will raise *it* and use *it* to take out every Christian left in this nation. When you're all gone, there will be no one left who can stand against him."

I shook my head, wiping the tears and snot from my face with my knee. A child born from a Christian to destroy the Christians; is that even possible? Still, my decision was final, "I can't end an innocent life."

Justin stood up cursing the situation, and then hit the tree a few more times. When he stopped, he stood with his shoulders back. "Get up," he pulled me to my feet. "You will help me save my sister."

I immediately resisted.

"If you do this," he said, "I'll help you escape with your child; even at the expense of my own life. But, not until I see my sister freed."

I stopped struggling. It didn't matter if he kept his promise. Inside, I felt compelled to help him rescue his sister. I felt God permitting me to stay. "Okay," I submitted.

"Thank you," Justin's grip on my arm lightened and he no longer walked me into the branches and thorns. His pace slowed when he saw me weeping. I wept for my friends. He stopped me and let me have a moment. He took his sleeve and wiped my face. What would become of my world without Steven's jokes and Jeffrey's protection? How would Jasmine's family cope, knowing someone murdered their daughter in the same country they came to, to find freedom? How was David going to handle losing his best friend's sister? What am I…?

CHAPTER 34

"Be strong and courageous. Do not be afraid or terrified because of them, for the L*ORD your God goes with you; He will never leave you nor forsake you."*
—Deuteronomy 31:6 (NIV)

Anthony met us in the trees with three men guarding him. The wind had ceased.

"Well, well," he smiled slyly, "looks like there's hope in your future yet, Farrell." With the snap of his fingers, the three men stood around Anthony in a triangle formation while Justin and I followed. We stayed in the cover of the tree line until two jeeps came to meet us. They weaved their way into the trees and Anthony rushed us to jump inside and sit down low. Anthony, Justin, and I all got into the back of one while the other three men piled into the second jeep. Justin placed me up against a set of bars that I could hold on to with my hands behind my back. Then, as fast as they had come, we peeled out of the forest, over rocks and mounds, bouncing us all over the place. Through the trees behind us, I could see smoke still rising from the earlier explosion. I shed more tears for the loss of my friends. I was grateful we had shared our faith in God. Through that, we would always stay connected.

A red dot appeared on Justin's back. I leaned in to block its path and turned in the direction from where it came. I couldn't believe I was trying to save him. I peered out into the distance searching for the gunman. God let me see someone crouched in the bushes. Anthony focused on the driver. Justin watched the terrain in front of us. No one saw the danger but me. Still, if someone was aiming for Justin, I had no guarantee he would kill Anthony too. If Justin died and Anthony lived, I would have no one on my side.

The laser mark moved and the jeep in front of us suddenly caught fire. The wheels turned and the vehicle began to roll. Our vehicle swerved, maneuvering out of the flying automobile's way, and we all ducked. Justin gripped my arm. I had a hold of the bar behind me but, as my body flung one way and then the next, I felt my grip loosen and was grateful for Justin's quick reflexes. My heart raced as I saw the gravel below. Justin helped me back to my seat. He placed me up against the bars and found a rope to fasten around me like a seatbelt. I gaped at the jeep engulfed in flames.

Anthony never ordered the driver to turn around and help their friends. He kept his eyes on the clearing ahead demanding they drive faster.

As we traveled, for what seemed like hours while the sun rose higher in the sky, I attempted to be an irritating splinter under Anthony's skin. "You murdered four American soldiers. No matter how much of a terrorist you've made me out to be as a Christian you'll be just as high on the government's wanted list."

Looking at me, Anthony smirked, "You still don't get it. They may have dressed in American uniforms, but any soldier who still claimed allegiance to America died during their attempt to save your pathetic people from that camp."

"Then, why did you kill your sister and those men?"

He laughed, "Erica was interfering with my plans. I don't know why father thought she could rule a country. He didn't even assign her his last name. Her life and the lives of the men who followed her are a small price to pay for my country. Father will approve."

"Still, how could your father approve of you killing his daughter?" I probed.

Anthony brushed off my inquiry with a huff as he turned his head away from me.

"You forget that America has allies," I shouted at him. "You'll never get away with what you've done. You'll lose the power you seek in less time than it took you to gain it."

"I wouldn't be too sure of that, Miss Monzel," Anthony said haughtily. "You haven't seen anything yet. This country is already beginning to bow to me and, soon, you will too. You and all of your other wretched little Christian friends will have no choice but to obey my commands."

"I'll never serve anyone but God. You'll have to kill me first."

"That's the plan," he said delightfully. He faced forward with his smug look held firmly in place.

Justin kept his distance but his eyes were always on me,

guarding me as ordered. I wondered how Anthony managed to pull Justin and his sister into this mess. An even better question is how did Justin expect to get us all out of it?

We pulled up to a large metal gate connected to an even larger brick wall that had razor wire spiraled across the top and camo netting covering its entirety. The gate opened after Anthony made his presence known. Inside, armed men and women guarded the wall and surrounded the jeep. They had on camouflaged uniforms, with a flag patched to both shoulder sleeves. It resembled an upside down American flag, with black and blue stripes and red stars on a white background. Five large bunkers in front of us had the same flag painted on them. Enormous equipment, covered in weighted down camouflaged tarps, sat all around the land inside of the wall. The same camo netting that covered the walls also covered every building in sight, and armed men stood at every visible doorway. A prison looked more inviting than this compound.

Approaching the middle of the bunkers with the flags painted on them, the vehicles stopped. The buildings looked like airplane hangars. Anthony forced me out of the jeep and Justin held my arm, guiding me on when to go and when to stop. He kept his grip firm but light. I would do my best to cooperate as long as he put trust in me. Anthony stood in front of the building and, again, the doors opened for him. There had to be at least fifty jets lined up on each side of the hangar. Each jet had the degraded flag painted on the tail fin. In the back of the building, a staircase led up to a room with glass walls, where Anthony had two guards standing at the door. One guard opened the door for us while the other stood straight, not making eye contact.

The room was a holding cell. I assumed the walls were made of glass so everyone could watch me, the new prisoner. A small stall in the corner to my right connected to the metal hangar wall. Inside, a toilet, shower, and sink crammed closely together. On the opposite side of the room sat a bed with a very fancy bedspread that didn't fit its surroundings. Beside it was a nightstand with a small box on top. The floor had a thick, red rug next to the bed, but everything else was the same metal as the bunker.

Justin released me into Anthony's custody and stood at the doorway. I wished to stay with him. I trusted him, not completely, but more than anyone else, for the moment. Anthony walked me to the center of the room. His hand gently slid down my arm. I shuddered. Trying to pull away, he forced my cuffed hands up to the center of my back. A searing pain came to my shoulders, forcing me to submit. Again, he brushed his other hand over my arm. I clenched my teeth, breathing heavily. Closing my eyes, I held the tears back. I tried not to imagine his plans. I felt the pressure of the cuffs leave my wrists. My arms pained as I jerked away from him. Spinning around, I readied for a fight. Anthony laughed while holding the cuffs up for me to see. All of that was just more of his games to instill fear in me. His laughter revolted me. I resisted the urge to rub my wrists as the pain in my arms subsided. I would not let Anthony have satisfaction in knowing what a relief he provided me.

"First things first," Anthony smirked grabbing the box off the top of the nightstand. He pulled from it a white, plastic stick.

"You're joking," I glared as I examined the item and the box. "I'm not peeing on that with you in here."

"You can close the door," he continued to hold that stupid smirk. "I need to know if you're actually pregnant with my heir or if we need to…try again." He opened the drawer to the nightstand and revealed several more boxes similar to the one he held.

Revulsion laced with curiosity filled my entire being. My heart slammed against my chest. I wanted to know, just as badly as Anthony did, but I didn't want Anthony knowing. He forced the pregnancy test into my hand and motioned towards the bathroom.

I refused to move.

"Let me make this easier on you," he pointed his gun at my head.

My heart exploded, but only for a moment. "You wouldn't kill me before knowing the truth," I chided.

"Maybe not," he then pointed his gun at my leg, "but I could make you suffer."

As if I wasn't already suffering. *Just do it,* a voice in my head said. *It's only a stupid test.* Taking baby steps towards the bathroom stall, I contemplated what to do next. I shut the door behind me and stared at the pregnancy stick. *If it's negative, then any chance I have at freedom goes out the window, and he may rape me again,* I shuddered. *If it's positive, I have to face that I'm pregnant with my enemy's child.* I realized my hand was shaking. *If it turns out positive, would Justin fulfill his end of our deal?*

As I sat to take the test, the room felt as if it were on fire. I started to sweat from head to toe. The harder I tried to urinate the less it felt possible. I resorted to turning on the sink faucet. Sure enough it worked. Now, I just had to wait. I wanted to pray, but didn't know what to pray for. "God, I need You," I finally whispered. "I can't do this." I closed my eyes as I washed my hands. I avoided looking at the *stick of fate* that I placed on the edge of the sink.

Breathe, I told myself. *Just breathe.*

Upon opening my eyes, I saw the results. It came up positive. I was now sure my life was over. I couldn't bear the thought of being raped just so he could have an heir. I stared at the stick. Would God change the results?

"I'm waiting," Anthony said outside the door.

Don't leave me here, Father.

Anthony shoved a set of clothes into my hands as I stepped out the door. "Make yourself at home. You'll be here for quite some time. Just about eight or nine months," he snickered.

I almost vomited. This would never be home. "I'd much prefer the floors of the cave and cellar than this prison."

Anthony chuckled, "That life is long gone. You may as well get used to it."

I dropped the clothes he handed me and crossed my arms.

"I really wish you'd warm back up to me. We were becoming quite the pair before… a few, minor setbacks."

"You mean, before you betrayed us all and murdered my friends," I glared.

He stared at me, as if I was supposed to have forgotten about all of that. I refused to look away this time. He kept my gaze, but ignored my comment. "You'll find a shower will do you some good. I expect you to look more decent before I return," he gestured to the clothes on the ground. With that, he attempted to leave.

"That's it?" I said, causing him to turn around. "You're not even going to look at the test?"

"I don't need to," he said slyly. "You're the one who needed convincing." He turned and walked with Justin out the door, leaving the two men standing outside to guard me. I watched for Justin to turn back or give me a sign that he would keep up his end of the bargain, but he gave none. The anger that began to settle in my soul turned to despair.

He had tricked me. Anthony needed me to know the truth, so I couldn't hold the 'what ifs' over his head. He needed me to know he now had full control over my life. Whether I stayed in this prison or escaped, he would forever have a hold on me that I couldn't evade. I glared at him as he walked out of the hangar. *If I play my cards right, you won't touch me for another eight or nine months. For what you're putting me through, I'll make your life more miserable every time I see you.*

CHAPTER 35

In my distress I called to the Lord; I cried to my God for help. From His temple He heard my voice; my cry came before Him, into His ears.
—Psalm 18:6 (NIV)

I stood for what seemed like an eternity pacing the room, searching for a weak spot in the glass, and watching everyone who walked by below. They stared at me as if I were a circus animal. When I tired of pacing, I forced myself to stand at the door and speak to the guards. They wouldn't reply, in fact they never acknowledged my presence, but it made me feel better to assume they heard me. I wanted to yell at them, or try to bribe them to free me, but the Spirit urged me to speak encouragement. Laughing at myself, I wondered why I would encourage my captors, but God's Spirit pressed me even more. With their backs to the window, I couldn't see their faces. Still, God reminded me that they aren't just soldiers. They're people.

These men may be fathers with families and pets, and do chores at home. They probably, at one time or another, broke a girl's heart or had their hearts broken. They may have friends, parents, and mortgages. Anthony may have even trapped them into serving him as he did with Justin. Humbly, I asked God to speak through me, "You are a man. A man made to change the world; a man with the ability to change a life. God created you out of love, to love. Built with the strength of an ox, you still have enough gentleness to tend to a child. Entrusted with the secrets of life, and given the key to success, you can do anything you put your mind to…"

I continued with positive things, telling them of who God made them to be, "As a baby, you were innocent. As a child, you were immature. You made mistakes, but you learned. You gained confidence with each fall you overcame. You are made for good." I repeated similar ideas and sayings, never seeing a response or change in anyone other than myself. My heart embraced a sense of stillness as I saw how God could love these men. I wondered, then, if they really knew they worked for a monster. Perhaps these men didn't know the full scope of their leader's plan and this was just another job to them.

The doors at the other end of the hangar opened. I immediately eyed the figure walking towards my cell. It was Justin, carrying a tray with food and water. My mouth started to salivate the closer he came but, when he got to the door, I stepped back and forced myself to stand in the center of the room.

"General Tereski sent these for you," Justin said, placing the tray on the nightstand.

General? I never heard Justin use Anthony's title before. "When did he become a General?"

"When he killed Major Simmons, Doctor Tereski, now the former General, saw his son fit for a promotion."

His family was more warped than I could have imagined. I looked at the food again. "Tell your *General* thanks, but no thanks," I begrudged.

Justin shook his head, "I leave when that tray is emptied." He seemed cold and distant, as if we never talked.

Getting nowhere with Justin, I stared at the tray. Sausage and cheese slices, crackers, and grapes all called to my empty stomach. It seemed like days ago since I had eaten. This meal was more food than I had in the past two months since the beginning of this nightmare.

"It's not poisoned," he said. I could almost hear a slight joke in his tone, but his facial expression stayed the same.

I reached out and popped one grape after another into my mouth. I chased the crackers and cheese with water as they sucked all the moisture from my mouth. The sausage I saved for last. It had been so long since I tasted the savory flavor of any meat, and sausage was one of my favorites. After cleaning the tray, I noticed an oval, pink pill in the corner. "What's this?" I questioned suspiciously.

"Vitamins for the child," Justin said. "You'll be required to take them once a day."

I contemplated a rebuttal before tossing the pill in the back of my mouth and finishing off the glass of water. There was no use in arguing. I knew I would either have to take it by choice or later have it forced down my throat. The latter wouldn't be pleasant and would only cause me problems. I needed to rebuild my strength.

Picking the tray up, I took it to Justin and placed it in his hands. "It's empty," I said. "You can leave now." If he wanted to be cold towards me, I'd return the favor. I hope that he hasn't forgotten about our deal so soon.

Justin grabbed the tray, and my hand with it. He whispered, very quietly, "You need to shower and change."

Taken back by this, I attempted to smell my clothes.

"If you don't start complying, Tereski will do it for you," he then let go of my hand and took the tray and cup with him. "The General will be by to see you soon," he said before opening the door. Was that his idea of a warning? I shuddered at the thought of Anthony touching me again, and nearly vomited when thinking of him trying to force me to change clothes. For that reason alone, I would comply.

I took the clothes with me into the stall and turned on the shower. Running my hand under the streams of water, I waited for it to get warm. Small, hotel sized bottles of shampoo, conditioner, and body wash were on a shelf in the corner of the shower. A washrag lay folded beside them. *I may as well make this count,* I thought to myself as I readied to take the quickest shower of my life. The bathroom door only had a twist lock on it, and was easy to open from the outside. I didn't want to give Anthony a chance to sneak in on me.

I stripped down fast and jumped into the shower, closing the door behind me. Throwing shampoo in my hair, I soaked the rag and began scrubbing every possible inch of my body. I watched the brown soapy water flow down the drain. The warm water grew hotter, relaxing my muscles as I took in a deep breath of steam. Scrubbing my arms and legs, I felt as if I was turning human again. For a moment, I forgot they had me in a cage. I imagined being back home, readying for another day with my family. I wanted to fall asleep in my daydreams, and never wake up.

I could feel the shampoo bubbles tickling my forehead, making its way to my eyes. I rinsed it out of my tangles and splashed water in my face. When lathering my hair with conditioner, I let my fingers run through each knot, pulling them apart. A few broken pine needles needed a forceful pulling before they let go of their nests. Had my mom seen these kinds of tangles in my hair as a kid, she would have shaved me bald. I laughed to myself, thinking about the time my sister had melted marshmallows in her hair. She was five. It appeared as if she took a marshmallow, squashed it in both hands, and ran her fingers through her hair from her ears down the strands. Her hair had been long and past her mid back. Mom gave her the choppiest looking haircut I had ever seen.

A creak of a door hinge brought me back to the present. I had showered longer than planned. Shutting the water off, I listened for footsteps. I held tight to the shower door. *Please don't let them in here,* I prayed. The towel hung just outside the door by the sink. If I threw my arm out, I could wrap myself before anyone could see me. *Three...two...*I reached through the small opening and made for the towel on the wall. It wouldn't pull off the hook. I shook it a few times and finally it popped loose. When I got it in the shower with me, I wrapped it tightly around my body, almost cutting off all circulation, and listened again. Slowly opening the shower door, I poked out my head. I stood alone in the stall, save for my reflection.

The clothes given to me were a set of undergarments, sweat pants, thick and warm, and a plain gray tee shirt. It was nice to be clean from head to toe. With it, came a hooded sweater made of the same material as the pants. None of the items had pockets, which made me wonder if Anthony got them on purpose so that I couldn't hide anything from him. Wrapping the towel around my head, I stepped out of the stall and into my cell, only to see water drops sliding down the fogged glass. The steam from my shower turned the place into a sauna.

"Ah, that's much better. Wouldn't you say?"

I jumped at the sound of Anthony's voice. I hadn't noticed him sitting on the bed. Seeing him brought all the anger that I had pushed aside, back to a white, hot flame that I knew I had to control.

"I brought you a full pitcher of water," he pointed to a pitcher and glass of ice placed on the nightstand. "It's best you stay hydrated while carrying my heir."

My stomach churned to think about it. I wish I could just forget and make it go away.

"How did you find your dinner? Filling, I hope."

I tried to ignore him, taking the towel off my head, and throwing it back in the bathroom over the sink.

Seeing I wasn't going to respond, Anthony stood and walked towards the door to leave. I stepped out of his way, keeping my distance. When he walked by the stall, he took the towel and my old clothes. "It's best we get rid of these," he smiled.

I watched as he walked out of the building. By that time, all of the fog had left the windows and people, again, watched me as they worked inside the hangar. I resorted to pulling the bedspread off the bed a little, until it touched the floor on the side facing the door. Then, I rolled myself underneath where no one could see me. I couldn't stand the thought of being comfortable when all my brothers and sisters in Christ were still running and hiding for their lives. There wasn't a lot of room for me under the bed, but it was enough to feel hidden.

My retreat reminded me of the morning of my first escape. I ran from Justin and Anthony, down the side of the mountain. Freedom was at the tip of my fingers, but something tripped me, causing me to have to hide in a hollowed log. Had I continued into the camp, I could have died in the explosions. Yet, God seemed to want to keep me alive. Then, Justin found me. He stood on top of the log, diverting everyone's eyes elsewhere. God seemed to put it on Justin's heart not to turn me in to Anthony at that moment.

God knew, even then, that I had conceived. He could have called me home at any moment that day, but He chose to keep me here.

I looked out from behind the comforter making certain that no one else was in the room. My little cave went dark as I draped the bedspread back. For a moment, I felt alone, away from human presence without guards, enemies, and onlookers, except I have a child with me. All feelings of solitary faded away. God is always with me, but that's different. I couldn't be alone at this moment or any moment in the future.

"God, I can't do this," I prayed. "I can't bring a child, created by sin, into a world of sin. I can't let it be the destruction of Your people. We've suffered enough. You, the God of the heavens and the earth, the Creator of all, You can end this. Just take my life and bring me home."

"I Am the only Creator," a voice came to me. It wasn't from in the room, but rather, from in my head. Still, it didn't sound like my voice.

I meditated, waiting in silence, wondering if I imagined things. Then, it dawned on me what the voice – God's voice – was saying. "Yes, You are the only Creator," I confirmed. "Which means this child, who has been *created,* couldn't have been created by sin." I took in a breath, trying to understand what this meant. "Even still, a sinful act was done and You allowed me to get pregnant because of it. Why?"

I wanted another spoken answer, but God didn't send one. I know He doesn't need to speak to give us an answer. Sometimes, He simply places the answers deep within us and lets us discover them at the right time. The answer to my question of "why," was one of those hidden answers.

"I will trust that You know what You're doing, but..." I paused. I had never been so firm with God and immediately lowered my tone. He didn't need my lectures. I still felt the need to remind Him of His promises, "...but, You have also told me that I can cast my burdens onto You. You can't lie and therefore, I ask You to let me give You this burden. I'll do whatever it takes to fall into Your footsteps of this plan, because I know You have already walked it. The battle is Yours and You have already won. Remind me of that constantly. I need Your guidance and wisdom. Alone, I'm not strong enough to go through with this but, in You, I know I can do all things."

I placed my hands on my stomach and allowed myself to imagine the child. Then, I prayed for him or her, that God's angels would protect us, and that the Spirit would begin to dwell in my baby even while in the womb. *My baby*...it was even more unbelievable to say. I felt the child was actually God's, not mine. I was His vessel. Keeping this in mind, I felt I would be able to rest.

I woke up to a brighter light than I could remember going to sleep to, but that was because I had pulled the bedspread down in my sleep and brought it underneath the bed with me. No one was in the room and only one guard stood at the door. The floors down below were vacant of onlookers. Continuing to feel God's peace, I drifted off to sleep once more.

CHAPTER 36

Be on your guard; stand firm in the faith; be men of courage; be strong.
—1 Corinthians 16:13 (NIV)

The door slammed shut, jolting me awake. I threw my head into a board supporting the box spring mattress. Rolling to my side, clenching my forehead, I could vaguely see a pair of black boots. Was Justin here to set me free? Anthony's face appeared below the bed as he bent down to see me.

"Good morning," he said obnoxiously. "Breakfast is served."

I didn't want to roll out, but I knew that if I didn't, he'd weasel his way under the bed with me. Anthony had two plates with him containing scrambled eggs, toast, and a glass of orange juice. "It's a lovely morning, isn't it?" He smiled.

"I wouldn't know," I frowned, moving my hands from my forehead to rub my eyes. "I'm a prisoner, remember?"

"You don't have to be," he sat the plates on the floor and gestured for me to sit.

I refused.

"I can make you," he reminded me sternly. "I'm giving you the option, for now."

I chose to avoid conflict and sat across from him as I yawned. I needed to use the restroom, but there was no way I'd go with Anthony still in my cell.

Anthony pushed the plate towards me. "Shall we?" He grinned.

A cunning smile crossed my face. "Yes," I said as I bowed my head and prayed. "Father, I thank You for this food, which only You have provided. Thank You for the sleep You also provided last night. I pray that You strengthen me during this time in prison. Help me to bring others to You just as Paul did. I also pray for Anthony, that You prick his heart and show him Your greatness as You did to Pharaoh. I love You, Father. Thank You for never leaving me. It's in Jesus' name that I pray. Amen." Smiling at Anthony, who tried hard to hide his frustrations, I took a bite of the toast.

"You're not going to change me," he said.

"You're not going to get me to fall for the nice guy act," I spat back.

"It's not an act. I just thought you'd like some company."

"God is all the company I need. I'm never alone, not even in death."

He laughed as he leaned back, "You are truly something else." His stance reminded me of the first time I saw him. He sat by me at the table, flaunting his arrogance with his sunglasses and eye watering cologne.

The wheels in my head began to spin, "How long were you planning this?"

"Since I woke up this morning," he reached down to get his first bite of eggs. "I thought you'd enjoy a home cooked meal after all you've been through."

"Not the breakfast," I corrected as I took another bite, though I assume he knew what I meant. "You knew exactly what you were doing when you first sat at the table with me and my friends didn't you? There was a reason you picked me."

Anthony leaned in, as if ready to divulge something important. I kept my distance. "Don't think so highly of yourself," he scoffed. "You were never the target, only a means to an end."

"No," I shook my head. "You had your eye on me everywhere I went. You befriended the members of my group to get closer to me..."

Anthony seemed amused by my scenario and shook his head.

I paused, "You... wanted David. Somehow, you knew he was close with my group. You weren't following me. You followed him." I should have seen it sooner. All this time I thought he was using David to get close to me, when it was the opposite. "Why?"

Anthony chuckled, "Your boyfriend isn't the end target either. He is, however, our key to getting there. With you at our disposal, he'll be more cooperative. He doesn't know you'll die before I ever let you go."

I suddenly lost my appetite, but continued to clean my plate out of fear of being force-fed. A moment of silence went by. "Do you plan to free him?" I asked, assuming the answer already.

"No," Anthony smirked, "but that's the joy of being in control. You can offer false hope for anything in the world, and people are bound to take the bait eventually."

"David won't," I finished the last bite of egg. "He'll never fall for your tricks."

"He already has, and so have you," Anthony reminded me of my past failures. He stood, grabbing our empty plates and left the bunker without looking back.

Anger and sorrow welled up inside. Anthony challenged everything I knew to be true about people. I could feel the walls closing in as hopelessness crowded my heart. I couldn't let him win, but it seemed as if he would. *No,* I told myself, *you cannot give up so soon. Keep fighting the good fight just as Paul told Timothy to do.*

Pushing my sorrow and anger down deep, I decided that I needed to use my emotions to build strength. I wouldn't be here forever. I'd find a way to escape. Though caged, I still had enough room to do pushups, squats, and stretches of all types. I even tried running in place for a little while, hoping it to prove helpful when the time came.

Over the next days, I exercised between meals and continued to encourage the guards. Anthony would bring the food, but he no longer ate with me. Instead, he stood and watched me eat, making sure I finished it all. I prayed over each meal, and then scarfed it down fast. The sooner I finished, the sooner Anthony would leave. Every dinner, he'd bring the prenatal vitamins. When he would leave me alone for the night, I'd crawl under the bed and drape the comforter over it like a curtain. With my nail, I would etch a line into the soft wooded side of the nightstand for each day I survived. The days seemed to grow longer and the scratches on the nightstand multiplied, but I never received message from Justin on when he planned to help me escape. Some nights I would sleep soundly, knowing God had not abandoned me. Still, the fear of being stuck here forever kept me tossing and turning in nightmares most other nights.

I often lay for hours before falling asleep, meditating on memories with my family and friends. The college years of fun and games seemed ages ago. Part of me wondered if those memories had actually happened. The Steven and Jeffrey I knew in college no longer existed. The boys trying to be men had become men, taking up the responsibilities placed upon them. I barely had time to get to know those men. I wasn't prepared to live life without them. I wiped the tears from my eyes before they could fall. It seemed a lifetime since I had felt carefree. Everything had changed more than I cared to see.

CHAPTER 37

Restore to me the joy of Your salvation and grant me a willing spirit, to sustain me.
—Psalm 51:12 (NIV)

"Khris," I heard my name called one morning. Half, awake, I couldn't tell if the voice was a dream. It sounded like Steven. "Khris," it came again. My eyes flew open wide. A hand pulled the comforter back and light burst into my refuge. I didn't know who belonged to the hand or the black boots. I scooted out, no longer able to roll on my stomach, slowly readying myself for the daily routine only to find Justin standing above me. I wasn't sure if he was any better. The guards at the door were gone. My first thought was to bolt out the door. Deal or no deal, I had learned I couldn't trust him. Not to mention, I hadn't seen him in weeks.

"Tereski sent me here to reason with you," that name reminded me who the real enemy was.

"What do you mean?"

Justin lowered his eyebrows, "You've been very hostile towards him. He wants to change that."

"He should have thought about that before he killed my friends and imprisoned me," I huffed.

"I can see why he came to me," Justin mumbled under his breath.

I'm sure he meant for me to hear him, but I didn't reply.

Justin sighed, "I've done everything I can to help your stay be more comfortable here. The closer to term you get, the more enticing it is for Tereski to call in a surgical team and raise the child in a tube. I've bought us time by reminding him that the child will be stronger if it can stay put. I've also assured him that kindness is the only way to get through to your people."

My people? I winced.

"He's tried his best, in his mind, but sees no response from you. I can't ask you to change how you feel about him, but what I do ask is that you try to show him a little more respect."

Respect? Cooperation, yes, but not respect. My conversations with God came to the forefront of my mind, and I knew that He would help me. If He planned to help me out of here alive, then

He could give me the strength to play the game. "Okay," I nodded, "I'll attempt to *cooperate* better."

"Good. Now," Justin lowered his voice. "I have to leave for a few days."

My heart raced. We had a deal. He just got here. When would he be back and set me free?

"I've been sent on a mission to go find a group of your people."

"You mean, Christians?" I corrected.

He confirmed without saying so and continued, "I have reason to believe that my mission is for a few... specific people... you may know."

I knew it. In my heart, I knew it. They're alive. As quick as I felt a shimmer of joy try to reach my face, I pulled it away and remained as before, "What will you do to them?"

"I haven't planned that far ahead yet, but it doesn't matter. I just need you to keep Tereski's wrath at bay. Now act hostile or shout at me to get out," he didn't give me time to ask more questions. The guard was returning. "Tereski doesn't need to see you responding better to my visits than his."

I looked at the glass of water on the nightstand and quickly threw the cup at him. "Get out!" I screamed as the glass shattered on the wall. It felt good to get out some of my anger. Justin still held partial blame for my situation, though his reason was better than Anthony's was.

After he left, I let my thoughts roam. Could my friends still be alive? I saw the explosion. I heard their screams. Perhaps it was all a trick. I felt the heat and force from it. The explosion may have only affected those of us above ground. They would have suffocated from the smoke even if they managed to keep the fire at bay. Oh, how I prayed that they would still be alive. I didn't know if Justin finding them would be better than them remaining hidden. *Lord, You know best. Let Your will be done,* I prayed.

CHAPTER 38

You believe that there is one God. Good! Even the demons believe that–and shudder.
—James 2:19 (NIV)

I couldn't go back to sleep after Justin left. I didn't have the desire to sleep. Hope kept me alert and awake. For hours, my eyes just stared at the bedframe. I prayed continuously for my friends' safety. I even caught myself praying for Justin's protection. I didn't want him to catch my friends, though. I wanted him to come back empty-handed and get me out of here. In order to do that, he'd need to see his sister free. So I prayed for her as well.

When Anthony finally entered the hangar, I stood in the center of the room waiting. He may have had me trapped in a box, but I wouldn't let him trap me in a corner.

Cooperate I kept reminding myself as he started up the stairs.

The two guards, who came with him, stood by the door dismissing the other guard.

"Wait," Anthony called to the guard he dismissed. He starred at the shattered glass, "Send someone to clean this mess." Then, he studied me, "Did you have a rough night?"

Justin's request stayed fresh on my mind, but it seemed impossible to cooperate with someone whose every breath repulsed me. "It slipped," I shrugged.

"I see," Anthony handed me my breakfast: yogurt, oatmeal, and a banana.

Digging down deep, I managed to find a, "Thank you."

Anthony stood speechless. I sat down with the tray, as usual, and readied to pray. I folded my hands and bowed my head. Instead of praying aloud, I kept my conversation with God internal. All that I accomplished by praying out loud, was further fueling Anthony's anger and hatred towards Christians.

"Are you sick?" Anthony asked me as I started to eat normally, rather than slopping everything down.

"No," I tried to act casual, but failed miserably as my outward responses contradicted my inward thoughts.

"Then you're plotting something," he accused.

I stared at him, putting down the spoon. "No," I sighed,

though technically the answer was probably yes. "I just realized things could be worse."

"Oh," he cocked his head, "how so?"

"You could have chained me up in a muggy dungeon, or placed me on an I.V. and feeding tube, but instead, you've given me the opportunity to still feel...purposeful. So, to that, I say thank you."

"I see Farrell's coercion worked."

He didn't coerce me, I wanted to say. *He just asked that I behave.* Something told me Justin didn't approach the situation the way Anthony planned.

"I wonder," he said. "Have you also come to terms with being the mother of my heir, or do you still need convincing?"

"I'm convinced," I said, attempting to filter what I wanted to say next. Some things were better left unsaid, but not right now, "It's obvious I'm pregnant, but don't fool yourself. I've promised this child to God, not you."

"If God were real, I may bother myself with a defense," Anthony blustered.

That's when I saw it – his point of weakness. I was blind to it until now. It made perfect sense. "You're scared," I said, throwing my conversation with Justin out the window.

He puffed up, "Have you seen nothing? A man with my status and power has no reason to be scared. It's the world that will fear me."

"The world may fear you, but that doesn't change the fear of God that I see in your eyes. You know He's real, or you never would've told me to call Him off when your men were dying right and left at the cellar that day." I let him know I could see right through him.

"Perhaps, for a moment, I considered you to be in touch with some sort of power. I assure you that idea was put to rest the moment we found and executed your sniper friend."

"Strike three," I mumbled. That was his third lie. First, he lied about Omar, telling me Justin stabbed him even though he lived to warn the camp. Next, he tried to make me believe that my friends had all died in the explosion, but Justin's assignment said otherwise. Now, he tried to convince me they killed the man that they so hastily ran from after the explosion at the cellar. Anthony was trying hard to make me feel alone and isolated. What he couldn't possibly understand is that God is always with me.

"Run that by me again," Anthony became very forceful. A guard interrupted when entering my cell to clean up the glass. Anthony paid him no mind and waited for an answer.

Kill him with kindness, I quickly reminded myself and corrected my error. I couldn't call his bluff or else he'd know that Justin revealed more than Anthony commanded of him. "That's the third time you've denied God's existence. Once in the cave, a second time right before you left to betray us, and a third time just now."

"Your point is?" He asked, stepping closer, trying to intimidate me, but God gave me the strength to keep speaking.

"It's only a matter of time before you have to admit God's existence. Even the demons believe in God."

"You compare me to a demon?" He stroked his chin seemingly amused.

"Only if that is what you choose to let control you."

"I wonder," he started to walk around me, still holding his chin, "what do you honestly believe about me?"

I thought before responding, trying hard not to fight evil with evil.

When I didn't answer in time, he repeated his question, "Who do you say I am?"

That question, so familiar, ran through my mind as it looked up the verse; Matthew chapter sixteen, verses thirteen through sixteen, Jesus asked His disciples the very same thing, "Who do you say I am?" Peter had the answer, "You are the Christ, the Son of the living God." It wasn't a mistake that Anthony used that specific phrase. He knew I would recall the reference and immediately be tempted to say Peter's answer. Not because I actually thought that

Anthony was my lord, but rather, because he wanted to trip me up. If he could make me stumble this time, he'd feel he had the upper hand. It didn't work; no, in fact, God gave me a different answer, "You are the prodigal son, still eating the food of the pigs. Your Father waits for you to return. He wishes to give you a feast, yet you haven't realized just how sincere His love for you is."

Anthony looked at the guard and when he turned back to face me, his demeanor had changed. There was a look of meekness about it. He removed his hands from his chin and dropped to his knees. The guard appeared as startled as I was. Anthony then folded his hands together and pleaded, "You're right. You're so very right. I'm tired of eating the pigs' food. I'm too scared to return though; too scared to give up all that I have…"

Though taught to forgive all and help all, I couldn't see how I could trust him now.

"I'm scared to give up my riches; my power; my control." He sat back up with a diabolic sneer and began to laugh. Then he stood to his feet, "Is that what you want to hear? You want to hear that I'm a lost puppy with my tail between my legs and you expect to find me a home. You can pray all you want and quote your religious nonsense, but one day you'll see that all you live for is nothing. Look around," he stretched out his arms. "I'm in control. I have more than I know what to do with. Not because any higher being gave it to me, but because I got it for myself." He brought his hands back down and regained his normal, creepy composure. "Now, eat your breakfast and keep my heir healthy."

In anger, I hastily finished the food. Justin asked me to cooperate, but Anthony made that nearly impossible. I had a hard time seeing how God could love Anthony. He treated God like a joke. Not to mention, after all he's done to God's people… I wanted nothing more than for him to suffer. Not just in this life but in the next. He wasn't going to change, but his death could help save the lives of others… *You need to stop thinking like this,* I reminded myself. *So long as he breathes, he has hope…*

CHAPTER 39

Salvation is found in no one else, for there is no other name under heaven given to men by which we must be saved.
—Acts 4:12 (NIV)

I made it a point, to keep uplifting the guards at my door. For the night shift guard, I would speak encouragingly to him right after his shift started and right before it ended if I'd wake up in time. One night, I felt the need to pray for the guard at my door instead of just talking to him. He had his head turned away from me, watching the stairs and the floor below just as every other guard had done. I didn't know if it was the same guard on watch every night, or if he was new to this position, but I couldn't shake God's Spirit urging me to pray. I stood next to the glass and put my hands near where his head was.

"God, watch over this man," I prayed. "You know what burdens his spirit. You know all the good and bad that this man feels in his heart." Suddenly, I filled with a fear for this guard's life. I didn't know why. I continued to petition the Lord. "Father, Creator of life, please let this man see that the only way out of evil is through You. Give him strength not to take any lives, including his own. Let him know that there's a reason to live. Let him know that that reason is You. God I ask –" the door pushed open, interrupting me. I looked up and saw the guard's pistol held in a very unstable hand. He walked through the door. I stepped back, attempting to keep the distance between us.

His hand shook so profusely that, if he pulled the trigger, there was a good chance he'd miss me completely. "Who told you?" His voice pulled my attention away from the gun and to his face. His eyes were red. His cheeks soaked in tears.

"God," I said, dropping to my knees. I took the most humble approach I knew. He may see any quick movement on my part as aggressive. I wasn't sure what he was talking about but he was talking and I knew God was using me as a tool to help this man.

He had a curious face as he said, "There's no such thing."

"Oh, but there is and He understands everything you're going through," I looked into the man's eyes. "He's revealed a hint of your pain to me, to show you just how real He is, and to tell you He can help you."

"Why? Why would He care about me now?"

"God has always cared about you. He loved you even before you were born and has been waiting for you to listen," I said.

The man dropped to his knees in front of me and sat the gun on the ground. He sobbed some more before saying, "I've lost them. Nothing I do can ever make up for this."

"Lost who?"

"My family," he cried. "My wife just had our baby and I can't afford to give her a good life. I've gambled all our money away. Every time I try to pay off our debt, I fail. Last night my paycheck was stolen and today was my last day to redeem myself. Tomorrow, they're coming for our house, and she doesn't even know. If I die, my debt goes with me. It's the only way."

I understood in an instant that he had been contemplating suicide. "There's another answer," I said hopefully. "You can turn to God. Acknowledge Him. Let His love enter your life. He has seen your struggles. He can get you through them. Suicide is not the solution. Your child needs a father. Your wife needs a husband. You may be able to end your own problems through suicide, but you'd be increasing theirs a hundred times over. It doesn't sound like that's what you really want."

"No. Of course not," he shook his head. "What do I need to do? Please, I need to know." His face hit his palms. The gun was there, on the floor, very near to me. This could be my moment of freedom that God has given me. The man wasn't watching and no one else was around to see me leave. It would be easy to grab the gun.

The guard sat up with tear stained eyes. I resisted the temptation of the gun and said to him, "God poured out His love into us when He created us. He gave everything to us, so we could share in His joy and His love. However, people sinned by pushing away from Him to indulge in their own plans and selfish desires. That sin kept us from being able to walk with God and be in His presence. Still, He loves us, so much so that He made a way for us to be back with Him.

"God literally put Himself in our shoes by allowing Himself to be born to a virgin. Jesus, who is God's Son and God, lived perfectly showing us how we ought to live with love and compassion for one another. Then, when He had finished what He came to do, He allowed men to kill Him in a terrible way. In doing so, He took the punishment for every sin we will ever commit so that we don't have to live in fear. Three days after His death, God raised Jesus from the dead to seal the deal and proclaim that we could, once again, walk with God because of what He did for us."

The guard listened intently, so I brought the story back to him, "Whatever sins you've committed, all the debt you owe, and all the disappointment you feel in yourself can vanish. The slate… your slate can be wiped clean. All you have to do is believe. Trust God and start letting His love into your life, He will help you work it out from there."

"Nothing ever comes free," the guard said skeptically.

"There's no catch," I smiled. "Choose to live for God; to live a life of love and forgiveness that says you know the Truth."

"What truth?" He asked.

"The Truth that Jesus is the son of God. With that Truth, you understand that Jesus has saved you from your sins, and calls you into a life of forgiving others just as He forgives you. It's not guaranteed to make life on earth easier, but when you follow Christ, you have the God of all creation helping you through your hardships. God also promises the reward of eternal life with Him, which is worth more than all the struggles we face. Will you choose to follow Him?"

Wiping his face, the guard said, "Absolutely, I will. The God you follow is nothing like any leader I've ever known. I want to follow Him. I want the salvation He offers."

"It's yours," I smiled, as I looked around the room. "Are you ready to take the first step?"

The guard looked at me cautiously.

"God asks nothing more than that you love Him and love

others." I stood up and walked over to where the pitcher of water sat on my nightstand. "Still, baptism is how you can easily and openly show Him you are ready to dedicate your life to Him. Jesus did it before starting His ministry. When we do it, it symbolizes that we are choosing to die to our old life and allowing God to raise us up into a new life with Him." I brought the jug to where the guard sat. "Usually, baptism would include full emersion in a larger body of water, but due to our circumstances this will do."

The guard looked at the water, and then at me with fearful eyes.

"What is it?" I asked.

"They warned us against your deadly tricks," his voice shook. "I wasn't even supposed to talk to you."

"I promise, it's just water," I got a cup full and drank it. "Well, to us, it's just water – and it can't technically clean anything except our skin, clothes, and hair – but to God, it's Jesus' blood that washes away all of our sin and makes us clean on the inside. That way, when we come to Him for help, He sees His perfect Son and not our sin."

"Then I want it," he finally relaxed, but now I found myself growing a little anxious.

I had never done this before. Though I've witnessed baptisms, they were always in deep water and the elders usually took a day or two to study with the person wanting baptized. Yet, as far as I can recall, Peter and Paul never postponed baptism to anyone who asked. They'd make sure the person confessed Jesus as their Lord and Savior, but the rest of the training came after baptism. "What's your name?" I asked as I stood next to him.

"Isaac Denver," the guard said.

"Isaac," I looked at him, feeling as if I was about to Knight him with a sword from shoulder to shoulder, "Do you believe in God, the Creator of the heavens and the earth?"

"Yes," he confessed.

"Do you also believe that Jesus is God's Son, sent to die for your sins?"

"Yes," he began to cry.

"Do you believe He is the only one that can save you and will you trust in Him the rest of your life, allowing Him to fill you with His love and guide you, no matter what happens?"

"Yes, yes!"

"Then with this water, I baptize you in the name of God our Father, Jesus His Son, and the Holy Spirit," I began pouring the water over his head and shoulders, "for the forgiveness of all of your sins – past, present and future. May you receive His Spirit and let Him guide you in the ways of our God for the rest of your life."

When the pitcher emptied, Isaac stayed knelt down in tears. I had no idea how to comfort him; a girl would take a hug or pat on the back, but men were sometimes different. Instead, I knelt beside him and placed a hand on one of his shoulders.

"God, You have heard Isaac's cry for help and You have witnessed his submission to Your will. He is placing his trust in the salvation that only You can give him. He now knows how to take Your Salvation to his wife and child. I pray Your Spirit guides him and teaches him how to trust You and love others. Give him the courage to explain to his wife, their financial situations, and give her the willingness to forgive him and stay close by his side. Provide another way out for them, as he is unsure of what to do if people come to take his house tomorrow. Help him to follow You the rest of his life, no matter what challenges he faces, so that he will get to see You in heaven. I send this prayer to You God, through Jesus' holy name. Amen."

Isaac reached his hand up to my shoulder at the end of my prayer and then pulled me forward to where our foreheads lightly touched.

"Thank you, oh thank you," he cried looking me in the eyes. A smile came to his face, bright and full of joy. I could see God carrying his burdens away right there in front of me. Then, Isaac brought me closer in for a hug and soaked my sleeve with joyful tears. Standing up, he left for the door.

"Where will you go?" I asked. His gun was on the ground still.

"To save my family," he looked at me with a smile. That smile faded as he saw me reaching for the gun.

He reacted quickly, jumping for it, but I had already pulled it in to myself. Isaac stood there for only a moment. No doubt, he wondered what I would do next. I held it by the barrel and handed it to him. "Don't forget this," I said. As the gun left my hands, I felt disheartened. I was afraid I had let my only chance of escape slip through my fingers.

"Come with me," he held out his hand. "My family can hide you."

I considered it, but had to refuse. I quickly told him the story of Paul and Silas in the book of Acts. They were in prison, praying and singing to God. Then God sent an earthquake that opened the prison doors and unfastened all their chains. The guard was about to kill himself when Paul spoke out, letting him know that not a single prisoner escaped. It was a great day of testimony, and God blessed their time in prison with that guard to where they ended up saving him and his family. My time would come. It was hard not to run with him, but I knew that if he were murdered for my attempt to escape, I'd never forgive myself. No one would question a guard walking around, but they'd certainly question a guard with a young pregnant woman out of uniform.

"Go, save your family, but don't come back here," I said. "Christians aren't safe. You've become an enemy to everyone who works here. Leave quickly and don't turn back."

Isaac pleaded with me but I refused to be the cause of any more deaths. "It's fully loaded," he said, handing me his gun. "Be safe."

"Thank you," I watched as he ran across the hangar. He stopped suddenly near the door. He just stood there. It seemed like an eternity before he moved. He looked back at me and then opened the door and was gone. I sat in prayer for God to protect him and his family.

Gun in hand; I contemplated what to do next. It seemed long enough since Isaac left that I could try to leave on my own. I reached for the door, just to test, and it easily opened. As I stepped out, I anticipated an alarm of some sort. Nothing happened. *You can do it*, I told myself. *Just breathe and sprint, that's all it is.*

I hesitated. *What would become of Justin and his sister?* Anthony couldn't pin my disappearance on them. Besides, I had a child to protect.

Darting down the stairs, I sprinted near to the first aircraft. No sirens or alarms sounded. Other than the echoes of my footsteps, all stayed calm. Again I ran, passing fifteen of the jets. A clicking sound brought me to a halt. I looked around and searched for the direction from where it came. I chose to take off running a third time but a giant squeal echoed down the hall, like a hinge that needed oiled. A light shined through my exit and scanned the room up to the back staircase.

"Denver," a man's voice called. "You better not be sleeping again." The man came in the door and I crouched behind one of the jet wheels. Dare I try to make it past him as he came up the walkway?

The door opened again, "Sergeant Barnet?" Men behind him awaited orders.

"Stand guard, I'm going to check it out. Have the others ready," the sergeant replied.

With the door blocked and more guards possibly on their way, I saw no point in continuing. The sergeant still had a lot of floor to cover. I turned and walked hastily underneath the jets, and back towards my cell. I couldn't believe I was willingly about to put myself back into that prison. This would all be so much easier if I could just use the gun; I looked at it again, placing my finger on the trigger and immediately removing it.

I came to the jet, closest to my cell. The sergeant was about ten planes away. He shined his light under each one he passed and with every step, he yelled Isaac's last name. As Denver's silence lingered, the other man's anger fumed. He began cursing Isaac for being lazy and threatening to have him fired. I tried to race to the stairs but my feet stayed planted. The sergeant stopped and called to another man. When the sergeant turned around, I dashed for the stairs. I crouched low as I ran. Entering through the door, I attempted to scoot under the bed. I saw the gun still in my hands. Quickly I placed it between the mattresses above and pulled the blanket down to cover me, just as I had done all the nights before. Seconds later the blanket ripped away from my fingers.

The sergeant bent down to see me. "Get out, now," he ordered.

I did as commanded.

"The woman's here," he said to the man at the door, who passed on the message to the ten men coming our way. "Where is he?" The sergeant asked.

I attempted a yawn and stretched my arms above me, "Who?"

"The guard who was at your door," he grabbed my shirt collar and stood me up. "Where is he?"

"I don't know. I've been asleep."

"Don't lie to me," he held up the empty pitcher. "This got here at some point." He threw the pitcher to the ground and raised his hand to hit me.

"Enough," a voice boomed at the door.

The man immediately stood in attention as Anthony came towards him.

"She obviously had no clue where your man went or she would've been long gone by now." Anthony then looked at me with curious eyes and whispered, "Unless, perhaps, she has nowhere else to go?"

I looked at him with repugnance.

"Go back to your stations," Anthony ordered everyone. "Call the next men in the rotation to post early," he instructed the sergeant, "then take a few others and go find Denver." As the sergeant left, Anthony looked back at me. He picked up the empty pitcher and gave it to one of the guards to refill. "You knew he was gone before we arrived, I can see it in your eyes. Perhaps Farrell was right about you. Tell me, is there anything else I can give you to help your stay seem more comfortable?"

"Free David," I said.

He immediately shook his head, "I said your stay, not his. He's not leaving. I told you this."

He's still alive. "Then, I'd like a Bible," I entreated as politely as possible.

Anthony winced, as if he already assumed I'd ask for one but hoped otherwise, "Of all the things you could ask for, you request a book."

"It gets quiet in here. I want to read. I'd finish any other book within a couple of days," I played innocent.

Anthony snapped his fingers and held his hand out behind him. One of the guards gave him a large stack of papers, with singed edges. Anthony then held them out for me to take, "You didn't say in what shape you wanted it."

I took the stack of papers seeing they were the pages of a coverless, burnt Bible. It wasn't all there, but I was grateful to have it nonetheless. I smiled, "Thank you."

Anthony wasn't pleased, "You should rest. I have a nurse coming to check on my heir."

CHAPTER 40

Sustain me according to Your promises, and
I will live; do not let my hopes be dashed.
—Psalm 119:116 (NIV)

The knots in my stomach tightened. I couldn't even bring myself to speak encouragingly to the guards. For hours, worry enveloped me. What would become of my baby if the upcoming checkup revealed any birth defects? Anthony would kill us. Of that, I am certain. It seems the more I prayed for God's hand of protection, the louder the troublesome thoughts emerged in my head and attacked every thought of hope.

Two guards eventually approached my prison. Between them was a young woman. I didn't need to look hard before guessing she was the nurse coming to check on me. She was dressed in a stereotypical nurse outfit – white skirt, white shirt, and green facemask. The guards with the woman dismissed the two at my door and invited themselves into my cell. The woman took a bag from one of the guard's hands and placed it on my bed. I had already sat. The need for social graces was long past and she would have me sit down anyway.

The woman opened her suitcase and pulled out a sphygmomanometer to read my blood pressure. "Uncross your legs," she demanded before strapping the cloth around my arm.

"I don't even get an introduction?" I said sarcastically. Of the two guards at my door, one had a very harsh look on his face from the moment he walked in, as if I had somehow inconvenienced him. I nicknamed him Grumpy, because I was tired of seeing nameless faces. The other had red tinted hair all over his face and arms. Though he probably shaved before coming to work, his five o'clock shadow had grown in early. It seemed only right to call him, Esau.

I decided to call the woman in front of me, Nurse Pain as she pulled out a stethoscope and placed it in her ears. She then began pumping too much air into the strap around my arm. I never liked those things under normal circumstances but here it was intolerable. She didn't have to make it so tight. Nurse Pain released the air and listened through her stethoscope, then pulled out a clipboard and wrote down a few numbers. Though everyone seemed calm and acted normal, my body remained tense.

"Why get to know someone who will die long before you can remember their name?" Nurse Pain finally answered me. I wasn't sure if she meant that about herself or me. She checked my heartbeat and lungs, ears and throat. What any of this had to do with my child, I didn't know. As far as I could see, it was a regular doctor's checkup. "I am, on the other hand, interested in learning how you did it," she gave a slight chuckle. "It seems the entire base is talking about your disappearing act with the night guard."

"Oh?" I was intrigued and surprised that everyone had heard about it already.

Not adding any more to the conversation Nurse Pain said, "You're very healthy."

I lay back in silence as she placed the stethoscope over my abdomen. She listened for a while, moving it to all different places. Suddenly, she pulled back. I sat up in anticipation, waiting. Did the pregnancy test lie?

"That thing inside of you has a strong heart beat," she spat.

Thing – What kind of nurse refers to a baby as a *thing*?

Nurse Pain then went inside of her suitcase, pulled out a syringe, and placed it inside a bottle. Holding it up, she used the handle to pull a yellow liquid from the bottle into the syringe. Then she came and pulled my shirt back up to see my stomach.

"What's that for?" I started to panic. I've experienced multiple levels of pain and fear these past months. I've been hit by the butt of several guns, stared down the barrel of many more, felt the sting of fists against my flesh, and had the scar from a bullet through my hand. Still, I could not calm myself enough allow such an immense, sharp object enter into my body, especially when it was that close to my child.

"The antidote," Nurse Pain said nonchalantly.

"Is the child sick?" I asked.

"Quite the opposite," she muttered as she brought the needle close to my skin.

I immediately grabbed her hand and knocked the syringe to the floor. Pushing her back, I jumped off the bed and stomped on the needle, breaking it off the syringe. I didn't like the tone in her voice. I panicked. I tried to grab for the gun but before I got my hand between the mattresses, Grumpy grabbed my wrist. I reached for the thing nearest to me, clawing for anything that would help me get out of Grumpy's grasp. My hand found the back of the mask on Nurse Pain's face. I ripped it off, along with a good chunk of her long brown hair. Esau grabbed my arm. Nurse Pain hollered her rebuke as I dropped everything.

It took both guards to pin me against the hangar wall. Even though they stood on my feet so I couldn't kick them, I was proud of the fight I put up. Nurse Pain searched her suitcase in haste, "This would be much easier if you'd cooperate."

"How can I cooperate with premeditated murder?"

"It won't harm you at all, except for a small sting," she lifted a new needle up, taking it out of its package, "although, you may find yourself a bit sick for the next twenty-four hours."

I pulled against Grumpy and Esau but they wouldn't budge. Nurse Pain turned towards me and ordered Esau to hold up my shirt. When she turned, I finally saw her face without the mask. In an instant I recognized her; a beautiful brown haired woman, about my age, and though she no longer wore a blue dress, she definitely had the same face.

"I know your brother," I blurted, trying to remember her name. "Justin." She stopped for a moment. "He showed me a picture of the two of you, when he received a medal."

"How do you know him?" She questioned.

"He's the one that brought me here," I'd hold nothing back if it kept us safe.

"You're lying. My brother would never work for these

monsters." She put her hand on my belly and readied to insert the needle.

I wiggled around, trying to buy time, "He's doing it to save you."

The woman removed her hand and looked up at me.

"He's been told your life hinges on his ability to follow orders. They have a tracking device on him that can inject poison in him if he fails."

"My brother left our family long ago. As far as I'm concerned, he's been dead for years."

"I don't know what happened with your family, but I know he's here for *you* now. He's doing everything in his power to set you free."

"If he's here, then where are they keeping him?" She put her hand back into position.

"I don't know, but he's on a mission, he should be back any day now," I waited for her to remove her hand again but she didn't.

"He's been in this hangar?" She looked around. Her breaths shortened. Then, she snapped back into character, "It doesn't matter. This thing cannot live."

"I know," I said. "I know what Anthony plans to do with my child."

"Then you know why it has to die," she demanded my cooperation but I couldn't give it to her.

"No," I protested, "it doesn't. I just need to keep my baby far away from Anthony."

"How do you plan that?" She mocked. "This fortress is covered with the General's men. The only entrance is the only exit. Even if you managed to sneak out of the hangar, you'll still find yourself imprisoned."

I tried to rationalize with her, "I know all of that, but Justin has a plan. He'll get me out when you're safe."

"What if he can't get you out, or the General never lets any of us go? What then?"

I thought on her question. Taking a risk, I told her to check under my mattress.

"Where did you get this?" She pulled out the gun, checking the clip.

"It doesn't matter," I said. "If all plans fail, that will be my final resort."

"You think you're brave enough to pull the trigger when you're too afraid to let me stick a needle in you?" She laughed and put the gun back under the mattress.

"Not on the child," I pulled my right hand from the guard and pointed to my own heart. "On myself, before he or she is born."

Justin's sister stared intently, as if waiting for me to recoil. I kept her gaze. "Let her go," she said to the guards. Suddenly, a look of uncertainty came over me. Grumpy and Esau could easily take this information to Anthony. While squeezing the needle back in the container, Justin's sister looked at the guards beside me, "These two men are being used in the same way you say my brother is." She gestured to them as they raised their arms to show me a similar tracking device to the one Justin has. "Their loved ones are being held hostage until these men complete their task."

I looked over each of them from head to toe. They carried a knife at their waists and a communication device, the same as Justin carried. It made much more sense now. Anthony didn't trust them with guns as he did his other *loyal* guards. These two men and Justin still had the potential to turn on him.

"These men have been assigned to guard me in the North Wing. These devices go haywire around some of the lab machines, so I can't wear one. Unknown to the General, the three of us have made a pact to ensure the fall of his reign, no matter the cost of our loved ones' lives. If you see Justin again, you tell him all of this. I'll continue to do my job of checking on that thing inside of you, but if we see any sign of trouble, I swear on my life, we won't hesitate to end this." She gave me no reason to doubt her sincerity. I let her know I understood and agreed to the plan.

As Justin's sister cleaned the broken vile on the ground from our skirmish, Anthony came through the doors, unannounced, with two of his own guards. My heart pounded with fear. Justin's sister immediately placed everything in her bag and turned towards him. She and the other two stood in attention.

"You started without me, Brittany," Anthony depicted himself distraught.

Brittany, I need to remember that for when I see Justin.

"I didn't see the harm in..." Brittany tried to defend her actions but Anthony quickly interrupted.

"Is my heir alright?" He walked towards me.

"It has a very strong heartbeat," she responded.

"Then there's no harm at all," Anthony proceeded my way. "Let me hear it."

Brittany grabbed the stethoscope back out of her bag and placed it on my abdomen. She moved it around a bit and then held it in place while handing the ear buds to Anthony. I wanted to slam my knee into his face, but Justin's request intruded my thoughts, *cooperate.* Brittany played the part very well and gave no indication of her recent attempt at treason and murder.

A smile lingered on Anthony's face while he stood. Brittany put the stethoscope back in her bag. Just when I thought we got away with our deception, Anthony placed his hand on the bed beside Brittany. It rested right above the gun.

"Is there anything else you need to tell me?" He looked at Brittany and, then at me.

I froze. Brittany drew his attention back to her, "No sir. We won't know more until I can get a machine in for an ultrasound."

Anthony ignored her and knelt to the ground, sliding his hand down the mattress, and picked up the mask I had pulled from Brittany's face. It still held a clump of hair. I wanted to give out a sigh of relief, but saw Brittany and the guards suddenly tense.

"Did we have some trouble?" He held the mask.

After a second of silence, Grumpy spoke, "Only at first, but she was easily subdued."

"Was she?" Anthony got up, walked towards Grumpy, and then put his gun up to Grumpy's temple. Looking at me, he asked, "Did they harm you in any way?"

"No," I quickly answered. He seemed all too ready to pull the trigger.

"Are you sure?" Anthony asked again. "I'll avenge you right here and now."

"No, they didn't lay a hand on me," I lied.

Anthony holstered his gun and looked at me with a laugh, "Even when you're all alone in this world, you're too weak to cause the death of another." Then he handed the mask to Brittany. "That is how I know you're perfect for this task." He demanded the guards and Brittany to exit the room.

Without question or hesitation, they left. Anthony's two guards stayed at the door. I watched another set of allies walk away and wondered just how long it would be before I could rid myself of this evil place.

The stress of Anthony's presence became unbearable, "Why do you keep testing me?"

He shook his head, "I don't know what you…"

"Cut the act and answer me."

He chuckled, "Every person can be bought."

I disagreed, but I waited for more.

"Most are bought with money. Others give in for love, pride, or revenge," he gazed at his jets, out the glass walls.

I wondered if I could get to the gun before he turned around.

"My people have spent over a hundred years in hiding, waiting for the day the government would slip up and give us access into their system. Without them even knowing, I've begun my rule over this country. America will cease as a nation and become a kingdom under one rule, my rule. Yet, how can a king reign when a large sum of his subjects claim to serve someone of a higher power?"

His question was obviously rhetorical. I kept listening for the connection to my first question. *Why did he constantly see a need to test me?* He wanted me to give him a reason to kill Grumpy earlier. *Why?*

"We've persuaded the governors, appeased their faithful subjects, and traded freedoms for loyalty. Most others we've instilled enough fear into that we'll never have to worry about them. Yet, there's one type of people we can't seem to break," Anthony walked my way, circling me, searching for a sign of fear. "If I can break you, I can break them."

"Why me?"

"You've watched your friends die. You've seen people you call your brothers and sisters murdered. You've had guns aimed at your own head and a stranger impregnated you. Allies have proven to be enemies and solitude has become your future. Yet, you keep your loyalty to your *God*. Others have denied it. Some have chosen to die. You refuse to deny or end your torment. I know there are others like you. I have a few of them in custody. Making them martyrs gives hope to others like them. Torture proves useful but slow, and your situation causes me to be a bit more creative."

My situation must refer to the pregnancy. He couldn't harm me physically, so instead, Anthony chose to toy with my mind until I choose to give in to his games.

"It'll be a lot more fun with less blood on my hands when I figure it out, so tell me," he peered. "What *is* your price?" With that, he left. His guards stayed on watch duty.

It wasn't enough that Anthony intended to force me to have his child. He needed to break me of my faith as well. "My soul is losing all courage," I cried to God. "I don't need to tell You why. You see how that monster continues to torment me day and night. Why am I still here? What else do You need from me? I let You use me as a tool to guide Isaac to You. I've stood firm in all trials, but I'm getting weak. My hate for Anthony is growing. I'm not just angry with him. I want him to die. I know You can still change him, but I'm not sure I want You to give him the chance. Father, get me out of here. Please, I beg of You, don't let me stay another night."

CHAPTER 41

There are six things the Lord *hates, seven that are detestable to Him: haughty eyes, a lying tongue, hands that shed innocent blood, a heart that devises wicked schemes, feet that are quick to rush into evil, a false witness who pours out lies and a man who stirs up dissension among brothers.*
—Proverbs 6:16–19 (NIV)

Without warning, four guards intruded into my cell and my prayers one mid-morning. It wasn't long after breakfast and I wasn't expecting anyone to show until lunch. One guard opened a bag and pulled out a squirt bottle and a pair of scissors. Another set a chair down and grunted for me to sit. When I didn't move fast enough, he quickly plopped me into the seat and promptly cuffed both my wrists to the chair arms. Like a wild stallion, tied to a stall, I kicked and pulled. They then cuffed my ankles to the chair legs.

I struggled against them while screaming, "What are you doing?"

With the scissors, the shortest guard began cutting away chunks of my hair. A spray bottle and comb were used to help pull at the hairs still left on my head. A big, brutish guard held my head firmly to stop my struggling, but the tangles still attached to my scalp put up a good fight all on their own.

The two guards on either side of me held my hands, clipping my fingernails and filing them down. They moved from my nails to my eyebrows, plucking the hairs one by one. Of all the things they did to me, this seemed to be the most pointless and excruciating. Every time they pulled out a hair, my eyes watered. Wincing and blinking didn't help. In fact, such rebellious acts seemed only to make it worse, especially when the sneezing started. Lastly, they clipped away at my toenails, cutting them as short as possible while still leaving some nail.

When the men were through, they cleaned up the floors and set me free leaving my prison sanctuary in the same order they entered – never answering any of my questions. Reaching up to the top of my head, I felt only a couple inches of hair left. Messing with it made my head itch. When I tried to scratch, I sat very disappointed with my newly filed down nails. "She's presentable," I heard one of them say on their radio before the door completely closed. I could barely see them through my swollen eyes as they walked down the hangar.

Stepping into the bathroom, I splashed water on my eyes to take down the swelling. As I looked at myself in the mirror, nothing was the same. My eyebrows curved evenly and were nearly too thin to see. My hair looked like they gave it an extra, long, buzz cut. *Is that…?* I reached to touch my cheeks. They even applied a layer of foundation. I'm not sure what they meant by calling me *presentable.* If anything, I felt more exposed. I left the bathroom, submitted myself to contentedness in my confusion, and again encouraged the guards.

"There's kindness in you; goodness in your heart. You have traces of love in your DNA. There's a plan set for you; though you've seemed to wander off its path, you can always find your way back. People may hurl insults at you, but they don't define you. Tragedies have struck in your lives, but they don't control you. God holds the key to the future. I know the plans He has for you are good, if you would just walk in His path."

Repeating Jeremiah's prophecy stung a little as it flowed out my mouth. *Where was the plan of good God had for me?* I thought about Isaac, hoping he had reached his wife. I only hoped she took to God's salvation as quickly as he did.

Feeling putrid and lightheaded suddenly, I darted to the bathroom. On my knees, I heaved into the commode. While waiting for the feeling to subside, I started to count back all the events that led up to this day. My stomach purged itself again.

This all started so long ago. After that first week when Anthony and his puppets captured Omar and me, everything went downhill. I thought it was all Erica's doing, but I was wrong. Then, the massacre broke out. I can still vividly recall the dead scattered across the camp. When we escaped and found shelter in the cave, I thought we had left the worst behind. I was wrong. We brought it with us.

In those few days within the cave, God gave me more red flags but I kept pushing them aside. I should have listened to Justin's warning about Anthony. We grew tiresome of one another, but I thought we had become friends. I should have seen through the lies. Perhaps we'd all be free today if I had.

The day we left the cave, we lost Justin…or at least we thought we did until he popped up again. We also reunited with Steven, Jeffrey, and Jasmine. My heart rejoiced in finding my friends. I felt as if we could accomplish anything once we had each other. David's family cellar gave us refuge for a few weeks while we searched for some sign of hope on the radio; it never came.

All of my days seemed to blur together after we reached the cellar. It had been months since I saw the sunrise and sunset; my ways of telling time were simply through my internal clock. Here, I could normally tell whether it was night or day depending on when the guards switched shifts and when Anthony brought me my meals. I had marked the days on my nightstand, but stopped counting them long ago.

I spent at least two months on the run, before Anthony betrayed us. Another two or three months have passed since then. That left me with between four and five months to figure out what to do. I hoped to be out long before then, but I had had also hoped for God to free me within my first week in this prison. Even if I got out, I had no way of knowing how to find my friends, or safety for that matter. I'd be alone, and helpless throughout the rest of the pregnancy.

No. God is with me. He promises never to leave me, or any of His followers. I need to remember this. My limits were continuously tested but, with God, I know I can make it out of this fiery test. "Still, why was I born if this is how my life would turn out?" I asked God. "Are You going to free me, or am I stuck in the hands of evil men until death?" I guess every other Christian in America, who's still alive, is probably asking similar questions. Even if God did answer me, I assume it would resemble the answer He gave Job after Job lost everything. God told Job that he had no right to question His plan. In fact, God reminded him of the billions of things He created and controlled. Job never really received the answer he wanted. He only found he needed to trust God. That, too, is what I choose to do.

My door opened. I still felt too queasy to want to turn around. I glanced over my shoulder and immediately sprung to my feet. Anthony had entered my cell. I couldn't let him have the advantage over me in my weakness. I walked out of the stall and into the cell. Behind Anthony stood an older man in a suit with a pin of the degraded flag on his lapel. Also in attendance were four men the size of tree trunks dressed in grey uniforms.

"Is this her?" The man said with a tone of disgust. His voice was strong but held a slight rasp, as if he was a long time smoker. "I expected someone a little more...plump."

"She isn't even past five months. Besides, the clothes are a little loose. The nurse confirmed it though; she's definitely carrying my heir."

"This child is God's," I declared, "not yours."

"Ha," Anthony clapped. "See father?"

"Father?" I looked at the older man realizing he's the reason Anthony wanted me to look *presentable.*

"Yes," Anthony smiled. "This is my father, Doctor William Tereski. Father, this *is* the Christian woman carrying my heir."

Neither of us extended hands for societal formalities. "I thought your father was a retired General who gave you the title after you killed your sister?"

Dr. Tereski stared at me, "I am. I am also one of the most highly educated psychologists in the world."

I smirked. *Of course, he'd have psycho in his title.* As he stepped closer, every impulse in my body told me to retract. Nevertheless, I stood my ground.

"She seems a little... comfortable," Dr. Tereski said to Anthony as he scanned my cell in distaste, ignoring me.

Puffed up, Anthony defended, "It's for my heir."

"Take the bed. Remove the nightstand. Strip her of her

garments. The longer you give her these luxuries, the more she'll rebel against you," the doctor said.

"I decide what happens to her," Anthony protested. "She hasn't attempted to escape, nor has she caused harm to any of my men…"

"Yet, one man is missing. Am I wrong?" His father reprimanded. "She'll take you for everything you have if you don't lay down the law now."

Anthony glared at me and then at his father, "I have it under control."

Dr. Tereski said nothing more on the matter, and changed gears towards me. "You've had three days to think on it. Have you decided your price yet?" Anthony must have reported our conversations to him.

Firmly, I stood tall, "I can't be bought."

Dr. Tereski walked around behind me, while Anthony stayed in front. Chills went down my spine. If Anthony was evil, his father was Satan incarnate. I turned to him, taking my chances of letting down my guard to Anthony.

"I'll never deny my God," I reaffirmed.

Dr. Tereski laughed, "We don't need you to deny him. We just need you to give up on him." He grinned.

As he said this, a memory from the horrors at the camp flashed back through my mind. They had us lined up, explaining to us that we had no hope left. The man in a red patch, the one who killed Agnes and tortured the husband before killing him in front of everyone, he gladly welcomed us all to Hell. He too, had a raspy voice… "You were there," my eyes widened.

"Come again," he leaned in closer. His breath smelled of tobacco.

"It was you. You wore the red patch. You killed them," anger, rage, contempt, they boiled in my veins, threatening to explode. I held my breath and clenched my fists.

He stood tall and smiled, "You remember me. Good. Then you will remember that I show no mercy. No one freely leaves.

Sure, you all managed to attempt an escape, but look where it's brought you. The others are dead or being tortured as we speak. Your confinement is only temporary until we can get from you, what belongs to my son. If you give up your god, it'll make your cooperation so much easier and in the end, it'll promise you a quicker death."

It took every ounce of strength left in me, not to try to strangle him. If I were closer to the gun, I would use it without blinking. "Telling me your plan will only make me fight harder," I spat.

"That's what we need," he took a step closer to me. "Without your full resistance, we'd never be able to completely break you."

Stand your ground, I said to myself. I desperately wanted to step away, but knew it would only show weakness. I thought of Psalm twenty-three, '*I will fear no evil for God is with me.*'

"I'll tell you what," he walked around me, standing back by Anthony. "If you tell us how to get your people to stand down and stop defending their faith, we will let you go."

"Father –" Anthony tried to interrupt, but the Doctor held his hand up to silence him.

Dr. Tereski then said, "This will be your only chance for freedom. I'm willing to part with one if it means capturing hundreds more. You and your child will have an eternal pardon. None of our men will touch you as long as you live... Answer wisely. What makes a Christian weak enough that they stop standing up for their God?"

Even if his question had an answer, I wouldn't give it. "'Though his speech is charming, do not believe him, for seven abominations fill his heart.'[14] I read this recently, and now I know it's about you. You can promise whatever you want to me, but you'd never honor your word. No mercy, remember? Christians aren't fickle like you suppose. God has prepared us for all trials and sufferings. We build our faith on a foundation that does not move and that

[14] Proverbs 26:25 (NIV)

human hands cannot touch. When you attack our weaknesses, we become stronger through God's Spirit. Lock us in a tower or throw us in a dungeon. Beat us and threaten us. Kill our families. God is everywhere. He sees everything. He will forever keep us strong and resolved."

I couldn't help but think about all the Christians who did fall away. We weren't all solid in our faith, as I saw at the camp during the attack. Jesus warned us about that in His parables, explaining that some Christians will take root fast, but in the end their faith is shallow and they fall away when the sun gets too hot or the rain brings a flood. I wouldn't tell Anthony and his father about this side of Christians. I wanted them to feel hopeless, even if it meant them never releasing me.

Anthony's father turned to look at him, without responding to me. "You're a fool if you think you can break her in such comfortable conditions. Remove it all or you'll be fighting a losing battle."

Anthony glared at me, enraged, as if his father's reprimands were my fault. "I will break her," he said to his father. Then, he looked at me again, "You will tell me what I want to know."

"Or what," I huffed. "You'll kill me like you did your sister? I think we've been over this enough times now."

With a bull's snort, he spun on his heels and marched down the stairs. His father narrowed his eyes and slyly grinned. He gave no response to my small comment about Anthony killing his own sister. Perhaps it's because he truly didn't care. After all, he promoted Anthony for it. He, too, left and waited at the bottom of the stairs. Anthony whistled loud. I looked out the glass to see five figures escorted in with brown feed sacks over their heads.

"Do you want to keep playing games?" Anthony yelled up to me. The guards kept the doors open so I could hear, but stood, blocking the way for any attempted escapes. "Let's play, guess who?"

My heart threatened to stop beating. A lump rose in my throat.

"These men and women were all caught, attempting to free the children taken from the camp. Two claim to be hunters, who can find their way through any terrain. Though they broke into my fortress, they weren't smart enough to know how to break out. Another, very young, said he was prepared to die for his faith. We'll see if that's the case. The fourth has a wicked arm with throwing knives, and will soon meet her wicked end if she makes one more attempt on my men's lives. Then we have the last victim... she is very near and dear to you. I'm sure you'd be happy to see her...if you play the game right, you just might get to talk with her."

I knew the names of the prisoners before Anthony ever ordered the removal of their sacks. They were the camouflaged brothers and sisters: Neil, Travis, Wesley, and Rebecca. The other was Bethany, who left our group to help them. They must have tracked the children to Anthony's camp.

I glanced at Dr. Tereski and saw him observing my reaction. He now seemed pleased with his son's vile work.

When the guards removed the sacks from the heads, Bethany and Rebecca began yelling at Anthony. Their guards practically had to hug them to keep them still. Rebecca bit into her guard's arm. He threw her forward and she rushed at Anthony. He pulled his gun and shot her in the shoulder. She fell to the ground. As she tried to get up, Anthony stepped on her wound and pointed his gun at her head. "What will it be Khris, her life or your god?"

I threw my fist into the glass. "You coward!"

Anthony pulled the trigger.

His father beamed with pride and clapped as if Anthony had accomplished some great feat. The display of his joy sickened me. The others grew louder behind Anthony. Both Neil and Travis struggled to free themselves. Anthony put the gun up to Neil's head, causing Travis to freeze and begin begging Anthony to shoot him instead.

"Give me one reason not to kill him," Anthony called to me

while ignoring Travis, and kept his gun on Neil. "Just one reason and I'll spare him. Haven't you caused enough deaths already?"

Tears rolled down my face. The guards kept my door barricaded, or I would have rushed at him myself. Another shot went off, but Travis fell instead.

"Oops," Anthony smiled, "I shot the wrong man." He put his gun back on Neil. "I remember you," Anthony said to him, still loud enough for me to hear. "You were the one so eager to kill me. You had your finger on the trigger, but the only thing that kept me alive was him," he pointed the gun at Wesley, the boy who stood horrified. He neither screamed nor fought for freedom. "You let me live so this child wouldn't die," Anthony said. He then turned to look at me. "Is that it? Are the children your weakness?"

I shook my head and beat the class, bloodying my knuckles. I yelled at the top of my lungs, "Leave them alone!"

"There's only one way to end this," he yelled back at me.

I shook my head and backed away.

Disappointed, Anthony frowned, "You're right. I can see this is a waste of time." He shot Wesley and then turned to Neil. I jumped to the mattress. Pulling the gun out, I aimed it at Anthony's head and fired. After the first shot, the rest kept coming. Two, three, four… they continued as I screamed out for justice. One of them had to hit him. My ears didn't ring this time, but my arms struggled to resist the kick of the gun.

Disarmed and thrown into the glass, I felt a jarring pain to my nose. Blood flowed down the glass as someone continued to force my head into it. I desperately searched for Anthony's lifeless body as my oppressor gripped my wrists behind my back. I fired off eight shots. Something had to hit him. Instead, I saw Bethany's body laid out on the floor. Because of her, Angelica lived. Because of me, Bethany died.

As they pulled me from the glass, my eyes came to focus on Anthony, blazing, rushing my way. *I missed…* Looking at the glass, I could see where every bullet hit, but not one penetrated it. My captor turned me abruptly and I lost focus again.

"You stupid girl," I heard Anthony's father right before a hand stung across my cheek. "Where did you get this?"

I saw him holding the gun in my face and then things blurred again.

He slapped me once more, "Where?"

"That's enough!" Anthony shouted.

"Get out of the way," demanded his father.

My vision came back as I saw Anthony stand his ground between us. The man behind me still held firm to my arms.

"No," Anthony said. "You're done here."

Dr. Tereski stepped back and called his men to formation. "I told you she was trouble. Let her live like this and she will be your demise."

Anthony turned to me. Any ounce of compassion I may have left for him disappeared. I scowled at him with pure hate. Nothing could change my mind. He needed to die. Anthony returned my glare and commanded, "Take it all."

Immediately, the men in grey took off with everything in the room; the rug, the nightstand with the burnt Bible, the bed – they even ripped the stall off the wall from around the bathroom and emptied it of all towels and cleansing supplies. They took it all and threw it over the stair rails. One of them approached to grab my garments but I stammered back. The guard behind me didn't let me go far, but Anthony gripped the arm of the man attacking me. "Don't touch her," he ordered. "She keeps the clothes."

He let the man go and the Doctor shook his head.

"You're weak," his father said.

"If she gets sick, my heir could die. The clothes stay."

His father said nothing more.

"The Father I serve would never treat His children like slaves as yours does," I mocked Anthony.

"I'm not his slave. This is my kingdom. My land. My rules."

His father kept silent.

"Besides," Anthony stood proud, "Who are you to talk of fathers? You've been abandoned by yours." He then ordered the man still holding me, "Lock her to the pipes."

The man walked me to the commode and snapped a cuff to my right hand. He then pulled me to the ground and cuffed the other side to the pipes on the wall. I didn't try to fight him. He wasn't my target.

As Anthony and his father turned to leave, I watched the Doctor let everyone walk past him. He whispered something to his guards. When they all cleared the room, he turned back to me. His four men stood watch at the door, holding Anthony and his men back.

"My son may have a soft spot for you, but I assure you, you will find no weak link in me. Step out of line once more and I will not hesitate to bring you more pain than you have ever known."

I pulled at my restraints attempting to take a swing at him. He stood too far back for me to reach. I played my last hand, "I know what the fortuneteller said about my baby. This child will never lead you to destroy God's people."

"Oh, I know," laughed the Doctor.

I sat confused.

"The whole prophetess scene was a scam from the beginning."

"But you…"

"I did what needed to be done, to build my son's confidence. You…just wandered into the crossfire."

I was still befuddled.

"I couldn't just let him find a wife and fall in love. He has a destiny to fulfill, granted I made it up," he said chuckling at my confusion. "Family is weakness. Love gets in the way. Why do you think I had to kill his mother? She made him weak. Having an heir creates power, but not when there's love involved. Who better to receive a child from, than the very people you hate? Once that child is born, I will have my son kill you. Nothing can stop him. Now you see just how expendable you really are. Try my patience, if you dare." The guards opened the door and Dr. Tereski stepped out to speak to his red, faced son, leaving me irate.

CHAPTER 42

Since the children have flesh and blood, He too shared in their humanity so that by His death He might destroy him who holds the power of death – that is, the devil – and free those who all their lives were held in slavery by their fear of death.
—Hebrews 2:14–15 (NIV)

Locked to the commode pipe, I watched guards come and go as they cleaned up Anthony's mess. There was no point in trying to break loose. Everything I did caused more death. *Your father has abandoned you*, Anthony told me. He was wrong. God doesn't abandon His children…or so I thought. Perhaps He has abandoned me. I assumed my purpose, here, was to spread God's message to the guards. I hoped that He would release me once I succeeded in that mission. The only positive thing that's come from my imprisonment is Isaac. Even then, I had no way to know if he kept to the faith or if Anthony's men tracked him down.

I unloaded my frustrations on God, "Show me You're still with me. Every time I try to save myself, somebody gets hurt. Every time I show my confidence in You, it costs someone their life. First Omar, then Agnes, and now five more brothers and sisters are dead. What have we done to deserve this? Why have You allowed Anthony to gain this power?"

I noticed the guards at my door whispering to one another. "Your fearless leader is a fraud," I yelled at them.

The man on the left slammed his fist up against my door. If that was his way of quieting the yapping dog, it wasn't going to work.

I barked at him even louder, "You're following a coward. Everything that man does is for himself. He'll kill anything that gets in his way, including you."

The guards stepped away from each other and my door opened. I immediately tried to jump to my feet. The cuffs forced me right back down to the ground.

"Well, that's a new look for you," Justin smiled.

Had I known he was behind the door, I may have spared my wrist the trouble and stayed on the ground. "It's the VIP. reserved spot," I muttered. "I'd be thrilled to trade places with you."

"I meant the haircut," he laughed, "but the whole toilet scene does make me wonder what you did to antagonize the General. I thought I told you to stay on his good side."

"That monster has no good side," I bellowed. Bethany's body, lying on the cold floor of the hanger in a pool of her own blood, stayed at the forefront of my mind. "Did you find my friends?"

He quickly tried to quiet me, and then asked, "Why do you worry about your friends when your predicament is obviously worse?"

"For the same reason you'd be asking about your sister if you knew I had seen her," I hissed.

"You saw her?" He took a step closer and leaned in for more information.

"More than saw her," I exclaimed. "She tried to kill me."

"She was here in this room…" He looked around as if searching for proof of her presence. In his frantic hunt, I remembered that Justin was just as much a prisoner as me.

"Yes, she was here," I tried to calm my desperate nerves. "What about my friends? Did you see them?"

"Only signs of them," he quickly replied. "Why did they have my sister here?"

"What do you mean by 'signs of them'?" I pressed. "Did you see remains or proof?"

"On our search I saw men tied to trees, just like the ones you all tied up above the cave. Someone has stolen a few of the military vehicles from men who were out patrolling, and their equipment has gone missing. This could have been done by others of your kind, but –"

"Christians," I interrupted. I had already corrected him on this once before.

He stammered, "Excuse me?"

"My kind; my people; the slimy filthy cockroaches you all refer to are called Christians. Stop avoiding that name, trying to make us sound like we're of any less value than you." I was at the end of my fuse.

Surprisingly, Justin didn't fight back. He just kept on talking,

"I realize this could have all been done by other *Christians*, but I'm almost certain that the descriptions fit your friends' profiles."

"Who gave you the descriptions?"

"The men they left alive," he said. "I'll never understand you… Christians. If you'd learn to kill, you wouldn't find yourself with half of your current problems. Now, why was my sister here?"

"To kill my child," I said bluntly. "Anthony had her making sure I was healthy. She had two guards with her," I lowered my voice to a whisper, "but they're on her side. Then, during the middle of the checkup, she tried to stab me with a needle to kill the child."

"You didn't let her?" He sounded angry.

"You said you could get me out of here. I'm not willingly going to let anything happen to this baby."

"What if I don't get you out?" He exclaimed. "What if something happens to me before I get that chance, or while I'm trying to help you escape? Did you ever think about that?"

I shook my head no, but wanted to defend my reasoning.

He kept on with his verbal attack, "Do you realize that if he's allowed to raise that thing, this will be the end of you…the end of all Christians. Not to mention, the beginning of another World War?"

"The so called prophecy that you heard of was a lie," I blurted.

Justin refrained himself from whatever else he planned to say.

"Anthony's father made it up to brainwash a boy into believing it would help fulfill his destiny. It was all a big scheme to blacken Anthony's heart even more. He didn't want him falling in love and starting a family, so he told him he needed to have an heir by the very people they hate."

Perplexed, Justin stared at me, "That doesn't make any sense."

"If Anthony actually loved someone, he'd be weak. His father wants him to have a successor so –"

"No," Justin shook his head, "I get his reasoning. What I don't get is why Dr. Tereski would have told you all of that."

I motioned to the splintered glass, still wondering why God didn't just let it break.

"You did that?" Justin asked.

"I didn't realize it was bullet resistant, or I'd be gone by now," I sighed, *and Bethany might have lived.* "Anthony only protects me because he thinks this child is his ticket to success. His father wanted to remind me just how easily all of that can change."

"Or, he's playing games with you, so you won't fight back. You should've let my sister kill that thing," Justin protested. "Then we wouldn't be left to wonder."

"If I permitted her to go through with the procedure, Anthony would have had all of us killed; me for no longer carrying his child, your sister for killing it, the guards for letting her, and you because he'd no longer have leverage over you."

"I'm prepared to die. I have no doubt my sister and those guards are too, if what you say is true. The life in question is yours. You, a supposed Christian with so much hope in life after death; why are you afraid of death? What's there to avoid?"

"I…I don't…" I stammered. His question cut to the heart. I used to be afraid to think about death. That wasn't so anymore. I know that when I die, I will be with God and everything will be perfect. Now, I had a different fear of death controlling me. "You and your sister may be ready to die, but you won't be ready for judgment," I said. "I want to do whatever it is that I can do to stay alive, to keep those around me alive, in hopes of bringing them to God so they don't have to fear that judgment."

"You fight a losing battle," he chided.

"The battle I fight is for a war that's already been won."

Justin's face turned to stone and any further conversation ended. "Where's my sister?" He asked with an icy tone.

"She's on base; some place called the North Wing. Two guards keep watch over her but they; too, have families whose lives depend on them following Anthony's instructions." I thought back, hoping I had told him everything he needed to know.

Justin seemed puzzled, "He's kept us in the same place all this time." He spoke more to himself than me. His eyes widened as he turned fast to leave the room.

"Wait," I stopped him. "What are you going to do?"

"I need to see her," he said.

"What if Anthony catches you?"

"He won't."

"If you find her, then what will you do?"

"I haven't forgotten my promise," he reassured me in a whisper. "I'll find a way to get you out of here." He left in a very professional manner and marched down the hall.

CHAPTER 43

And the dust returns to the ground it came from,
and the Spirit returns to God who gave It.
—Ecclesiastes 12:7 (NIV)

I wanted to believe Justin, but the longer I stayed chained to the toilet the harder it was to hope for anything. Soldiers covered the entire base. As far as I knew, I was Anthony's top priority. His men may pass over Justin leaving with his sister, but they wouldn't have to double take when seeing a pregnant woman trying to leave.

New soldiers arrived to relieve their comrades at door. They brought with them one of the gray guards from Dr. Tereski's team. He entered my cell and a sudden chill entered the room. He set a bowl of something on the ground and slid it towards me with his boot. He then crossed his arms saying, "I'll leave when the bowl is empty."

"You want me to eat that?" The acid in my stomach threatened to make a sudden appearance. The substance in the bowl was an orange mixture. "It looks like vomit."

"I'll leave when the bowl is empty," he repeated.

"Then you'll be up here for a while," I pushed the bowl towards him.

He shoved it back in my direction, "You're going to eat it one way or another."

"I'll tell you what," I smirked. "You take the first bite. If you can keep it down, then I'll try it…" I paused and added, "Assuming you're still alive."

He refused to humor my request.

"Your boss revealed his little secret to me. I know he has no reason to keep me alive. This could be poison for all I know. Then, when I'm dead, he'll tell his son you did it. Where does that leave you? You'll be dead too." I realized, "Then again, if you don't feed this slop to me, there's a good chance Dr. Tereski will kill you. Either way, I'm not eating it," I said defiantly.

"The Doctor doesn't kill," the man gave me an evil grin. "He makes you beg for death. Now eat."

"Is that why you follow him, because you're afraid of him?" I asked.

"I follow him because his son is the future king. They take care of their own, and we take care of them. Eat," he demanded.

"What's that monster ever done for any of you other than threaten your families?"

The guard raised the sleeve on his jacket. I expected to see another tracker. He had the numbers 4168-18 tattooed on his arm. His evil grin became more sinister, "What families? Most of us only have our fellow convicts to lean on. That man you call monster provided us with all the family we need. So, if he has to use force to take what he wants then we, my brothers and I, have no problem applying it."

"You can't justify murdering innocent men, women, and children."

The guard shook his head at me and laughed, "Our definition of innocent is different. Now, eat… before I make you."

I felt the truth in his threat. Seeing that we were never going to compromise, I picked up the bowl and stared at it. Pretending, I pulled it closer to my face and quickly dumped it into the toilet bowl. Whoosh! It was gone.

"You stupid girl," he growled, rushing towards me with his hand drawn back.

"She's not to be touched," a strong voice sounded through the room. "Stand down soldier." Both guards outside my door had their guns drawn.

The gray guard stopped himself and jerked the bowl out of my hand. He tried handing it to the guard on the right, "Make yourself useful private, and go get the cook to refill this."

"We have our orders," my guard at the door tried to stand his ground.

"I'm giving you new orders. Both of you go, now."

"With all due respect," my guard had beads of sweat on his forehead, "we answer only to our commanding officer."

Angered, the guard in gray stormed out of the room, pushing the man aside as he cleared the doorway. He was already down the stairs by the time my door guard's comrade helped pick him up off the ground. They holstered their guns and looked at me.

"Thank you," I whispered. The guard on the left smiled, but the one who stood up for me wouldn't acknowledge me. As usual, they went back to their duty of ignoring me and keeping me caged.

"In case anyone has forgotten," I said frustrated, "I'm chained to the toilet. My hand can't slip out of my cuff. My body can't detach my wrists. I – can't – escape. Take the day off and enjoy whatever freedoms you claim to have. I'll still be here when you get back." As sarcastic as I was being, I acknowledged the truth of my statement. *I am trapped. I have no escape and no chance at life outside of these walls. I'll spend my last days here. I'll eat my last meal here. I'll even breathe my last breath here…except, this is not the finale. There is another life.*

That small reminder sparked a thought. It wasn't one to be proud of, but it was the best option I could see. I told Brittany I could pull the trigger during a time I wasn't quite sure if I really could. Now, I'm sure that I would. It wasn't worth it to be in Anthony's hands. *I refuse to be a pawn in his evil games any longer.* That's it... I decided my fate. Staring at the toilet I thought, *I could drown myself.* Sadly, the idea of sticking my head in the bowl was too gross to accept. *If the chain around my wrist were longer, I could–*

The prison door barged opened. I glanced up to see Satan's spawn. Anthony stared at me not saying anything. I didn't have the strength to fight with him. He won, but I wouldn't let him win completely. I'd be dead soon, and so would his child. *No,* a voice fought back, *it's not your time.*

"Is this what it has come to?" Anthony had a bowl in his hand. He brought it closer to me. I could see the same slop as what the other guard tried to get me to eat. "You're choosing chains over comfort even though the end remains the same. Is this what you want?"

"What I want doesn't matter."

"You're right," he sighed. "It doesn't. No matter what, in the end, I'll still have my heir. Now eat," he closed the toilet lid and sat on it.

Heir... That label for my baby entered my ears like a poison. I began to laugh, "He's really fooled you, hasn't he?"

Anthony didn't look amused. He scooped a spoonful of slop and tried to shove it in my mouth. I knocked it away.

"This so called destiny that you're fulfilling is all a big hoax," I bellowed.

"How do you know about…? Never mind, eat," he fought with me over another spoonful.

"Your father made it up," I said. "He didn't like you being a momma's boy. He knew you'd be too weak to do what he wanted. So, he killed your mother and gave you false hope for a fake destiny."

"Enough of your lies," Anthony growled. "Eat."

I refused, "He hired a phony 'gypsy' to fool you into his stupid plan. He doesn't want you falling in love."

"I said that's enough."

"What about the girlfriend you told me about when we were in the cave, the one killed in a car accident, who do you think caused it? Your father sees you as weak and pathetic. Even I can see that with the way he treats you."

"Silence," Anthony flared, slamming down the bowl on the back of the commode. Some of the slop splashed on me.

"You know it's true. You're his puppet. He controls everything you do."

"I am not his puppet!" Anthony threw his fist into the wall beside me while dropping down to my level.

I startled, but raised my voice even more, "He admitted it to me in this very room. You stood outside those doors. He's living vicariously through you to get what he wants. The man is a monster, and so are you."

Anthony gripped my jaw. I tried to pull his hand away, but

he was too strong. "My father is a man of integrity and honor. He has never lied to me. You, on the other hand," Anthony spit on the floor, "you have been nothing but trouble. Deny it all you want. It doesn't change the fact that I own the child inside of you. When I get my heir, and I will, I assure you it will be a pleasure killing you, slowly." He released my jaw. "Until then, you had better learn to listen. Now, eat." He held out a spoonful for me to grab.

I refused.

"Cordell, get in here," Anthony ordered. "Vickman, you stay at the door."

The guard who stood up for me earlier marched into the room. He waited for his orders never making eye contact with me.

"Hold down her arms," Anthony commanded.

I struggled, but couldn't go very far chained to the pipe. He pulled my free arm behind my back. He gripped the other as best he could so I couldn't lift it. Anthony placed his weight on my legs. Before I knew, I was choking down slop. Anthony forced every bite into my mouth and clamped it shut until I swallowed. It tasted like a mix of foods blended together. I wanted to vomit. I wished I could, but my body wouldn't let me.

When they finished, Cordell went back to his post. Anthony stood mocking me, "You never could put up a good fight. Best keep your lies and comments to yourself from here on out Miss Monzel." With that, he disappeared.

I couldn't hold my tears in any longer. I felt weak and defeated to the core. "I want out," I cried aloud to God, slamming my head back into the wall. "I hate this place!"

You have a way out, temptation called to me.

I stared at the guards and the walls. I pulled at my cuffs. I had no nearby weapons or sharp objects.

It's not your time, I heard again.

"Maybe not," I whispered, "but I've had enough. I'll make it my time."

Forcing myself to vomit into the toilet bowl, I heaved out as much food as possible. *I'm done,* I sighed. *I'm leaving this place and I'm taking my child with me.*

For the next few days, I didn't observe anything going on around me. I fed myself when Anthony would come. I'd wait for him to leave. Then, I'd force myself to throw up. I felt my body shriveling to nothing. I cried until I had no tears left. Ashamed of myself, I wouldn't talk to God. I couldn't. I knew I was wrong, but I couldn't live here any longer. I hoped He'd understand.

One day, people entered my cell and I didn't even notice. It was as if I were asleep. I could hear their voices though. Anthony's stood out among them all. "Call in the nurse," I heard him say. Then, I felt the chain fall off my wrist. I couldn't move. The door creaked. I didn't attempt to open my eyes. I no longer cared who came or went. Nothing mattered.

"Fix her," I heard Anthony say.

A gentle hand felt my forehead. Semi curiosity caused me to make slits of my eyes. Brittany turned and made a request to Esau. He left. Then, she came closer to me. I could see her holding her breath as she moved her hand into her bag. She pulled out a light and stuck a stick in my mouth. I didn't resist. I couldn't. "She needs to get cleaned up," Brittany said.

I heard Anthony remark, "Then clean her."

"Not with all of you in the room," she defended. "Help bring up the stretcher and supplies. She also needs new clothes."

I didn't care about my privacy. I wouldn't be around much longer, but she didn't know that. They must have done as she requested because I could feel her struggling to lift me alone. I wanted to tell her not to, but I couldn't speak.

"This would be better if you would stand," she begrudged.

I attempted to help, but it didn't seem like much.

She sat me down in the shower and removed my garments.

"It's cold," I startled through the water flowing down my face.

"Oh, now you can talk?" Brittany said adjusting the temperature. "What in the world are you thinking?"

I stared at her and mustered the strength to raise my hand up like a gun. I touched my head with my finger. "I'm keeping my promise." I didn't want to say it aloud.

"Are you mad?" She exclaimed using a cloth to wash me down. "This is worse than suicide. You're condemning yourself to life on a machine. Tereski is dedicated to taking your child," she leaned in close and the water soaked her even more. "Are you really going to give him your baby that easily?" She whispered.

I pushed her away. "I'm done," I groaned. "He's won."

"Not a chance," Brittany sat me up higher and continued to rinse my skin. "As long as I'm here, you're going to live."

A knock came at the cell door. Brittany left me in the shower and returned with soap, rags, a towel, and new clothes. She cleaned, dried, and dressed me. The soldiers returned to help her lay me in a stretcher type bed. Anthony didn't wait long before cuffing me to its rails. Brittany struggled to place an IV in my hand, but she eventually succeeded. I continued to ignore my surroundings. Even at death, I had failed.

I closed my eyes and when I opened them again, there was only one person in my room.

"Welcome back," a woman said.

My eyes focused on Brittany at my feet.

She checked me over and made notes on her chart. Then she listened to my heart. She moved the scope down to my belly.

I raised my head and waited, but for what I didn't know.

"Your baby is doing fine as far as I can tell," she said. "You've been in and out for about a day now, but all your vitals seem good. Your God must really be looking out for you."

I cringed, knowing what I tried to do was wrong. I hoped He would forgive me.

She put a straw up to my lips, "Sip. You need to start eating and drinking again."

I drank the water slowly. My throat was dry. As she pulled the straw away, I wanted to say something.

Brittany silenced me, "My guards will be back soon with Tereski. He wanted to know when you were awake. Stay strong. It's not your time yet."

A surge of life pumped through me. *It's not your time,* I had heard repeatedly. Now, Brittany said it. What was God trying to tell me? *Ask Him,* the thought ran through my head. I couldn't. I was too ashamed.

Anthony entered the room with a smile. Grumpy and Esau stood behind him, and Brittany went to their side. Two guards still stood outside my door. "For someone who believes my destiny is a lie," Anthony walked closer to me, "you sure tried hard to kill my heir." He placed his hand on my stomach.

Another surge of energy rushed through my veins as I tried to push him away from me. My wrists couldn't budge.

"I've been thinking about baby names," he grinned. "What do you think about Drake?"

I clenched my teeth, unsure what kept me back from cursing at him.

"Never mind," he laughed as he removed his hand, "I don't care what you think." He turned to Brittany, "Results?"

"We caught her early enough that no harm came to the child." Brittany said. "Now, she needs to get some exercise."

"Not going to happen," Anthony said. "She's had enough chances."

"I'm not asking for her," Brittany replied. "I'm asking for your heir. Pregnant women who lay on their backs too often usually end up having defected children." I couldn't tell if she was bluffing.

"Alright," Anthony caved, "but keep your guards close. If she tries anything, I want her strapped in that bed."

"Absolutely," Brittany agreed.

The next thing I knew, Brittany was standing over me removing my cuffs. As she sat me up, every joint felt rusty. Anthony stood at the door taking pleasure in my pain. I couldn't look at him. Lying back down I heard Brittany speak her frustrations against me.

"I'll get her to stand," Anthony said annoyed.

"Not by force," Brittany stopped him. "Give me time. Three days tops."

"You have a day," Anthony said.

I could hear the door close, but I never saw him leave. I didn't want to look at him.

Brittany forced my head in her direction, "You need to sit up."

I didn't want to, but I couldn't get the thought out of my head; *it's not your time.* I hadn't listened to it before, but it meant something different now. It was no longer a life sentence. It was hope.

"You need your strength," Brittany growled. "Get up."

Repeatedly she ordered me to sit until I couldn't take it any longer. I forced myself to sit upright. From there, I strained to stand. I ate what she gave me, I drank what she handed to me, and as the day went on, I walked where she told me. I don't know why. I just did. All the while, I disregarded my heart and I ignored my thoughts.

CHAPTER 44

Two are better than one, because they have a good return for their work: If one falls down, his friend can help him up. But pity the man who falls and has no one to help him up!
—Ecclesiastes 4:9–10 (NIV)

Anthony was pleased enough by the end of day one that he let me stay in Brittany's care. Grumpy and Esau only hung around when Brittany had to go somewhere. Other than that, they did whatever Anthony had them do. Other guards still stood post at the door. By day three, I was practically back to my normal health. I still didn't talk much, but I'd answer Brittany's questions. Finally, I had to ask her a question of my own.

"Why didn't you just let me die?" I looked her in the eye.

She paused what she was doing. "I honestly don't know. I hate to say it, but I felt sorry for you. I couldn't even see a flicker of the fire you showed me the day we met. All I could think is that Tereski was getting what he wanted. I couldn't have that."

How ironic, I thought as I gave a slight chuckle.

"There's that flicker," she grinned. "This isn't over yet. Stay strong."

Her comment sent my mind back to the woman who handed me a tortilla at the campground. That woman had also told me to "stay strong." Even though she had lost everything, she still encouraged me that night. Brittany, who wanted the child dead the first time I met her, saw reason to keep me alive. Whatever God had in motion, I needed to stop fighting against Him.

The doors opened. "Tereski needs you at the nurses' station," Grumpy said to Brittany. "More soldiers were attacked in the woods."

"I'll be just a minute," Brittany began to gather her things. She looked at me.

"I know," I said, walking back to the stretcher. "Lay the cuffs on me."

She snapped the cuffs over my wrists, but left the bed sitting up. "Work out those legs while I'm gone."

Lifting one leg at a time, I counted to ten and then I would switch. My thoughts ran wild. I could feel the change inside me. I knew what I needed, but I was scared. The Spirit overwhelmed my heart. "God, I'm sorry," I finally blubbered. "I don't know what came over me. The time I needed to show the most faith in You, I've proved a failure. I can't assume that You have left me just because things aren't going my way. I know that, but I forget it. I wanted out of here. I wanted my old life back. Now, all I want is You. It's killed me not to talk to You. I'm sorry it took so long to come back.

"There's a reason You put it on my heart to stay when Isaac gave me the chance to leave. There's a reason You didn't let me die. I submit myself to contentedness in You, wherever You choose to place me. All I ask is that, no matter where I am or how long I live, You let my child go with me or die with me. Please, don't let Anthony have my baby. Don't give him the opportunity to pass on his lies and hate to such innocent ears."

Later in the night, the next set of guards came for their shift. I recognized them from the first time Anthony force-fed me. The guard on the left kept turning to look through the glass of my cell door. His partner, the one who helped hold me down, would nudge him and make him turn around, but it didn't stop him. Once, I stared at them too long. The guard on the left caught my gaze. He cracked the door, deciding to pay me a visit. His partner grabbed his shoulder, but he shrugged it off and walked towards me.

My breaths shortened with every step the guard took closer to me. My mind ran through all of the worst possible scenarios. Chained, I had nowhere to go as the man crept closer. My pulse quickened as my heart rate skyrocketed. Perspiration trickled down my forehead. I attempted to shrink as far away from the man making his approach. "*Even though I walk through the valley of the shadow of death, I will fear no evil, for You are with me.*[15]"

I took a breath and asked, "What do you want?"

"I'm not going to hurt you," he said, stopping a few feet from me. He crouched down and stared at me on the stretcher as if I was an animal at the zoo.

---

[15] Psalm 23:4 (NIV)

"Then why are you in here?" I asked. *Where is Brittany when I need her?*

"Why don't you talk to us?" His voice was that of a boy.

I shook my head, confused.

"He wants to know why you haven't talked through the door like you used to," his partner explained.

"Why…?" I began to ask, but then realized it didn't matter why he wanted me talking to him. What mattered was that he desired the encouragement. "I'm sorry," I looked at the man in front of me and lightly pulled at my cuffs. "I'm kind of too chained up to go to the door."

"It's okay," he smiled, showing off his eagerness through very yellow teeth. After seeing the way he walked, talked, and laughed, I wondered if he had a mental handicap. "We can hear you now."

I smiled back and asked, "What's your name?"

"Jeremy," he said blissfully. Then he pointed to his partner, "And that's Ralph."

For a moment, all I saw in front of me was a child. He had a gun at his waist side, which meant, to me, that Anthony wasn't forcing him to work for him. My eyes began to well up, wondering how someone who seemed so innocent could be working for someone so evil. Before letting a tear fall, I shoved it all aside and started encouraging him as I had done for the other guards in the past, "You are young, but you are intelligent. You are good, better than the world tells you. You are a friend. You are a son. You are a child of the highest King, though you do not know it yet," I felt a little rusty, but God's words flowed through me.

Jeremy's grin nearly reached his eyes.

"You are good, made to do good things, though this world tries to pull you the wrong way." I looked up and saw Ralph in the doorway. I may be wrong, but it looked as if Ralph noticed his reflection on the door glass, finding disapproval. "Though your reflection is not as it should be, you have the ability to change. The person inside may not be who you want it to be, but you have the strength to mold that image."

Ralph lowered his head. Jeremy watched me with intent, soaking in everything. I leaned forward, getting closer to Jeremy. Ralph's eyes shot up with his hand at his side; no doubt, he stood prepared to draw his gun.

"Your life has seemed purposeless, but there is One who has given you a purpose. He wants to share it with you. He is the One who can show you how to be the person you need. He will never harm anyone because of his differences. To Him, no one is insignificant." I could almost hear God saying these same things to me. From the corner of my eye, I noticed Ralph's curiosity. "He is God. Not a make believe character or fancy Greek or Roman god. He is the Creator of the universe. He made the sun, moon, and stars, and He made you. Even though He loves everything that He created, there is only one thing He called 'very good'. That one creation is you. You, Jeremy, are very good."

Jeremy's bright smile expressed sheer delight.

I turned my head towards Ralph, "You, Ralph, are very good."

Ralph quickly stood straight. His head turned and he warned Jeremy to get back on guard. Jeremy did so immediately and the two stood without moving a muscle. Whatever it was that had them back to work wasn't visible to me.

I felt the joy of God's Spirit filling me up again. Through Jeremy, God reminded me of my purpose here. I prayed loudly, for them to hear, quoting David's psalm as its truth refueled my spirit, "Lord our Lord, how majestic is Your name in all the earth! ...what are mere mortals that You are mindful of them, human beings that You care for them?[16]" I finished the rest of it proudly, and then began to explain what it meant, "You see, none of God's creation compares to you; not in His eyes. You are far more important." I noticed the door at the entrance of the hangar open. Jeremy and

[16] Psalm 8:1,4 (TNIV)

Ralph suddenly stood at attention. It was too dark to see who was approaching, but I guessed it was someone to be wary of by the way Jeremy and Ralph reacted.

I summed up what I wanted to say, "There are forces seen, and unseen, which constantly try to pull you away from the purpose God has for you. He has given you strength to do all that you need. The question is, when given the opportunity; will you use that strength to do what's right?"

I kept still while waiting to see who would come through the door, but I wouldn't focus on them. I would focus on the joy of God's overabundant peace expanding in my heart. I had convinced myself that Anthony was ruining everything God had planned for my life. Now, after meeting Isaac, Ralph, Jeremy, and even Brittany, I began to think that this is right where God wanted me.

"Be strong," I said. "Don't give into the hate. Know that even though you are employed by those who are evil, you don't have to be evil."

CHAPTER 45

"You will not have to fight this battle. Take up your positions; stand firm and see the deliverance the Lord *will give you..."*
—2 Chronicles 20:17 (NIV)

The ground shook below me and, for a moment, I thought that my body had tricked me; perhaps a strange feeling every pregnant woman feels. Jeremy panicked. He felt it too. Ralph steadied him. The two looked at me and attempted to say something. I focused on the earthquake caused by the army rushing in towards us. Staring wide eyed, my heart skipped a beat. All three of us gaped at the soldiers who marched our way. I couldn't see Anthony or his father.

Ralph opened the door and took my cuffs off the stretcher, but left them on my wrists. "You need to come with us," he said. The army stood, waiting impatiently below.

"What's going on?" I asked as I maneuvered out of the bed. When I stood, he put one cuff on his own wrist.

"There's a threat on the base," Ralph grabbed my other arm and handcuffed it to Jeremy. "Protocol; we're to keep you safe. We are to give our lives to save yours."

What happens if both of you die? I'll still be handcuffed to you.

We reached the bottom of the steps and the mass of soldiers pulled and pushed us to the middle of them all. Jeremy said to me, "All forty of us have the same order; protect you at all costs."

Jeremy and Ralph stopped. Brittany, Grumpy, and Esau stood in front of us. "Why are you here?" I asked. "I thought you were needed elsewhere."

Before Brittany could say anything, Ralph answered, "They go where you go. General Tereski has ordered that a nurse be near at all times, just in case."

In case of what?

"Don't worry," Jeremy said, he looked with a smile and spoke in his child like voice. "We'll protect you." The way these two acted made me feel as if they actually believed that keeping me safe for Anthony was the best thing for me.

The guards surrounding us began to walk forward, taking us with them. Brittany and her men kept close. The soldiers led us towards the main entrance where someone hoisted open the large hangar door. The hazy morning blinded me. I lifted my hands to my face, dragging the men's arms with me to shield my squinted eyes.

The smell of burnt rubber and metal offended my nostrils and I immediately forgot about the blinding sun. I could hear the crackle and pop of a large roaring fire. Heavy black smoke engulfed us. The acid cloud burned my eyes and nose. Just before I closed my eyes to the burn, I saw flames rise from behind the base wall. Boxes of what appeared to be supplies were in full blaze. Men scrambled everywhere. Some attempted to return fire but, at who, no one seemed to know. It seemed the gunfire was random. While some of the men attempted to stop the fire, others pulled off large tarps to uncover several tanks and other types of weapons. Chaos ensued. The surrounding guards herded Brittany and me towards a parking area full of Jeeps.

As the smoke cleared, the silence became deafening while the militants waited to see their attacker. No warriors dressed in black came to raid the camp; no cavalry came to save us. All that stood behind the smoke were trees, rocks, and blown up rubble. The men around us began to part, as if they were the Red Sea, and an armored vehicle moved into the open circle where I stood. Justin jumped out of the SUV. His right hand was missing. A thick bandage wrapped around the end of his stump. He yelled for us to get in the vehicle.

"We are to wait for General Tereski," Ralph said, not letting us go with him.

"My orders are to bring you to him," Justin persuaded.

Multiple explosions rocked the hangar. Jets and fuel exploded in a mass of fire. Brittany and her guards didn't hesitate. They hustled into the SUV. Suddenly, Jeremy and Ralph dragged me in behind them. The moment the door shut, Justin peeled out of the crowd of guards. He drove straight towards the open exit. The gate, no longer attached, lay in pieces a hundred feet from the entrance. Justin gunned the engine and we burst through the opening before anyone could stop us.

“You’ve left the perimeter,” Jeremy exclaimed, reaching for his gun.

Quickly I pushed his hand back down on the seat and practically sat on him. “No,” I pleaded, “Please, don’t make me go back there.” I would do whatever it took to keep us out of that evil compound.

Then I heard Anthony’s voice, “Vickman, what are you doing you worthless peon?” It came from the radio receivers on Ralph and Jeremy’s belt. “Bring me that girl.”

They both looked hesitant until Brittany’s guards each pulled a knife on them.

“Stop it,” I struggled to remove Grumpy and Esau’s hands. Brittany, who had scooted herself up front to the passenger seat, turned and grabbed my cuffs. She pulled me foreword, which yanked Ralph and Jeremy’s hands with me. Brittany’s guards forced Ralph and Jeremy to give up their guns, along with all other weapons on them.

“This is ridiculous,” I exclaimed as Brittany let me go. I slid myself down to the floorboard at everyone’s feet, keeping my hands above me. Nothing was comfortable. “Can no one talk out issues anymore?”

“What is going on here?” Ralph’s frustration came out, knowing Jeremy and he were the ones left most in the dark.

“We aren’t going to General Tereski are we?” Jeremy said timidly.

“Only if you want to die,” Grumpy threatened.

Again, Anthony’s voice blared on the radios. This time, Justin ordered Ralph and Jeremy to throw the receivers out of the vehicle. When neither of them budged, Grumpy and Esau reached for the radios and took them by force.

“Wait,” Brittany said as she grabbed one from Grumpy. ”We

need to know what they're planning." They threw one out the window as she kept the other.

"What did you do to your hand?" Brittany exclaimed as if she had just now noticed Justin's arm pulled into his chest.

"Sacrifices needed to be made for the greater good," he said, paying it no more attention.

We all flew towards the right side of the truck. Justin had taken a hard left and struggled to get the vehicle under control. The area we would have driven over, if we stayed straight, blew up into thousands of pieces. The explosion separated trees and threw dirt clumps all around our vehicle and on top of it.

Brittany, who had braced herself up against the dashboard, looked all around for the cause of the explosion. Out of nowhere pulled up two vehicles similar to ours with their guns ready to fire. The rocket launchers fired constantly, blowing up the trees around us, forcing us to take two more sharp left turns. The gunmen on the other vehicles were herding us straight with each new explosion. Every time we tried to turn and outrun them, they forced us to stay on their course of choice.

"Did you set up those bombs in the base?" Brittany asked Justin.

"No."

We were all shocked.

"Then who did?" I could see the frustration on Ralph's face.

"Judas," Justin said prosaically. Apparently, he expected everyone to know who Judas was. The only Judas I could think of was the one that betrayed Jesus. All four men in the back leaned forward with shock and disbelief in their eyes.

"He's still alive?" Brittany said astonished.

It was as if, in that moment, no one realized we were in the middle of a war zone. They all shifted eyes at each other as children do during a ghost story.

I couldn't hold it in any longer, "Who's Judas?"

"The only man who ever got away," Jeremy said pale faced, still leaving me perplexed.

"What does he want?" Grumpy asked.

"His son," Justin tilted his head in my direction. "I had a little run in with your friend,"

Brittany slammed her palms on the dash, "Watch out!"

I braced for an impact just as Justin hit the brakes and swerved. Someone's knee jabbed into my ribs. Another's heel pressed hard into my toes. The vehicles around us began to sandwich us in together. Justin had no other option but to follow their moves at their pace.

"Your ally, the sniper, paid me a visit," Justin continued as if nothing had happened. He kept his eyes in front of him this time. He wouldn't say the sniper's name. "He took out nearly all of the troops on my most recent mission. He spared me because he knew I'd have information. I didn't tell him everything, but I told him enough. The moment I mentioned you, Judas revealed himself. They'd have killed me, too, had I not explained our deal. An ex guard from Tereski's men was leading them here. All they needed from me was passage onto the base. Once I parked the vehicle, they went about their plans but I only had one goal; to rescue the two of you."

"It's a fine job you've done *big brother*," Brittany said sarcastically as she stared out the windshield. We stopped, suddenly, in a smoky field where Anthony stood with his father and all of their soldiers around them.

Justin kept the engine running. The doors remained locked as Anthony raised his radio receiver to his lips, "Release Khristy to me and the rest of you can go free."

I held my breath out of fear that their answer would be, *for the greater good*. Ralph reached to open the door. To my surprise, everyone in the back jumped to stop him, including Jeremy.

"It's a trap," Justin whispered, as if fearing Anthony could hear him. "The moment those doors open, we're all dead."

Brittany spat into the radio, "Get her yourself you lying, no good–" Justin stole the radio from Brittany's hands and smashed it on the dash before she could infuriate Anthony any further.

"You don't know what he's capable of," Justin said, scanning the barricade around us.

Anthony sent four men to each door. When they couldn't come through by the handle, they awaited Anthony's orders and then hit the windows with the butt of their guns. I tensed for the shattering of glass and shielded my face. My heart hammered with each thud. I raised my head. This time, I was thankful to have bullet resistant glass between Anthony and me.

Justin threw the vehicle into reverse, turned it to face Anthony, and dropped it into gear. Spinning out, he peeled forward. My head whipped back as the SUV flew on its side, tossing us all on top of one another. We rolled once more, landing topside. My head pressed up against the window while my body lay underneath everyone else. My ribs began giving in to the pressure. Suddenly, I remembered my child. My heart hammered. A mother's instinct kicked in and I used my arm and leg strength to keep as much pressure off my abdomen as possible.

The same explosion that flipped us had also scattered Anthony's men and overturned the other vehicles around us. Quickly, we untangled ourselves from each other and tried to kick out the doors. Grumpy's side opened first. We piled out as a group as fast as possible. Brittany and her men ran off with Justin the moment their feet hit the ground. I tried desperately to follow, but the metal shackles around my wrists held me back. Jeremy stood with his head hung, while Ralph took charge.

"We can do this the easy way, or the hard way," Ralph said, pulling the hand cuffs just light enough to see if I would come with them.

"I'm not going back there alive," I stood, tugging harder for him to follow me. The smoke was too thick to tell where Anthony had gone, but I refused to stick around long enough to find out.

A silhouette figure came from behind Jeremy and Ralph. My eyes widened, my feet begged to run, and my heart jumped up to my throat. As the two turned to see what was going on, they each fell to the ground unconscious from a gun butt to the head.

The silhouette now became clear and revealed Lorenzo inside its shadow. Quickly and quietly, he searched the bodies until he found the keys to my handcuffs. The moment he freed me, I threw my arms around him.

"Thank you," I cried.

He pulled me away urgently, "Follow me." He moved swiftly without making a sound. His body stayed crouched and yet he still managed to move at a pace that kept me short of breath behind him. Something told me that Lorenzo was a higher rank in his unit than Private before going AWOL to help my friends and me.

We tracked around a few other flipped vehicles and came upon the devil himself. Anthony desperately tried to lift rubble off the top of someone. I could only assume that someone was his father from the pain in his voice as Anthony begged him to stay awake. I watched for a moment, wishing I had a gun. My hesitation caused me to fall behind Lorenzo's lead. Quickly I tried to close the distance. I succeeded only in stumbling over my own feet.

Anthony turned in a flash with his gun pointed right at me, "You!" He said, shocked to see me.

I stood paralyzed, *run!* I told myself. Nothing happened. He took a step towards me and finally my arms found their way beneath me to push me up.

"This is your fault," Anthony pulled the trigger. I braced for the bullet but found myself thrown to the ground. I half expected to see Lorenzo. Jeremy lay before me bleeding from his shoulder. He struggled to push himself up to stand. How or why he had chosen to save me now, I didn't know. What I did know is that I needed to get him out of here before Anthony took another shot.

As I helped Jeremy to his feet, I noticed Anthony hitting the side of his gun, jammed. I thanked God as Jeremy and I began to run. Lorenzo brought up the rear. He fired a couple of blind shots towards Anthony as some of Anthony's men came into view. We didn't stop running to find out the results and synchronized our steps as best we could. I refused to turn back and look. I had enough looking behind me. I chose to look ahead to the freedom that awaited us.

CHAPTER 46

Place me like a seal over your heart, like a seal on your arm; for love is as strong as death...
—Song of Songs 8:6 (NIV)

Lorenzo led us through fire, ash, rubble, and mud, until he found a spot far enough away that we could stop and temporarily wrap Jeremy's bullet wound. He never asked who Jeremy was, nor did he explain where we were going. Frankly, I didn't care. My focus stayed on our environment. Every branch that moved, every foreign sound, every distant cry, caught my attention. Jeremy clasped his mouth with his good arm, trying not to howl out in pain as Lorenzo put pressure against Jeremy's shoulder. We didn't have time to dig out the bullet but at least, for now, he wouldn't bleed to death.

Within a couple of minutes we were back on our feet racing through more pine trees. After nearly driving half a day the day Anthony kidnapped me, I was almost positive that Anthony's base was miles away from the old location of the Salt Creek Mountain Pass Christian Camp. Yet, the terrain seemed very similar. Pine trees stood tall all around. Their old needles and pinecones covered the ground and moss grew on rocks wherever moisture built up. Shrubs completed the ground cover, growing wherever they could find sunlight.

A vehicle approached behinds us. I preparing for the worst. If they spotted us, I was ready to run in the opposite direction. Perhaps we could get out of sight while they attempted to turn around. A van, painted like forest camouflage, drove straight at us. I crouched and readied to run. The van passed us about ten feet away and then skidded to a stop. That was our sign. I sprung to my feet to start running but Lorenzo grabbed my arm and spun me back around. The van doors flew open and Lorenzo rushed Jeremy and me inside despite my struggles.

The driver turned to see if we were all in and threw the van into drive. I recognized him. It was Gunner, from my original mission group. He barely acknowledged our presence with half of a salute before stepping on the gas. *Some did survive.* I had assumed them all killed. I didn't brace myself for the sudden lurch of the van and hit the back door with a crash. Lorenzo and

Jeremy were both smart enough to grab hold of the side of the van to keep from tumbling. Two other men held tight to a stretcher thus, keeping it from rolling. One of the men was Gunner's friend, Richard. He, too, gave a slight nod before returning to work. Stabling myself, I stared at the bloodied man on the stretcher. It appeared his injuries covered him from head to toe. He lay lifeless. The man wiping a wet rag across the wounded forehead caught my attention. Glen Roach sat with tears in his eyes.

"It's Judas," Jeremy gazed in disbelief. Judas, who I knew as Glen, looked back at Jeremy in recognition. He went back to cleaning the body in front of him.

Judas is Glen, my head spun. He's the one who helped us escape; who set off the explosions at the base. I wonder if David knew his father's secret. I recalled the conversation from the armored vehicle when Justin told the others that Judas wanted his son. My eyes locked onto the battered body. My heart drummed. *No, please don't be...*

Lorenzo stole my attention. "Khris, I need a scalpel, gauze, and tweezers," he said to me.

"There are supplies in that bucket," Richard pointed to a small pail beside me.

Jeremy removed his uniform and shirt, per Lorenzo's request. When I handed Lorenzo the utensils, I noticed scars all over Jeremy's arms and chest. Meeting his eyes, I managed to ignore the marks and muttered out, "Thank you for saving me."

Jeremy smiled grimly before Lorenzo laid him back on the floor. There wasn't much room but they made it work. Lorenzo then folded up his belt for Jeremy and let him clamp his teeth on it.

"This is going to hurt," Lorenzo said bluntly.

Jeremy nodded and kept his jaw locked.

"Khris, be ready to put pressure on the wound the moment I pull out the bullet," Lorenzo said as he poured water over Jeremy's shoulder and tried to wipe away as much blood as possible.

"Have you ever done this before?" I asked, but Lorenzo had

already begun digging in the bullet hole. His focus needed to be on Jeremy. The scalpel allowed for a slightly larger space for him to work with as he inserted the tweezers. The bumpy drive didn't help our circumstances. Sweat ran down Jeremy's forehead. His eyes welled. He began taking in short, deep breaths.

"Several times," Lorenzo answered my question as he pulled out a small piece of crushed metal, "but never in a moving vehicle."

I jumped into action, throwing gauze on the open wound, resting my body weight on my arm to keep pressure as requested. Lorenzo flashed a partial frown.

Jeremy used his good arm to reach up and pull the belt from his mouth. "When you get shot, I get to do your surgery," he laughed.

Lorenzo gave a slight chuckle as he eyed the metal scrap in the tweezers.

"It's a hollow point," Lorenzo snarled.

"What does that mean?" I asked. So long as the bullet was out, Jeremy could heal.

"This isn't the entire bullet," Lorenzo held the red coated metal closer to my eyes. It's only a piece. Hollow points split apart on impact."

"It allows for more suffering," Jeremy said through clenched teeth. I looked at his chest and wondered if Anthony was the cause of his scars.

Lorenzo threw the shrapnel into a bucket. "They're illegal in war time for that very reason. Then again, you can never expect evil men to fight by the rules. You'll have to deal with the pain until we can get you better help," he said to Jeremy.

Jeremy shrugged with his other shoulder, "I can manage." His gaze focused on Glen, who seemed to ignore our exchanges. "After all this time," Jeremy said.

"We'll get him all the help he needs," Glen said to Lorenzo while ignoring Jeremy's stare. He tried to smile, but it didn't quite meet his eyes. Jeremy eyed Glen like a hawk. He didn't seem very trusting of him.

The more I eyed the man on the stretcher the less focus I put on tending to Jeremy. A hand over mine brought me back to my duties. Lorenzo smiled gently as he replaced my hand with his. He'd be better for the job at any rate.

Glen brushed his rag up and down the battered man's arm. I couldn't see his face from where I squatted, "Is that…" I paused, wondering how I should react if the answer was yes. Curiosity drove me forward, "…David?"

Glen nodded his head, "I should have never kept him in the dark."

Slowly maneuvering around the supplies on the ground, I managed to make my way near them. Richard gave a faint smile, but I couldn't focus on him. I stared at David and tensed. Aside from the sheet covering his middle, he was completely exposed. Every inch of his skin had some sort of laceration or contusion as further proof of the torture he endured. I placed my palm on his forehead and noticed a fever.

"This is my fault," Glen said. It was as if he was confessing his sins aloud and not to us. "I should have told him more."

"You've been a good father to him," I grabbed the antibacterial ointment that I saw between us, along with some gauze. Too many thoughts whirled around my head. Helping tend to David's injuries would let me focus on something else right now. I didn't want to think. I just wanted to do.

"I let them in under my nose. My own staff…I never tried to prepare him for what would come," Glen kept his eyes on David.

"You knew this would happen?"

Glen batted his eyes, as if to remember something, and then shook his head. He held one hand on David's, but used his other to wash David's side. "Not exactly like this," Glen said nostalgically. "I knew the persecution would come, but I didn't expect it this soon. It was supposed to come in five more years. I would have trained him by then," he paused. "Yes, by then he would have been ready."

"How did you know?" I knew I should wait and filter my thoughts before they spewed from my mouth but, as I looked down at David's tortured body, I didn't care if I came across as prying. I wanted answers.

"Some secrets will be better made known when David wakes," Glen sat in silence.

Furious didn't even describe the explosion of emotions that threatened to burst forth. After the suffering we've endured, he couldn't answer a simple question.

Glen stood, "Please, watch him. We need to go up front for a minute." He left, avoiding the onslaught of inquiries that I was about to rain on him. Richard went with him and slid the door shut that separated the two sections of the van. I turned my mind back to rubbing the healing salve on David's cuts. Some of the bigger lacerations I found best to cover with gauze and lightly swathe it with the bandage wrap. I tried my best not to wrap too tight or too much. Everything I did overlapped other sores. Even though he lay unresponsive, David's skin still twitched and tightened when he felt the pain. I put a wet rag on his forehead to try to keep the fever down.

I dabbed ointment on the scabs and cuts on his scalp. It looks as if this is where the torture began. Some cuts had begun to heal and others were still raw flesh. I brushed the side of my palm across his forehead and down his left cheek. My hand rested against his skin. I used the rest of the ointment on my thumb and rubbed it over a few more cuts. It looked as if Anthony's men had beaten David with a bat, or worse. The gentle face I remember first seeing was now unrecognizable. His nose had been broken and fixed, his eyes swollen, and his lips were extremely dry and cracked. I took my finger and rubbed some of the ointment on his lips.

I remember the first time I heard his voice as he prayed. *Oh David, how I wish I could hear your voice again.* All my other friends were unaccounted for; I prayed fervently for David to regain consciousness. I missed him. When suffering in the pits of hell, I never thought I would see him again, or anyone for that matter. Lorenzo was one of the last people I ever expected to see. I assumed he would have found his way home, and yet, he came to my rescue.

"Yes?" Lorenzo asked as he caught me gawking. He and Jeremy were having their own conversation before I interrupted.

"You're the sniper, aren't you?" I asked.

His grin gave him away.

"What's your military rank?"

"Well, right now, I'd guess I no longer have a rank unless it's number two traitor," Lorenzo smiled playfully.

"Last I remember you were only the rank of Private and taking orders. You have impressive skills for a Private."

Looking amused, Lorenzo chuckled. "Guess I gave it away," he paused. "I was special ops for thirty-four years."

My mouth nearly dropped to the floor. A special ops soldier was with us all this time. That explained everything. He could rock climb, fight hand-to-hand combat extremely well, use a sniper rifle accurately, and apparently, he was adept at tracking down missing people. The only thing it didn't explain is how neither Justin nor Anthony knew this about him.

Lorenzo saw the question on my face before I could ask, "My commander placed me undercover in the squad I followed to your camp. He wanted to uncover some of the illegal activity going on within our unit. In the middle of my mission, someone transferred the team to your camp. My commander told me to stay. He thought the perpetrators would slip up and reveal themselves once they were away from base for a while."

"Well, I'm glad God brought you to us," I smiled.

"That's what Darius always said," he stayed silent for a minute. "He kept telling me God was the one who led me here, but I don't know how to believe it."

"It's pretty simple," I replied hoping only to help God's work on Lorenzo, which Darius started, and not hinder it. "You just trust that God knew we would need you here one day. So, He made sure that every path you walked helped lead you to us."

"If that's so, then why would your God lead Darius on this path if He knew it would end in his murder?"

That seemed to be the question everyone asked; some form of why, followed by an event of unexpected death. "I don't have an answer for that," I said confidently, "but, I know the God who does. I choose to trust there was a reason He took Darius home when He did."

"Do you really believe that?" It was as if Lorenzo expected me to fess up and admit I didn't really know what I believed.

"Yes," I refused to waver and waited in the silence for his response while I continued to doctor David's wounds.

Lorenzo switched out the blood soaked mess on Jeremy's shoulder with new gauze. He blinked back up at me and said, "I think Darius would agree with you."

Jeremy cleared his throat and cautiously said, "I was told that Christians were terrorists; monsters waiting to take us out the moment we show weakness."

"Who told you that?" I asked assuming the answer already.

"Everyone, they all tell me you have powers to control minds. That's how they won Judas to their side. General Tereski told us to make sure none of us listened to your lies, but I guess I was too weak." He looked frightened, like a child caught in the dark.

I wanted to inquire about Glen since Jeremy brought him up, but needed to address his way of thinking first, "You aren't weak and I'm not lying. The one that has lied to you is Anthony. He's a tyrant, willing to do anything to get what he wants."

Jeremy shook his head, "No. He's not a tyrant. He does a lot of good; he gives us a home."

"Then he shoots anyone who doesn't do what he says," I added while pointing at his shoulder.

"He was shooting at you, not me," Jeremy excused Anthony like a defensive son.

I then asked, while trying not to lose my temper, "Why did you jump in front of that bullet if you're so loyal to him? You deliberately interfered with his actions. Isn't that bad?"

"My orders are to protect his child at all costs." I could see Lorenzo's eyes widened as Jeremy let the cat out of the bag.

This is not his child. I felt my blood coming to a rolling boil. Before I could stop myself, I blared, "So you think that it's okay that Anthony raped, beat, kidnapped, and murdered all so he could have a child?"

"He would do anything for his children, whether adopted in or created by him," Jeremy sounded brainwashed. He made it seem as if Anthony had himself playing the role of a god.

"Does he always take care of his children by beating them?" I stared at his scars. One in particular traced from his stomach, around his ribs and stopped midway up his side. It bulged out, looking as if someone did a terrible stitching job on it.

"Sometimes children need disciplined," Jeremy began fidgeting his fingers.

"He treats you like a slave," Lorenzo refuted. "Discipline and abuse are two different things. No good father would ever treat his children so cruelly."

"Absolutely not," I confirmed. "Fathers teach their kids how to act by their own example. They discipline out of love, and not anger or hate. They raise their children to be a help to society, not a hindrance."

"Oh, we are helping," Jeremy tried to reassure us. "We're purifying the land. We even–"

"That's the same speech Hitler made while killing six million Jews," Lorenzo blurted. "It's not right. No war created by man can bring peace to all men. There will always be someone to start up another battle. Purification of the land is going to have to start with setting aside our differences; willingly."

Jeremy furrowed his brows. He seemed bewildered. I wanted to add that the land already had a Purifier. Before I could open my mouth, David's body started to shake.

"What do I do?" I panicked. David's body convulsed more wildly. I grabbed his shoulders to keep him from bouncing off the stretcher. His arms swung and pushed me back.

"Lay your chest on top of his and keep your body weight on him," Lorenzo said sternly. "Can you hold pressure, here, for a moment?" He said to Jeremy.

Before Lorenzo could get over to help me, David lay still. He didn't just stop shaking; he stopped breathing. I panicked. Lorenzo felt for a pulse. He folded his hands over David's chest and began pressing down repeatedly. "One…two…three…" he spoke aloud the number of compressions. At fifteen, David came back to us. His eyes opened wide as he shrieked out in pain.

"Help Jeremy while I check him out," Lorenzo instructed. I resisted the urge to wrap my arms around David's neck.

Repeatedly, David tried to get off the makeshift bed but Lorenzo gripped his arms and kept him on the stretcher, "You went into shock. You can sit up but don't try to stand."

"Where am I?" David frantically looked around the van. His eyes locked on me as if he had seen a ghost.

"You're in a van," I said. "Your father saved us."

"My…father?" David whispered. "Yes, God…" His eyes still linked with mine seeming dazed.

"Glen Roach," I added.

"I know who my father is." David tried rubbing his eyes but jerked in pain. Like a whirlwind blast, I watched as he began to feel all of the sores on his body. He voluntarily lay back down in the bed. "You died…I'm dreaming…you died." With that, he closed his eyes and looked as if he'd gone to sleep.

"David?" I whispered.

The silence lingered.

Lorenzo looked at me, unsure of what just happened. All

three of us sat confused. "David," Lorenzo said tapping David's shoulder. David jolted awake. Scared, I jerked, slightly adding pressure to Jeremy's shoulder. He flinched. Thankfully, Jeremy's kindness outweighed his anger as he attempted a grin.

David sat up again, but didn't try to stand. He appeared fully alert as he stared at Lorenzo. "Where am I?" He asked again.

"In a van," Lorenzo repeated my answers. "Your father saved you."

"My father?" David whispered to himself. I feared we were about to go through the same conversation all over again. "Yes, my father…so that means…" He slowly turned, looked at me, and went pasty white. Looking back at Lorenzo he asked, "Can you see her?"

"Who? Do you mean Khris?" Lorenzo said.

David turned to me and twisted back to Lorenzo, "How is she here?"

"Ask her yourself," Lorenzo traded me places once more. I felt awful putting Jeremy under so much change.

Every move I made towards David caused his eyes to grow wider. I could practically hear his heart beat out of his chest. Finally, when his facial expressions could no longer stretch, he held out his hand and touched my arm. Was this how Thomas reacted when Jesus appeared to him after He rose from the dead? When the tension on David's face started to dissipate, he squeezed my hand. I turned and sat next to him so he didn't have to stare at me the whole time. It didn't help.

"How are you here?" He repeated.

"Unlike you, I walked…" No reaction. "Who told you I died?"

"The guards…they threatened and beat me, wanting the whereabouts of the Ichthys. I didn't have it. They brought you out with a sack over your head and started to beat you. They told me they were going to kill you. That was the last thing I remember. The clothes were the same, down to every bloodstain and tear. You were crying, hands bound behind your back," David choked, "I couldn't get to you. They demanded I give up information I didn't know. They tortured you in front of me for days. I fought them, all of them. I tried to get to you…" He began to sob.

"That wasn't me," is all I could repeat. "I was given a room with a bed, where guards watched me day and night. No one hurt me; Anthony didn't allow it. I promise you, that wasn't me."

"She looked like you," he squeezed my hand tighter. "I'm so sorry I couldn't reach you."

His grip became unbearable. I placed my other hand on his to get him to loosen up. Grabbing his undivided attention, I argued, "David, that body wasn't mine. Anthony gave me a change of clothes after capturing me. He must have forced another girl to wear them. I promise you, I'm fine."

David looked me over a couple of times. He rubbed his hands up and down my arms as if he needed to confirm that I was flesh and blood. Goosebumps rose under the hair of my skin. His hand rested on the side of my face as he pulled me in close. His lips pressed gently against mine. My heart raced. Before I could reciprocate anything, he pulled away in pain.

"I'm sorry," I reached for the ointment, seeing his lips slightly start to bleed.

"No, no," he attempted a smile, "that was definitely my fault." He let me rub more of the medicine on his lips and face. "Will you take a rain check?"

I blushed, "Absolutely."

Lorenzo and Jeremy pretended not to notice.

Then, David asked, "Why would Anthony keep you alive?"

I took in a deep breath and let my chin drop to my chest. As I pulled my shirt tight against my stomach, I revealed my baby bump.

I could see the confusion on David's face, "Did he…is that… are you…"

"Pregnant," I gulped, suddenly at a loss for words.

"You don't have to explain anything," he said grabbing my

hand. "I'm just thankful to know you're still alive." He tried to embrace me again, this time without the kiss. I gently wrapped my arms around him, but pulled back upon hearing the sting of pain in his breath.

I sat straight, took another deep breath, and exhaled slowly. David was a trusted friend. I owed him something. If not for him, I owed it to myself to talk about all that had happened. Beginning with the day that I hiked the mountains to call my parents, I told them everything. I told of Anthony playing us for fools and Justin's predicament. I tried to explain that he, too, was a prisoner but David wouldn't hear it. I hated having to talk about Anthony raping me. I was embarrassed and couldn't look them in the eye. While making them understand Anthony's plan to use the child for the destruction of Christians, I kept Jeremy's reactions in view. He didn't seem shocked or worried. It was no small feat getting David to understand that the importance placed upon me, because of the baby, meant I was never in real danger. All of that would have changed after my baby was born. The hardest part of all was telling them how I tried to take matters into my own hands. Again, I asked God for His forgiveness.

As I talked, I watched a plethora of emotions change in David's face. He was angry and sad, then furious, and wanting to seek justice. He would show sympathy and understanding, but mostly he was enraged. I tried to reassure him that I trusted God to get me through it all. David allowed his fury to cloud his judgment. He let go of my hand and slammed his fist into the stretcher bed suppressing any pain he felt.

"David," Lorenzo said steadily. His voice resembled Darius' when trying to calm David in the cave. "I haven't known you long, but I know you well enough. You're not a man to deny a godly explanation." Lorenzo stunned me.

I thought that David would come unglued, but he soon exhaled, "You're right." He looked at me with regret, "I'm sorry."

The door to the cab slid open as the van came to a stop. The sun was nearly down, giving us very little light to go by. Glen smiled upon seeing David but he never approached him for a hug or handshake. "It's good to see you awake, son," is all Glen could muster before telling us we would have to walk from here. I scooped up all the medical supplies I could and put them in the pail. I didn't know how far we planned to walk, but it made no sense to leaving it behind.

"Gunner has volunteered to take the van far away from our destination, rerouting anyone tracking us," Glen said. "We need to be cautious. Those of you who have been in the compound may have trackers."

Had I not seen the tracking devices in the water jugs back at the cave, and the one on Justin's arm, I would have thought Glen to be paranoid. Richard handed us clothes that looked like camouflaged scrubs. Lorenzo and Jeremy had no problem stripping to their underwear and putting on the pants and shirts provided for them. David only had a sheet wrapped around him, so he, too, slipped the clean clothes on quite easily – other than struggling against his constant pain. I kept my eyes averted, feeling my cheeks redden. As for me, I struggled to change, pulling my arms through the inside of the sleeves of my old shirt, and then turned my back to them all to slip my arms into the new one. I put it over my head the same time I pulled off the old shirt. Then I wiggled it over my head and through the neck hole of my new shirt. The pants were a little trickier, but every man present was respectful enough to have turned himself away.

Once we changed, we threw the old clothes into the van. Jeremy was hesitant to give up his old uniform, but Lorenzo reassured him that that would be the only way he could stay with us to keep my baby safe. It made me uncomfortable to use the child, like a pawn, to persuade Jeremy. I wondered if he would turn us in if given the opportunity. Still, we couldn't just leave him to die. We needed to give him a fair chance.

Glen ran a hand wand over each of us, scanning for electronics.

Anxiously I waited for the process to end. I didn't like standing around. The sooner we started moving, the harder it would be for someone to find us. We all scanned clean. It was time to move.

I overheard Richard talking to Gunner before he left. The way they talked made it sound as if they didn't expect to see each other again. "God speed, my brother," Richard said. The two gripped arms and hugged. Gunner drove off through the woods after that. Then, Glen led us in a direction none of us knew, except maybe Richard and special ops Lorenzo. I still couldn't get over the excitement of having such a blessing at our side. There was no doubt in my mind that God brought him to us.

"Keep close and stay alert," Glen said. "We have two miles to go."

David stumbled as he tried to walk. I rushed beside him to give him extra balance. It seemed odd that neither David nor his father made an advance towards one another. What confused me most was how Glen seemed to have so much fear of losing David while we were in that van. Now that David was awake, Glen showed none of that emotion. Men are different from women. I get that. What I don't get is how a father and son couldn't even hug after not knowing if they'd ever see one another again.

CHAPTER 47

Men will flee to caves in the rocks
and to holes in the ground...
—Isaiah 2:19 (NIV)

We trekked through the woods as quietly as possible. Two miles sounded easy compared to all we've already endured but it was far from it. Every muscle ached. The beginning stages of cramps stung in my legs. I extorted what little energy I could find within, and used it to power each foot forward. As long as we moved, I was able to ignore most of the cries from my lungs for a full breath. David and Jeremy had the toughest time out of all of us. I lagged behind with them, helping David when he would let me. Having someone to help gave me the strength to push forward... Tears stung my eyes as I thought of Angelica. I needed to help David as much as I needed to aid her after the massacre. Glen suddenly held his hand in the air, bringing us all to an abrupt stop. He motioned for us to gather around a large tree stump. What little strength I had was waning fast. I breathed heavily while trying not to fall.

"Watch in every direction," Glen whispered. "If you see movement, tell me."

Each of us listened intently for the slightest proof of onlookers. My eyes peered through the trees. Even though I was supposed to be looking around, all I could see was the field of death where all of this began. Surely, I was mistaken. My mind couldn't comprehend why we would ever come back. A crackling sound suddenly pierced the silence. It wasn't loud. It was out of place.

I spun on my heels ready to bolt. The middle of the tree trunk opened like a cellar door. Richard stepped down into the dark abyss. He turned and put a hand up to help me go down. I stepped back. Jeremy and David went instead. Once they were safely down, I took Richard's extended hand and felt my way through the dark. Lorenzo followed me. I reached my hand out to touch the wall. It was cold and harder than any dirt I had ever touched. I couldn't even scratch my nails into it.

"Tungsten," Glen said turning on a flashlight, "the toughest metal there is. Often compared to Titanium but it's a lot more malleable. It lines the entire trunk of this old pine, protecting us from most natural disasters and heavy attacks. You'll find it outlines the rest of this tunnel as well."

Richard and Glen lit up our way through the steep tunnel. "The path will take us about fifty feet below ground. There are a few steps to look out for when we turn corners, but other than that it's a pretty smooth path," Glen explained.

"What is this place?" Jeremy asked.

Glen answered very optimistically, "A safe haven for all Christians."

"How long has it been here?" David's question tinged with the sound of distrust.

"We started it a little over nineteen years ago," Glen said. Then he added, "It's not finished, but it'll work. I planned to show it to you when we completed it."

"Who's 'we'?" David investigated.

Glen didn't answer.

David seemed just as furious with his father's secrecy as I was. He eyed Glen like a hawk and kept his teeth clenched as if trying to hold his tongue. His brows furrowed. Though tempted to repeat David's question I, too, kept silent. Something didn't feel right, but if we pressed Glen too hard, he may show more of his cards than we're prepared to play.

At the end of the tunnel, we came to a flat wall. No marks indicated an opening or way through. Glen knocked on the wall twice. It echoed behind us. Another knock returned his from the other side of the wall. Glen knocked three more times and turned out his light. Click. A small burst of light came from a hole in the flat wall and blinded us briefly. It then snuffed out just as quick. From the other side of the door I could hear the sound of a dial turning with a snick and a spinning wheel followed by another tick. Grinding gears set my teeth on edge. Glen had us stand back as the wall in front of us pushed open.

Once we were all through the doorway, two men pulled the door closed and turned a giant wheel until it locked in place. The room was dark. I could hear faint whispers, like a gentle breeze on the sea. Lights slowly flickered on in four corners. The rest of the room dimly lit up from lights on pillars. Hundreds of eyes stared at us around the room: men, women, and most surprisingly, children.

Glen stood in the middle of everyone with his hands held high. "Mission accomplished," he exclaimed. Everyone clapped and cheered, praising God. Then, Glen waved his hands to get their attention once more. As the people quieted down, he added, "God blessed us with a few others as well. The rest of the team should be back within the hour. We need to prepare more places for the injured."

Men and women stood up and began to move things around and pull out supplies, while others stayed huddled in small groups. I recognized some of the people from the camp. It was obvious that those who knew each other were sticking together. A group of women watched the children. I wondered about their parents and if they had been lost to the slaughter. A familiar face approached from the crowd. It was Thad; the same generous man who walked with us in the mountain until choosing to join our camouflaged brothers and sisters. Sadness took root in my heart.

"You're alive," he said, coming to shake David's and my hands.

I tried to smile, but I couldn't. I couldn't even offer a proper handshake. I had to tell him about Bethany.

"Lorenzo told us about what happened to you guys. He also told me about Darius. I'm sorry."

I swallowed the lump in my throat.

Thad gripped my shoulder, "He was a good man. We'll see him again."

I tried to offer a grin.

"You should see what they've done here," he changed subjects. "They've planned for everything. There's a pantry full of nonperishable foods. They've had enough first aid gear to tend to everyone's wounds, and plenty of blankets to keep us warm. I've even heard rumors that someone supplied books for the kids to keep up with their studies."

I looked around at the room, "Where did they all come from? I thought the soldiers took off with the children."

"A few days after we all parted ways, the group I followed found several locations where the soldiers had taken the kids. We've been infiltrating their bases ever since. We brought in five last week. Bethany and a few of the others stayed behind to check out the rest of the area. We're waiting to hear from them."

I lowered my head, "Thad, they're not coming back." The joy of victory fell from his eyes. He leaned in as I explained. "Anthony's men caught them breaking into his main base. He murdered them all right in front of me. Everyone was there except you and Teresa. I…I wanted to stop him…but…"

"Hey," Thad tried to comfort me. "It's not your fault."

"He killed them because I wouldn't cooperate."

"They knew the risks. We all do. The enemy also killed Teresa two days after we parted ways. We can never forget those whom we lose. Thank God, they're never really lost."

Two other familiar faces approached me and Thad could see the joy in my eyes. "I'm going to let the three of you visit," he smiled. "It's good to have you here."

Jasmine and Angelica came and embraced both David and me. I soaked in their warm hugs, not wanting to let them go. They looked amazing. They were no longer the dirty, beat up girls I thought died in the cellar. Jasmine's strong hug and Angelica's beam let me know that God had taken good care of them.

"What about…?"

"We've been praying for this day," Jasmine exclaimed. "Come, let's get you bandaged. Khris," she looked at my stomach, "you need fluids and something to eat." They took David and Jeremy to the back of the room. I followed close behind, but made sure they got the attention they needed first. Lorenzo stayed back to talk with Glen. I wanted to know about Steven and Jeffrey. I looked around as I trailed behind David and his caregivers. I saw both fear and hope in the faces that we passed. A young girl stood out as she sat, playing with a raggedy stuffed animal. She held its arms and moved it back and forth making noises I couldn't understand.

"Hello," I smiled down at her.

She looked up at me embarrassed.

"Who's your friend?"

"Greg the g'rilla," she mumbled.

"He seems very nice," I patted it on the head. "He looks like a good protector."

The girl laughed at my comment and looked me in the eye, "He's not real, silly. He's only pretend. God protects me."

"That's right," the woman sitting next to the girl leaned in while holding a baby in her arms and gave the young girl a kiss on the forehead.

"You've taught your daughter well," I grinned.

"She's actually my niece," the woman's tone became sullen, "but I'll take care of her as my own."

I didn't need to ask about the rest of her story. This child didn't need to hear a repeat of her families' tragedies. I noticed that this woman didn't have a scar on her hand. Many others did. Still, several seemed to have evaded the enemy's mark.

I watched as Jasmine dug shrapnel from Jeremy's wound. She prepared to stitch it closed while Angelica redid some of the bandages that I put on David. He, too, needed a few stitches. David struggled to stay still. "I guess I should've taken more time on my dressings."

"Relax," David smiled at me, "you did great for being in a moving van. I held together all the way here didn't I?"

"Don't be so hard on yourself," Angelica added as she poked a needle into David's upper arm. "Jasmine had to teach me most of this."

David flinched, "Well, she better continue to teach you." He rubbed his arm playfully, "You could be a little gentler. What was that for?"

"Hepatitis shot," she smiled waving the needle in front of his face. For a moment, I thought he'd pass out. "We're giving them out to everyone here before we have any epidemic breakouts."

I laughed at David's pale face until she turned with a new needle in hand. I shook my head, backing up slowly. A brick wall stopped me in my path. I looked up. Lorenzo stood behind me, holding me still with a smile, "It's not going to hurt but for a second," he laughed. I panicked. My world went dark.

Kicking and screaming, I yelled, "You can't have her! She's mine." My arms were pulled tightly across my chest albeit unwillingly. "Stay away," I yelled. The more I struggled, the less I could breath.

"Khris," a voice whispered in my ear.

No...no, it's a trick. I slammed my head back, trying to get free. Something warm and wet trickled down the back of my neck.

"Khris, it's okay," the voice came again.

I clenched my fists, pulling hard against my restraints. They tightened even more.

"Khris," one more time the voice came with others saying the same things, "easy, it's okay."

"Easy," Lorenzo's voice came into focus as his grip loosened. "It's okay. You're safe."

Short breaths came and went as I flushed with embarrassment. He let go completely. The eyes of the entire room were on me.

"Nothing to see here," Lorenzo said to the crowd as he wiped blood from his nose. He lifted his head and pinched the top of his nose between his eyes.

"We can do it another time," Angelica put the needle down.

"I'm so sorry." Shame covered me.

"It's okay, you just need some rest," Angelica handed me a light blanket from a pile they had up against the wall. "We can get you situated later."

No, I said to myself. *You can do this.* "I want the shot," I said, holding up my sleeve. Angelica approached with caution and wrapped an elastic band around my arm. She cleaned off a little spot on my skin before poking it. I cringed, but forced myself to stay still. Lorenzo requested his shot right after me, seeming to have gotten his bloody nose under control as if it didn't faze him at all.

"I…I'm…" Sorry couldn't explain how badly I felt for hurting him.

"I'm alright," he grinned removing his hand from his nose. "See, I'm fine."

Attempting a smile, I looked back at Angelica and Jasmine. I didn't know what else to say, "How did you two get out of that cellar?"

"Lorenzo didn't tell you?" Angelica looked at him.

He shrugged his shoulders, "No time."

Angelica stepped closer with excitement, "We were all huddled into that little bathroom with the door shut. It felt like an eternity in there. All we could do was pray. Jeffrey's prayer reminded us of Shadrach, Meshach, and Abednego. 'The three of them were thrown into the fire,' he prayed, 'but You, oh Lord, sent Your angel to bring them through it. Send us an angel, please.' Sure enough, God sent an angel who pulled us through a pathway of flames. Lorenzo had bulldozed everything off the top of the cellar door and burnt half of his body to save us. God rewarded him though…" As she said this, I searched Lorenzo's body for scars. "…his burns were only minor blisters."

"Glen found us a few hours later," Jasmine added. "He led us to this shelter. Others were already here to help get us situated. He and Lorenzo immediately began looking for you and David. We never thought it would take this long."

"Where are Jeffrey and Steven?" I asked. "Are they safe?"

"They were part of your rescue mission," Jasmine smiled.

"They've been taking teams out on missions ever since we got here. Don't fret. They should be back any time now."

"They were tired of sitting around," Angelica laughed.

Steven always was the first one to jump in with both feet, and Jeffrey would follow him anywhere.

Two knocks echoed through the room. A few people bolted in all directions. All voices hushed. The room went dark. The man on our side knocked once and three knocks followed his. Again, you could hear the sliding open of the peephole door, followed by the turns of a spin wheel and three different clicks. The grinding of the gears came as the man at the door turned the wheel.

"We need medics," someone hollered as the door opened and on turned the lights. Several of the women in the room, including Angelica and Jasmine rushed to the scene. I stayed back, unsure of how to help.

Thirteen people came through the door looking just as bad, if not worse than David did when I first saw him. Bruises and cuts covered them from head to toe. Some were even missing large sections of skin. A few healthier looking men carried in the injured who couldn't walk for themselves. The rest of the people in the room stayed back and watched as the medics went to work.

"Khris," I heard Jeffrey say my name. Before I could turn around, he had me in a giant bear hug. "I never thought I'd see you again." A second grip came from behind as I saw the side of Steven's face join the picture.

"I'm so glad you guys are alive," my eyes started to water.

"Now don't get all sappy on me," Steven tried to joke.

"No, no, it's just the pregnancy hormones," I laughed. There was no hiding it and, besides, Jeffrey knew about it before Anthony split us apart. Steven had to know by now. Still, they looked surprised.

"I don't want to talk about it right now," I said as I reached out and hugged them both, again, as tight as I possibly could.

"We are here for you through it all," Steven said in my grasp, "but only if I get to be called Uncle."

I laughed through the tears of joy running down my cheeks, "Yes, definitely. I insist. It really does mean a lot to have the two of you here. I didn't want to do this alone. Tell me," I released them and became serious, "I've heard a little about the items stored down here, but what's the plan? We're not expected to live here forever, are we?"

"I'm not too sure," Steven said. "Glen has been searching for David. Now that he's here, we'll be able to get more answers. We've searched the woods through and through. The past five days we haven't found any refugees. Except a couple of days ago, when we met a man who said he knew where Anthony was holding you as a prisoner. He told us everything in exchange for giving his wife and children a safe place to hide. We sheltered them and took him with us. Had he not known the layout of the base so well, I don't think we would have made it out alive. We found all of the injured people brought in today in an underground prison. They're in pitiful shape. If we can get them back on their feet, I'm convinced we can do anything."

Jeffrey added, "I'm assuming Glen has a plan since he already had this hideout, but–"

He reminded me of a question I felt needed answered, "Does anyone know how he knew to build this place?"

"Maybe he discovered it," Jeffrey suggested.

"Impossible," I remarked. "In the van, he said a few things that made me think he knew the attacks were coming." I filled them in on everything he said while David was unconscious. A jab came to my side as David approached our company with a limp. The warning had come too late.

"Don't worry," David said. "I know as little as you three. Frankly, I'm questioning if I ever knew who my father really was. The man I'm seeing is not the man I grew up calling 'Dad'."

"Well I hope I can convince you otherwise," Glen surprised us all. Apparently, sneaking up on conversations ran in the family. He appeared, lightly placing his hand on David's shoulder. David flinched away, but I couldn't tell if it was out of pain or bitterness. "Son, can I speak with you?" Glen attempted to pull David to the side privately.

"Anything you need to say can be said in front of them," David gestured to Jeffrey, Steven, and me.

"Very well, follow me," Glen didn't hesitate to heed his son's wishes.

CHAPTER 48

Do not be afraid of those who kill the body but cannot kill the soul. Rather, be afraid of the One who can destroy both soul and body in hell.
—Matthew 10:28 (NIV)

Glen led us to the back right corner of the room, through a door cloaked to look like part of the wall. In the room, he placed a small lantern on the table, which lit up the ten chairs circling it. The four of us sat on the side opposite Glen. The tension between us thickened.

"Well?" David rapped his fingers on the table.

"I'm struggling for where to begin," Glen's voice shook.

David furrowed his brows deeper.

Steven broke the silence, and calmly asked, "Why not explain where we are?"

Pulling away from his son's gaze, Glen answered, "Geographically, we're underneath what's left of the campground's activity fields."

My heart sunk. I was right. I leaned forward furious, "You're telling me there was a shelter we could have run to when all of this started. How many lives could have been spared?" I felt Jeffrey pat my arm to stop me from exploding further.

"Yes," Glen lowered his eyes, "but it wasn't supposed to happen so soon. I had a couple more years to build up the camps' attendances and spread the message. By then, these shelters would have been completed and their locations would have been made known to Christians."

"There are other shelters?" Jeffrey inquired.

"How did you know this would happen?" David spat.

Glen chose to answer Jeffrey, "All three camps have a shelter beneath them. There are twelve others in various locations, but I don't know where. I specifically told the other men and women not to reveal the locations for safety reasons. Next year, we were supposed to touch base."

David stood, slamming his fists on the table, "Again, how did you know this would happen?"

"Son, there are a lot of things . . . I kept secret from you, and I'm sorry. I would have told you, but it was for your safety that I did not."

"Look at me," David shrieked. "Does it look like your secrets kept me safe?"

I wrapped my fingers around David's wrist, trying not to hurt him, and gently begged him to sit.

"No," Glen said solemnly.

"Answer the question," David demanded, gritting his teeth.

"Please remember, as I reveal these things, that you were the one who didn't want to talk in private."

David sat, still clenching his fists.

"I told you, long ago, that I didn't have any living family. I lied. I have a father who may or may not still be alive. I also have a brother." I saw David's entire childhood crumble before him as his father continued to reveal their ghastly family dysfunction. "My father became an abusive drunk after our mother died. He always found trouble at the bars, which left my older brother, William, and I to tend to him. When he got in too deep, men came for him. They didn't try to take the house, or car, or even what money my father had left. They wanted us kids as payment. My father let them take us. They called themselves the RA – Rising Ambassadors. I was nine and William, eleven. We had no way to fight back. They took us away but our father never came for us. The RA put us into combat training courses and classes that filled our heads with lies, namely against the government and Christians. When Will turned nineteen, they took him from the barracks in the middle of the night. They kept us apart until I, too, turned nineteen. Then they took me. The RA placed me in the middle of the desert with hundreds of other young adults and they finished our training. Will became one of my trainers. They trained us to live among Christians. They set us up to live in our assigned areas until they called us for *The Awakening*. That was supposed to happen five years from now. I should have seen the signs when the border locked down…I should have warned you all then… but, I didn't.

"I hated every day I was with the RA. They had won my

brother over, but not me. When my training in the desert ended, I made plans to escape. They provided everything we would need to live while we waited, but I threw it all away. I had to fake my own death and change everything about me."

"Is that why they call you Judas," I asked, "because you betrayed them?"

Glen smiled as he shook his head, "Ironic, isn't it, that I would have the same name as Jesus' betrayer. However, it was my birth name. My plan was to leave the country. I didn't get very far before I met your mother."

"You and Mom knew each other in high school," David denied the whole tale.

"No," his father shook his head. "We met in a diner. She stole my heart the moment she walked through the doors. I stayed in that town longer than I had planned. I couldn't leave. I had to marry her. There was only one problem; she was a Christian – the very type of person the RA trained me to hate.

"On our fourth date, she took me to church with her. I remained cautious and on guard. I also never felt more welcomed by a group of people in all of my life. God was working on my heart and I didn't even know it. The following week, her father baptized me. Three months later, she and I married. Your mother loved the mission field. It bothered her to come back from a trip and see the Christians in the states who weren't actively living their faith. That's when she and I came up with the idea for the spring break camps.

"Strange things started happening though. Her father's barn caught fire. Someone ransacked our house. Then, threatening messages showed up on our answering machine. I knew the voice. My brother had found me. He swore that if I didn't come back within the week, they'd kill your mother. There was no way I'd go back or leave Whitney's side. I took the biggest risk by telling her everything from my past. She was distraught, to say the least, but stayed faithful to me. She believed it was God's plan for us to be together and that He would give us wisdom on what to do.

"Her parents revealed, to us, some land they owned – the very land we're on right now. Apparently, her family had secrets of their own. They had amassed a great deal of wealth throughout the ages from different family lines. They gave every penny to us to build the camp with one stipulation; we had to prepare Christians for the persecution that was inevitably coming.

"Whitney's willingness to leave her life behind only made me want to work harder to further the Kingdom of God. My own faith began to grow and strengthen. It was then that I knew my devotion to God was solid." Glen took a moment to gather his thoughts, and then took in a deep breath, "We traveled to her family's land, and settled fast hoping to get started as soon as possible. While builders worked on our house, we surveyed the property. We mapped it out in search for a good location for the camp. When we started the building process, we also had men working on this shelter. That's when David was born. Then..." Glen took a breath, keeping his composure. "Your mom left for her last mission trip. She wanted to say goodbye to her friends in Africa. She planned to spend the rest of her days here."

Glen held David's gaze, as if debating on how much more he wanted to reveal, "When I told you that your mother's plane was shot down in the mission field, I wanted it to be an encouragement to you to strengthen your faith. I was too scared to tell you the truth... too scared that you would blame her death on me."

David gripped the table. His knuckles whitened.

"Again, I'm sorry I lied," Glen could no longer look at any of us. "Whitney never made it out of the states. The safety of our unlisted property kept us hidden from the Rising Ambassadors. We always used cash for every purchase. When Whitney's name entered the system for the plane ticket, an RA suicide bomber joined her flight. She called me from the plane, explaining that she saw someone with the RA flag tattooed on his arm. I prayed and prayed for God to let it be a coincidence, but…" he couldn't hold the tears back, "in the middle of trying to comfort her…the line was cut. The news reported that the plane had a malfunction, but I knew better.

"For Whitney, I continued with our plans. Still, I worried about protecting you, David. I wanted to keep you home, where the RA could never find you. You had your mother's spirit, but I had to keep you safe. When I met Joy, I knew she was a Godsend. She couldn't do much on her own, physically, while I was away. With you tied down helping her, you would be kept out of harm's way until I could prepare you for what was to come…"

"You never prepared me for anything," David growled. "I spent day after day, cutting trees, chopping logs, hauling wood, digging trenches, and all other grunt work you assigned me and never once, did you try and prepare me for genocide or should I say, mass extermination."

"I wanted it all to be ready. I didn't want you to have to carry my burden…"

"No, instead, you inflicted a whole new set of burdens on me. This entire time, I thought the attacks were somehow my fault. I thought I should have been wiser; that I should have seen some sort of hint that our own staff was plotting against us. I blamed myself for all the people who I had to watch suffer and die. Now, I know their blood is on your hands."

"David," his father desperately pleaded, "you have to understand…"

"I don't have to do anything," David begrudged.

"A house divided cannot stand," I said softly as I grabbed David's hand. "Your dad knows he was wrong. He can't change it. None of us can, but we need to move forward. We're all frustrated and angry, but anger will get us nowhere."

"I wish I could change how I handled things with you..." Glen tried, again, to show David his sincerity.

"They kept looking for something called the Ichthys," David

stopped his father's apology. "They tortured me looking for it and planned to use me as bait to get you to reveal where it's hidden. I've heard you use that word in secret before, and I want to know what it is."

Glen nodded his head, "This shelter and the others are the Ichthys."

"No," again, David assumed his father a liar. "They sought after it as if it held some form of monetary value; as if it were an object they could hold."

"That's because your mother and I were very keen on keeping the strongholds discrete. When hiring builders, we made sure they knew never to call it a shelter and never to reveal its coordinates. Along with that, they had to record every yard as an inch, every foot as a centimeter, and every inch as a millimeter, in order to confuse the enemy. No doubt, they knew the *object* could help Christians, but they never knew it could be this large. Most likely, they assume it's a weapon. Your mother and I came up with the name Ichthys because it would be a place to hide Christians, just as it was a sign to help them back in the days of the first persecuted church."

"Sir," I interrupted. He had told me not to use that name back when I first met him but it slipped. I had a question gnawing at me that needed answered. "You said you changed your name and that your brother's name was William. What's his last name?"

"Tereski," he said. "Why do you ask?"

Everyone's eyes were on me. I was speechless.

"I'm kin to that scum?" David exclaimed rising from his chair. Meanwhile I sunk further down into mine.

"How do you know him?" Glen asked, confused.

"We met briefly as he watched his men torture me. His son, *your* nephew, is the one who betrayed us." David then looked at me, "He's the one that Khristy warned me against, but I was too stupid to listen. Because of my stupidity, Darius is dead and Khristy is forced to carry that monster's child."

"This is not his child!" I lashed. Jumping to my feet, I said with all the fury of my being, "My baby will be a child of God. Anthony will have no claim over him or her."

"I'm sorry, I didn't mean..."

I stopped David after realizing I had blindsided him. "I just need you all to understand that my baby is God's and I will raise him or her in that way. David, I don't know what's going on in your heart, but the truth is that now isn't the time to question your past or that of your family. God has brought you here for a reason. He has you in His plan. Glen did what he thought was best. Now we have the option to either let those secrets become a curse or we can turn them into a blessing."

"Khris is right," Lorenzo stepped out of the shadows. "The RA will be more overzealous now that they think they have world power. Their evil is rising up and the US government is destroyed. All through your history, your God uses suffering to bring more people to Him. Every time the world attacks, more Christian's rise up, not just the fake ones who wear their Jesus on Sundays only to take Him off that night. Rather, the ones that truly have a heart to love their God and love others. You have the opportunity to train Christians now, in a world that will more easily see how much they need salvation. This is where Christianity flourishes."

I wondered why Lorenzo wasn't, yet, a brother in Christ. He was right and everyone in the room knew it.

"If everything about the RA is true, then where do we start?" David asked.

Jeffrey's eyes lit up, "The Pentecost."

The whole room now turned to him.

"Hear me out. After Jesus' last appearance on Earth, came the Pentecost. Once the people reformed, Peter preached. He taught about the hope brought through Christ's sacrifice and convicted them all. Three thousand people joined the body of Christ that day. We have members of the body here with us. Most of them are tired and feeling lost. Let's remind them where to find hope.

Speak to them about their salvation and assure them that this is not the end."

Steven tapped in, "We do as the Apostles did. We've already seen the diversity of people coming together to retrieve Christians on the run and take care of the wounded. There's a lot we still need. Finding food, water, and other supplies is a good start."

"Right," Glen tried to take control. "All of that is brilliant. We can come up with a list of things needed and let the people fill in where they best wish to join..."

"Not before we tell them the truth," I interjected. "Unless you have already told them about the RA, they deserve to know what they're up against. Jeremy can teach us about some of the RA's tactics and secrets to better equip ourselves. If we can't be honest now, those still weakened by these past events will fall away the moment the rug pulls out from under their feet."

Glen opened his mouth in protest, but David caught him. "She's right," he said. "Nothing good has come from keeping secrets. If we're expected to work together as one, then we can't hide things from each other."

Glen rubbed the back of his neck, mulling over things. "Alright," he submitted, "let's go check on the wounded and I'll talk with everyone after that."

We stood to go, but Jeffrey stopped us, pulling us together for a prayer. He prayed for wisdom, guidance, and strength to get us through the next few hours. He also prayed for unity, and for God to open our hearts to His plan and love. At the end, he prayed that we would only speak God's message and not one of our own agenda.

I grabbed David's arm as the others left the room. His eyes revealed the pain of his heart. "If you need to talk; I'll listen," I said softly.

"Thanks," he smiled faintly. With his finger, he gently brushed back some of my hair behind my ear. His eyes revealed that he wanted to say something, but was scared.

I reached up and took his hand into both of mine, "What is it?"

He sighed, "During my imprisonment, knowing everything they were doing to me, I kept praying for God to release you from the torture. When I thought they killed you, I…I felt relieved knowing you didn't have to suffer. I never once thought you would be dealing with something so… permanent." He looked at my baby bump. "My bruises and scars will heal, but you'll have this for the rest of your life. You say the child is God's, and I realize that you're the one carrying the burden, not me, but I can't wrap my mind around how well you're taking this."

"David, I struggled with this for months. So much so, that I tried to kill myself. The only way I made it through was because of God's grace. I know there will be times I feel as if I can't handle it, but this is going to have to be something I take one day at a time. I think that's all that any of us can do now."

"You're right," he said, maneuvering his hands to where he now held both of mine. "I just don't want you to think you have to take on this challenge alone."

My heart raced.

"If it's alright with you…"

Panicking people suddenly started to crowd in our little room, pushing us apart. David tried to pull me in closer to him but we couldn't keep our grasp. I could still see him through the blurred faces. Someone fell at my feet. I reached to help them. When I stood, David was gone. The room darkened.

CHAPTER 49

Finally, brothers...Aim for perfection, listen to my appeal, be of one mind, live in peace. And the God of love and peace will be with you.
—2 Corinthians 13:11 (NIV)

After losing David, I pushed against the flow of the crowd to find the cause of the chaos. One light shined at the entrance. Ten or fifteen men stood in the light by the closed door with makeshift weapons in hand. Several knocks echoed. It wasn't the secret knock. Silence grew as if everyone in the room were holding their breath. A sudden chill filled the air. The knocking became more frantic. I thought I heard the word help, but no one was moving, only listening.

"Someone, help them," I couldn't take it any longer.

Jeffrey snuck up beside me, quieting me, "We have to take precautions. Anyone could be on the other side of that door. This could be a trick for all we know."

Glen quietly gave the order for all men to stand ready for defense. Everyone stood on high alert. The ones nearest the door crouched, ready to leap into action. Lorenzo and three others huddled directly in front of the door's opening. All four of them looked at each other and then to the man standing guard at the door's lock. The clicking, wheel turning, and gear grinding began. The light dimmed. The door slowly cracked open.

"She needs help, please," a familiar voice burst through the silence, echoing in the room. *It couldn't be…could it?* Lorenzo kept the man from entering and sent the three behind him to check out the tunnels for traps. The door closed. Again, we waited. This time, I held my breath with the others. *If it is a trick, where could we go?*

It seemed like hours had passed before a series of knocks resurfaced with a pattern. One…one, two…one…one, two, three. The door reopened.

"Coast is clear," Lorenzo called. He had a limp body in his arms. "We need Jasmine. This girl is in bad shape."

Someone turned on the lights. Those who had been hiding in the back began to ease their way forward to look at the new arrival. Men and women searched to see if the girl was someone whom they had lost.

Jasmine and Angelica retrieved the body from Lorenzo and took her to the back of the room. I followed to help, ready to do anything they asked. As they lay the girl on the ground over a blanket, shouts came from the entrance.

"No. I swear. I'll do anything. Please, just help her," the familiar voice cried.

I turned to see Lorenzo and the three men apprehend a blond headed man. He had bruises and cuts everywhere.

"How did you find us?" Lorenzo growled as the others held the man against the wall.

Suddenly, David recognized him too. "Traitor," he yelled as he broke through the crowd and ran towards Justin with clenched fists.

"David, don't!" I shouted, rushing to interfere.

Lorenzo caught David's punch midair and pushed him back. "This is not your fight," he said firmly.

I made it to Lorenzo's side, standing between David and Justin.

"He can't be here," David bellowed. "He's one of them."

Gasps came from all around, followed by multiple mutters of condemnation. Fear gripped me. These people suffered greatly. There was nothing to stop them from taking all of their revenge out on Justin.

"Are you taking his side? He kidnapped you," David spat.

"He also saved my life, more than once," I defended.

"Who's to say this isn't another trick?"

"Everything he did was to save his sister. She's here, in the back, with the medics. Tell me you haven't gone to extreme measures to save your loved ones."

"How did you find us?" Lorenzo repeated to Justin, turning both our heads. The whispers stopped as everyone desired an answer.

"We were in a wreck," Justin breathed heavily. "The trackers on two of the men with us set off. The dead driver slammed us into a tree. I carried my sister through the woods, hearing footsteps all around. I thought it was Tereski's men coming to finish the job. When I recognized Jeffrey and Steven leading a group of injured men and women, I followed. I thought that maybe they could lead me to help, for Brittany." He quickly added, "They didn't know I was behind them."

"Why did you feel the need to hide?" A burly man accused. "Why not ask for their help above ground?"

"You saw the group they brought," Justin came across both desperate and irritated. "Every person with them was in terrible condition. I didn't want to add to their troubles. When I saw them go through the tree trunk, I knew there had to be something for my sister."

"I'm not buying it," said the burly man. "Who's to say this isn't a plan to find our weaknesses? That woman could be acting for all we know." He strode towards Brittany.

Justin shouted at the top of his lungs, "Don't touch her."

Immediately, Angelica stood between the man and Brittany, while Jasmine continued to work on her. Angelica met the man's stance without wavering.

"Step down," the man said.

"If you plan to hurt her," Angelica spoke loudly for all to hear, "then remember that whatever you do to her, you do to God."

"You're trying to tell me that this woman is a messenger of God?" The man practically spit in her face.

"'The King will reply, "I tell you the truth, whatever you did for one of the least of these brothers of Mine, you did for Me."'[17]" She quoted Matthew twenty-five. I noticed her hands starting to shake.

The burly man violently pointed his finger to Brittany on the floor, "She's not hungry. She doesn't need clothes. Nor is she without a place to stay."

"You don't know that," I said, trying to help Angelica. "Are you going to let your heart become like that of a Pharisee? Jesus

[17] Matthew 25:40 (NIV)

constantly preached about the sins of the heart. It's not about the sustenance or beds. It's not about the laws you follow on a checklist. Whatever you do within your heart towards another person, whom God *has* created; you have also done to God."

Angelica smiled at me, relieved to have some of the pressure off her. I paused, letting everything I said settle. He wasn't the only one that felt that way. We all needed to check our hearts, including me. I'm convinced God wasn't just speaking through me, but to me. I did my best to step back from interfering with the Spirit's work, "Now, if you can tell us that your heart is pure in what you're about to do, then Angelica will step aside." Angelica tensed. "If not, then I refuse to let a brother in Christ stumble."

"She's right," David said, finally seeming to trust me. "I feel as if a lot of us have lost touch with the heart of God since our persecution began. We've allowed anger to reside where love should be. Hate fogs our judgment. We need to draw closer to God in our suffering and follow Jesus' example. The lives we had are gone. These people, right here in this room, need to be our priority. Friend or enemy, they are here with us now and we need to take care of each other. We need to encourage and strengthen one another for the battles to come."

A woman asked, "How long is this going to last?"

"Isn't someone coming to help us?" Another questioned.

"We don't know," David said.

Murmurs started to rise from all corners of the room.

"Calm yourselves," Glen's voice rang. "My son is right. We can't let our fears separate us. We need to stand strong, together. The men we're up against aren't lawful. In short, they're terrorists who are working to overthrow the government and to, in their words, purify the world of Christians. If we can't stand together now, they will destroy us one by one."

"Who told you all of this?" I could hear the accusations begin again.

Glen breathed in deeply, "They're called the Rising

Ambassadors, also known as the RA. Long ago, they trained me to be part of their cause. I ran away, refusing to follow their system. I planned a way to counter their attacks and protect as many Christians as possible." The room was oddly silent. I expected a riot or, at the very least, someone to hurl a few insults at Glen. He continued with beads of sweat gathering on his forehead, "This year, we planned to spread the message of where Christians could find shelters like this one, if they ever found themselves in trouble. I never meant for it to stay a secret. I only wanted to keep the wrong people from finding out. The fact of the matter is, I messed up, and I need your forgiveness. We can make this work, but…"

"What's to say there aren't more secrets in your closet?" A young man asked, letting Glen feel the sting of his past decisions. "How do we know that this shelter isn't just another place to gather us up for a second slaughter? If this RA group is out to destroy us, and they've been hiding among us for this long, how can we trust anyone here?"

"If you can't trust your own brothers and sisters," a lady responded, "then maybe you're the one we have to watch out for. Who's to say *you* won't give us up to the enemy?"

Whispers increased among the crowd and people started to take sides.

"Enough," Lorenzo shouted with authority. "Can't you see that this is exactly what the RA wants? If you start fighting against yourselves, they've already won."

The young man threw his hands in the air, "So what do you expect us to do? Team up and follow Glen Roach. Devote our lives to him, and just trust that he's leading us right. I don't think so. I've seen enough of my friends and family murdered."

"No," Jeffrey stood tall. "We aren't calling any of you to follow anyone other than the God of all nations, who has brought us together for a purpose. No man is in control here. Glen won't be leading you, unless asked by you. We need to listen to him though. He has more information on the RA's plans than anyone here does. If we expect to live through their attacks and threats, then we're going to have to hear what he has to say."

"Not me," the young man walked to the door. "I'm not going to stay down here forever. I have family I need to help."

"If you leave now," Glen said, "you and your family will die."

"Is that a threat?"

"It's a fact. The Rising Ambassadors have monitored Christians for years. Everyone claiming to be a part of the faith is on the RA's watch list. They didn't just pose as staff at my camps. We aren't their only concern. They placed themselves in all Christian camps, retreats, and expeditions before the attack. They made it look like, to the rest of the world, we were terrorists bombing civilians and attacking military personnel who tried to help. Once the RA manages to convince the majority of the nation that we are the enemy, the people you once called friends and coworkers will do their work for them. They will kill and arrest Christians in every city and town. Maybe your family did survive and are in hiding right now, but with that mark on your hand anyone you come in contact with outside of these walls will be put in danger."

"What does this scar have to do with anything?" The man held his hand in front of his face staring at it.

"It's your brand, so to speak," Glen said. "They've already announced it. They say we've marked ourselves like a gang. That scar will cause others to treat you like a threat the moment you step into the public. They'll kill most of you on sight, but others will be taken in for questioning; tortured for information, as they did my son. The RA will give anyone without that scar one chance to clear his or her name. If you fail, they'll either kill you or give you the same mark and send you to prison. The freedoms we once knew are gone. We are fugitives now."

The young man stood by the door, but didn't make another move to leave.

"What can we do then?" A scared teen said from the crowd. I could feel the hopelessness in the room as our situation sunk in.

David's voice resounded, "'He who has an ear, let them hear what the Spirit says to the churches. To him who overcomes, I will give the right to eat from the tree of life, which is in the paradise of God.'[18]" David walked until he was in the center of the room with his father. "In the book of Revelation, Jesus declares this right after telling a church in Ephesus that they have done great things except one; they had forsaken the love that they first had. If we love, in the midst of our suffering, we have not lost.

"We are foreigners in our own land. We no longer have the distractions of a daily schedule as an excuse. Our work will now consist solely on taking care of one another and furthering God's kingdom. There are things we can do for each other here, to show our love. It's time we offer up the talents God gave us, and use them in service to each other. Our hearts no longer have to wait in fear for help. We can rejoice in love. We've seen the medics stand up valiantly to take care of the wounded. We've witnessed brave men and women willing to rescue those of us who the RA held captive. Yes, we've seen death and suffering, but we've seen God's hand bringing us through it all." Like a rally leader, David threw up his fist, "Will you choose to stand together as God's people?"

"Yes," a few of the people said.

"Will you help to strengthen one another?"

"Yes," more men and women shouted.

"Will you look out for the good of each other, no matter your differences? Will you choose to stand against the forces of darkness and live a life filled with love?"

Nearly everyone gave a resounding yes.

"Brothers and sisters, today we unite under one God for one cause: To show His love is burning in our hearts. No matter what circumstances we face, no one can defeat us. They will try, but they will not succeed. God has heard our cries and He will answer. Trust in Him to deal with our enemies in His time. Vengeance is

---

[18] Revelation 2:7 (NIV)

His, not ours. God calls us to stand against the forces of darkness in love. Let God Almighty do the rest."

Everyone cheered, encouraged and renewed in spirit by what David had to say. Then, one of the men pinning Justin took us three steps back, "What about people like him?"

Lorenzo didn't hesitate to answer, "He, and others from the RA who come here for refuge, can give us Intel. They can help us prepare for attacks and guide us on how to rescue your other brothers and sisters."

"He's not one of us," Justin's captor refuted. "How can we trust anything he has to say?"

"One of us or not, he doesn't deserve to be treated like an animal," I said sternly, making my way towards them. I had to do something. "We are called to bring others to Christ, not shut them out, or kill them." An arm stopped me in my tracks.

The man blocking me stood between Justin's captor and me. Isaac Denver's face came into view. Awed, I stepped back and listened to what he had to say, "I'm new to this faith in God," Isaac began. "I don't know all of your laws and regulations. What I can tell you is that if it weren't for the kindness that a young woman showed me during her own torture, I would never have considered becoming a Christian.

"This man," he pointed to Justin, "worked for Anthony Tereski, but his work was involuntary. Several of Tereski's men are forced mercenaries. He finds their weaknesses and uses that to keep them in line. I was one of those men. He threatened my family to keep me under his control. Coming to Christ, I found my chance to run away as a free man with my family. Everything changed. Farrell," he gestured to Justin once again, "worked to save his sister. Obviously, she's out of Tereski's hands. I'd be willing to bet my life, that without her under his evil control, Mr. Farrell will be more than willing to keep peace with the people here."

"So we have three, willing to vouch for the good of this man's character," Justin's captor huffed. "Would anyone else be willing to stand alongside them and risk everything to see him freed?"

"I will," David said, standing with Isaac and me.

"I will also," Angelica stepped forward.

"Five?" the man holding Justin mocked. "Only five of you, compared to a room of maybe five hundred."

"Since when have numbers ever mattered to Christians?" Lorenzo questioned. "Didn't your God call Gideon into battle with only three hundred men against the Midianites? Didn't your Savior call only twelve men to begin His mission with Him? If I recall right, even in ancient Israel's days only two witnesses were required to condemn a man. Wouldn't you also only need two witnesses to absolve a man? Nevertheless, if you condemn Farrell for his guilt, condemn me also. I, too, worked alongside Tereski before joining you."

You could hear a pin drop as the room went silent. No one threw the proverbial first stone. When the silence lingered, Lorenzo stared at the men holding Justin. "Well?" He spread his arms wide, giving them full control. The men let Justin go and stepped back. Lorenzo lowered his arms and met Justin's eyes. "Can we trust you to work with us?"

Justin had every reason to lie. His sister's life was still in jeopardy, along with his own. He had no way to escape without our permission. People may have still wanted to see him suffer for all the pain inflicted on them and their loved ones.

"No." Justin said. As men stepped forward to apprehend him again, he added, "But, you can trust that my sister and I won't work against you either. We'll tell you everything we know about the RA."

Lorenzo nodded, stepping aside for Justin to make way to his sister. "There's work to be done," he said to everyone else. "Let's get to it."

Some were unhappy with Justin's freedom, but no one outwardly challenged Lorenzo's actions. It became apparent that

Lorenzo had more respect from the masses than anyone else did in the room. The murmur of voices began again. It had become second nature to whisper.

I checked on Jasmine, praying she had been able to help Brittany. Justin was kneeling beside his sister as Jasmine gently shook her awake. She stirred a little, and then half smiled upon seeing Justin's face. "You made it," she said.

"We both did," he beamed. "How do you feel?" Justin brushed his hand up against her cheek.

"Fine," Brittany replied. "I'm a little tired."

Jasmine whispered to Justin before Brittany dozed off again, "Ask her some questions with easy answers. We need to make sure she's remembering things."

A brief look of concern crossed his face. He sank down and made himself as comfortable as possible. He wasn't moving any time soon. He asked when she was born, what their mother's name was, and for her favorite food. That last question threw me off; favorites change too often. She answered, "Veggie pizza, with anchovies and blue cheese."

Jasmine and my disgusted faces made Justin chuckle. "She's an odd fish," he said, "but I'd do anything to keep her safe."

"After all I've seen, I believe it," I smiled. I stared down at his arm and missing hand. He cut it off to remove the tracker. 'Sacrifices needed to be made for the greater good,' Justin had told Brittany when she asked him about his hand before. He knew cutting it off was the only way to get Brittany out safely. That, in and of itself, confirmed his devotion and love for her.

"I'll be back shortly," Jasmine said. "She has a concussion. She needs to rest. Have her sip water when she wakes, but mostly she needs to let her brain rest," she handed him a water bottle.

"I can do that," Justin stared at Brittany. It made me wonder where my sister was and if she was being well cared for.

Isaac Denver approached me. With him was the young woman

whom I had met when I arrived at the Ichthys. The young girl with her still held to Greg the Gorilla as tight as before.

"Praise God you made it out," Isaac smiled. He was a completely different man than I first met. "Heather," he said to the woman next to him. "This young woman is the reason we're here today."

"I'm Khris," I smiled at her.

Heather pulled me in for a warm hug, "Thank you God for sending us Khris." Then she looked down at the young girl with the Gorilla. "You already met my niece Venus, and this is Amber," she said about the baby in her arms.

"She's beautiful," I grabbed her little hands with my fingers, "Hello, Amber." I looked back at Isaac. "How did you find this place?"

He grinned, "After leaving you, I had no idea how to give my family what they needed. I hoped that the Christians would have an answer. We searched for a church, but the RA already had them heavily guarded. That's when I remembered the rumors on base about where they were losing track of the Christians. I didn't want to put my family in more danger by going there, but we had to find a safe place to hide.

"When we reached the forest, Jeffrey found us wandering. He nearly killed me when he saw me in my uniform. He agreed to shelter my wife and the kids if I lead a group of their men to you and David. We ran into Justin on the way, who said he could help smuggle us into the base. Everything fell into place so well. Every doubt about God's power left me. I watched Him protect and bless those men who rescued you and the others. I used to think no one would beat him, but Tereski is no match for God."

I smiled and thanked God for showing me why the past few months were worth everything I went through. God doesn't always allow us to see the fruit of our toils, but I'm grateful He revealed this one.

CHAPTER 50

Therefore, if anyone is in Christ, he is a new creation; the old has gone, the new has come!
—2 Corinthians 5:17 (NIV)

The Ichthys is where my new life began. Due to my pregnancy, my friends wouldn't allow me to leave the safety of my new home. At first, I saw it as another cage. I was envious of my friends. They left the Ichthys weekly, hunting for food and gathering other Christians in need of refuge. Even David, who seemed to heal quite well, had his turn to help the hunters. Every time they returned, Jasmine would rush to meet Jeffrey with a hug. David would search me out among our brothers and sisters in Christ.

I was nervous about beginning two new relationships, one with David, and the other with my baby. When David went hunting, I waited anxiously for him to return but tried not to show it. My misgivings didn't deter David from trying to win me. Steven and Lorenzo seemed to become good friends while on their excursions. They often sat with Justin and Brittany, getting to know them better. Angelica and Jasmine focused on all medical needs and looked to Brittany's vast medical knowledge for help. There were always cuts and scrapes that needed mending and, with my pregnancy, I was a regular visitor.

The eighty-two children who were with us couldn't go above ground either. Isaac's wife, Heather, and I were able to round up a few others to help teach the children to read, write, and do basic math. Amazingly, we had a college professor who taught Bible at a Christian University. He gave lessons on the History of the Church and Christianity that encouraged everyone, including the children. The people found strength while learning about how our Christian ancestors endured their persecution.

Along with teaching Scripture, we came up with multiple activities to help them learn what it means to work as a team. We would give them different life scenarios, working with them on how to respond in a godly manner. It all boiled down to love. If we didn't respond in love, then we let the enemy win.

Justin would sit in on most of our classes, to learn how to use his left hand. He would get frustrated for having to do things slowly. "It's a long process worth going through," I'd remind him.

It didn't take long before I learned that the best way to calm him was by bringing him new work. I'd turn around and untie his shoe, making him tie it back if he grew tired of trying to write. If he became frustrated with tying his shoe, I'd place a blanket before him and have him fold it. Eventually, I'd get him back to writing. He often used his right arm to help balance or hold things down but every now and then, I'd watch him stare at it as if he could still see his fingers.

"Does it help?" I asked him one day when I caught him staring at his nub. The kids were all working on their scripture readings.

"Not at all," Justin stayed fixated. He twisted his arm back and forth as if he was turning his palm back and forth. "If anything, it's holding me back."

"Then why pretend it's there?"

"For the same reason you still pretend that you'll see your family again," he put his arm down.

My eyes narrowed. I always considered the possibilities of them not surviving, but this was the first time anyone told me to face the facts. The next time I'd see my family will be in heaven.

"It lets me smile when hoping it may grow back some day. Then, perhaps, I could be of use."

I understood, but disagreed, "You are of use here. You give these children strength to grow up in this new age. They see the sacrifices you made to save your sister and they understand they may have to make similar choices someday. To see someone recovering from a wound like yours allows them to know they, too, can recover."

"Let's hope these children never have to see the war out there," Justin shook his head. "Let's hope it ends before they grow up. No child should have to experience this kind of hate."

"It's inevitable that they will," I sighed. "Christians have been persecuted all around the world for centuries. It finally festered into America. We had ample warnings to prepare ourselves.

Instead, we chose to complain and continued our daily lives. It only makes sense for it to be our turn now."

"What's the point?" Justin rolled his eyes. "Why go through all of this torture and raise kids to do the same when they could have an easier life out there, raised by families who aren't being attacked?"

I smiled as I looked out at the children. "Because," I said, "one day, when this life is over, their suffering will end. They have a home waiting for them, made by the God of all creation... I guess that's why I pretend that my family is still alive. Whether they're still here on Earth or not, I will see them again." I saw him look back down at his arm. "If you had my hope, you'd know that you would get your hand back one day too; though, that would be minor to all of the other blessings waiting there for you." I had his attention. "In Heaven, everything will be as it should. God will give us all new bodies without flaws… It's just something to consider." I went back to monitoring the kids, leaving Justin to finish his task.

Three weeks into our new life, Jeffrey approached me before he and the others went out on their weekly escapade. "We need you to come with us today."

I had just started gathering the kids together. I hadn't seen Heather, but a few of the other women reassured me that they could handle things without me.

"What's going on?" I asked Jeffrey, hoping everything was all right.

"It's a surprise," he smiled craftily.

Leaving the Ichthys, my body soaked in the evening sunset. I didn't realize how backwards our schedules were. Fresh mountain air filled my lungs. We hiked passed the trees towards what used to be the camp. Ten men and women scouted the open fields first. The hairs on the back of my neck rose. We waited, crouched in the bushes. The leader gave the signal and we set out across the fields. Everything seemed so different. Though the RA forced us to clean up, the ground had not fully recovered. I could still spot out the potholes and bare ground where grass had yet to grow.

We passed where the Tent of Meetings used to be. Images resurfacing of the mutilated bodies scattered all over haunted my thoughts. I gritted my teeth, remembering the torment they put us through that week. I'd never forget what the soldiers did to my brothers and sisters in Christ, how they brought us to our knees, forced us to burn our loved ones, and then murdered others who were too weak with sorrow and fatigue to continue.

Suddenly, a faint smile found its way to my lips as we approached the pond. God reminded me of the morning that I sat on the pier with Jasmine. The pier was gone, but the memories still lived. The men stopped us by the pond, completely exposed. Seven of us gathered in a circle. David, Jeffrey, Steven, and Lorenzo were the people who I knew were with us. I hadn't seen Justin and Brittany until now. Suddenly, two other familiar faces joined in, Isaac and Heather. All other men in our group scoped out the area, keeping us safe.

"This is a big decision you have all decided to make," David spoke.

My heart raced with excitement. He didn't need to say more. I knew why we were here.

"We're in a time crunch and can't risk being seen, so I want to ask you each this question here. Then we'll take you to the water."

They all looked at David and nodded that they understood.

"Do you, Lorenzo, Justin, Brittany, and Heather, believe in God; the maker of heaven and earth?"

In unison they said, "I do."

"Do you also confess that you have sinned against Him in your life?"

"I do," they each responded.

"Do you believe that Jesus the Christ is the Son of God?"

Again, they each proclaimed, "I do."

"Do you believe He came to earth as a perfect man to die for your sins?"

"I do," they said.

"Then will you, in just a moment, willingly face the death of your old life and resurrection of a new life in Christ through baptism?"

Again, they all agreed and then walked down into the water in pairs. Lorenzo followed Jeffrey, David led Justin down, and Steven helped Brittany while she held to her brother's hand. Last, Isaac took his wife in hand and they followed beside the other.

Jeffrey, David, and Steven almost synchronized when saying, "Based upon your confessions, I will now baptize you in the name of the Father, the Son, and the Holy Spirit that you may receive the Holy Spirit and the forgiveness of your sins." Isaac listened to what they said and repeated it to his wife; he not only dunked her but himself in the process.

Submerged into the water they all came back up as new creations in Christ. Tears of joy streamed down my cheeks as I hugged each one of them coming up from the pond. "Welcome to the family," I congratulated. We didn't get much visit time before our lookouts rushed us back to the Ichthys.

I later asked Lorenzo what finally changed his mind.

"Darius," he grinned. "I avoided baptism because I didn't want to seem weak. Darius used to say it was the faith that made the man, not his physical strength. Last night, while we studied through Hebrews, everything Darius had said resurfaced, especially when reading chapter eleven. Those men and women listed are some of the strongest people to have ever walked the Earth, not because of their actions but because of their faith. I talked with David after the study. He only helped confirm that I needed to make this commitment now."

It thrilled my heart to see God at work. Jeremy was the only one left uncommitted to the faith within the Ichthys walls as far as I knew. Christians surrounded him, but the longer he stayed in the Ichthys, the more stir crazy he became. I talked with him often about God and he seemed interested, but I wondered if he saw this place as a prison. He would help us with the children's activities, but sat in a corner during the lessons. When I returned from the baptisms, Jeremy was hysterical. He had no idea where I had gone or where to find me. A few people tried to reassure him that I would be back, but he wouldn't listen. He stayed near my side after that, as a lost puppy found in the woods.

"Jeremy," I sat him down to talk, thinking that the reason he acted so dramatically was because he still held firm to protecting my baby, "do you realize that my child has a Protector who goes with me no matter where I am?"

He looked at me, "Where?"

"You can't see Him. The Protector is God," I smiled.

He faintly grinned, "So what do I do then?"

"What do you mean?" I saw dread in his eyes.

"If I can't watch out for you, what do I do? You're my only friend," he muttered.

My heart dropped. His mental impairments kept him from being very open with others, but it never crossed my mind that he needed my help to meet other people. I leaned in and gave him a hug, "Let's change that today." I brought Jeremy to my friends and quietly asked them all to help him feel included. They did so and immediately I saw a change in him. He truly was like a child; all Jeremy needed was a little attention for his day to get brighter.

CHAPTER 51

The LORD God said, 'It is not good for the man to be alone. I will make a helper suitable for him.
—Genesis 2:18 (NIV)

Over the next few weeks, I noticed sparks of attraction between Steven and Brittany. It started in the Bible studies when he would help answer her questions. They began to talk and hang out during down times throughout the day. Justin gave them space and took more time to hang around Jeremy. They became quite the pair of troublemaking friends, but it was all in good fun. They would joke with the younger kids by tickling them or hiding their pencils, but in the end, their pranks only bettered their relationships with the children. David and I also grew closer over the days. We talked about having a relationship, but I still struggled with the whole idea.

"What point is there in making any kind of commitment when we have no idea what tomorrow will bring?" I asked Jeffrey one day. He had pulled me aside to ask why I was stringing David along. He knew me better than that, but he also knew it would get my attention.

"We've never known what tomorrow will hold, Khris. That never stopped you from committing to the missions in China, Africa, and Mexico. I know you're not meaning to, but from an outsider's point of view it looks like you're playing him."

"I'm not. It's just that…"

"That what?" Jeffrey obviously wasn't interested in my excuses. "You're going to have to raise a child. If tomorrow doesn't come, so be it, but if it does then who's going to have your back when the child gets grumpy or starts disobeying? Who's going to teach your son how to be a good father to his kids, or your daughter what kind of man she should seek after? We've all promised to help you, but we can't all take on the role of a father. Your child is going to need someone he or she can count on and talk to when he feels unable to come to you. That's what we are here to do. You have someone godly who's not only willing to love you unconditionally, but who's ready to take in your child as his own. Don't push that blessing away."

"David understands…"

"No," Jeffrey said, "he doesn't. What he tells you and what he feels are two different things. This stays between us, but it says a lot that he had to come to Steven and me for advice. He puts on a good face because he truly loves you, but your distance is killing him. You've friend zoned him, Khris. I don't know what I'd do if Jasmine started to distance herself from me. Right now, she tells me everything and I her. It's relieving to know I have someone praying for my safety every time I leave this place and waiting to be the first one to greet me when I come back."

"I have that..."

Again, he interrupted, "No, what you have isn't even half as good as what I'm talking about. You have someone giving you his all, but you selfishly burden yourself with guilt and fear of being fully open with him. With that, you burden him with fear and rejection. He's giving up, Khris. Not on God, but on you. Still, his fire for God would burn so much brighter if he had your full support and undivided love. I'm willing to bet, yours would too."

I tried to hold back the tears of truth that threatened to flood my eyes. I never realized that I was hurting David. Jeffrey was right, but I didn't want to tell him. I wanted to be angry with him for making me feel so foolish, but I knew I needed it.

"Hey, Jeffrey," I heard David's sweet voice from behind me. "Could I borrow Khristy for a minute?"

I didn't turn around. I needed to regain my composure or I'd blubber uncontrollably the moment I looked at him.

Jeffrey looked at me while answering David, "She's all yours." His subtle hint made me laugh just enough to gain the courage to face David.

"What's up?" I tried to say nonchalantly.

"What's up...?" He muttered twice under his breath. He raked his hand across the back of his neck. "Khristy, I...I've been thinking..."

My heart dropped, if I even had one. Jeffrey said David was giving up, but I didn't realize it would happen so quickly. "David,

I'm sorry," I cried. The floodgates opened. Suddenly I felt weaker than ever before. David reached out and pulled me in to his chest. I crumbled in his arms, as he gently sat with me on the floor.

"Tell me what's wrong?" He whispered.

I wanted to, but I didn't want to hurt him… Jeffrey was right. I was being selfish. I was scared of opening up, scared to see what doors it would open, but David deserved to know the truth. I apologized to him for everything, though he may not have understood it all through my sobs. I told him the truth of how I felt, "You've said it to me a hundred times but I haven't… David, I love you. I don't want to lose you. That's what scares me. There's no promise we'll live long lives, but if there were I wouldn't hesitate to spend mine with you. I just didn't want to embrace that hope because if our future ended too soon, I don't know what I'd do. Now I realize that even if our future only consisted of three more days, I'd rather have that than nothing at all."

I pray that I never forget the look of pure love and joy on David's face. Grasping my hands, he swallowed and blurted, "Then marry me."

My jaw practically dropped to the floor.

"I promise never to leave your side, never to look at another woman, and never to be anything less than what you need me to be. I'll learn to love you more each day, and when the time comes, I'll be as devoted a father as I will be a husband. I'll take care of all your needs, no matter how bad our situation gets. I'll listen to all your thoughts and carry all of your burdens. Most of all, I'll lift you up to God every day in prayer, just as I have since the first day we met. I'll never move forward without God's blessing. I'll never retreat without His command. I will always put Him first, so that He can guide us even when we feel there is nothing left for us."

I didn't know what to say. I wanted everything he said, but marriage… "David we haven't even attempted to date."

"I don't care," he maneuvered to where he sat on his knees, while still holding my hands. "Dating is what people do to get to know one another. You've seen me at my worst, and at my best. I've been an open book. You may feel like you've held back, but anything that you feel could push me away from you is a myth. If you still wonder whether God means us for one another, then just tell me. Go, and *date* other men if that's what you desire. If not, and you feel the same way I do, then there's nothing to fear. We'll work everything else out with God's guidance. If that is something you're willing to do with me then, I ask," he pulled one knee up off the ground, "will you marry me, Khristy Monzel?"

My heart beat faster than a thousand stallions racing across a plain. I wanted time to think but really, I didn't need it. I didn't want to date other men. I wanted David, or else I'd choose to stay single forever. He wanted me too. He said so himself. He's willing to take me for who he knows me to be, and work through everything I've chosen to hide from him. I had my reasons to say no, but none would win out in the end. "I will," I smiled, and suddenly a weight lifted from my shoulders.

David grinned, "Does this mean I can cash in that rain check?"

I laughed and nodded as he stood and pulled me in for a kiss. This time, neither of us pulled away in pain. As he held me in his arms, I felt more secure than ever before. I knew, then, without a doubt, that God planned for us to be together.

Howls and applause brought us back to our surroundings. I flushed with embarrassment, but couldn't hide my excitement. David stood with me and held my hand high, while gripping my side with his other hand and pulling me in close. "We're engaged," he hollered at the top of his lungs. Now, just about every man, woman, boy, and girl added in their applause. I buried my head into his chest, laughing. Glancing towards my friends, I could see Jeffrey and Steven pull in their loves for a kiss and fist bump one another behind Jasmine and Brittany's backs. I couldn't contain my laughter as I saw both women grab Jeffrey and Steven's hands and pull them back into their embrace, away from each other. *You brought us together, thank you, God.*

CHAPTER 52

...for I have learned to be content whatever the circumstances. I know what is it to be in need, and I know what it is to have plenty. I have learned the secret of being content in any and every situation, whether well fed or hungry, whether living in plenty or want.
—Philippians 4:11–12 (NIV)

I went into labor three days after David and I married. It was a short wedding, but it was perfect. Glen proudly did the ceremony, and Lorenzo did the scripture readings and prayer. We didn't worry about having bridesmaids and groomsmen, we just wanted to say our vows and celebrate. Our friends knew of their importance to us. They were family, both by choice and through Jesus' blood. They didn't need a place by our sides to know that.

I was glad that most of my friends weren't around to see me in labor. They were out hunting and gathering as scheduled. Still, I wished David hadn't gone with them. Thankfully, Jasmine was able to leave Angelica and Brittany in charge of the sick, and Heather left the other teachers with her class. The two of them took me into the meeting room with the lantern. They helped me through the whole process. Five hours I waited for my child to be born. The birth pains were horrifyingly unexpected, but it all went away in the end when I held my crying son. He cried and cried as they cleaned him off and swaddled him into a towel. I soothed his screams while humming *Amazing Grace*. I pulled him in close to my chest and stared at his precious face. He was bald as could be with the tiniest hands I had ever seen. Two deep, blue, innocent eyes stared into mine before he fell asleep in my arms. I loved him. No matter the means by which he came to me, I knew that I would love him for all eternity.

Sitting with him, cradling him in my arms, Heather helped me prepare for my friends' arrival. I wrapped myself up and let a giant grin cross my face as a rapid tapping came at the door. David was first to my side. He kissed my forehead and clung to our child's hand. Jeffrey and Steven came in close, making small jokes while playing with my boy's tiny fingers and toes. They all congratulated David and me.

"What's his name?" Angelica asked.

David and I had talked about it, and had come up with two names. Ricky, after my father, or Darius, who we wanted to honor after giving his life for us. If I had a girl, we would have settled for

Miracle. For a boy, we decided on mixing my father's and Darius' names into one that neither of us had heard in a while. "Derrick," I smiled at him in my arms. "His name is Derrick."

Steven picked on me for a bit, telling me I was ruining my boy's life by giving him an old man's name. We laughed and joked back and forth, but fear gripped me in the midst of our conversation. I blurted out, "He's never allowed to know about his relationship to Anthony; ever."

"Khris," Steven started to refute, but I needed to make myself clear.

"He can never know he came from someone so evil. I won't let him grow up thinking he could have Anthony's traits. Please," I begged. "As far as he and the world will know, David is and always has been his father. Of course, above all else, he will know God as his one true Father."

They agreed to my requests and then let David and me sit with Derrick alone for a few minutes.

"Can I hold him?" David asked. As I handed Derrick over, David cautiously cradled Derrick's head and scooped him up into his arms. Immediately, I saw David become a dad without hesitation. "Hey son," he whispered, "you don't really understand this yet, but I'm your dad. That means I'm the one who's going to teach you everything there is to know about becoming a man. I may also be the one who butts heads with you the most but, when we do, I'll make sure you never leave feeling unloved. Every day of your life, your mom and I will love you more. We'll raise you right, you'll see."

He held him for a minute longer before handing Derrick back to me. Then, David leaned against the wall and pulled me in close. I rested my head back on his chest and he wrapped his arms around both Derrick and me. The lantern dimly lit the room, but I could see Derrick's face perfectly. A cold chill came over me. I pulled Derrick in close and David draped a blanket over us. It wasn't long before I could hear David taking in softer breaths. He had fallen asleep.

Feeling safe in David's arms, I found contentedness…I found tranquility. I could almost sleep. First, I needed to talk with God, "I may never see my family again, Father. For whatever reason, You've allowed us to be separated. Yet, You've given me a new family. I don't feel I am deserving of them, but I will forever show You my gratitude. How You managed to bring David and me together in the midst of all of the chaos still baffles me, but I will never forget it." I pulled the blanket tighter around us and stared down at Derrick. "As for this little blessing You've given me, I'm sorry I first saw him as a burden. Thank You for not giving up on me and not letting me give up on him. I promise we will love Derrick unconditionally. Please, help us to raise him right. He will grow up in a world without religious freedom. It's a world we know very little about. We will tell him of Your wonders, so that he will be aware of every miracle that You show him first hand. Let him be Your witness. Please, don't let him stray from Your truth. Give me wisdom to be a godly mother, and David the wisdom to be a godly father. Provide us with the right nurture, care, and discipline. Remind us to let our friends be of help. I thank You that they are willing to aid us in raising Derrick right. We'll teach him to walk in Your ways from today until the end of his journey. Let his heart be fully open to Your truth and love. Father, this is my dedication of Derrick to You."

I looked down at Derrick, enthralled with God's tiny blessing, "I love you, my baby boy. You will grow up in the ways of God. May you never seek a life apart from Him." Kissing him on the forehead, I felt the need to remind Derrick of the hope we have from Second Corinthians. A hope, I would never let him forget, "We have been 'persecuted, but not abandoned…'[19] We will never be abandoned."

---

[19] 2 Corinthians 4:9 (NIV)

Follow the story in, *Persecution: Insurrection*, coming soon.